INTO AUTUMN

A Story of Survival

INTO AUTUMN

A Story of Survival

A Novel by

Larry Landgraf

To Tom,
Life will throw you curves.
Go with them and learn.

Larry Landgraf

Fresh Ink Group
Roanoke

Into Autumn: A Story of Survival

Fresh Ink Group
An Imprint of:
The Fresh Ink Group, LLC
PO Box 525
Roanoke, TX 76262
Email: info@FreshInkGroup.com
www.FreshInkGroup.com

Edition 1.0   2015
Edition 2.0   2017

Book design by Ann Stewart / FIG

Cover design by Stephen Geez / FIG

BISAC Subject Headings:
FIC000000   **FICTION** / General
FIC055000   **FICTION** / Dystopian
FIC028070   **FICTION** / Science Fiction / Apocalyptic & Post-Apocalyptic

Library of Congress Control Number: 2017930907

Paper cover ISBN 13: 978-1-936442-54-6
Hardcover ISBN 13: 978-1-936442-53-9
Ebook ISBN 13: 978-1-936442-55-3

Table of Contents

This book is dedicated to Ellen, whose numerous editing skills have made a profound difference in the quality of this book as well as the quality of my life.

Introduction

Lars Lindgren sat on the front porch of his country home. He rubbed his hands together and winced a little at the pain of arthritis, which seemed to get a little worse every year, as the cooler weather set in. A cool north breeze teased the wind chime hanging from a rafter at the end of the porch, producing a pleasant tinkle. Lars looked at the calluses on his hands, then rubbed his hands together, to produce a little warmth, and touched the palms to his face. The eastern sky began to glow brightly, as the sun was preparing to peek above the gentle slope of the landscape. Lars hated getting up early, but these days, he could never sleep in. He reached over and grabbed his rifle, a small can of oil, barrel rod, and an old washcloth. The lever action 30-30 needed cleaning badly, but no matter how much he scrubbed and oiled, the gun would never be new again. It belonged to his dad. Though past its prime, the weapon still had plenty of years left, provided he kept it well oiled. The task completed, Lars shoved in five 180 grain cartridges, and leaned it up against the porch railing.

Lars leaned back in his chair and stretched out his arms. He closed his eyes, and his mind drifted back to the old days; the old days of three years ago, before he went off the grid. Going off the grid was not his choice. The choice was not his to make; just something that happened rather suddenly one day. There was plenty of warning, but he did not see the signs. He had just assumed everything would always be the same. Over the years, presidents came and went, the stock market went up and down, taxes went up on a regular basis, and there always seemed to be a war somewhere, but everything always remained the same. Not this time though; how could he have known? The grid just suddenly shut down. No more electricity, no more mail, no more well stocked grocery store shelves, and probably the worst, no more gasoline for his aging truck. He had a full tank of gasoline when the grid shut down and a 55-gallon drum about half full of the fuel, but didn't use the last of the precious liquid in the truck. He could do without his truck, but he needed his tractor to plow and plant his garden. His feet replaced his truck, but losing the tractor would mean a lot of extra back breaking work to plow the garden so he could plant the crops he needed to survive, now that his only source of food would be what he could produce himself. There was no telling how long this would be the case, maybe the rest of his life. He just didn't know.

Lars didn't just have to fend for himself; he had two mouths to feed. Lars was not married, but Eileen came to live with him about the time the grid went down. Lars did not care so much for himself. If he could not take care of himself, maybe he would just waste away and die. Lars had lived a relatively long life, and his health was headed downhill. Nothing serious, just a little arthritis, and he tired more easily and seemed to need much more sleep than when he was younger. He was just beginning to feel old, much like his dad's old gun. He didn't have a lot to live for, with most of the modern conveniences he had gotten used to over the years, now a thing of the past. Long-distance travel was certainly no longer possible, even if he did have the money or gas, which he did not. If it were just him, he probably would not care, but he did care for Eileen very much. She gave him strength and courage to press on and work hard, to provide as best he could for both of them. She gave him a sense of purpose. He did not want her to be cold when the chilly air blew down from the north. He did not want her to be hungry when times were lean, so he worked harder to provide what he needed to provide. He did not want her to sleep scared at night or worry someone would come along during the day and take everything she and Lars had worked so hard to accumulate. He wanted her to feel she had a future; they had a future; life was still worth living. Lars' job these days was to take care of Eileen, and with a little help from her, he would do so. He would make her feel safe, keep her belly full, and give her all the love she needed.

Lars' thoughts turned to his past year's crops. They were not nearly as good as he had hoped they would be. If they had been, he would have had something to barter with the neighbors. At the moment, they had all the food they needed, but little to barter with. Lars would have to get up soon to chop some wood, but he just couldn't stop thinking about his situation. They would need the firewood tonight, as the chill in the air meant it would be colder tonight than it was last night. Yes, he would have to get up soon. Well, not just yet, but soon. Lars rolled a cigar from some of the tobacco leaves he kept in a small cloth pouch in his chest pocket. The leaves were fresh from the day before, when he peeled them from the full leaves hanging in the barn to dry. His tobacco crop was meager this year, like all the other crops, so he rationed the leaves. They would not likely last until the next year's crop came in, so he enjoyed every puff of every cigar. No more cigarettes for him. He had no papers to roll them in, and you certainly could not buy them, as all the local stores had closed down long ago, so cigars it had to be. Maybe he would just quit when he ran out of tobacco. This would certainly make Eileen happy; she never liked smoking. He knew it was a nasty habit, but Lars enjoyed smoking. He thought it helped him relax, and there were many things to relax from these days.

Lars took his last puff from the cigar, thumped the butt into the dirt just off the porch, and slowly got up. The sun was already up a little higher than usual. He would need to get after his chores soon. Eileen was still in bed, and he needed to get her up. He had decided to let her sleep a little longer this morning. It would be a full day of chores with the colder weather bearing down upon them. There were many things which needed attention before winter set in for good. Lars grabbed his gun, walked to the front door, turned the knob, and slowly pushed the door in. There was a little squeak in the hinges. Lars took the can of oil, set his gun just inside the door, and gave the hinges a little squirt. "Ah, that's better," he said softly. *Can't be waking Eileen up with a squeaky hinge*, he thought. Lars went into the bedroom and the covers were still high over Eileen's head. He slowly pulled at the covers, revealing her blonde hair, then her closed eyes, followed by her cute little nose, and the luscious full lips he loved to kiss. He just stood there for a minute. My God, she was beautiful. She just didn't seem to get any older, and every day she seemed to be more beautiful than the day before. Lars leaned over and gave her a gentle kiss on the forehead. She stirred a little, and then her eyes opened slowly. Then, there appeared that lovely smile he fell in love with the first day they met.

"Is it time to get up already?"

"I wish I could let you sleep a little longer," Lars said, "but we have a lot of chores we need to get at." Lars walked back into the living room. Eileen followed shortly, all dressed and ready to get to work. She had never been lazy, one thing Lars really liked about her. She always carried her load to help provide for both of them, and sometimes, she even surprised Lars with how hard she worked.

Lars could see that Eileen missed the city life, as she stuffed the old wood stove with kindling. She was a city gal at heart, unlike Lars who spent as much time in the country as possible. Living just outside town most of his life was not really living in the country, but Lars made up for this with numerous hunting and fishing trips every year. He didn't like cities much, though cities did have their good points. But, no more. Cities were very dangerous these days. They were off the grid too, as was everyone. When there was little left to loot from the local businesses, the survivors lived on what they could take from others, who generally were killed for their meager possessions. Eileen was smart enough to leave the city long before things got really bad. She must have known the nation was going to shut down. She was not just a pretty face, she was smart too, very smart; city smart, school smart. How she found Lars, he didn't know, but was very glad she did. You couldn't tell Eileen was a city gal now by looking at her. She looked like she was born and raised in the country, much like Daisy Duke on the old television show. But Lars could tell she wasn't, because of her lack of typical country skills, like shooting, old medicine, how to deal with wildlife, and knowing what and how to do all the everyday tasks, which most country folk seem to know instinctively. But Lars didn't care about what she knew or didn't know. What he cared about most was that she was eager to learn, worked hard to learn, and never gave up trying. Lars also remembered how lonesome he'd been before Eileen showed up.

Eileen got busy on breakfast, but before Lars went outside to get started on chores, he walked over to give her a big hug and a tender kiss. Eileen liked his bear hugs, and this was a daily ritual. Women need to know they are appreciated, loved, wanted, and needed. Lars wasn't much for words, but he let Eileen know daily she was loved and needed. He learned a long time ago that women need to know someone wants them and that their hard work is appreciated. Lars made certain Eileen knew this, every single day. He was not certain he could survive, with or without her, but he let her know every day that, with her help, he would give it his best effort.

Chapter 1

In the beginning...

Lars Lindgren had worked hard for many years, building an auto dealership in a neighboring city, with a population of about twenty thousand. It was tough, but with a lot of hard work, he managed to build a very profitable business. He worked in town but lived on the outskirts on about an acre of land. He hated living in the city when he was growing up. Now, he wasn't very far out of the town, but at least he was away from the traffic, noise, and the hustle and bustle of city life. He longed to move even farther away from town, to be able to support himself on the land, and to just get away from everything. To this end, Lars planned carefully and worked hard every day.

When Lars was in his twenties, he knew what he wanted. He worked as a mechanic for a while at a small automobile dealership in the city. He was a diligent worker and was soon promoted to shop manager. Eventually Lars was asked to manage the entire dealership. Every spare dime he made was invested heavily in the stock market. The stock market treated him well, and when the aging owner of the dealership said he wanted to get out of the business, Lars, who was in his early thirties at the time, jumped at the chance. To Lars' surprise, the owner accepted his offer, even though it was a bit low, because it was all Lars had to give. Lars became the owner of Lindgren Chevrolet.

Through the remainder of his thirties and forties, Lars grew his business, expanding it every chance he got. He picked up the local Ford franchise only a couple years after purchasing the Chevy dealership. A few years later, he acquired the local Chrysler/Dodge franchise. His business was booming, and Lars bought into blue chip stocks with much of his profits. Lars was doing well financially, but he became bored with the business. It was the same thing every day. Nothing changed, but he could not deny the money was good.

Lars began watching poker on the television and liked the action. He had played poker here and there most of his life, and knew the game very well, but *no limit hold'em* was new and even more exciting. He played poker on the computer regularly and found he was pretty good at the game. One day a friend of his invited him to go to Las Vegas.

"You think you're pretty good. Let's go see how good you really are," said Andy Prentiss.

Lars had never been on a jet, and certainly had never been as far away from home as Las Vegas, but it didn't take him long to decide he really wanted to go to Vegas. It only took a few minutes to say, "Sure, why don't we just go to Vegas."

To his surprise, and especially to Andy's, Lars did quite well. Well enough, in fact, that Lars went back again and again. Some trips were not all that great, but more often than not, Lars won. After a year or so, Lars slowed his travel to Las Vegas to only a couple times a year. After all, he had a business to run, and—oh yeah—he had a wife. He and his wife hadn't gotten along for many years, but she did like the money from his business and investments. Rachel Lindgren hadn't complained much up until now, but he was neglecting his business and their financial future. She certainly did not like his going to Las Vegas. "Well, you won't go with me," he would say on a regular basis. He asked her to go several times, but after her repeated refusals, he stopped asking. *To hell with her*, he thought.

Finally, Lars reached his fifty-fourth birthday. It was time for him to seriously pursue his dream. If it was ever going to happen, now was the time. He could feel the clock ticking. For years, Lars had wanted to get as far away from the city as he could. He had worked hard for over thirty years towards his dream. His kids were grown now and had moved away to pursue their own dreams. It was time to pursue his.

Lars found about forty acres of undeveloped land along a small river. There were trees, plenty of animals, a good water source, and—best of all—no one around for at least a couple of miles. It was perfect—but pricey. The cost didn't matter though. Lars fell in love with the place and bought it on the spot. He did not tell Rachel about the property for a couple months, long enough to build a small cabin big enough for two, with only the basic necessities. This would do until he could build a larger, more permanent home.

One evening, when he returned home from the dealership, Lars decided it was time to inform Rachel they were moving to the country and that he had put the business up for sale.

"I don't think so," said Rachel.

"The business is up for sale, and the cabin has been built on our new land. We're moving alright!"

"The hell we are!" exclaimed Rachel.

Then the fight really got going. They hadn't said ten words to each other all week. Well, the words were flying now, and many of them Lars had never heard come from Rachel's mouth before that day. The fight went on for about twenty minutes, and then Rachel stormed off into the bathroom. Lars could hear the water running. *Maybe she is trying to drown herself*, he thought. Then he came to his senses; he couldn't be that lucky. In about an hour, Rachel slowly walked out of the bathroom, went into the bedroom, and slammed the door. Lars had gotten on the computer and was playing a game of poker. He waited for her to come out so he could resume the fight. He was ready.

It was about thirty minutes before Rachel came out of the bedroom. Lars could see she had tears in her eyes, and she choked a little when she said, "I'm going to Mom's. I won't be back." She just walked out without another word. Lars didn't say a word and resumed his game of poker.

The following week, Lars heard a knock on the door. He got up, turned the knob and slowly pulled the door open. Uniforms! Cops! Lars didn't like cops. "What!" he exclaimed.

"We're here to serve you with divorce papers," said the stocky, manly female officer.

Lars looked down at her hand. She had several sheets of paper stapled together. Lars looked at the other officer and then back at the female. The thin male officer just stood there with a grim look on his face. The female officer handed Lars the papers, a pen and a receipt. Lars signed the receipt and handed it back. They turned and walked away, without a thank you, kiss my ass, or other acknowledgment. Lars just turned around, walked back into the house and shut the door. "Assholes," he murmured under his breath.

Lars walked over to his favorite recliner and began to read the papers. He knew it was going to be terrible; divorce always was. When he got through, he shrugged, thinking *This is not so bad.* It was bad though. He got all of his newly purchased 40 acres and the tiny cabin. The entire house, most of the stock, and 75% of the business! That was all Rachel wanted! Seemed a little too much, but he would have to sleep on it.

The next morning, after a long and restless night, Lars woke up with a headache. He didn't mind Rachel leaving, but how much of his hard work over the past thirty years would it cost? He did come to a decision though. He would not contest the divorce. It probably would cost him even more money to do so. He would be able to keep his dreamland and could build a modest home. There would even be enough money left over to tide him over for a couple years, if he spent it wisely. *Well, I hope the bitch is going to be happy!*

Chapter 2

October, two and a half years later...

    Lars climbed onto his small tractor and began plowing up his garden. Lars liked riding his tractor. No one could bother him, and the engine drowned out all other sounds. He couldn't do anything but drive and think. His crop was meager at best, just like he had thought it would be. At least the two-acre garden produced much more than his little garden at the old house, just outside the city. No more business to worry about, no more stocks to worry about, no city noise—just peace and quiet, except for the groan of the tractor, as it strained a bit to plow the rich black soil. Lars plowed and thought about the investments he had made in precious metals. He had doubled his money. *Good thing too*, he thought. Food was a struggle, at least the vegetables were. There were plenty of animals around, so he wasn't starving for meat. He just hadn't put on any weight. Guess he would never gain weight while he was working so hard. He did gain muscles though. All the time he worked at and then ran the dealership, he had kept in pretty good shape. He never went to the gym. But Lars worked hard; he was always on the go, running from one dealership to another, taking care of this and that. Even around his old house, he always had an endless number of necessary chores that needed to be completed. *You have to keep in good shape when you are constantly running around all the time*, he decided.

    It had been a little over two and a half years since his wife left. *I guess the marriage was a failure*, Lars thought, *just like much of my garden*. It at least felt like a failure to Lars, except for the two beautiful kids he and Rachel produced. They were both smart and successful. I guess this is all you can ask for in kids. Lars saw them regularly, and they seemed happy. He loved his kids very much, and as long as they were happy, Lars felt good.

    Lars really liked his new home, his 40-acre property, and his garden. This was his dream. But was he really living his dream? He was living where he wanted to live; he was living how he wanted to live, but still something was missing. He knew exactly what it was. *I guess you're never too old to learn something new*, and Lars certainly learned something new today. Lars' tractor gave him the solitude to think and to learn. But, he didn't realize until today that a dream can only be totally fulfilled if you have someone to share it with. Lars needed a woman. He parked his tractor, and then stood and looked at the freshly plowed ground. He walked over to the garden, bent down, and grabbed a handful of the rich black dirt. He put it up to his nose and took a deep breath. You could smell the richness of the ground. Good rain made great crops; poor rain made poor crops. If he could only make it rain when he wanted… but he could not. It takes more than just good dirt to make good crops. It takes more than a dream and a lot of hard work to make your dream come true.

Lars walked back into the house and took off his clothes. He got into the shower and just stood there, letting the shower head do all the work. The gears were turning in his head. What was he going to do to complete his dream? Twenty minutes later, he figured he had wasted enough water, and quickly soaped himself up and rinsed. He got out, dried quickly, and hurried over to his computer. He pressed the on button and walked over to the kitchen. He made a glass of tea, grabbed some jerky out of the glass jar in the cabinet, and got back over to the computer.

Lars brought up a website for airline flights. Destination: LAS (Las Vegas). Then, he started to type in the date. But for how long? *Ten days should be long enough,* he pondered. The available flights came up on the screen. The prices were really high for immediate flights, but much cheaper for later flights. If he were to postpone the trip for a couple weeks, he could cut the cost in half, so he booked a later flight. He was going to Las Vegas again, but this time not just to play poker. He was on the hunt for a woman.

As it turned out, Vegas was a bad idea. There were too many gals—old gals, young gals, uppity gals. Maybe they'd be good for a fling, but they weren't really suited to bring back home. Some of them even laughed at him when he brought up the idea. They seemed okay at first, but when he mentioned taking them home, their tune changed quickly. They did not want him; they wanted his pocketbook.

Lars met Brittney at the poker tables during one of the games, and they struck up a friendly conversation. She was a pleasant looking school teacher from Montana. She was smart, plenty good looking, and just a little younger than Lars, he imagined. Every time the dealer would place the *flop* on the table in the *no limit hold'em* cash game they were playing, she leaned over the table a bit to see the cards better, and in the process, pressed her breasts against her crossed arms on the railing. Every time she did this, Lars would take a look at her breasts, which appeared to be on the verge of popping out of her low-cut dress. Brittney had really nice breasts, from what Lars could see, and imagined he would soon see the remainder of her lusciousness. Finally, Brittney caught Lars' eyes fixated on her breasts when she was pressing hard against her arms. "Are you staring at my boobs?" she asked rather indignant.

"Yes I am," Lars replied. "If you are going to keep showing them to me, I am certainly going to keep looking."

Everyone at the table chuckled. Brittney clammed up and would not talk to

Lars after this. It wasn't long before Lars and Brittney were playing against each other in a hand. They both had a pair of queens, and when Lars made a mediocre bet, she pushed *all-in*, betting all her chips. Lars called the bet. They both ended up with top pair after the river card was dealt, but Lars had her out-kicked and took the pot. As Lars had more chips than she, he busted her out and she left the table. Everyone at the table was upset with Lars for running the busty lady off. Lars cashed out soon afterward. He never saw Brittney again.

Lars also ran into Megan at the Carnival Buffet at the Rio. She was eating lunch alone, and Lars asked if he could join her. She accepted, and after a pleasant conversation over their meal, Lars invited her to accompany him to a show later that night. She accepted. They went to see Terry Fator and both enjoyed the show very much, but Megan shied away when Lars hinted at taking her back to Texas with him. This relationship went nowhere just like the others.

Lars decided to stroll over to Harrah's on the strip the following day to look around. He played in a *no limit hold'em* cash game all afternoon and into the early evening, then went up the escalator to Toby Keith's *I Love This Bar & Grill*. Lars didn't care to drink much, but thought he might find some country ladies who would be more agreeable to moving back to Texas with him. It was a long shot, but so was his entire trip. Lars arrived at Toby's place at 8:00 P.M. There were several empty tables, and he chose a table for two; himself and hopefully a nice lady who didn't like seeing him drinking alone. Lars ordered a margarita and sat, sipped, and waited. An hour went by before anyone approached him. Laura asked if he would buy her a drink and Lars quickly obliged. They chatted for a while and Laura soon propositioned Lars for sex. Lars passed on the proposition and Laura moved on after finishing her drink.

By 11:00, Lars was working on his third drink and an equal number of propositions. Sheila was a gorgeous lady and Lars saw himself getting nowhere with a lady to take home. Lars decided to take Sheila up on her proposition, if she was willing to take the shuttle to the Rio where he was staying. She was. Lars hadn't had any good nookie for longer than he could remember and was enjoying his second orgasm at 1:00 A.M., more or less. Lars wasn't keeping track of time. Sheila appeared to have an equal number of orgasms, and after a shower, she left Lars' suite. Lars didn't awaken until noon, but he did have a big grin on his face, that is, until he saw how much money he had left in his wallet, or more correctly, how little he had in the wallet. *It was an expensive night,* Lars thought, *but damn, Sheila was a wonderful lady.*

His ten days in Vegas went by before he knew it. Lars packed his bags and took a cab to McCarran Airport. His flight was on time and Lars headed home. *I guess Vegas is not really the place I should be looking for a good woman,* he thought. Lars pretty much broke even on the tables this trip, and he did enjoy the poker, but went home empty-handed when it came to the women.

When he got back home, Lars did light chores around the house for a couple days, while he rested up from his trip. Then he got on the computer again. He found some dating sites and worked these for a couple weeks. There were some really nice ladies, but after a few weeks of chatting with literally hundreds of women, none really seemed right for him. There was one lady who caught Lars' attention due to her interesting moniker, *Icelandic Sword Goddess*. She liked to be called Jordy, though her real name was Icelandic, Hjordis. Lars really liked her. She was sweet and seemed to like him as well, but she was not about to move to Texas.

"It's too hot in Texas," she explained.

Well, it is too cold in Iceland for me, Lars thought. "My arthritis kicks up when it gets down to 60 degrees. I don't think I could take the cold weather," he explained when she asked if he'd move there.

Olga in Russia was really anxious for Lars to visit her, as was Natalia in the Ukraine, but Lars couldn't see himself living there and having them visit or move to Texas would be really difficult. He really didn't know what he was going to do. Maybe he had better get used to being alone. A lot of people make out just fine alone. He couldn't think of any at the moment, but there had to be some. Maybe his dream included being alone. Maybe that just went with the territory. No one else can really share your dreams. Rachel certainly could not, would not, or whatever.

Lars buried himself in work the next couple weeks. If he was tired, maybe he wouldn't lie in bed thinking about his needs—what was lacking in his life. The roof needed a little work, and the fall rainy season was here, so he took care of that chore first. Fall would be followed by winter, and Lars had no wood cut to keep the fires burning.

It seemed like the rain would never stop. It wasn't a hard rain, just a light to moderate drizzle. On the driest day of the week, the sun actually peeked out and it warmed up enough to reach a comfortable temperature. Lars grabbed his ax and made quick work of ten trees, felling them and cutting all the small limbs off. He then let the trees lie there and waited for a dry spell so the wood could dry a bit before he cut them up to haul to the woodshed.

There were four fruit trees with ripening pears and persimmon, which needed picking now. He didn't know how the trees got on the property but was happy they were here. The trees had to be twenty years old. Lars harvested what he thought would get him through the winter. Of course, he had to taste a few to make certain they were ripe enough. The Bartlett would be mighty tasty in a month or so. The two varieties of Asian pears were really good right now. There were not many persimmons, and they would not last more than a couple days.

They did not keep very well, so Lars ate half the crop immediately. He saved a few for next day and maybe even the day after tomorrow, if the fruit would stretch that far. Lars cut the grass around the house, worked on his tractor, pulled a few weeds in the garden, and whatever else he could find needed his attention.

After a couple of weeks, the place was in pretty good shape, but the work did not get rid of his needs or stop him from thinking about them. Lars was not the kind of person who could live alone. Maybe he could be alone in the short term, but for the long term, Lars needed more. Unless women started falling out of the sky, it seemed Lars' dream would die, just like the crops died when the rain refused to fall.

Lars was a rather handsome man. He had dark hair with a little gray around the sides. He was six feet tall and around 200 pounds—not an overly big man but certainly no small man either. He was muscular and in pretty good shape and kept himself reasonably clean. Of course he stank to high heaven when he worked, but so did everyone else. Work stink washes off. As Andy said when they took their first trip to Las Vegas, "Boy, you clean up real good." *Guess maybe I do, but it didn't get me a lady*, Lars thought.

Chapter 3

In San Antonio, Texas...

Eileen Branson was up at 6:00 AM. She put on her robe and slippers, and then neatly made her bed. She stretched her arms, let out a big yawn, and walked slowly to the bathroom. She turned the heat lamp on and started the hot water in the shower. She grabbed her toothbrush and squeezed a little toothpaste onto the bristles and began to brush her teeth. She took a pee and then slipped out of her robe and got into the shower. The water was hot, almost steaming. *Just right*, she thought. She soaped up quickly and rinsed off. She was not one for long showers. Eileen slipped her robe back on and slid her feet into the slippers.

Eileen looked into the partly fogged up mirror and began her morning routine. She didn't need much makeup, but felt there was always something to cover up a bit. She wasn't the young girl she used to be, but still looked great for her age. She celebrated her 50th birthday last month. *Another milestone*, she thought at the time, but Eileen really wasn't too concerned. She still looked great and felt great—much younger than she was. Eileen grabbed the hairbrush and quickly brushed her blonde shoulder length hair. It really didn't make much difference for her naturally curly locks, but she felt it just wouldn't be right to not brush it at all.

Eileen picked out the blouse she wanted. She didn't know whether she wanted to wear a skirt or slacks, so she laid both on the bed. She chose a pair of shoes from the neatly arranged pairs on the floor of the closet and dropped them by the bed. She then stood back and eyed the skirt and slacks. She thought the weatherman said it would be a bit windy today, so she settled on the slacks. She grabbed a bra and panties out of the dresser drawer, slipped into them, and then finished with the slacks, blouse, and shoes. *How did my swimsuit get into the underwear drawer?* She would not need it anymore this year. Maybe in January or February, if she decided to take a tropical vacation. Before she put it in its proper place, she held it up to her body and looked into the mirror. *This is a great bathing suit*, she thought. She got a lot of second looks this past spring when she was in Cancun. The suit wasn't very old. She would definitely keep it for another year; she placed it in its proper drawer.

Eileen then walked over to the mirror on the door to the bedroom and took a look at herself. *These slacks and blouse really don't look that great*, she thought, *but they'll have to do.* Eileen never thought she looked great, but the truth was she had a body any man would enjoy staring at. She was a little on the thin side, though she always thought she looked a little too plump. Her skin was smooth and a creamy white with a few freckles. She thought she needed a bit of a tan, but she always burned; she never tanned. "Well, I guess this has to do," she said and walked out of the bedroom. Her purse was on the dining room table. She put a few things inside, which she thought were necessary to get through the day, grabbed her keys and went through the door to the garage.

Eileen got into her Volvo and inserted the key. The engine turned over and started immediately. The odometer showed the car was getting up in years, but like Eileen, the car looked and drove like it was in its prime. The Volvo had been kind to Eileen over the past eight years, with few problems. She always took good care of the vehicle and always took it in for the required maintenance. She slipped the gearshift into reverse, backed out, eased the lever into drive, and depressed the accelerator. The Volvo responded quickly and sped forward.

Eileen had thirty minutes to get to work. It was only a fifteen-minute drive, so she had plenty of time to stop by Starbucks for her morning dose of caffeine. She ordered her usual café latte and off she went. She soon arrived at the stock trading firm, where she had been a stock analyst for as long as she could remember. The building was as warm and inviting as her latte for a change. It was usually a little too cool inside for her. She flipped the light switch on in her office and started her computer. Then she sat and leaned back to sip on her drink as the computer booted up.

This was Eileen's life since she began her career so many years ago. Day after day, week after week, and year after year, her routine seldom changed. She was committed to her job and rarely took a sick day. She had four weeks of vacation every year, and usually took a couple of week long trips a year somewhere, as she really loved to travel and see new places. She usually spent the other two weeks around home, seeing what the city had to offer. There were concerts on a regular basis, and she would buy tickets when she found one she really liked. An occasional cooking class was always fun, and numerous trips to the library took up a lot of time. The rest of the time she spent around the house and in the backyard with her tiny garden. She went on shopping sprees trying to find clothes that would make her look better, though she never thought she achieved this objective. Occasionally, she would take a trip out of the country, usually a tropical vacation, as she loved the sand and sun. Not much sand where she lived in Texas, but she did have plenty of sun. There was usually a little too much sun in the middle of the summer with her light skin, but she liked it nevertheless. The spring and fall were much better suited for her complexion, provided she kept up the protection with sun block, which she did religiously. A lady had to protect her skin, if she wished to remain a lady and not turn into a prune.

Eileen's life, for many people, would be considered pretty boring. She was a workaholic, but she had her hobbies and her vacations. She didn't feel bored. Eileen lived alone and took solace in her tiny garden. She didn't have much room; her backyard had space for two planters and two fruit trees. Her patio table and chairs, as well as a few potted plants, fit very nicely on the back porch. She also had a few herbs planted along the back fence. It wasn't much, but the plants provided some healthy and tasty additions to her meals. Eileen was a good cook and took great care in preparing recipes she found in her several cookbooks. When she wanted something to soothe her desire for another tropical vacation, Eileen would search her computer for new and different exotic recipes.

Her computer was a little slow booting up this morning, but finally her stock program was displayed. As Eileen scrolled through the list of stocks on her computer, she noticed something a little disconcerting. As she continued to scroll further down through the list of stocks, it became increasingly difficult to find one that had risen. Almost all the stocks were falling. She checked the blue chips, and they had all dropped one to three percent. Could it be the President's speech night before last? Was it a small slow-down due to the impending winter? The holidays were upon us—was it due to lack-luster sales? Maybe there was a new report out she hadn't seen. She began checking reports. No new reports. What was going on! *This is unusual*, she thought.

Then the talk around the office began to filter in. The Dow Jones lost four hundred points just after the opening bell. Eileen got busy checking and then double checking. She could not find one rising stock; everything was falling! An hour went by and the Dow lost another six hundred points. Eileen became concerned, and then she got scared. She had heard all the apocalyptic talk the past few years with the saddening economy, the growing crime rate, unstable fuel prices, and a President who seemed even more incompetent than the last one. She recalled that president severely aggravated the country and economy years back, due to his incompetence. Eileen was always optimistic and tried to shrug off all this talk. Our economy was bad, but it couldn't be this bad. Maybe there would be an apocalypse one day, but not now. Eileen kept checking and double checking. No change. Everything continued to fall. Then Wall Street abruptly shut down the Stock Exchange. This was a measure put in effect years ago to try to prevent a market crash, and to let things simmer down a bit and prevent panic trading. The Dow had lost 1,546 points, or 10%, in only a few short hours, and it was shut down for one hour. Eileen sighed.

Eileen walked to the break room to grab a soda. The room was empty. She got her drink out of the vending machine and walked back to her office. The office seemed rather quiet in spite of the market. People were not talking. They were busy at their computers trying to figure out what was going on. Eileen sat down at her computer and got busy too. She checked the precious metals. Metals were rising. They had been rising for weeks. *This is good*, she thought. *No! This is bad*. She continued checking. She checked commodities, futures, reports of every kind—anything that might give her a clue as to what was happening and where things were heading. Eileen didn't have time to read all the details in every report, so she printed most of them out so she could read them later.

Eileen worked hard the remaining hours of the day, checking everything she thought would give her a clue as to what might be happening. Quitting time came around with no solid clues emerging from the reports she had read. There was still a huge pile of reports she found and printed but had not read. She stacked these reports in a neat pile on the end of her desk. Eileen put her phone into her purse, grabbed the unread reports, stuffed them into a folder, and then walked to the door. She didn't say a word to anyone, as she walked out the back door to her parking space and climbed into her Volvo. Her phone rang. The screen said it was her mother. "Hello Mom," she said. Her mother lived in Lexington, Kentucky.

"Eileen, what is going on with the stock market? I heard on the radio the market crashed!"

"No, Mom, it didn't crash."

"They said it did!"

"No, Mom, it just had a little drop as it does occasionally. It was just a little adjustment," Eileen explained. "The market does that from time to time. It doesn't mean anything," she continued.

"Are you sure?"

"Yes, Mom," Eileen assured her.

"Alright, if you say so. When are you going to come out to visit me, dear?"

"Not for a while, Mom. I'm really busy with work now, and I've used up all my vacation time, so it will be a while"

"You could take off if you really wanted, sweetheart."

"No Mom, I can't. I'm just getting off work. I had just gotten into my car and was ready to head home when you called."

"Okay, dear, I won't keep you, but you should come out to see me. I won't be around forever. You really need to come see me more often."

Eileen rolled her eyes back in her head. They had a terrible fight last time she was there. Mom accused her of abandoning her in this mediocre dump halfway across the country from her favorite daughter. Eileen was her only daughter. She didn't have any choice in the decision. Mom wasn't about to live in Texas. "It's too hot in Texas," she said at the time. *Lexington is not much better, but that is where she wanted to live,* Eileen recollected. *The independent living place she is living in is really comfortable and the food is better than most, but Mom always finds something to complain about,* Eileen thought. *One minute she can be so sweet, and the next she's yelling at me about a problem she imagined or created. Mom's getting so bitchy in her old age.*

"Yes, Mom. I love you," Eileen said in an irritated voice.

"I love you too, dear. I'll talk to you later."

"I'll call you soon, Mom. Bye."

"Bye, dear."

They hung up and Eileen started the car, backed out and headed home.

She didn't turn the radio on during the drive home. All she could think about was the stack of reports lying on the passenger seat as she drove. Eileen pulled into the garage of her suburban home. Her home looked just like every other house on the block. It was not an expensive residence, but it was comfortable in every way and close to her work. The brick structure was sturdy and required little maintenance. She wished the front yard was a little smaller and the back a little larger, so she could have a couple more fruit trees and maybe a few more planters to grow more vegetables. But, she had what she had and was reasonably comfortable where she lived.

She had been single since her second divorce. She didn't remember how many years ago that was, but she felt reasonably safe here. The neighborhood was nice and she was comfortable taking her walks after work. The neighborhood was in a low crime area, but in spite of this, Eileen was always careful and paid attention to her surroundings. She had grown up in Houston, in an area that was not so safe.

Eileen closed the garage door and then opened the door into the house and stepped inside. She turned off the alarm and set her folder of reports on the kitchen table. She quickly changed clothes and then reset the alarm, walked out the front door and locked the door behind her. She checked her phone for the time and then proceeded on her routine walk. This time, though, her walk was a little different. She didn't pay too much attention to the changing leaves on the trees and the other beautiful sights in the neighborhood. She had a lot on her mind and her thoughts occupied most of her walk.

About an hour later, Eileen returned from her walk, took out the keys to the front door and then went into the safety of her home. She turned on the television, grabbed a soda and curled up in her recliner with the reports. The local news had already gone off, so she tuned in to CNN. She listened to the television while she read reports. All the talk on television was about the stock market, but she heard nothing she didn't already know. There were some stories about oil prices, rioting in the big cities, and the war against terrorism, which had been going on for years. Nothing new, just the usual. Eileen finished the reports, made a meal out of leftovers, grabbed a book and curled back up in the recliner. She reached over to the table, hit the off button on the remote to the TV, and opened the novel she was about halfway through. She read her book until her eyes got heavy, and then went to bed.

The next morning Eileen was back up at 6:00 AM. She finished her morning routine and was back at work just before eight o'clock. She hadn't slept very well. She kept waking up during the night with the thought of all the reports she had read popping into her mind over and over. She didn't feel tired or sleepy, though, as adrenalin was flowing through her veins. She was anxious to see what the morning would bring. She got back to her computer. As she scrolled through the stocks, there was little change since yesterday. It wouldn't be long before the stock exchange rang the bell for another day of trading. Eight-thirty came around, and Eileen kept scrolling through the stocks to watch the early morning action. The Dow lost another two hundred points in early trading, and then slowed to a crawl—a crawl downward. *Maybe the worst is over*, she thought. Most of the day was uneventful, but about thirty minutes before the final bell, the stocks took another tumble—more like a crash. Another 1,600 points before the bell sounded. Eileen got goose bumps. She felt a chill run through her and pulled her sweater hanging on back of her chair over her shoulders, though it wasn't cool at all in the office. Why was this happening? The reports she had read were not good, but certainly not bad enough to warrant the crash in the market. There had to be a reason, but what was it? She didn't know, but would search for an answer.

Quitting time rolled around again, and Eileen went home. She took her usual walk but cut it a little short this time. She wanted to look over the reports she had collected from the previous day, plus a few more she had brought home today. She ate a light dinner and curled up in her recliner with the reports. She did not turn on the television. She knew what the newscasters would be saying, but they would not know *why* either. Eileen went over report after report. Still, there was nothing to indicate why the market was falling. Maybe there was not one specific cause. Maybe it was a cumulative effect. None of the reports were overly bad—just none of them were good. None of them!

The next day, Eileen was again up at her usual time and performed her usual routine without exception; she arrived at work at her usual punctual time. It was Friday. *What will happen today?* She asked herself. She hoped today would be a better day—that the market would turn around. Usually there are plenty of buyers in a bear market, which tends to drive stocks back up. Just a small upturn would give her hope. What if it continued to fall? She would know by the end of the day. The morning bell rang and immediately the stocks began to fall. After an hour, trading was stopped. Were there no buyers? Trading resumed in an hour, and again the stocks tumbled. Trading was then stopped a second time for two hours because the stocks lost 20%. This was the first time anyone could ever remember this happening. Finally, an hour before the final bell would sound, trading started up again. There seemed to be nothing anyone could do. The market took a final nose dive, with all stocks losing at least half their value since the start of all this mayhem just 56 hours ago.

Eileen loved working with stocks. It was fascinating to watch the market rise and fall, rise and fall. But this was not a rise and fall; it was a crash, a disaster. Eileen had money in stocks. She couldn't sell now. That would be giving her money away. This was the time to buy! She knew this, but she didn't have the money to buy. Her mortgage and utilities took a big chunk out of her paycheck. Her yearly trips took much of her excess cash, along with all the extras she felt she needed to live a comfortable life. Eileen did live a comfortable life, but she had little savings other than the money she had stuffed into the stock market. Much of that was now gone. Her goose bumps turned to chills. She was a strong woman, but she was getting scared—really scared! Monday was a holiday. Eileen saw the reminder on the bulletin board.

She quietly went to her car and headed home. For a change she altered her trip home. She stopped at Starbucks for an extra dose of caffeine. The line at the drive-thru was long. Maybe there were a lot of others who felt today was a double Starbucks day. *Well, at least one business seems to be doing okay,* she thought.

Eileen finally got her drink and drove home. She would have plenty of time for a long walk tomorrow, so she altered her routine once again. She went straight to the television. By not taking her walk, she was able to catch the local news. This was a holiday weekend, but there was no celebrating. Instead, there were riots and several stories about armed robberies. One store clerk was killed over a six-pack of beer and a carton of cigarettes. The bad news went on and on. The local news showed bits and pieces of national news in their program, and it looked and sounded just like the local news. Maybe a little worse in some areas of the country, but still an awful lot of death and destruction everywhere. Finally, Eileen turned off the television. She didn't want to see or hear anymore. Eileen didn't need to read the reports anymore either. She felt in her gut that terrible things were going to happen in the coming days and weeks. She didn't need the news or reports to tell her this. Maybe this was the apocalypse and maybe it was not. It really didn't matter. Whatever it was, it was going to be bad.

Eileen went out to her backyard. She had some Asian pears on her young tree which were ready to eat. She walked over and pulled off a big one, then went over to her patio table and sat in one of the chairs facing the evening sky. The sun was almost down, but there was plenty of light for a little while. Eileen nibbled at her pear and gazed at the clear blue sky overhead merging into the yellow western sky. A high band of cirrus clouds were brightly colored by the setting sun. Eileen was in awe of the beautiful sunset. Suddenly, she heard a gunshot in the distance. *This can't be happening in my neighborhood,* she thought. She didn't know what was happening out there, but she could guess. *It could be a car backfire.* It didn't matter what it was; it still scared her. *No! It was a gunshot.*

Most businesses would be closed on Monday due to the holiday. She imagined almost as many would be closed Tuesday and afterward as well. She wished she had gone to the bank before she came home. Suddenly, Eileen sprang up and ran into the house. She had to get to an ATM. She grabbed her keys and purse, raced to her car and headed out. It wasn't far to a nearby bank. *Good,* she thought, *there is no one here.* She inserted her card into the machine and entered her pin. She wasn't certain the machine would work, but it did. *Yes!* She tried again and it worked, taking out the maximum amount each time. It worked three times before it would not let her withdraw any more. At least she had some cash for a few days. Then she heard several gunshots in rapid succession. She looked around and saw no one, but as she pulled out of the bank parking lot, she saw a pickup truck chasing a car. There were men leaning out of the windows and they were shooting at each other. *What the hell is going on?* She asked herself. Eileen pulled out of the parking lot, as the vehicles faded into the distance. In the direction of downtown, she noticed several plumes of smoke rising into the air. *Shit!* Eileen rushed home, shut her garage and set the burglar alarm. She was relieved a bit but still very scared. She was locked up in her home, but she didn't feel safe anymore.

Eileen read a lot of books. She always carried one or two with her. She had even read a couple of apocalyptic books. She knew what could happen—what might happen. She could not believe this was actually coming true, but it was as plain as the nose on her face. She needed a plan. She did not turn on the television. She fixed a nice, large meal. After eating what she could, Eileen was thankful there were enough leftovers for a good two or three days. She packed the food in plastic containers and went outside with a plastic bag to pick the remaining dozen pears off her tree. There was nothing else in the garden she could use. She double checked the locks on the rear and side gates to her backyard, went back inside, locked the door and reset the alarm. Eileen decided she had to leave town. It was too late to leave tonight, but she would be ready by daylight tomorrow.

Damn! She had forgotten gas. She grabbed her keys and hurried out to check the fuel level. She inserted and turned the key. The gauge edged up to three-quarters of a tank. *That will have to be enough,* she thought. Eileen got her large suitcase from the closet and put it on the bed. She packed plenty of underwear, and then all the slacks and blouses she could easily fit into the suitcase. She also had a couple pairs of jeans and three old flannel shirts which had belonged to her ex. She had planned to rip the shirts up for cleaning rags, but had never gotten around to it. There hadn't been the need yet. She hurried into the kitchen and grabbed a reusable grocery bag and stuffed it with all the shoes she thought she might need. She kept out a pair of tennis shoes for tomorrow. A pair of jeans and a tee shirt went onto the bed for tomorrow as well. Eileen then went into the kitchen and grabbed a pen and paper, and then stretched out in her recliner. She started a list of other things she might need. Toiletries were first on the list. Once the list was completed, she got up, dragged out all the items on the list, neatly organized them, and put them into the Volvo. She then crawled into bed and tried to get some sleep; she would need it tomorrow.

It was hard, but Eileen did manage to get a few hours of sleep. There were more gunshots during the night. She was up at her usual time; she showered and grabbed some last minute items. Most of what she had packed last night was already loaded neatly into the trunk of the Volvo. She grabbed some nutrition bars, yesterday's leftovers and a large drink in an insulated mug. She also filled an empty plastic milk jug with drinking water. The sun was just about up as she secured the house and backed out of her driveway. Eileen still did not have a plan. She had tried to come up with one as she tossed and turned in bed, but to no avail. She wanted to drive south, as north would take her directly into the city. She definitely wanted to avoid the city and anything that might be happening there. Probably not much would be going on in town this early in the morning, but you just never knew. South was her destination.

There was little traffic, as Eileen pulled out of the suburbs and onto the main highway. She noticed that she smelled smoke and realized what she had thought was fog was in fact smoke. She instinctively looked into the rear view mirror to see the downtown area completely obscured by smoke. She tried to tune in a local radio station, and finally found one. In fact, there were only three stations on the entire band that she could understand. All the stations had static, as if they were transmitting on limited power. There was no news—only music. There was no talking on the station even between songs. Eileen expected a DJ to say at least something between songs, but there was only music. It was like there was no one at the stations—as if everything was on automatic and unattended. Eileen drove for a couple of hours, avoiding the larger towns as best she could while maintaining her southerly direction. There was very little activity even in the small communities. She would see people every now and then sitting in their car or checking to see if a local business was open. It didn't look to Eileen as if anything was open. It was still early, but she expected something to be open, especially gas stations. She was wrong.

After about three hours, Eileen came upon a roadside park. She decided to pull into the empty park to have a snack and stretch her legs for a bit. She didn't stray far from the car in case someone happened by. There were almost no cars on the road. Maybe one or two every hour or so. Eileen looked about at the trees and landscape; it seemed so serene. The birds chirped and there was a gentle breeze blowing through the trees. The leaves rustled a bit, as they were dry and changing color in preparation for the coming winter. It seemed so peaceful out here. There was no sign of the brewing disaster in this country. Eileen took the last bite of her snack and then a sip of water before getting back into her car and driving on.

After hours of driving, Eileen had no idea where she was going or what she would do when she got there. She only knew she had to get out of the city; her life depended upon it. Her gas gauge was going down and down. She had just over a quarter tank of fuel left. *This is getting serious*, she thought as she eyed the gauge. Then she began to cry. Eileen was a tough lady, but she had just left her entire world behind to head off into only God knows where. Had she lost her mind? She mulled the question over and over in her head, while she continued to drive south. The sun had passed the midday point, and all Eileen had accomplished was to get out of the city and into the middle of nowhere. She decided to pull over again but had to find someplace she thought would be safe. Finally, she found a side road in a flat area that she could back down, which would allow her to see behind her, as well as down both directions of the main road. She backed about a hundred feet down the side road and cut off the engine. Her tears had dried, but she could feel them coming back. "You've got to be strong," she murmured. Eileen took a deep breath, "suck it up", and pulled herself together. She had to make a plan. Up until now, she had no plan. A bad plan would be better than no plan at all, which is what she currently had. The fuel gauge registered less than a quarter of a tank now. It would not take her much farther. Eileen got out her phone and checked the signal. The phone was fully charged but she had no bars. *Not even one,* she thought. She had to make a plan.

Eileen leaned back in her seat and closed her eyes a moment to go over her options. She could not go back; there were no gas stations open. She would get stranded on the open road and that was not an option. She was far enough from the city that she wasn't familiar with the terrain, so she didn't know what to expect if she continued on. An old map she found in the glove compartment didn't reveal much. The past few hours of driving hadn't presented any good options for her. Would the next couple of hours be any different should she drive on? She could only hope. "Think," she said to herself. Eileen finally decided she couldn't drive on. She would be out of gas, and then what? She'd be dead in the water, so to speak. That wasn't an option. But what then?

Next thing she knew, she was waking up from a sound sleep. *Damn!* The last thing she should have done was to fall asleep, but she just couldn't help herself.

What time was it? She looked around. At least the sun was still up, but it was getting rather low. "Shit!" It would be dark in an hour. Should she risk getting back onto the highway? She didn't think so. But she couldn't stay where she was, and the only viable option she could come up with was to see where this side road led. Eileen cranked up the car, turned around and then headed slowly down the side road. After a few minutes she began to have some crazy thoughts. *Wow*, she pondered. *This seems to be a scene in a very bad horror film.* Was she crazy? Maybe so. Was this the only reasonable option she could come up with? *I should have stayed in the city* was the thought that came to mind. It was too late now. She imagined there would be a little farm at the end of the road, where there lived a crazed murderer who chopped his victims up and fed the body parts to his pet pig. Then she really got scared. She had to stop this thinking. She would be okay. That was just a movie. Things really didn't happen like that in real life.

Eileen had to have driven four miles down the road and still there was nothing but more road. The sun had gone down and it would be dark soon. There were a lot of trees, which made it even darker than it would have been out in the open. A couple more miles and still there was nothing. It was really dark now. She had to stop, so she pulled off the road and killed the engine. When she turned the lights off, it was really dark—darker than in her bedroom when she turned the lights off. It must have been overcast, as she could see no stars. The moon, if there was a moon, could not penetrate the heavy blanket.

Eileen checked to make certain all the doors were locked. Then she reached back to find another snack. She refilled her mug with water and opened the plastic container in which she had packed some of the leftovers from home. She wasn't all that hungry but continued to nibble at the dish, as she mulled over her situation and options. She checked her phone again and still had no bars. Eileen had always been a very rational girl, but she had gotten herself into a really bad situation. No matter how long and hard she tried, she could not come up with any rational solutions. She finished her snack, took another sip of water, and continued to mull over her options. She tried and tried to come up with a viable course of action and a new plan. Finally, frustrated and tired, she began to cry again and soon dozed off.

Eileen awoke the next morning well rested. *It's hard to believe*, she thought, *I slept better last night out here in the wilderness than I have the previous two nights at home.* The sun was already up by the time she woke up, and Eileen had to pee. She looked around the car, and everything looked all right, so she unlocked the car door and got out. The air was heavy and moist. She could feel a slight breeze through the thick trees and brush. The air felt warm too. It was fall, but this morning felt like a very nice summer morning. She listened a bit, as she continued to monitor her surroundings. Except for the sounds of a few birds, there was an eerie quiet in the woods. She heard the screech of a hawk in the distance, but there were no city sounds, just peace and quiet. Eileen walked around to the front of the car, just in case someone came down the road. Maybe they wouldn't see her squatting there. She unbuttoned and unzipped her jeans and reached for the seam at the hips. Then she took another look around before pulling them and her panties down to her knees. She squatted down in the tall grass and let go with some past due relief. The grass tickled her underside and a smile developed on her lips, partly from the grass, but mostly from the relief she felt. There was no toilet paper to dry herself. *I knew there was something missing from the list*, she thought. Too late now. She would need to work on this. Next time it may be more than a pee she needed. She pulled up her panties and jeans, and then took another look around. She was still alone.

Eileen walked around to the back of the car and looked up and down the road. She couldn't go back to the highway. She didn't have enough gas to go very far. Going back just didn't seem to be the best option. But what was down this road? Maybe it was a road to nowhere. Where would that get her? She didn't seem to be in a hurry to get anywhere at this point. She wasn't going very far regardless of whatever decision she made, that was certain. After a while of taking in the beautiful scenery and the peace and quiet, Eileen finally decided to continue down the road and see where it took her. It seemed to be her only sensible option, regardless of how irrational it might be. She got back into the car and turned the key. Nothing happened. She turned it off and then back on again. Still nothing. What could be wrong? She pressed on the horn and it sounded loudly. *Dammit! That was a bad decision. What if someone had heard me? Too late now.* She just sat there looking around and up and down the road. After about thirty minutes, everything was still the same. No one came around. She tried the key again, and again nothing. She got back out of the car and looked around some more. Only the birds chirped. Everything was peaceful and quiet. *Maybe no harm has been done*, she thought.

She filled her mug with water, put a few nutrition bars into her jacket, locked the car, folded the jacket over her arm and headed down the road. She walked slowly and constantly kept looking over her shoulder. It was nearly noon by now, and the day seemed to be shaping up into a wonderful summer day, just not quite as hot as it usually got during the summer. A stiff breeze had picked up, and since it was warm, she assumed it was from the south. That would make her direction of travel to the southeast. After an hour of walking, her situation had not changed one iota. Another hour passed, then two. The road narrowed a bit, but it did look traveled, at least on occasion. There were no recent tracks, but someone had been using the path.

She was at the point of no return now. She couldn't see any reason to turn around. The trouble was, she couldn't see any reason to continue on. If she went back to the car, she would have a place to stay the night, but where would she go tomorrow? The choice of going to the highway or returning down this same road to this same spot would have to be made all over again. She couldn't just keep walking back and forth between here and the car. There really was no option. She could only continue down this road, regardless of how unproductive her journey had been thus far. She continued forward. If the situation were a little different, she could be taking a leisurely walk in the beautiful countryside on a gorgeous day, but the situation was not different. She was stranded and lost. Her bad situation had turned into a nightmare. *You're so stupid*, she thought to herself. Another hour, then two hours and still little changed. The scenery did not change. Her situation did not improve. She had another hour or so before sundown, and then a little more and she would be in total darkness. She walked a little faster, and then she ran a ways. She slowed back to a normal walk after a while, and she could feel the tears welling up in her eyes again. Eileen remembered having nightmares when she was a child. None of them were as bad as the nightmare she was now living.

It was getting dark, and rather quickly. "Now you've done it," she muttered to herself. There was only one thing she could do—find a soft place to lie down and go to sleep. Eileen could just barely make out a large tree just off the road. She walked over and checked out the ground with her hand. She couldn't see the ground very well, but it felt soft. She didn't feel any burrs. She laid down, curled up, and went to sleep. She woke up rested, but she was sore from sleeping on the hard ground. The grass didn't soften up the dirt enough to make any difference.

Eileen felt tired, and she had a nasty taste in her mouth. *No toothbrush!* She had about half her mug of water. She took a swallow and swished it around in her mouth. She started to spit it out, but then thought that she couldn't be wasting her water, and swallowed. She continued down the road, and it wasn't long before she had to pee. She found a nice spot just off the road, took a quick look around, and then pulled down her jeans and panties. Before she pulled her britches up, she looked at her panties; she didn't know why and wished she hadn't, but it was too late now. They were stained yellow from peeing yesterday. She pulled them up quickly. She had always kept herself clean, but having looked at the panties, she now felt dirty all over. She grabbed another nutrition bar out of her jacket, ate it quickly, and then headed down the road.

After several hours, she stopped to eat an Asian pear she took from her jacket and to rest for a while. She found a log alongside the road to sit on. Then she dug around in her jacket to find only one more nutrition bar. That would be supper. Her mug was down to one-quarter. She had better find something soon. *I will tomorrow*, she thought. Eileen continued on her way and began looking at the scenery again. There might be something she could eat. She did not recognize most of the trees. They all seemed to be just trees—no fruit; no berries; nothing. So far, she had not crossed any streams. There were no puddles and no water sources. She was in trouble, and her situation seemed to be getting progressively worse. "You're an optimist," she kept saying to herself, but being an optimist in her current situation was not easy.

Maybe I should have stayed in the city, Eileen thought. *No, I had no gun; no way to protect myself if someone broke in. If I had a gun I would have probably shot myself. The city was burning and people were shooting at each other. I would have had to stay inside and would have starved to death in a week or so. I didn't know my neighbors. I didn't take the time to get to know them. I worked all the time, and though some seemed nice and waved hi when I took my walks, I did not take the time to really meet them and get to know them. They may have helped, but I don't know that. Maybe I should have been a little more outgoing. Yes, I did the right thing by leaving the city, though the more doesn't seem so right at the moment. The apocalypse books I've read tell of endless horrors in the cities when things go terribly wrong.*

Yes, I did the right thing, Eileen thought as she walked and continued to ponder her decision to leave the city. *No matter how wrong the decision might seem to be right now, I did do the right thing. I wonder how Mom is doing. Do I really care?* Eileen took her phone out again and checked the signal. No bars as she expected. *Well, I have a very nice clock*, she thought.

Another day was about gone, and no progress. Eileen pulled out her last nutrition bar and ate it. She chased it down with about half the water she had left, which was only a couple swallows. She would save the rest for later tonight before going to sleep. She had to remember, though, to save just a sip to rinse her mouth in the morning. Eileen found a reasonable place to sleep, and after a bit of tossing and turning, she dozed off.

The next morning, Eileen rinsed her mouth with the last of her water and pressed onward. Finally, something changed—not much, but a change nevertheless. There was a tree across the road! It wasn't just any tree though; it was a huge tree and it looked as though it had recently been cut down. But what did this mean? *Eileen, think dammit!* One, there was a freshly cut tree. She could see footprints, no, shoe prints but with no heels, among the chips of bark and wood from the tree. Two, someone intentionally cut this tree, but why? Three, there were no tracks behind her except her own. Someone had come from down the road and deliberately chopped down this tree. She could see footprints leading from somewhere down the road and then back, but why? Four. She had no four.

Eileen stepped over the tree and continued down the road. She walked a little slower now, trying to come up with four but could not. The only thing she could think about was that her options had not changed; she still had no recourse but to continue forward. It didn't matter what the tree meant, she still had to stay her course. The only thing she now knew was that sooner or later she would run into someone. It was getting late again, and it looked like she would be spending another night in the woods. *Great!* She thought. Now that the sky had darkened, she could see the flashes of lightning behind her. There must be a cold front coming in. That's all she needed, as if her situation wasn't bad enough. Eileen continued to walk in the dark, but after a little bit, she could not tell where the road ran. She didn't have a choice now; she was sleeping in the woods again.

Eileen could just barely see what appeared to be a large tree at the side of the road. She walked in that direction until she touched the bark. She could not reach around the tree, which made it quite large. She knelt and felt the ground, and it felt like grass. She sat down and leaned back against the tree. Eileen stared into the darkness seeing nothing but black, and then nothing but trees when the lightning flashes lit up the night sky. Suddenly a cool breeze began to pick up from the direction of the lightning, and a light rain began to fall. All of a sudden, the sky flashed brightly and a clap of thunder rang out really close. Eileen zipped her jacket up tightly and pulled the collar up around her neck. She tried to catch a few raindrops in her mouth, but they just barely wet her tongue and lips. The rain did not fall hard or for long, and she was thankful for that except that she could have used a drink now that her mug was empty. The wind continued to blow harder and got quite a bit colder. She curled up in a fetal position and tried to stay warm. She didn't know how, as uncomfortable as she was, but it wasn't long before she fell asleep.

When morning came, Eileen was up early. She was really cold and wet through and through; her jacket wasn't waterproof. Another misstep on her part. It must have rained more after she had fallen asleep. The temperature had to be around forty and she was shaking. She was really thankful she had slept through what had to be a miserable night for her body. The morning was plenty miserable as well. Eileen had to pee again. At first thought, she considered peeing in her pants. It would certainly feel nice and warm for a bit, but even though her panties were already stained yellow, it probably wouldn't be the wisest thing to do. She had been shaking from the cold even before she had gotten up from her sleep. Now she was much colder and shaking severely, as she quickly pulled up her pants.

Eileen walked over to the road. She dug around in her jacket pocket for a nutrition bar. She had forgotten she ate the last one last night. Her mug was empty. She had finished it off as well. *I should have left the top off last night to see if it would catch some rainwater,* Eileen thought. *Another misstep on my part.* She dropped the mug to the ground. In one of the apocalypse books she had read, she remembered the mention of drinking pee. She thought about it for a second, but it didn't take more than an instant to dispel that idea. Eileen was now hungry, thirsty, and colder than she could ever remember being in her entire life. She was also sore and quite a bit more tired than yesterday. In spite of all this, she decided a little running would be in order to warm up a bit, so off she went at a moderate pace for a while. This worked quite well. She stopped shaking; and though she was still cold, she wasn't nearly as cold as she was earlier. After about fifteen minutes, she slowed to a walk. Her legs were getting a little shaky; it must be from lack of food and water. In her present condition, it would now take several days to get back to the car. It wasn't really an option anymore, but if she didn't improve her situation by mid-day, she thought she could still make it back to the car before she starved to death. Her situation hadn't improved much, but at least she could see where she was walking.

After what seemed to be about an hour, Eileen heard a gunshot. She stopped and squatted down in the road. Then she looked around and listened carefully. Another shot rang out in the direction she was headed. Was someone shooting at her? She ruled that out. Texas folk don't miss, and she was still alive. Maybe a hunter? Was it hunting season? She didn't know. After a few minutes, she moved off the road and squatted next to a tree, and then leaned back to watch and listen. There were no more shots after her estimation of a half hour. Eileen got up and walked back to the road. She thought she may as well head in the direction of the shots. She walked slowly and kept her eyes and ears open for the slightest irregularity. The shots had seemed to be a good distance off, and after another hour or so she had not seen anyone or any sign of civilization. It wasn't much longer though, until the trees began to thin out and there appeared to be a clearing up ahead. She slowed her pace and looked more intensely for any sign of people. She also kept an eye over her shoulder. As slow as she was walking, someone could sneak up behind her.

Indeed, there was a clearing ahead. The trees opened up to a valley, and she could see a bit of smoke on the far side of the clearing. She stopped for a minute and looked around. She didn't see anyone. Eileen continued ahead, until she could see the house with a little smoke coming from the chimney. A wood fire was burning inside. She was cold and someone was very cozy in their comfortable house. She couldn't just walk up though. Even though she was cold, hungry, thirsty, and exhausted, that would be a good way to get shot. Eileen edged up a little closer to get a better look. There was a tree only a couple hundred yards from the house, and Eileen thought this would be a good place to sit a while and see what she could learn about the inhabitants. She eased up on the tree, keeping it between herself and the house. She sat down with the tree covering about half her body and watched. Eileen checked her phone for the time. An hour went by, and she saw nothing. It was still fairly early in the afternoon, so she decided to sit for another hour or so before she made a move.

As Eileen sat half concealed behind the tree, she looked around the property. It was hard to miss the large garden, neatly plowed and ready for the upcoming winter, or maybe it was about time to plant a fall garden. She didn't know which. The tall fence around the garden was in good shape, and there was a large gate on the one end. She assumed it was there so the tractor could be used to work the field. This was obvious with the tractor nearby. There was a small rain gauge on the corner post nearest the house, which glistened in the sunlight, probably due to a little water in the bottom from the rain last night. The house looked nice enough; not quite what she would expect of a crazed murderer, but what did she know? She didn't know any crazed murderers. There was a brown truck at the side of the house. It appeared to be only a few years old. The metal roof on the house looked pretty new, too; it still had the shiny look of a new one. There did not appear to be any dogs around. This was good for her; if there were dogs, she would have been found out by now, since she was only half hidden by the tree, and a dog could likely smell her body odor for miles. There were chickens, but they were not very good guard dogs. Why was there no one outside? Was it too cold? Certainly not for country people, especially country people with dry clothes. Where was the wife, if there was one? Maybe the wife was inside preparing a meal for her hunter, who would be returning soon with his fresh kill. There didn't seem to be any kids. No tricycles or bicycles around. No swing set or other indication there might be kids. If there were kids, they would be noisy. Kids always made a lot of racket. Did this place belong to an old hermit? With such a large garden, there had to be a family. But where were they? Maybe there was no one at home. But there was a fire in the fireplace, and certainly the shots she heard earlier had to come from here, or at least nearby. She just didn't know. Should she just walk down like she owned the place and see what happened? That didn't seem like the best option—as if she had been making good choices over the past few days! Maybe she would sneak just a little closer. She thought about it for a bit, and finally decided sneaking a little closer was the only decent idea she could come up with. Besides, it was damn cold and she was wet. She would likely die of hypothermia tonight if she didn't do something pretty damn soon.

She climbed up to her feet, using a low hanging tree limb for help, and stood behind the tree for a few minutes. Her legs were stiff from the cold and being in one position for such a long time. They were a little weak from her lack of food too. She angled well to the right of the house and walked bent over with her head down, as if someone were watching, they would not see her. Right! If someone was watching, of course they would see her. She was not wearing camouflage, not her; ladies don't wear camo. Her jacket was not red, but it was relatively bright. She could be seen from a mile away! Then she stood up as straight as she could and just walked. Occasionally she would peek around and behind her to make certain no one was sneaking up on her. She cut her distance to the house in about half, and then angled toward the side of the house.

There were no windows on this side of the house. There were a few shrubs, and the brick base and column of the chimney, a little trickle of smoke still rising from the top. This side of the house gave her some protection from the wind. Eileen was bordering on hypothermia now. She had stopped shaking for a while, but it had started again. She had run out of adrenalin. Maybe it was blood sugar she had run out of. She was certainly hungry, and shivering was burning calories. She had probably run out of everything judging by the way she felt. If she didn't know better, she'd think she was dying. That might very well be the case. As she reached the side of the house, she squatted and leaned against the house and brick of the chimney, in the little corner made by the chimney. She already felt warmer, but she continued to shake. She still had not seen anyone, so she sat down on the ground and listened. If there was someone around, she would certainly hear them.

After about fifteen minutes, she finally heard something. It sounded like someone opened and closed the front door. She could not see the front porch, but she heard footsteps, and then nothing. Was she hearing things? She did not think so, but in her condition anything was possible. Finally, she got up the nerve to crawl over and peek around the corner to see if someone had, in fact, come out the front door. She was shaking badly again as she crawled to the front corner of the house. Very slowly she peeked around. As soon as her eyes made it around the corner, she found herself peering straight into another pair of eyes. She quickly ducked back around the corner. Had he seen her? It was a man's eyes—not young and not old. She couldn't tell precisely, as her glance around the corner was only for a second. Of course he saw her; she was the one that was delirious. What would she do now?

As she squatted there trying to come up with a plan of action, she heard a voice from around the corner.

"You know I saw you, right?"

She said nothing. Then she got her nerve up to peek around the corner again. As she edged closer to the corner, her body began to shake more than ever. As her eyes rounded the corner again, once more her eyes met his. But this time he had gotten down on his knees and made his way to the corner, and just as their eyes met, he said, "boo!" She jumped and screamed at the same time, and about halfway up to her feet, she began to fall backwards. She could not catch herself and fell hard. A small shrub did not break her fall but only made her roll to the side as she fell. She landed hard on her left arm, which slowed most of her fall except for her head, which continued toward the ground. Her head fell mostly on grass, but there was one small rock about the size of her fist which caught her just above the left eye. She felt a sharp pain as the edge of the rock cut into her skin. She felt herself going limp, her eyes closing, and then she was out cold.

Chapter 4

Eileen woke up feeling warm and cozy. Where was she? Why was she here? It took a minute but the memories began to return—sneaking up on a house, or at least her version of sneaking. Her head hurt and she was hungry. At least she was no longer cold. She was beginning to get her senses back and quickly peeked under the covers. Yes, she still had most of her clothes on but no shoes and no jacket. Everything else was intact. Her body and clothes still felt damp, but she wasn't shivering. Then she noticed her body's odor! It wasn't just stink, but the smell of sweat, dirt, mud, and grass. It was the odor of gym socks and dirty underwear that had been left in a clothes hamper a day way too long. She reached for her left eye. It was covered with what felt like gauze and tape. Then she looked around the room. It was dark, but she could tell it was daylight outside. A little light came in around the heavy curtains which blocked most of the sunlight. She could make out a large dresser with a mirror hanging above. Eileen then spotted a chair beside the dresser. That was about it. There were two doors—both of them closed. Eileen climbed out of bed. The room was warm. She didn't feel the slightest chill when she got out of bed. Eileen moved to the smaller of the two doors and turned the knob. She found a light switch just inside the door. Click. It was a large sized bathroom. Towels had been laid out, as well as a soft bathrobe and some furry slippers. *Were these laid out for me? Who else would they be for? Did he lay these out for me? Maybe his wife did?* There was gauze and tape on the counter. Those had to be for her. She turned around and looked at the door. It had a lock. Eileen reached over and locked the door. As she turned back, she caught a glimpse of herself in the mirror on the medicine cabinet. She continued to look in disbelief. *Damn! Double Damn!* That pretty much described what she saw. She had never seen herself look this bad. She had always been concerned about looking old or having dressed badly, but what she saw in the mirror was death warmed over! She quickly turned away from her reflection.

Eileen slowly took off her clothes. There was a bruise on her left arm and it was sore. Where she had fallen, no doubt. There were also some scratches on the back of her right hand. She didn't remember getting these injuries, but they were real. Her right knee also hurt, and she looked down at it. She could not see any surface injury, but it hurt nevertheless. She wiggled her toes and moved around a bit to see if anything else hurt. Nothing, except her eye. She leaned toward the mirror and picked at the edge of the tape holding the gauze. Her nails were chipped and scratched, she noticed, as she picked at the tape. She managed to get a corner of the tape free and pulled. Some gauze fell into the sink below. Looking down to the sink, Eileen saw a big dried spot of blood in the middle of the gauze. There was still some gauze stuck to the tape around her eye. She pulled at the tape until the gauze was free of the wound. There was blood on this piece too. Then she looked at her eye. About an inch to the side of her eye was a little cut. It was swollen and red. As she looked closer, it looked like it had been sewn closed. On further examination, it looked like some sort of tape. At least the bleeding had stopped.

She turned to the shower, and then turned the hot water on. After a moment, the water got hot and she adjusted the temperature to her liking and stepped in. There was soap, a washcloth, and shampoos and conditioners only a woman would use on the little ledge inside the shower made for these things. As she immersed herself into the warm water and lathered up her hair with the lilac shampoo, she began to think about what she was going to do when she got out of the shower. The shower felt so good! This guy was not going to hurt her. He could have done that earlier. What day was it? She was not certain. She felt rested but could not tell how long she had slept. After her hair was clean, she put the conditioner on sparingly, rubbed it through her hair, and rinsed. She picked up the yellow bar of soap—not the same brand she usually used, but neither was the shampoo or conditioner. How could she even think of being picky at a time like this?

She stepped out of the shower and grabbed a towel. She blotted the cut by her eye first. *Good, still no blood,* she thought. It was sore, but at least it wasn't bleeding. She wrapped the towel around her hair, and then grabbed another towel. She dried herself from top to bottom. Her nipples were a bit sore. Again, her thoughts returned to her host. Was he a pervert? She was still mostly dressed when she awoke, but did he take a good look before he put her to bed? Did he pinch her nipples? Damn! *He is a pervert*, she thought. *No,* as she further considered the point. *No, her nipples were sore because they had been irritated by the dirty and wet clothing. This had to be the correct assumption.* She was getting riled up over nothing. She had to calm down. Then she thought, *what guy wouldn't want to take at least a little peek? Stop it!* She was jumping to way too many conclusions. She didn't have a clue about this guy. *He could have a wife. She could have put me to bed. Maybe not carried me in, but at least finished the task of tucking me into bed. But if this were the case, the wife definitely would not have let me fall asleep in wet, stinky and dirty clothes. The man must have put me to bed. This has to be the answer.*

Now she was scared again. She had just calmed herself down and now she was getting all upset. Finally, she finished drying off and checked her eye again. It was still not bleeding. This was good. Eileen pulled on the soft robe. Then she took the towel off her head and brushed her hair with the brush lying by the lavatory. The brush didn't help much; her hair was still a little too wet. *Oh well,* she thought, *my host is probably going to end up killing me anyway, after he rapes and has his fun with me.* Her mind was going crazy, and still she didn't have any idea who this man was or what his intentions were. *Boy do I need Valium.* There was only one way to find out. She piled her clothes and towels up in the bathroom and walked back into the bedroom. She checked the bed and the sheets were wet. They reeked of whatever Eileen smelled like before her shower. She peeled the sheets and pillow cases off and put them in a pile, and then made the bed with just the spread and comforter.

She looked around the room. There was nothing else she could do in here. Eileen walked to the larger door and then back to the chair beside the dresser and sat down. She had to get herself under control before she left the room. She took a few deep breaths and told herself she was in good hands. She tried to believe this with all her heart. It wasn't easy. She gritted her teeth, got up, and headed for the door. Her slippers made a scraping sound on the wood flooring, as she cautiously walked across the floor to the door. She slowly turned the knob and carefully opened the door. The large room looked pleasant. It was an open style with a bar, separating the kitchen from the living room and dining room. She peered around the edge of the door trying to see *him.* Whoever this guy was—whatever this guy was—she needed to meet him now. She needed to know if she was going to die now. He didn't appear to be in the house. There were two windows in the front of the house and one in back. She looked out all the windows as she walked to the center of the room. She couldn't see anyone.

Eileen took a deep breath. The room smelled homey. There was the definite odor of burned wood—not a harsh smell, but a pleasant aroma you would expect in a country home with a wood burning stove. There was also the smell of coffee. Suddenly she heard a noise at the front door. He must have been sitting out front and heard her come into the room. He had gotten up and was coming in to check on her—or rape and kill her. *No! No! Quit thinking like this,* she said to herself. *Girl, do you want to die? Just keep thinking you are going to die, and you will certainly get your wish.* The way things had been going the past couple days, this was a distinct possibility. She could see the door knob turning. Then the door suddenly swung open and there *he* stood. She thought her heart stopped; it was certainly in her throat. Was she breathing? She didn't think so. He had a big smile on his face.

"It's about time you got up and cleaned up! You hungry?" he queried.

Eileen noticed she was breathing again. She stood there in a daze and tried to speak, but the words would not come out. Her heart was still beating, and back in her chest again. She pulled the robe a little tighter and tried to speak again. "My name is Eileen." She felt the tears begin to flow again. This was all she could say. Again, "I'm Eileen," and the tears began to flow as they have never flowed at any time during her entire life. She began to tremble. He just stood there looking at her, smiling. *Oh my god*, she thought. She was definitely going to die. Just what she deserved for leaving the relative safety of the city and suburbs. *The stench of my body kept me alive until now, but now I smell like a bunch of lilacs—probably his favorite flower,* Eileen thought. Yes, she was definitely going to die. Then it—he— spoke again.

"My name is Lars. You were in pretty bad shape when I found you, day before yesterday."

Two days ago, she thought. Had she really been here two days? Had she been asleep for two days? That would most definitely account for the stench she smelled when she awoke. "What day is it?" she asked.

"Friday," he said.

If it really was Friday, he was right. *How could it be*, she thought? She did feel well rested. Other than a little soreness, she felt fine. *Well, not fine. Better, but not fine yet.* She was hungry though.

"You must be hungry," Lars said, as though he could read her mind. "I'll fix you some breakfast."

Eileen nodded, and then sat down at the dining room table. She didn't say another word. She just kept crying and crying.

"Let it all out," he said. Then Lars said probably the only words she wanted to hear, "You're safe here." The crying didn't stop, but she did feel better.

These are the best eggs I've ever eaten, Eileen thought. Toast—even butter on the toast—bacon, and jelly and syrup sitting on a wooden turntable in the center of the table. There was also salt and pepper, artificial sweetener, as well as real sugar and honey. Lars poured a cup of coffee and set it in front of Eileen. She hadn't looked Lars in the eyes since he first walked in through the front door. The food really tasted good. She looked up into his eyes and then gave him a grateful smile.

He smiled back and said, "You look like you're going to be alright. I'll get your clothes and clean them up." He walked into the bedroom and back, and then out the back door.

Eileen was alone again. She ate, looked around and ate some more. Okay, she was not going to die—not yet anyway. She began to relax, but the ordeal was a long way from being over. Who was this guy? Where was his wife? Questions! Questions! She ate until the last bite was gone. Then Lars walked back in, and with a big grin on his face, sat down directly across from Eileen and looked directly into her eyes.

Suddenly, Eileen heard, "When will your wife be back?" blurt out of her mouth.

"Oh, I'm not married," he said.

She felt the *I'm going to die* phrase swelling back up in the back of her head. "Oh!"

"No, I live here alone," Lars said. She smiled. Lars' smile had not let up since he first sat down. "Are you okay?" Lars asked.

"I think so," she responded. They just sat there looking at each other for a moment sipping their coffee. He had so many questions; she had even more.

Lars could see Eileen's wanting, questioning look on her face. He did not wait, but began to explain how he had worked hard most of his life to be able to move here from just outside a nearby town. He bought the place without his wife's knowledge and built a small cabin. When he informed his wife they were moving to the country, she packed up and left. He received the divorce papers the following week. She was just along for the money at that point, most of which she got in the divorce, but he got this place and enough money to build the house. He was self-sufficient, or at least he thought he was. With the state of the country like it was, he would soon know for sure. Lars explained everything he could think of, including that he had two grown kids he had now lost touch with, but he knew they would be fine. They were strong kids.

"Now for your story," he asked. "How the hell did you find this place?"

"It wasn't easy," she explained. She told him the entire ordeal, with a few exceptions, which primarily dealt with her panties. Lars asked if she needed a doctor, but she didn't think so. He didn't know if there was one to be had, considering the state of things, but he would try. "No," Eileen assured him she felt she was all right.

"Oh, and before I forget again," he said, "I owe you a deep and sincere apology for scaring you on the porch." Eileen gracefully accepted his apology.

Once they had gotten to know each other a little better, and the health issues and apologies were out of the way, Lars pressed her for more details about what was going on in the country. Hopefully she knew more than he did. After all she had fled the city like it was burning down. She told him she was a stock analyst and described what was happening before she left. She told him it was apocalyptic, or almost so, at least that's what she believed. "The city was going to hell, and I wasn't going to burn in hell," as she put it. She thought getting out was her best option. "Didn't look like such a wise decision, up until now," she added.

Lars got up and said, "I'll be right back," and walked out the back door. When Lars came back, he told her he had to hang her clothes outside on the clothes line, and they continued their conversation. He said he was sorry he didn't have any ladies' clothes, and she was the first lady who has been on the place.

"Your lilac shampoo?" Eileen queried.

"No, I got a box of my ex's stuff by mistake," Lars laughed. "You can thank her for the robe and slippers too," he added.

"Oh, by the way," Eileen said, "I took the sheets and pillowcases off the bed, and they're on the floor beside the bed."

"Yeah, I got them when I grabbed your clothes; you didn't have to make the bed, not in your condition," Lars said.

"I just felt I needed to," she responded. Lars smiled and they continued talking.

After a while Lars told her, "Your clothes should be ready by now." Once again he went outside and returned with Eileen's clothes. "If you would like to change into your own clothes, we can go outside and take a walk. I'll show you around the place."

"I'd love to," Eileen readily agreed. She took the now clean and fresh-smelling clothes from Lars and walked back into the bedroom. She quickly dressed and then went into the bathroom. Eileen checked her face. She didn't look too bad, considering what she looked like earlier in this same mirror. Her hair needed brushing, so she ran the brush through her hair once again. It looked better but not by a huge margin, in her opinion. There just wasn't much she could do to her hair to make it look better—brush or no brush. Eileen joined Lars in the living room, and there was that big smile again. It seemed a little strange, him smiling all the time, but at least it brought a little smile to her face as well. Lars got up and held out his arm. Eileen walked over and hooked her arm into his, and they walked toward the door. *This is so sweet*, Eileen thought.

Eileen felt more presentable for her host now. She was clean, dressed, well-fed and she didn't feel tired anymore. She was still a bit sore, especially her left arm. At least she felt comfortable walking with Lars. Was this guy real? He seemed real and honest thus far, but it would take a while before she could be certain. They walked out the door and it was cool, but she didn't feel cold anymore. Her dry jacket insulated her against the cool air—much better than when it was wet.

"By the way," Lars said, "I saw you before you got to that tree," as he pointed toward the large tree Eileen hid behind for a few hours, watching the house for activity.

"Really?" Eileen asked.

"Yes ma'am." Another smile from Lars. "I saw you as you made your way down to the big sycamore tree. You couldn't see me, but I saw you. I wondered how long it would take you to make it to the house."

"Why didn't you come out?" she queried.

"I didn't know who you were or what you were going to do. I wanted to see what your intentions were, and I didn't know you were a lady from that distance."

"Okay, fair enough," Eileen said.

They walked toward the garden and Lars explained he planted corn, potatoes, green beans, beets, onions, and carrots. He had bought some heirloom seeds from a friend of his a few years back. This type of seed will re-grow from seeds produced the previous year. Lars also explained the seeds did not produce like the hybrids, but this way, if you were not able to buy new seeds every year, you could still provide for yourself. "It seems this may be the case for a while." Eileen nodded agreement. They walked over toward the fruit trees, and then around behind the original cabin, now the wood shed, and the adjoining smokehouse and root cellar. There was also a 30x60 metal shed where he kept his tractor most of the time, along with a little gas in a drum, and all sorts of tools, lumber, and more odds and ends than you can count. There was a storage room on the backside of the barn where Lars stored more sensitive items, such as food and cooking and canning items. Lars stored a lot of stuff. Anything he thought he would eventually need one day was stored. Then they walked around to the truck which was, as Lars explained, only good for the gas that remained in its tank. Lars would save this fuel for his tractor, as long as it would last. Lars then pointed to the trees, which would supply him with protection from the winds to some extent, and all the firewood he would ever need. Finally, they walked down to the river. It wasn't a big river, but there were plenty of fish to be caught most of the time. This was his favorite source of food. Venison was plentiful, as were rabbits and squirrel, but they were so cute. "I really hate to kill them, but when necessary, they make a very tasty meal."

"I heard a couple gun shots the other day," Eileen said to Lars. "Yes, I got a rabbit and a squirrel. They are salted down in the smokehouse. Maybe we'll have some tomorrow, if you like?"

"I've never had them, but I'll give them a try."

Lars nodded his approval with a smile, and they walked back to the house. "I'll get some fresh sheets and pillowcases for the bed," he said as they walked back through the rear door. "I'll sleep on the couch. It folds out to a bed." Eileen smiled and nodded her agreement.

"I'll help you make them up," Eileen offered.

The next morning, Lars was up a little earlier than usual, just in case Eileen was an early riser. She wasn't this morning but came out of the bedroom fully dressed before Lars had finished cooking breakfast.

"Smells good in here," she said.

"Thank you. Have a seat. It will be ready shortly." Again, like yesterday, he smiled that never-ending smile. Lars served Eileen eggs, bacon, toast, and coffee. Eileen and Lars sat and ate. They had no further words this morning during breakfast. Lars felt they both needed time to think a bit. When they finished, Lars said he had chores to do outside. It had warmed up a bit, and the sun was out. It was shaping up to be a gorgeous day. "Relax and make yourself at home," said Lars as he walked out the door.

Eileen got up from the table, looked around the room, and walked over to a bookshelf. There were about a hundred books, including how to garden, how to cook, a lot of novels of all kinds, and some masterpieces like *War and Peace* and *Tom Sawyer*. The books seemed nothing out of the ordinary. There were no pictures or photos on the walls, she finally noticed. This seemed a little odd. The wood stove seemed to be the only method of cooking in the house. There was a wood box beside the stove with kindling and larger chunks of cut wood at its side. There appeared to be running water at the sink, and there was definitely running water in the bathroom—and hot water. There must be some type of water heating equipment, but there was little electricity.

All the light, except in the bedroom and bathroom, came from candles and oil lamps. Eileen hadn't noticed up until now; guess she had too much other stuff on her mind. There was a door to the left of the bedroom she had slept in. She walked over and turned the knob and pushed. There was what appeared to be another bedroom, but it was piled high with junk. She could just barely see the bed, but it was there. There was also another door inside this bedroom, which obviously led into the bathroom she had used. She had not noticed the other door from the bathroom, but it must have been there. Eileen closed the door and looked around the living room. A desk in the corner of the room had a laptop computer lying on top, the lid closed. The house was wired for electricity but didn't really seem to depend upon it. There was nothing else particularly interesting in the house. Everything just seemed so normal and ordinary for a country home.

Eileen walked out the front door and looked around. *Where is Lars?* She wondered. Then she heard chopping at the side of the house. She walked over to the end of the porch. Lars had his back to her. His shirt was off and he was splitting firewood. He had a good stack of wood going, but there was a lot more to cut. It was a little warm today—much nicer than just a couple days ago. The muscles rippled in his back as he sat each log on the stump and split each piece. *My!* He looked like a man twenty years younger than he really was. *He looks good!* Eileen had not been with a man for a really long time; how long she couldn't quite remember. *Has it been that long?* She asked herself. Maybe if the situation had been a little different, she would take a liking to this man. But things were not different; she was in a predicament, one she did not know how to get out of.

Eileen cleared her throat and Lars turned around. "You feeling better?" he asked.

"Yes, much," she replied. Lars laid the ax down against the stump and walked over to the porch.

"You about ready for the long talk we need to have?"

"Yes, I think so," she replied. He jumped up on the porch and led Eileen over to the chairs, and they sat down facing each other.

"Do you know what you want to do?" he asked.

"No, not at all. I have nowhere to go. My car is down the road a ways, past a tree that was cut down. Did you cut the tree?"

"Yes," he replied. "I cut it down a few days ago when the computer servers went down. After all I saw on the computer, I figured it was best if I closed the road."

"There was not much traffic on the highway," Eileen added.

"Yeah," Lars responded, "but you just never know." Eileen nodded agreement. "The server has not come back on, so I assume the world is going to hell in a hand basket," Lars told her.

"You're probably right," Eileen responded.

"You married?" Lars inquired.

"No, I've been divorced twice, and just never got around to finding anyone else. I wasn't really looking, and no one happened along. I worked as a stock analyst in San Antonio. It looked like disaster was headed my way, and having read enough doomsday books, I thought getting out of the city should be my first priority. Little did I know; I wasn't nearly prepared for what happened." Lars nodded and listened. "After I made it out of the city, I really didn't know what to do, so I just kept driving. I got off the main road when my gas gauge got down to about a quarter tank. After I drove down your road—I don't know how many miles—my car quit. I spent one night in the car. I went farther down the road on foot and spent three really miserable nights in the woods. Then I came to your place. I think you pretty much know what happened from there."

"Yep," Lars nodded.

They just sat and looked at each other for a bit. Eileen had a lost look on her face. "How about a drink?" Lars said.

"Yes, I could use a drink."

Lars got up and went into the house. He came back shortly with two glasses of tea. "Sorry, I don't have ice."

"This is fine, thank you," Eileen said. She sipped her tea and stared out across the little valley and at the garden. "You going to plant a winter garden?" she asked after a bit.

"No," Lars replied, "I would have to plant mostly greens, and I really don't care for greens much. I have some vegetables stored in the root cellar, though. Those will be enough for me."

Eileen finally got up the nerve to ask Lars if she could stay with him until she figured out what to do and where to go. "I know we don't know each other very well, but I will help out around here to pay for my stay. But if you'd prefer, I do have money to pay you."

Lars didn't hesitate, "I think that would be just fine. A little company will be good. Your money is no good around here though. Not just your money, but all money. There are no stores out here and no place to spend money. I'll clean out the other bedroom, and you can sleep in the master bedroom," he added. "I'll get right on that tomorrow."

Suddenly Lars caught some movement at the edge of the woods, not far from the sycamore where Eileen had spied on Lars' house. Lars got up. "We have company. Let's go into the house." Lars opened the door, let Eileen in, and grabbed his rifle leaning just inside the doorway as he followed her inside. He pulled the door shut and walked over to the window. Lars watched the area he had seen the movement for a while. He saw nothing.

"I don't see anything now, but I know I saw someone," Lars said. "I guess I better go see what he is up to. You stay inside."

Lars hurried out of the back door and ran over to where his truck was parked. Lars peeked around the side of the truck, eying the edge of the woods where he had noticed the movement. After a moment, Lars saw the movement again—it was definitely a person. Lars backed away from his truck, keeping it between him and the intruder. He backed up to the edge of the woods at the back of the house, always keeping his eye on the tree line where he spotted the intruder. He then quickly made a big circle through the woods until he got close to where the person had to be. He didn't see any movement, so he still had to be close to where Lars had first spotted him.

Lars squatted down and looked and listened. Soon Lars heard a muffled cough, revealing the intruder's location. Lars stayed low and concealed as he worked his way closer to the sound. Finally, Lars saw him squatting behind a tree. He eased up behind the guy with his thumb on the hammer of his rifle and his finger on the trigger. Lars was forty feet from him, but the guy had not heard or spotted him. Lars stood up and eased the business end of his rifle in the direction of this fella, and then watched the guy jump as his ears picked up the distinctive sound of Lars working the lever on his 30-30 and a fresh shell sliding into the cylinder. The gun was cocked and ready for action.

"Don't shoot!" was the immediate reply, as the youngster turned to face Lars. He threw his hands up into the air and repeated the plea for Lars not to shoot.

"What are you up to?" Lars inquired.

The kid was probably in his mid-twenties, with the dictionary picture of the word *scared* on his face. His clothes were dirty and he was dirty. He had long hair and a scrubby beard that didn't look like it had been shaved for a month. He looked to weigh around 150 pounds—not a big threat if he was unarmed. He had a small sack which he immediately dropped to the ground. He was visibly shaking.

"What are you up to?" Lars insisted again.

"I'm lost," was the response. The intruder seemed harmless, just a hungry scavenger trying to find a meal. Lars told him to back up, and when he complied, Lars picked up his sack and looked inside. A couple pieces of smoked meat, a pear and a slightly rusty knife. Lars dropped the sack back to the ground. Unless he had a gun concealed on his body, which it did not appear he did, he was no threat to Lars and Eileen.

"There's nothing out here for you," said Lars. "You have one option. You know that road you came up here on? Well, that's your only way out."

"Yes sir," the kid said.

"You get back up that road as fast as you can, and you don't stop. Make your way up to the highway and keep on going from there," Lars said. "You come back this way, and I've got a bullet with your name on it."

The kid responded with a shaky "yes sir," picked up his small sack, and started to move in that direction.

"You mess with that car up the way, and I'll come looking for you. You know what I mean?" Lars added.

"Yes sir."

"Now git," Lars finished. The kid took off as fast as his legs would take him. Lars slowly let the hammer back down on his gun and took his finger off the trigger. He then followed a ways to make certain the kid would keep going. He never looked back. Lars stood on the old road for about ten minutes, and seeing no sign of the boy, he headed back to the house.

Other than Eileen, this was Lars' first indication the problems with the country were expanding into his neighborhood. He didn't think there would be a lot of problems way out here, but he would need to keep a careful watch. Lars returned to the house, went inside, and told Eileen what had happened. "Do you know how to shoot a gun?" he asked her.

"No, I've never shot a gun," she replied.

"Well, if you're going to stay here, I guess I need to teach you. You can't stay out here and not be able to shoot. There may be more intruders and they may not all be harmless." Lars went into the spare bedroom and grabbed a rifle and a pistol. "The 30-30 is probably a little too much for you, so I'll start you on a .22 caliber rifle, and then we'll try the pistol." Lars got the oil, barrel rod, and rag, and said, "Let's go back out to the porch. I'll clean these guns while we talk a bit more."

As Lars cleaned, he explained a little about the guns to Eileen and how to keep from hurting herself and Lars. "A gun is supposed to protect you, not kill you or the ones helping you, and especially me," said Lars, with a smile. "This gun is not nearly as loud as my 30-30, and there is no kick. There is absolutely nothing to be afraid of as long as you don't shoot yourself." Lars continued to clean, working on the pistol after he finished the rifle. "This pistol is a .32 caliber. It does have a little kick to it, but not nearly as much as most pistols. I don't have a .22 pistol. This is the smallest caliber I have, and it will have to do," Lars continued. When Lars finished cleaning both guns, he went inside and got a couple boxes of shells, one for the .22 and one for the .32 pistol. "Let's go out back," Lars said. "It's time for your first lesson."

Lars found a few cans and set them up along the top of a log he had placed across his log sawing cradle. He loaded the rifle, showing Eileen exactly how this task was done. "This is a semi-automatic rifle," he said, "which means when you shoot, another round is automatically re-loaded and is ready to shoot again. This is quite handy but makes the gun more dangerous, because it is always ready to shoot again, immediately after you fire a shot. Always remember this, and never point it at me or anything else you don't want to shoot," he added. "It's best to point the gun up or at the ground when you are not intending to shoot at something."

Lars explained the sights to her and how to hold the gun. He then handed the rifle to Eileen. Eileen was a little wobbly as she held the gun up, but after a moment of checking out the sights, she steadied and squeezed the trigger. She hit the first can. She put the sights on the second can and squeezed again. Another hit. She squeezed the trigger six times and hit five of the cans. "Very good," Lars said. "Now let's try the pistol."

Lars took the rifle and handed Eileen the pistol. Again, he showed her how to load, handle, and sight the gun. Lars set the cans back up on the log. The handgun was a single action revolver and did not load automatically. Instead, she had to pull the hammer back each time she wanted to shoot. This was a little difficult for Eileen, as she did not have the hand muscles Lars did, but she managed to get the hammer back safely. Eileen fired six times again—no hits. Lars told her she did well. He explained that it's harder to hit targets with a pistol due to the short barrel and the fact that it's more difficult to steady a small handgun. Eileen nodded in agreement. "Well, that is lesson one," Lars said, as he took the pistol from her. He grabbed the rifle and then they went back to the front porch. "You did fine for your first time," he said, as he started cleaning the guns. She smiled at the compliment.

Eileen began thinking as she watched Lars clean the guns. *Little more than a week ago, I was sitting behind a desk working on a computer. Now here I am in the middle of the woods shooting cans with a strange man. It is beautiful out here though; quiet and peaceful too. What will tomorrow bring?*

Chapter 5

"If you are going to stay here for a while," Lars said, "we need to have some rules."

"Yes we do," Eileen agreed.

Lars started, "I don't want to feel crowded by your presence. We both need our space, and I don't want to feel I need to be constantly stepping around you. I have my ways, and I don't want to feel I need to change to make room for you."

"That seems fair enough," Eileen agreed.

"You will have to take care of yourself most of the time," Lars continued. "We will also have to work together to provide for our mutual needs, but you need to take care of your personal needs." Eileen nodded. "You must practice your shooting on a regular basis and not shoot me when I come in from a hunt or whatever. While I don't expect you to chop wood or do any of the heavier chores, I do expect you to help keep this place clean. I don't expect you to be my maid. I do housework too and will continue to do so. I only expect you to help."

"Before we go any further," interrupted Eileen, "I have things in my car—some more clothes and toiletries I need. I'd like to get those things, but I'm afraid to go alone."

"Okay," Lars said, "we'll go get them together. Maybe we'll do that first thing in the morning."

"Thank you," Eileen said with a smile.

"I'm not sure what kind of rules we need, just that we need some rules. Let it suffice to say that you need to help out around here and not pester me with every little thing. If something comes up and there is a need for more rules, we'll cross that bridge when we come to it, okay?"

"Okay," Eileen agreed.

"How about you?" Lars asked, "Are there any rules you need?"

"I'm willing to help out as much as I can, and I need my privacy too, but as far as rules, I can't think of any more off the top of my head. I guess we'll come up with them as we see fit," Eileen responded.

Lars added, "Let's be sure to communicate with each other. Let's not let problems fester. Come to me if you have a problem, and I'll do the same."

"Sounds good to me," said Eileen.

"Now let me show you a few things before we go any further," said Lars. He led her outside through the back door and away from the house a few yards. He showed her the solar panels on the roof. "These provide electricity for the bathroom and bedroom lights, as well as for the hot water heater." He showed her the battery array which stored the power. "The grid should provide adequate electricity for all the hot water we need, as well as enough lighting. Keep the lights off if you are not using them. There are outlets in the rooms, but use them sparingly. The main thing is not to waste electricity. The supply is limited."

"Alright," Eileen said. "All I have is a dead phone, and the charger is still in the car." Eileen didn't expect to use the phone much, if any, as she hadn't had a signal since she left the city and the battery went dead while she was asleep in Lars' bedroom. No one called her before the battery died, and her mom was the only one she needed to phone. If she couldn't get a signal, she wouldn't even be doing that.

"The only outlet in the living room is where I have my computer. It was intentionally part of the house design," Lars added.

Lars also pointed out the cistern, which stored water. He explained the cistern only stored rain water. "See the glass tube on the side? This tells you the water level. If it bottoms out, there will be no water for a shower. There's a well over by the woodshed, but the main way to get water is with the hand pump. We will always have drinking water. You just have to work for it. I have a small electric pump, but if the sky is cloudy for a day or so and we use the pump to fill the cistern, there may not be enough electricity to heat the water. You could end up with a cold shower."

Then they walked around to the woodshed. Lars showed her the dry wood and the racks of salted, dried, and drying meat in the smokehouse. He also showed her the root cellar. As they walked back out of the smokehouse, Lars pointed to the metal barn where he kept seldom-used necessities and his tractor. "Things you may need one day," as he put it. Lars also pointed out two halves of a metal drum alongside the barn. "Coffee and tea grounds go in the left drum. Scraps of wood go in the right one. I have earthworms in the left bin and wood grubs in the right," he said.

As Lars led Eileen back into the house, he explained the heating system. "There are brass pipes in the chimney. A single pipe comes in through the wall from the outside. The pipe then runs into a fan motor compartment goes through the brick into the chimney. It runs up and down and then back out the chimney into the attic. There the pipe splits into several ducts to warm the bedrooms, bathroom, and far side of the living room to even out the heat. These vents help reduce the amount of wood needed while keeping it very cozy in here without overheating the living room. The fan motor also runs off the battery array."

Eileen yawned.

"Am I boring you?" Lars asked.

"Maybe a little," Eileen responded. "I drifted off thinking about my mother in Lexington. She is old and completely dependent upon electricity. She is probably dead by now. Talking about the phone and charger made me think of her. We never got along very well growing up, but that is another story entirely."

"I'm sorry about your mother, but I'm just showing you stuff you need to know about. If you want to learn on your own, that's fine with me. But if you screw up and I have to take a cold shower, I'm going to be pissed at you," Lars said.

"Okay! I'm listening," Eileen said.

Lars continued to show Eileen where the utensils and cooking supplies were in the kitchen. Then he instructed her how to light the stove. Eileen was listening, but Lars could tell she was getting bored with his instructions.

"Well," Lars said, "that's enough for now. If we are going to your car in the morning, what do you say we get started cleaning out the spare bedroom? The couch is not very comfortable." Lars headed into the spare bedroom and Eileen followed.

Lars began grabbing items and putting them into the living room in the center of the floor. "We can take these out to the metal building," he said. Many of the items were not needed in the house and just kept getting in the way. Over the last couple years, the stuff found its way into the spare bedroom. There were some things that weren't suited for the metal shed, like linens, winter clothes, and the like. They had a place but Lars hadn't put them back after their last use. He instructed Eileen to store these things here and there, in their proper place. Eileen did so without hesitation. There were bed clothes on the bed, but they needed to be changed. Eileen helped Lars remake the bed with clean sheets and pillow cases. She then instinctively grabbed a broom she had seen earlier in a corner of the living room and began to sweep.

Lars got out of her way and went to the kitchen to fix a couple glasses of tea. Eileen got the dust pan and finished the task. Lars walked back in, "Glass of tea?"

"Yes, thank you, Lars," she said with a smile.

Lars held out the glass. "This should be good for now," he said, also smiling.

Lars thought Eileen seemed to have been sincere when she said she would help. She seemed to want to please Lars and she did, without question. Lars lit a couple oil lamps. *It's getting late*, Eileen thought. *Where did the day go? It must have been a fun day, as the saying goes,* she thought. *But was it fun?* She asked herself. She pondered the question for a moment, and in spite of her situation—their situation—she thought it had been fun.

"We need to get up early if we're going to tow your car back tomorrow," Lars said.

Eileen agreed. She finished her tea, put the empty glass in the kitchen sink, and walked to the master bedroom door. She stopped. "This is your bedroom. I should be staying in the spare bedroom," she said.

Lars thought for a minute. "No, you go ahead and stay in there. The bed in the spare is comfortable too. I'll stay there for now. Maybe we'll switch in a few days."

Eileen smiled and said thanks, and went into the bedroom and closed the door.

Lars went out onto the porch and rolled a cigar. Lars could hear a few coyotes in the distance. A great horned owl hooted nearby. Lars smiled and blew a few smoke rings into the calm night air. He certainly liked living in the country. *Peace and quiet*, he thought. *Just like I like it. It's also good to have someone to talk to from time to time. I hope Eileen is a quick learner. She certainly has a lot to learn.* Lars took a last puff off his cigar then snuffed the butt out and tossed it into the darkness. He then went inside, locked the doors, and went to bed.

Chapter 6

Eileen awoke to the sound of a rooster crowing. Light was coming in from the one window in the bedroom on the backside of the house. The dark curtains blocked out most of the light, but there was just enough shining in around the edges to tell it was already daylight outside. What time was it? There were no clocks. Her phone was of no use and there was silence in the house. Eileen got up quickly and got dressed. She opened the door to the living room and there sat Lars sipping a cup of coffee.

"How about a fresh cup of java?"

"Yes," she replied. "What time is it, anyway?"

"You have an appointment?" Lars asked.

"No!" Eileen replied.

"Then it doesn't really matter, does it?" he replied. There were no clocks in here either.

"I guess not," Eileen said.

Lars said he never knew the exact time—didn't really have a need to know it. The only two times that it did matter were the time to go to bed and the time to get up. The body will give you those times; therefore, no need for clocks. "I'm pretty good at approximating the time of day," he said. "You will get better at it after a while too."

They finished their coffee and Lars got up and put their empty cups into the sink. "Well, we had better get on our way," Lars said. "We'll have jerky for breakfast," he said grabbing a handful, and out the door they went. Lars had a pistol on his hip and his trusty 30-30 across his arm.

Lars checked to see if his tow strap was still in the back of his truck. It was. He climbed in the driver's seat and cranked his truck up for the first time in quite a while. It hesitated briefly, then started right up. Eileen walked around the truck to the passenger side. Eileen paused for a second. *I guess he's not going to open the door for me,* she thought.

"Something the matter?" Lars asked.

"No," she said, "I just thought country gentlemen opened the door for ladies."

Lars opened his door and started to get out.

"Never mind," Eileen said as she opened the door and got into the passenger seat.

"I thought you wanted me to open the door for you?" Lars asked.

"I wanted you to think of it," she replied. "I didn't really expect you to think of it. I just thought it would have been nice."

"Uggg," Lars growled.

Eileen hadn't had anyone open a door for her for a long time. *I don't know why I expected Lars to open the door,* she thought.

Eileen was no longer tired and most of the soreness was gone. She felt good and was happy to be going to her car to get the items it held. "I'm sorry I expected you to open the door for me," Eileen said.

"Do you expect me to open the door for you from now on?" Lars asked.

"Not really," she said.

Lars was already beginning to have second thoughts about Eileen. *Is this how big city women are?* He thought. *Rachel was a city gal too; a small city gal, but she had a lot of country in her as well. I never opened the door for her and she never complained. She also walked out on me.*

"Are you testing me?" Lars asked.

"Maybe," Eileen replied with a smile.

Lars smiled too. *Eileen is certainly no Rachel,* Lars thought. Maybe this was a good thing. He and Rachel had not gotten along for many years and finally went their separate ways. Lars backed the truck up and turned toward the sycamore tree and up the road. Eileen talked most of the way, asking Lars question after question. He answered as best he could.

"Do you always wear those moccasins?" she asked.

"Yes," Lars replied. "They are comfortable and good for sneaking up on stuff like deer and rabbits—and people these days."

"Did you make them?" she probed.

"Yes, out of deer hide," Lars responded

"Do you always carry two guns?" Eileen asked.

"Yes, and you will too as soon as I'm certain you won't shoot me," he asserted with a smile.

Lars told her about his longtime buddy who lived a couple miles away, Reggie Carston and his wife Emily. "You'll like Emily," Lars said. Reggie was a sort of weird character but was Lars' best friend and mercantile store. Reggie was a prepper, having devoted ten years to accumulating everything he thought he could possibly need should the apocalypse show up on his doorstep. He told her how Reggie built a huge bunker, into which he stored probably ten times more stuff than he could or would ever use. He had to have a hundred guns, tons of ammo, heirloom seeds by the case, oils, fuels, and more survival items than one could count. He had enough non-perishable foods to feed an army, which he had also sold for many years. His stock of survival gear was better than any Wal-Mart store Lars had ever shopped at.

Reggie had worked as an army contractor when he was younger. He had access to things the average person did not, including explosives and heavy weapons. Reggie had made millions of dollars, but unlike most rich people, he didn't live just to make more money. He lived to be free. His version of free was to live in the middle of nowhere and not be dependent on anyone. He didn't even have a road to his place. Everything he built and moved in was airlifted to his homestead. The pilot and men he hired to help build his house, barn, and bunker had to sign a contract to keep his place secret. According to Reggie, his guns were a better contract than the piece of paper. After all, Reggie was crazy, or at least he made most people think he was. Lars would have to visit him soon. Maybe Eileen could meet him and Emily before long.

There was also Ronald and Sara Weston and Samuel and Sally Lin. Both couples lived a little farther away than the Carstons and in different directions. They were all good and necessary friends. "Ron and Sara are about my age," Lars said. "They pretty much stay to themselves but are always ready to help when needed. They love each other very much and spend a lot of time reading. They're continually borrowing books from me. Sara is very beautiful and appears much younger than her age. They have no children and no family that I know of," Lars continued.

"Samuel and Sally have two children—Sean, who is nearly two years old, and Debra, who is almost three months old. Sam and Sally are youngsters compared to everyone else in the valley. At first glance, Sam may not appear to be overly smart, but he really is. For one reason, if no other, Sam and Sally never fight or argue. It's difficult for most men to learn who really rules the roost. Whatever Sally wants, if humanly possible, Sam gives her. It doesn't make him less of a man for Sally to appear to wear the pants in the family. Maybe it makes him more of a man. Sam has learned that some of the most important words he will ever use, are *yes* followed by *dear, honey*, or *darling*. Sam knows his job is to keep Sally happy. Her happiness ensures his happiness. They work well together providing for their every need—much like a well-oiled machine. If you stay around long enough, you will meet them all," Lars said.

Lars told Eileen some of Reggie's planning had rubbed off on him. He had stocked up as well, just not nearly as much as Reggie—not even close. Lars, even though he had less land, worked harder and often bartered with Reggie to provide himself with things he did not have. Also, Lars was able to give back to Reggie some of the things he and his wife needed. Reggie didn't care for Lars' pickled beets, but his wife Emily couldn't seem to go long without them. Every time Lars made a trip to see Reggie, Lars would take a jar or two to trade. Reggie was always happy to trade most anything for those beets to keep Emily happy.

As they drove, Lars told Eileen about his ex-wife, his car dealerships, his kids, and pretty much everything else about his life, mostly as answers to her questions, but some things he offered without her asking. After a while they reached the tree Lars had chopped down. He tied his towing strap to the tree and truck and then easily pulled the log off the road. They continued up the road and a short time later came to Eileen's car. A window was busted out and a few things were missing from the front and back seats, mostly food. *Probably that kid*, Lars thought. Eileen noticed her phone charger was still in the power socket. Nothing else of importance was inside. She looked for the keys; they were not in the ignition. She felt her pockets. They weren't there either. She had no idea where they were. Lars said it didn't matter. But it did matter. There were things in the trunk she needed. Her suitcase was in the trunk. Lars reached under the front seat and felt around a bit. Suddenly the trunk popped open. Not many people know it, but there is a trunk release well hidden under the seat on this particular model, if you know where to look. Eileen didn't know. She was pleasantly surprised and very happy that Lars did. *This guy is amazing*, she thought. Lars grabbed the suitcase and sat it on the ground.

"The bag of shoes too," Eileen said. Lars obliged. Eileen grabbed the bag of pears. "That's it," she said. Lars shut the trunk and they put the items in the back of the truck.

"How much gas do you have in the tank?" he asked.

"About a quarter tank."

"Oh yeah," said Lars, "you already told me that, didn't you?"

Eileen smiled but didn't say anything.

Lars hooked the tow strap to the back of the car and instructed Eileen on how to steer the vehicle so he could pull it back onto the road. Eileen followed his instructions and they soon had the Volvo on the road. Lars unhooked the car and then moved the truck to the front of the car and hooked it up again. He then instructed Eileen further on how to steer the vehicle and to brake when he held his hand out of the window. She got in her Volvo and Lars tightened the towing strap, then proceeded up the road. After they had towed the car just past the tree Lars had moved off the road, Lars held his hand out of the window for Eileen to stop. Eileen stomped the brakes and the car and truck jerked hard to a stop. Lars got out of the truck and walked back to the Volvo. "What the hell are you doing?" Lars demanded.

"Just stopping the car like you instructed me," Eileen replied.

"Well, you don't have to cram the brakes so goddamn hard," Lars growled and walked off before Eileen could reply.

Lars then unhooked the car, tied the strap onto the tree again and moved it back so it blocked the road. He hooked the car up again, and they proceeded to Lars' house. A few minutes later, Lars felt Eileen's car jerking against the tow strap and Lars' truck. They stopped and Lars got out.

"What's going on?" Lars asked.

"Nothing, just practicing braking," she replied smiling.

Lars just shook his head and got back into his truck and proceeded toward the house. But every so often he would feel the tow strap jerking against his truck again and again all the way home. Lars looked into his rear view mirror each time and could see Eileen smiling. *Damn that woman!*

They made it back to the house mid-afternoon and parked Eileen's car to the side of the house, alongside Lars' truck. Lars grabbed the suitcase and bag of shoes from the back of the truck, while Eileen got the pears. She also took her phone charger out of the car and they both went inside with their loads. Lars put the suitcase and the bag of shoes on Eileen's bed.

Eileen plugged her phone in and checked the signal when the screen lit up. Still zero bars. *Guess I'm doing without a phone for a while*, she thought. *I guess I can at least use it for a clock as long as it will last*, and she left it plugged in.

Eileen could see Lars was visibly upset.

"Are you mad at me?" she asked.

"No," Lars said a bit harshly; he and she both knew that was a lie.

"You admonish me for hitting the brakes a little too hard and just walk off and you are going to pay for it, Mr. Lindgren," she said sternly.

Admonish, Lars thought. He wasn't certain he had ever heard that word before, but he could guess what it meant. "Is that why you kept pumping the brakes?" he asked.

Eileen didn't answer.

Lars didn't want to fight with Eileen; though if he wanted to fight, Eileen was ready and willing to give him all the fight he could handle no doubt. Lars calmed down and worked up an "I'm sorry" to which Eileen accepted his apology.

Eileen wasn't trying to be mean to Lars. She felt better than she had all week. She was happy with Lars' hospitality and the fact he had not turned out to be a crazy man. She was especially happy to have her suitcase. Maybe she was getting back at him for scaring her when they met at the edge of the porch. Maybe she was testing him to see if he was really the man he appeared to be. She was not certain why she was acting as she did. She just knew she was feeling a little capricious.

"How about some tea?" Lars asked.

Eileen didn't say anything at first. She was beginning to calm down too and even worked up a smile. "A glass of tea sounds good," Eileen responded.

Lars fixed two glasses and handed one to Eileen. "Let's go have a seat on the porch and watch the sun go down," Lars said. "I think we've done enough for today."

"A pleasant ending to a productive day," said Eileen.

They sat and continued their earlier conversation. Eileen told Lars about her job and her mother in Lexington. "It's probably best if Mom is dead. I'm an only child. A brother died during childbirth. Mom couldn't have kids after that. She became a terrible person to be around and drove me and Dad away. When I got old enough, I ran away from home and Mom and Dad divorced. We kept in touch but were never a real family. Dad remarried and helped put me through college. Mom never remarried."

They talked about the surrounding forest, the weather, and Eileen's stamina. They also talked about the possibility for the need for a few more rules after what had happened today. In the end, they decided they would both try to get along better and wait and see if more rules were really necessary. It was nearly dark when they felt the conversation dying. They were not hungry, as they had eaten a couple of nutrition bars Eileen had retrieved from the side pouch of her suitcase and two pears each, which had been in the trunk in a plastic grocery bag. They were tired and both decided to go to bed early.

Eileen closed the door to her room and began to undress. As she did, she could not stop thinking about Lars. He seemed so kind and gentle on the inside yet so rough and tough on the outside. *He definitely has a stubborn side, but I guess I do too*, she thought. She definitely felt safe now with him around. She knew she could trust him but didn't really know why. It was the air about him and the way he projected himself. *This is the kind of man I could fall in love with*, she thought. *Don't jump to conclusions so fast. How many good decisions have I made lately, thinking back over the past week or so? None! Exactly!*

Eileen's thoughts suddenly were directed towards her panties. She popped open the suitcase and still neatly stacked in the back were at least twenty pairs of fresh panties. *Yes!* Eileen couldn't stand wearing dirty panties. Over the past few days she washed her panties every day, going without half the time as the only pair she had was drying. Eileen didn't like going without panties, but she had to keep as clean as possible. She knew she smelled as bad as she looked that first night. Eileen peeked out into the living room and asked Lars if it was okay if she took a shower.

"Of course," he replied.

Eileen slipped off her bra and panties, grabbed her own toiletries, and stepped into the shower. She made sure the shower was as short as possible, remembering what Lars had said about the solar panels. She got out and toweled herself dry, wrapped the towel around her hair, and then turned to the mirror. She dug through her toiletries finding her moisturizer. There was not much else she could do after applying the cream sparingly. She went into her bedroom and slipped into a t-shirt and crawled into bed.

Eileen kept thinking how nice Lars seemed to be. He answered all her questions and then some. *Maybe I need to be a little more considerate of Lars*, she thought. *He has not been around a woman for years. He is very nice; maybe I need to let him get used to having a lady around again.*

Then her thoughts returned to her suitcase and the multiple outfits which were now in her possession, and especially the numerous pairs of underwear. She could now easily keep herself clean and wear something different every day. The next thing she knew, it was morning as she heard the familiar crowing of Lars' rooster.

Eileen had been an early riser for more years than she could remember, but this morning she didn't feel the need to get up right away, and there really wasn't a need. She lay there thinking about what the coming day would bring; whether Lars was up yet and what was happening with the country. After about twenty minutes, Eileen finally decided she would not have any answers until she got up. She crawled out of bed, dressed, and started her day.

Chapter 7

Eileen opened the door into the living room and looked around. Lars was not there. She checked the doors; they were still locked. Lars had to be in bed. Eileen got a fire going in the stove and immediately a little smoke began seeping out of the seams of the stove. As she found bacon, eggs and bread to prepare, the smoking stove grew worse and she opened the front and back doors. She did not know what else to do, but fortunately most of the smoke was sucked out of the front door. As the fire got going, the smoke slacked off and she decided to start the coffee. Then she put plates and silverware on the table, along with two coffee mugs. The stove continued to smoke, but the smoke was not unbearable. She did not know how to stop the stove from smoking completely. She thought she had done everything just as Lars had shown her.

Eileen then heard Lars stirring in the spare bedroom. She had hoped to have breakfast ready for him when he came out, but she was afraid to put the food on with the stove smoking. Lars emerged shortly.

"What the hell!" Lars exclaimed as he entered the living room.

"I can't stop it from smoking," Eileen said with a whimper.

Lars walked over to the stove and opened the damper up fully and immediately the smoke stopped coming out of the joints of the metal stove.

"All you have to do is open the damper," Lars said in a raised voice.

"I didn't know," Eileen replied.

"It's not rocket science," Lars asserted. This was the wrong thing to say.

"I do not know how to do every damn thing you do around here," Eileen screamed. Her face was getting red. "I was trying to fix you a good breakfast, and I did the best I knew how to do," her voice still very loud and beginning to crackle. "Excuse me for trying," she said as tears began to trickle down her cheek.

"I'm sorry," Lars said.

"If you want me to do things like you want me to do them, maybe you should teach me better. I can't learn everything overnight."

"You're right," Lars admitted. "How about we finish fixing breakfast together?" Lars asked. "I'll show you exactly how to prepare the fire and keep it going properly."

Eileen began to settle down a little and agreed to Lars' proposition.

The coffee was ready and Lars poured a cup for Eileen and then himself. Eileen had built the fire correctly. "If you had only opened the damper, there would not have been a problem," Lars said. "You really did well," he continued.

"You only made one little mistake. Don't worry about it; you'll do it perfectly next time."

Lars then started the bacon and Eileen sliced the bread for toast. Lars cooked the eggs in the bacon grease and Eileen started the toast. He asked Eileen to sit down. He slid the eggs onto her plate and added four slices of crispy bacon while she added the toast. Lars then filled his plate as well and sat down across from Eileen. Eileen looked up to see Lars. She had a smile on her face—a smile which no doubt would melt ice. Lars smiled back with a weird look on his face. He had a fuzzy feeling in his chest, and opened his mouth as if to speak, but nothing came out. She picked up her mug, took a sip and looked into Lars' eyes again. He still had that strange look on his face. He tried to speak again. This time he managed to get two words out, "I'm sorry."

She smiled, "You'll do better, and I'll do better."

After breakfast, Lars went outside and tinkered with Eileen's car for a while. He wiggled some wires here and there and then stood back and scratched his head. *What can be the problem?* He thought. Lars then crawled under the car and tugged at the power cable to the starter. It was loose. He tightened the nut holding the cable to the starter and then went back inside to get the keys.

"Eileen, did you find your car keys?" he asked.

"Yes, I found them on the floor," she replied.

"I need them," Lars explained.

"They're on the dresser in the bedroom," Eileen said.

Lars went into the bedroom, picked up the keys and went back out to the car. He inserted the key into the ignition and turned. The car started right up. Lars returned to the house, put the keys back where he had found them, and told Eileen her car was fixed.

"Really?" Eileen asked.

"Yes, really," Lars replied.

Wow, Eileen thought. *This guy is a farmer, hunter, a good cook, and apparently a great mechanic. What can't this man do?*

Lars then asked, "How about another shooting session?"

"I'm up for it," Eileen replied.

Lars grabbed the .22 rifle and .32 pistol, along with a couple boxes of cartridges, and they headed to their new shooting range. Lars didn't say a word. He just handed the .22 to Eileen, along with the box of .22 shells.

She loaded the gun, put one in the chamber, sat the butt of the gun on her foot with the barrel pointing into the air, and said, "Are you going to set the cans up?" She gave him a smile, which he returned immediately, and then dutifully walked over to the log and picked up the cans. He set the cans up, as he did the previous session, and then walked back to Eileen. She raised the gun and bam,

bam, bam—six in a row. She raised the gun, putting the butt on her foot again, spread her legs, and hooked her thumb into her waistband. She gave him that *I'm good* smile he knew was coming.

"Okay! Okay!" he said. Lars took the .22 and handed her the pistol along with the box of ammo. She loaded the gun almost expertly and then looked at the cans.

"Sorry," Lars said as he hurried over and reset the cans.

Eileen raised and cocked the pistol, gripping the pistol in her right hand and putting her other hand under the grip of the gun, just like Lars had shown her, and fired. Again and again she fired. After six shots, she hit two cans. She reloaded and fired another six shots—hitting two more cans. Eileen handed the butt of the gun to Lars, and they walked back around to the front porch. Eileen sat in one of the chairs while Lars went inside. He returned with their two mugs and handed one to Eileen filled with the coffee leftover from breakfast.

Finally, he looked her square in the eyes and said, "I'm really proud of the way you handled the guns this morning; so much so, I think I'll leave you here alone today to guard the property. I've been meaning to go see Reggie. You think you can handle it?"

There was a slight pause, and then "Yes, of course I can."

Lars walked back inside and came back with his pistol on his hip and a back-pack with a jar of pickled beets. "By the way, it's time you clean your own guns. Remember, try not to shoot yourself or me when I return this evening." Lars smiled and then walked off past the garden.

Eileen twisted her face into a smirk but knew Lars was right. If you're going to learn to shoot, you also need to learn to take care of your weapons. Eileen went in and got the oil, cleaning rod and rag. She wasn't certain she remembered exactly how Lars had done this, but, *it's not rocket science*, she thought. After determining the guns needed different wire brushes to clean the barrels and how to change them, the rest was rather easy. Eileen finished the task in good time and went inside to fix herself a glass of tea. She returned to the porch with her tea and the .22 and some shells. She loaded the gun but didn't put one in the chamber. Instead, she leaned the rifle against the rail as she had seen Lars do and sat back to drink her tea. Eileen gazed off in the distance, looking first to where Lars had entered the tree line and then around the remainder of the valley.

Lars followed the river upstream. The river valley opened up to a meadow from time to time where large trees grew only directly on the riverbank. The surrounding meadow was a good place to hunt, as deer liked to feed in these open areas. Lars spotted a doe and its spring baby in the second meadow. Reggie had his home in the third meadow. Reggie had a lot more acreage than Lars, but it was mostly trees and brush. Reggie's meadow was only a third the size of Lars'. Reggie had a lot of animals on his plot, though—more than Lars.

It took Lars nearly an hour to get to Reggie's place due to the rough terrain, but he finally made it to the third meadow. Lars walked up to within a hundred yards of Reggie's house and looked around. Not seeing Reggie, he let out a long wolf howl and waited. Directly, Reggie walked out onto his front porch and looked around. Lars hollered, "Don't shoot!" Lars could see Reggie's smile from a hundred yards away. As he approached Reggie, Lars held out his hand and gave him a firm handshake, followed by a big hug. Reggie invited Lars inside the house. Emily was on the sofa reading a book. Lars walked over to Emily and gave her a kiss on the cheek. Then he turned back to Reggie and said, "What's going on, brother?"

"Nothing much," he responded.

Lars removed his backpack and took out the jar of beets. He held it up for Emily to see.

"Eeeee!" Emily squealed. She got up and ran over and gave Lars a big kiss on the cheek and a hug. "Thank you!"

"You're very welcome," Lars said.

Then Emily asked, "What do you want in return? Whatever it is, it's yours."

"I didn't come for anything," Lars responded, "but if I think of something, I'll let you know."

Lars turned to Reggie, "It seems like it's been forever since we last talked. What I came over for is to hear what you've heard about the country on the ham radio."

"Well," Reggie said, "it's not good. The story is the same from all my radio buddies. It doesn't matter whether you're talking about New York, Houston, San Francisco, or New Orleans. The story is the same. There is no law and order—rioting and killing everywhere."

"That's sad," said Lars. "You seen anyone snooping around?" said Lars.

"No," Reggie replied, "but I expect sooner or later there will be some desperate souls coming around when the cities become barren. How about you?"

"Yes," Lars said. "A few days ago, a lady showed up. She was from the city and in pretty bad shape. She got caught in the cold and rain the other day. Looks like she's going to stay with me for a while."

"A lady!" Reggie exclaimed with a big smile. "Did love finally find you old man?"

"No, nothing like that," Lars responded. "She's smart and educated, but taking off like she did to get out of the city wasn't so smart. She was clearly out of her element and cold, wet, and hungry. I just couldn't let her go. She would have died, and I couldn't let that happen. She's doing much better now. Quite a handful actually."

Reggie looked over to Emily, "She must be good looking."

"Yes, that too," Lars grinned, "but that wasn't what made me help her."

"Right!" said Reggie.

"Then there was this kid in his mid-twenties. He had long hair and a red shirt. I don't think he'll be back, but keep your eyes open. If you see him, put a bullet in him; he's been warned once."

"Gotcha," said Reggie. "Let's take a little walk."

The two walked out the front door. Lars explained he hadn't really come over for anything but to see how Eileen would handle herself being alone. Lars thought she would be fine, but you just never know until you throw it out there for a test.

"You sure you don't need anything?" Reggie asked.

"No, I don't think so," Lars responded. "To tell you the truth, I may need something eventually, but not right now. I just don't know how Eileen is going to affect my life. She seems great—a little bitchy at times—but she really takes the edge off the loneliness. Maybe I'll want her to stay on for a while, but that will be her decision."

Lars rolled a cigar and handed it to Reggie, then rolled one for himself. They continued to talk about what had been going on since the last time they got together. Reggie had a lot more gadgets and things than Lars. He had accumulated a wind turbine, several more solar panels, and numerous appliances, so he and Emily lived very comfortably. Lars was happy for his friend. He wasn't jealous. He was very contented with the way he lived. Lars could take care of himself, but he was concerned about taking care of Eileen too. Could she live the way Lars did after living in the city most—if not all—her life? Lars could only teach her so much. Reggie understood where Lars was coming from but assured him he was up for the challenge. Lars knew this; he just needed someone to talk to, and his buddy Reggie was the only person Lars felt he could talk to about such a touchy situation. Reggie gave him the assurance he needed.

As Lars and Reggie worked themselves back up to the house, Emily met them on the porch with glasses of tea with ice.

"This is a real treat," Lars said. "Thank you, Emily."

Lars and Reggie sat on the porch and talked for a while longer as they drank their teas. Emily soon joined them and shared in the conversation.

"When are we going to meet your new lady?" Emily asked.

"The next trip over here, I'm sure," Lars replied.

"What is her name?" Emily queried.

"Eileen," Lars answered.

"Such a pretty name," Emily said.

"For a pretty lady," Reggie chimed in.

"That's enough guys," Lars demanded.

"I need to get going," Lars said. "Before I go," Lars added, "I could use a bottle of fuel stabilizer."

"Say no more." And with that Reggie ran out to his bunker and immediately returned with the additive.

"Thanks, bro."

"My pleasure," Reggie said. Lars gave Emily a big hug. He and Reggie hugged and shook hands as they said their goodbyes. Lars thanked them for their hospitality and fuel additive, and stepped off the porch.

Lars turned back, "Oh, by the way, I haven't heard anything from my son, James, or my daughter, Georgia. If you have a buddy on the ham radio around Conroe or Gonzales, put the word out, will ya?"

"Of course," said Reggie.

Then Lars walked away for his return trip down the river.

Lars returned home about an hour before dark, as he said he would. He let out his usual wolf howl and what he got back in return sounded nothing like a wolf. It did, however, manage to get a smile out of Lars. Eileen was sitting on the porch and saw him as soon as he cleared the woods. He inquired how Eileen had made out while he was gone. "Fine, I didn't shoot you at least," she said, with a giggle. "And I have a surprise for you. I dug through your root cellar, meat supply and pantry. Come on inside." She led him inside and Lars could smell the surprise. Eileen had prepared a big meal for them. "It smells great!" he said.

"And no smoke this time," Eileen added with a smile. "Have a seat," she said. Lars complied. The table was already set. Eileen poured tea and then set a big pot in the middle of the table. She then spooned out a good serving of meat and potatoes with gravy for him. The rabbit was much better than any Lars had ever made. The potatoes were tender and the gravy was delicious. Lars ate his fill and wiped his face. He then told her that it was the best meal he ever had. He got up and walked around the table. As he did, Eileen got up as well. Lars reached for her hand and brought it up to his face. He kissed the back of her hand and saw the tears forming in her eyes. His eyes weren't exactly tear-free either. They just stood there for a minute, and Lars finally asked her to go sit on the sofa. She had done enough today. Lars put the leftovers away, washed the dishes and then joined Eileen on the sofa.

Lars and Eileen sat and talked about what he had learned from Reggie. He told her about the chaos in all the cities across the nation. He then told her more about Reggie's survival preparations. Eileen looked saddened about the news of the chaos in the country but cheered up a little when Lars began to discuss his and Reggie's survival plans. After a few hours of talking, Lars asked Eileen if she would like to meet Ronald and Sara Weston. Ronald and Sara lived about three miles in the opposite direction from Reggie and Emily's homestead. "I think tomorrow will be a nice day for another trip."

Eileen agreed.

"Well, let's get some sleep," Lars said, so they both went to bed.

Chapter 8

Bright and early the next morning, Lars and Eileen got dressed and ate a hearty breakfast. Lars dug out a holster for Eileen's pistol and handed it to her. He strapped his pistol on and filled a small bag with jerky, while Eileen put her holster on. Lars handed her the pistol she had been using for target practice; then he grabbed a canteen of water, his rifle, and they headed out the door.

Lars pointed out the direction to the Weston homestead and told her to lead. "I want you to practice drawing, pointing, and aiming your pistol," Lars said. "Aim at anything that catches your eye. I just want you to practice drawing and cocking your gun, and then lowering the hammer and putting the pistol back into the holster. It will help build your hand muscles and you will get faster and better at shooting. When you get better, and I'm certain you're not going to shoot me, I'll let you follow me." They walked along, Lars watching Eileen as she handled the pistol and also giving additional instructions from time to time. Lars was pleased at how well Eileen was handling the pistol after such a short time. "You're doing very well," he said. She looked back and smiled.

The path to the Weston's place was not nearly as difficult as the route to Reggie's place, and they made good time. It took about an hour to get to the edge of the clearing where Ronald had built his home. Lars told Eileen to put the gun away and take a position behind him. They then stopped behind a large tree at the edge of the clearing. Lars could not see anyone stirring around the house and gave out a big wolf howl. Seconds later, one, two, and then a third man stepped out of the already open front door to the house. Lars didn't recognize these men. He just knew Ronald was not among them. The three men looked around for a few seconds and then went back inside.

Lars instructed Eileen to stay where she was and to keep well hidden. He then worked his way to the left of the house. Not seeing anything, he moved closer to the rear of the house. Near the woodshed, Lars could see a body beside the woodpile. It was Ronald. Lars moved back around to the front of the house and took his position behind a large tree stump, which hid most of his body. Lars pulled the hammer back on his rifle and aimed at the front door. He let out another wolf howl. The three men came out again. This time the first two men out the door had guns. Lars aimed at the first man and squeezed the trigger. He quickly reloaded and fired at the second. Both men fell immediately while the third ran back inside the house. Lars hurried back toward the rear of the house and caught the third man running out the back door, heading for the woods. He made it halfway to the tree line before Lars dropped him. Lars ran up with his rifle ready to shoot again, if necessary. It wasn't. The man was dead, blood oozing out of the hole in the center of his back. Lars hurried back around to the front of the house to check the other men. Lars had been dead on when he shot those two as well. Lars poked the bodies with the end of his rifle. There was no movement.

Lars cautiously peered inside the front door and then walked in—ready to shoot if necessary. The house was silent. There had been only three men, and Lars had taken care of them in short order. He went into the bedroom and found Sara on the bed lying face up, naked with a gunshot wound on her forehead. The pillow under her head was soaked with blood. He moved closer to the body. There was blood between Sara's legs and she had marks on her arms and face. Bastards! Lars shook his head in disgust and covered Sara with a sheet. He then headed back to the woodshed. Ronald was lying face down in the dirt beside the wood pile. There was blood on the leg of his jeans and two blood spots on the back of his shirt. He still had the ax in his hand. Lars guessed the men had sneaked up on Ronald and shot him in the back. Then they raped and killed Sara.

Lars walked back to where he had left Eileen. She had watched Lars cut two men down in a heartbeat, and she had heard the shot ring out from the back of the house. She was crying when Lars reached her. "We need to call the police," she said.

"And how do you suppose we do that?" he replied.

"I don't know, but we need to call someone." Eileen cried, as he led her all the way to the house.

"That's not how the world works anymore," Lars informed her. "There is no law anymore." Her tears let up as she thought about what Lars said. Eileen was shocked at how a man who could be sweet and gentle could be so cold-blooded. But she knew Lars had done what he had to do.

Lars took Eileen into the bedroom where Sara lay. He pulled the sheet back. He wanted Eileen to see what he had seen. He wanted her to know exactly why he had done what he did to those men. When Eileen saw Sara, she became hysterical. She screamed and her whole body began to tremble. Though she only looked at the body a few seconds and then turned away, Eileen saw the bruises on the arms, legs and neck of the pale and slightly bluish body. She saw the blood and matted hair between her legs. Eileen then understood the trauma Sara had suffered through. Lars grabbed her by the shoulders and pulled her toward him. He gave her a big bear hug, but a bear hug was not going to comfort her much now. They just stood there for a while and Eileen finally began to calm down and her trembling lessened. Lars pulled the sheet back over Sara's body, and then went back outside. Eileen followed, softly crying.

Lars found a shovel and chose a nice spot to bury his friends. He began to dig. As Lars dug the graves, Eileen sat on a stump and thought about what had happened. *Sara was such a beautiful woman. That could be me*, she thought. *Lars is right, there is no law out here to help us. We must help ourselves, and if we fail we will die just like Ronald and Sara.*

Eileen got up, drew her pistol and found a target to shoot at. It was only a discolored spot on a nearby tree, but to her it was an attacker. She pulled the hammer back and fired at the spot. She fired again and again until her pistol was empty.

"What the hell are you doing?" Lars demanded.

"I'm killing an intruder," she replied.

Lars just stood there in his hole looking at Eileen as she reloaded her gun. Again, she fired at the spot on the tree. When her gun was again empty, she walked over to the tree to check on her accuracy. Lars got out of the hole he was digging and walked over to the tree as well.

"Well done," he stated.

"Thank you," she replied.

Eileen could see ten holes in the tree, all within the dark area she had chosen as her target.

"What brought this on?" Lars asked.

"I'm not going to end up like Sara," she replied. "Hell no! That is not going to happen to me."

Lars smiled, then returned to his hole digging leaving his red-faced partner to her target practice. Eileen reloaded her pistol three more times and unloaded it on the tree. She then reloaded the gun again and stuck it in her holster.

An hour later, Lars had dug two holes side by side near a large elm tree. Eileen couldn't help Lars wrap the bodies in blankets for burial. She was still very distraught and her crying continued intermittently. As Lars placed the bodies into the makeshift graves, Eileen picked some flowers she found at the side of the house. Lars began to fill the two graves with shovelfuls of dirt. When he was finished, Eileen gently placed the flowers on top. They both just stood there for a moment. Lars mumbled some words, and then turned to Eileen again and gave her another hug.

Eileen followed Lars back into the house. He looked around and gathered all the ammunition he could find and placed it into a cloth tote. Lars also found two .357 magnum pistols, which he put into the bag. He then gathered up the guns lying beside the dead men and a couple rifles Ronald had that Lars didn't want to carry all the way home. He hid these in the woodshed where he figured no one could find them. Then Lars went back to the dead men. One by one he dragged them out into the yard. Lars closed the doors to the house, turned to Eileen and told her it was time to get back home.

"Are you going to just leave these men out here in the yard?" she asked.

"Coyotes and buzzards need to eat too," he said. "Now let's get home."

Again, Lars seemed so cold-blooded, but she did not say a word.

Lars led the way back home, and for a long time, Eileen didn't say a word to him. Finally, about halfway home, Lars stopped. He laid his bag and gun down against a log and turned to Eileen. He took her by the arm and pulled her close to him and gave her another bear hug. Eileen still felt shocked, hurt, and sad for Sara and Ronald. "I'm sorry," he said. Eileen began to whimper a bit, and Lars gently pushed her back and looked into her eyes. "I'm sorry you had to go through this," Lars said. "It couldn't be helped. If I had not done what I did, the same thing might have happened to us. We could have ended up just like Ron and Sara." Eileen nodded her understanding, but she could not help feeling the new feelings she was now experiencing.

Eileen had never seen anyone killed. She saw people killed on television and never gave it a second thought. To see two men buckle as bullets tore through their flesh, splattering blood everywhere, became very real for Eileen today. She felt their pain as she jumped from the echoing report of Lars' rifle. She felt the pain of the man who ran out of the rear of the house as well, though she never saw the man get shot. This was something she would never forget.

The one feeling she was not having was fear though. Her stomach was in knots, but she felt safe with Lars. Lars was a gentle man, but when necessary, he transformed into a killing machine. He could take care of himself, and he could take care of her, she imagined. *Or can he? Ronald couldn't protect Sara. I can learn to shoot like Lars,* Eileen thought, *but can I kill another human being? I must. I don't have a choice now, unless I want to end up like Sara.* Eileen managed a small smile and pulled Lars back to give him a hug. "We had better get going," he said, and they continued their trip home.

Lars and Eileen worked together to make dinner. They didn't mention their ordeal throughout the meal. When they were finished, though, Lars suggested they go out on the porch. "We can talk some more while we watch the sunset," he said. Lars refilled and handed Eileen her glass of tea, got his, and together they walked onto the porch.

Eileen was first to talk, "I know why you did what you did. It's hard for me, but I know it was necessary."

"We can't take our safety for granted anymore," Lars said. "We cannot assume everything will work out for the best around here. We need to get real serious about our safety or we may not live long."

"Do you think we'll have more intruders?" Eileen asked.

"We need to assume the worst," he replied. "Tomorrow morning, we'll have another shooting session," Lars said. "We need to be prepared and keep our eyes open around here. I can't leave you here alone anymore," Lars added. They were quiet for quite a while, just sitting there sipping their teas.

"Sara was the sweetest lady in the world," Lars finally said. "She and Ronald lived there most of their lives. I don't know when they moved there, but it was a long time ago. After Reggie, Ronald was my best friend. He and Sara were quiet people, unlike Reggie who talked all the time. Reggie always carried the conversation when he and I were together. It was much different with Ronald. But when he had something to say, I listened, because it was important." Eileen just sat, listened and nodded.

"Ronald and Sara were survivors. Not survivors in the way Reggie and Emily are, but still survivors. They didn't have a lot of guns, but they had plenty of ammunition. They didn't have a large garden, but they always seemed to grow as much as I did. They didn't have tons of prepackaged foods like Reggie and Emily. The Westons lived off the land and were very good at providing for themselves. They were never short of food."

"Ronald and Sara had no kids that I'm aware of. They were just a couple loners who loved the woods. They had their hobbies, and when they were not working at surviving, they worked at their hobbies. Ronald loved to carve things, like duck decoys, rocking chair parts, and spare ax handles. If he was going to carve something, it had to be something useful. I've got several duck decoys from him, and he taught me how to carve a good rocking chair. I'll need to make me one someday."

Eileen never interrupted Lars. She could see he was hurting, and he needed to let it all out. He didn't cry much, but talking about his friends was his way of relief. Eileen went back inside and refilled their glasses. When she returned, Lars continued to talk about Ronald and Sara. "Sara was meticulous in keeping her home clean. There was never a speck of dust in the house. The stove was always clean. If Ronald tracked in the smallest speck of dirt, she was all over him. 'You get those damn dirty boots outside, and then you can clean up your mess,' she would say. She was quite a lady."

"That was mean and nasty what those men did to her. She didn't deserve to go like that." Finally, Eileen could see some tears in Lars' eyes. He was really hurt by what those men did to Sara. "If I'm going to go, a couple shots in the back would be the way. Not like Sara...terrible!" Lars could not talk about his friends anymore. He was quiet for a long time, his head hanging down, as if he were looking at the floorboards on the porch. But he was not seeing the boards; he could only see Sara's pain. Finally, he raised his head. "Beautiful sunset, isn't it?" Lars asked.

"Yes, it is," agreed Eileen.

"It's hard to believe there can be so much beauty yet so much ugliness in the world," Lars said. Eileen nodded her silent agreement.

Lars finally said, "We need to go check on Samuel and Sally Lin tomorrow. They live about the same distance from here as Ronald and Sara, but out toward the back of the house across the river. I can't leave you here alone, so you'll have to come with me." Eileen readily agreed and said it was not a problem. *I'm not about to stay here alone,* she thought. "We've had a long day," said Lars. "Let's go get ready for bed." Eileen got up and headed inside, with Lars following. "Take your shower first, if you'd like," said Lars.

Lars went over to the kitchen and poured another glass of tea. As he headed back to the sofa, he noticed Eileen had left her door open and was standing outside the bathroom undressing. He instinctively stopped and watched Eileen, with her back toward him. She took her bra off and tossed it onto the bed, and then her white panties, which she let fall to the floor. She just stood there for a moment. *Her creamy white back looks soft,* Lars thought. *Her butt is smooth and round, and just the right proportion for a woman her size.* Her legs completed the perfect ensemble. Lars cleared his throat, and Eileen turned toward the bathroom, revealing her small but firm breasts. Then she walked out of sight. She did not look toward Lars. Lars walked over to the sofa and sat down to sip his tea.

As Eileen got into the shower, she smiled. She could not believe she did what she had just done. She was certain Lars had seen her. Why did she do this? Was she so hungry for a man? It had been a long time, but this was silly. She was already having second thoughts about what she had done. *It's too late now,* she thought. *I wonder if I turned him on. How could I not have turned him on?* Eileen finished her shower, dried off and put her robe on.

Lars thought about Eileen as he sat and sipped his tea. *Did she mean for me to see her? She didn't look at me. Did she know I was watching? She had to have known I was there,* he thought. *Was this an invitation?* It had been a long time since Lars had been with a woman. A long time! There had been no one since Rachel. That was three years ago. *Has it really been that long?* Lars certainly liked the way Eileen looked. Lars realized that as he watched her, he had felt the excitement and pressure rising in his pants. The feeling was gone now, but the vision in his mind lingered. Lars smiled and then finished his tea.

Eileen came out of her room, "Your turn now."

Lars got up, took his glass to the kitchen, and walked into his bedroom without looking at her.

Eileen fixed herself a glass of tea and went to the sofa. She sat down and waited for Lars to finish his shower. Lars was in and out of the shower quickly and came back out and joined Eileen on the sofa. Not a word was said about what had happened. Lars began talking about Ronald and Sara.

"Ron and Sara were much more than neighbors; they were good friends. Ron worked hard to provide for Sara. He didn't have a mean bone in his body. Sara was a great cook. I'm going to miss them."

Eileen could see tears forming in Lars' eyes as he looked straight ahead, never looking toward her. "I'm sorry," Eileen said.

"We better go to bed," Lars said. "We have another long walk ahead of us tomorrow."

Eileen got up first and headed toward her room while Lars followed.

"Good night," Lars said and went into the spare room.

"Good night," Eileen softly murmured as she went into her room. Not another word was said.

Neither slept well that night, and they got up a little later than they had planned. After breakfast they readied themselves, just as they had the day before, and walked out the front door. Lars took a good look around, especially along the tree line. He then led Eileen around to the back of the house in the direction of the Lin homestead. Suddenly, Lars noticed some movement and put out his arm to stop Eileen. Someone was coming through the trees. Lars raised his rifle and instructed Eileen to draw her pistol. As they stood there, the intruders emerged into the clearing between the house and tree line.

Sam saw Lars and Eileen pointing guns at them and raised his arms, yelling, "Don't shoot!" It was Sam and Sally Lin.

"It's alright," Lars said to Eileen. "They're my neighbors. Lower your gun." Lars headed out to meet Sam and Sally, and Eileen followed closely behind.

Lars was so relieved to find his friends in good health. He gave Sam a firm handshake and an even bigger hug. "We were just on our way to see you guys," Lars said. He then turned to Sally and gave her a big hug too. Lars turned to Eileen, "This is Eileen; she showed up on my doorstep a few days ago. Eileen, this is Sam and Sally and, of course, Sean and little Debra."

Eileen shook their hands and gave them a welcome smile. She hugged Sean and then took Debra from Sally's arms.

"You are a beautiful little girl," Eileen said. "And my, aren't you a handsome young man, Sean."

"Come on up to the house," Lars said, and they all walked up and around to the front porch. Lars grabbed a couple more chairs from inside the house and offered refreshments.

"Thanks," said Sam and Sally simultaneously.

"I'll get it," said Eileen, and she excused herself.

"It's good to see you, old friends," Lars said, though they were only in their mid-thirties. "My, the kids are growing so fast," Lars added. Eileen returned and served the tea.

Lars told Sam and Sally about Ronald and Sara, which deeply saddened them. They had been neighbors to Ronald and Sara much longer than Lars. Lars explained all the non-gory details of the ordeal. The conversation then turned to Eileen. Lars didn't let on there may be a romantic connection between them, only that Eileen would be staying a while until she could figure out what she wanted to do.

Lars got up and invited Sam to take a walk around to let Sally and Eileen have a chance to talk woman to woman for a while. The men started off toward the garden and then around back and down to the river. Lars picked up a few pebbles and tossed them into the water one by one as they continued to talk.

"You had better keep a close eye out; you hear?" Lars said. "If you run into trouble you can't handle, you and Sally get the hell out of there. You can come here, and we'll figure out what to do. Don't hesitate." Sam nodded, indicating he understood the seriousness of the situation.

Sam was of Asian descent. This didn't matter to Lars. They helped each other a lot over the past couple years, especially when Lars first moved here. Sam was strong and, at his age, didn't tire like Lars. Lars felt Sam was an indispensable friend and the feeling was mutual. "Will you stay for lunch?" Lars asked.

"We would love to," Sam said, "but we're on our way to Reggie's. I need some .357 magnum cartridges."

"I have some here, Sam. I took all of Ronald's ammunition I could find so someone wouldn't use it against us. I hid the guns we couldn't carry back in the woodshed. You're welcome to the two boxes of .357 cartridges."

"Thanks," said Sam. "In that case, we'll stay for lunch."

Lars and Sam headed back to the house. They went in the back door and Lars got the ammo.

"Eileen, we're having guests for lunch," Lars said as he and Sam walked out the front of the house onto the front porch. Eileen and Sally and the kids were seated on the front porch drinking tea and enjoying their new found friendship. "I'll get some meat and vegetables out of the smokehouse," Lars said.

When Lars returned with venison, potatoes, and beets, Eileen said, "You men continue your conversation; Sally and I will take care of lunch." Lars smiled and nodded his approval. The ladies got up, and Eileen took the meat and vegetables from Lars. The ladies disappeared inside with the kids while Lars and Sam went to the garden.

"I'll head back over to Reggie's in a few days," Lars said. "We need to keep an eye on each other from now on." Sam agreed. "I'll have to take Eileen along," Lars continued. "We can't be leaving the ladies alone anymore. It's just not safe for them to be alone." Sam understood completely. "I'm instructing Eileen on shooting," said Lars. "Be careful when you come around. I don't want you or Sally to get shot. She's doing pretty well, but she still has a lot of city girl in her. It'll take her a while to get used to the guns."

"Will do," Sam assured Lars.

After about an hour, Eileen stuck her head out the door and called the men in for lunch. The guys strolled over and went inside.

"That didn't take long," Lars said.

"You guys do like your venison raw, don't you?" Eileen said jokingly. Lars smiled. *This gal is something else*, Lars thought. They all sat down and had a delicious and healthy meal. The table talk was minimal, and the meal was quickly finished. They then went back out onto the porch and chatted a bit longer before the Lins said their goodbyes and headed back into the woods.

After the Lins left, Lars explained to Eileen that Sam and Sally always seemed a little queer to him, but the Lins provided one of Lars' favorite commodities. They raised chickens, goats, hogs, and a few ducks. Lars had chickens and could get his own ducks, but he needed the Lins for their hogs. Lars liked bacon a lot, and while the wild hogs in the area made very good eating, it was the fat tame hogs Sam raised that made excellent bacon. This made the Lins vital neighbors. Sally milked their goats, which provided some good milk, butter, and cheese, and these were added delicacies. Lars traded with the Lins mostly for bacon, but occasionally for a little butter and cheese. The area where their home was located was in the woods and didn't have a meadow. It was difficult for Sam and Sally to grow corn where they lived. Lars provided them mostly with corn. Sam was always ready and willing to trade bacon for corn. This arrangement worked perfectly for both Sam and him.

Lars also explained he didn't really understand the Lins. Maybe it was because of their Asian culture or background. Sally didn't look as Asian as Sam and though they both had Asian characteristics, they seemed to be of a mixed heritage. While they spoke good English, conversation always seemed difficult with them. The words were perfect, but the way they were put together always seemed strange and their accent always threw Lars off. Maybe it was also due in part to the fact that Lars didn't hear quite as well as he did when he was younger. Their mutual love of the woods and privacy, however, kept them close friends. Sam and Sally were young, with strong backs, and they worked very hard. They seemed to know nothing but work. They were also as sweet as the candy Sally made often, and were always ready and willing to help their neighbors. Just like everyone else was, here in the valley.

Chapter 9

Over the next few days, Lars and Eileen hung around the house. A fresh northern wind had blown in during the night, right after Sam and Sally left. The air wasn't all that cold, but it rained heavily with a little thunder and lightning, followed by a lingering light rain that lasted for two days. *Good thing*, Lars thought—it was getting a little dry and the rain was welcome. The rain filled the cistern, and because the rain wouldn't evaporate quickly due to the cooler weather, he imagined there would be plenty of moisture for the winter grasses. Winter grasses bring the deer to the meadow. More deer meant more food for the table. He wondered if he should have planted some greens in the garden and maybe some carrots and a beet or two. *Too late now*, he thought.

Lars went over a few chores he needed to do as soon as the weather dried things up a bit. He needed to chop more firewood and he needed to take another trip to Reggie's. Eileen would need to go with him and meet Reggie and Emily. He could not leave her alone to fend for herself. Anything could happen, and Lars didn't want whatever might happen to be on his conscience. More important, though, he was getting to like having her around. Lars told Eileen this trip would be a little more difficult than the recent trip because of the terrain. She assured Lars she was up for the trek.

The wet and miserable weather mostly confined Lars and Eileen indoors and they used the opportunity to get to know each other a little better. They spent hours on the sofa just talking. It seemed they had quite a bit in common. They both liked to travel and both considered themselves workaholics. They also thought of themselves as loners, but neither wanted to live completely alone. The more they talked, the more subtle similarities they found. Even though they had come from different worlds, it didn't drive them apart. In fact, it seemed to be bringing them closer together. Lars was certainly beginning to feel at home with her around. Eileen seemed to be fitting in very well with Lars' sharply different lifestyle, now that she had gotten the hang of building a fire in the stove.

Finally, after two days of rain and drizzle, the sun peeked through the clouds on the third morning. At about mid-morning, Lars told Eileen the two of them should make the journey to Reggie's. He also warned Eileen the trip would be a little wetter due to the rain, but also because the area was naturally a little swampy in places.

With a grin, Eileen said she didn't have a problem. "I'm not afraid to get dirty or muddy. Not quite what you would expect from a city girl, huh?" Eileen said.

Lars just smiled.

When they were both ready to leave, they headed out the door. On the porch, Lars asked Eileen if her gun was loaded.

"Of course," she replied.

"Then let's get going," he said.

At the beginning of the second clearing, about halfway to Reggie's place, the swamp was at its wettest. Eileen got stuck in the mud and Lars had to help her out. She was stuck pretty good. So stuck that Lars nearly got stuck himself. If this had been yesterday, they both would have been miserable. In spite of the cold mud, the day was warm. It helped that the sun had been up for a while.

Lars grabbed Eileen underneath her armpits and began to pull her up to a grassy knoll. He slipped on the wet ground but kept a firm grip on Eileen as he landed on his back with Eileen on top of him, with Eileen's back towards him, having worked free from the mud. She raised herself up a bit and turned over on top of Lars. Now they were face to face. Lars looked into her eyes for the first time. Not really the first time, but this time he really searched into her eyes—deep into her eyes. It was as if he could see her soul. Her eyes were a deep brown with tiny specks of yellow and they burned into his heart. Eileen bent her head down and gave Lars a kiss, not on the cheek as you might a friend, but on the lips. The kiss was so tender, her soft and warm lips pressing gently against his. The kiss lasted for only seconds. When she rose up and started to stand, Lars lay there stunned.

As Eileen stood up and looked at Lars lying there, she smiled and asked, "Are you okay?"

"Yeah," he responded, "you're just making it a little hard to be a gentleman."

She gave Lars a little wink. "Whoever said you needed to be a gentleman?" she said. "Come on, get up." She reached her arm out to give him a hand up. Lars took the hand and pulled himself to his feet.

He took his pistol out of the holster to check if he had gotten mud in the barrel and instructed Eileen to do the same. The guns were good. Lars checked the rifle barrel, which was also good. Eileen then took off in the correct direction as Lars followed behind. After a couple minutes, Eileen looked back to check on Lars. He was following about ten feet back.

"What are you thinking back there? I can hear the gears in your head whirring." She smiled and continued on.

Lars said nothing. As he walked though, he could not help noticing that he continually focused on Eileen's butt. The wiggle in her walk was mesmerizing. She had a nice butt too—round and firm. *Perfect in every way*, he thought.

The only talk from here on out was about directions. Finally, they reached Reggie's place. Lars asked Eileen to hold up a minute while he gave out a long wolf howl. Within seconds, Reggie opened the door and stepped out onto the porch.

"Come on in, bro," Reggie yelled. Lars led the way now, with Eileen close behind. Emily came out as Lars and Eileen walked up the steps.

"This is Eileen," said Lars. "This is my best friend, Reggie, and his wife, Emily," Lars added, looking at Eileen. They shook hands and exchanged greetings.

"My, you two are a sight!" Emily exclaimed.

"Yeah," Lars said, "the rain the past couple days really softened up the swamp. We'll be alright," Lars added.

"Nonsense," Emily replied. "We've got to get you two cleaned up. Come on, Eileen, we'll get you a shower and some dry clothes." She led Eileen into the house.

While Eileen was getting cleaned up, Lars quietly told Reggie about Ronald and Sara.

Reggie held his head down. "They were good friends," he said sadly.

"Yes, they were," Lars added. "I just wanted you to know what happened."

"Thanks, man," said Reggie.

"Have you seen anyone around?" Lars asked.

"As a matter of fact, I did," Reggie replied. "A couple days ago, this kid came by. I ran him off, but a few hours later he came back and took a shot at me. I killed him and buried him out near the tree line."

"It is getting really dangerous around here now," said Lars.

"Yes, it is," Reggie replied.

"You and Emily need to keep your eyes open. You don't want anyone sneaking up on you like they did Ron and Sara. You and Emily also need to stay close at all times," Lars added.

"We will," assured Reggie.

"I don't stray far from Eileen these days," Lars said.

"That kid was so stupid," Reggie said. "He only had a pistol and took a shot at me from a hundred yards away. You can't hit anything at a hundred yards with a pistol. Why didn't he heed my warning?"

"People are hungry," Lars said. "Hungry people often do stupid things."

"I never told you this, but before I came out here, I got into politics for a while," Reggie continued. "I was on the local city council. Most of my life, the people I had dealings with were smart. When I got on the council, this changed. It seemed like I was dealing with dumb people on a daily basis."

"Oh yeah?" Lars probed.

Reggie went on, "There was an incident where an elderly man ran into the back of a stopped garbage truck. The council wanted to require orange cones to be placed behind all garbage trucks at all stops. These trucks are constantly stopping and starting. The extra time to set out and pick up a couple cones at each stop would be significant. We calculated the fuel and labor cost would increase 20%, as would the amount of time to collect the trash. It would take too long to pick up all the trash and we would need to buy more trucks. 'Are you stupid?' I said. If people can't see a large, brightly colored truck with flashing lights, do you think they are going to see a couple little cones? I nearly went ballistic that day. This was just one of many incidents. This one, though, put me over the edge. I knew I had to get away from these people. When my term ran out, I quit. The next day, I began my plans to move here.

"Take that kid the other day," Reggie continued. "Now these stupid bastards are following me out here!" Reggie exclaimed. Reggie was really getting peeved at this point. His face was getting redder by the second. "I'll just kill every one of the mother f…" Reggie stopped mid-sentence, as he heard the doorknob turn and the front door opened. Eileen and Emily walked out onto the porch. Emily had given Eileen a dress to wear; they were about the same size. Lars had not seen her in a dress up until now. *She looks like a new woman*, he thought and let out a big smile.

"I'll take that smile as your approval," Eileen grinned.

"You look fantastic," Lars said.

"You all right?" Emily asked Reggie, noticing the color of his face.

"Yeah, I'm okay," Reggie said.

"Alright, Reggie, get Lars some clothes," Emily instructed.

Reggie led Lars into the house and dug out some overalls as Lars showered. Lars finished and got dressed, and then joined Reggie, who had returned to the porch with the ladies.

"You've got a great girl here," Emily blurted out.

Lars turned a little red and smiled. He had no words.

Emily washed and dried Eileen and Lars' clothes in a couple hours and stacked them in the living room.

"You guys need to stay the night. I won't take no for an answer," said Emily.

"Emily's right, you guys can't go back across that swamp today," Reggie added. "You must stay."

"Eileen, come on inside," Emily encouraged. "We'll get started on dinner. We'll let the men talk a while." Eileen got up, walked over and kissed Lars on the cheek before following Emily inside. She left Lars sitting there with a strange look on his face—a look which led to too many questions from Reggie.

"So it's getting a little juicy over at your place, huh Lars?" Reggie asked.

"No!" Lars replied.

"Could have fooled me," Reggie said, laughing.

Lars couldn't deny things were heating up between him and Eileen, but Reggie didn't need to know the details.

Reggie led Lars out back to his bunker where Reggie kept all his assorted toys. Lars thought he had seen most of Reggie's goodies, but Reggie had reserved many of his favorites. Due to the economy and the murder of his friends, Ronald and Sara, Reggie wanted to share some special toys with Lars. His prize was a sniper rifle, which according to Reggie could take a man's head off at two miles.

"Wow!" exclaimed Lars.

Reggie also showed Lars the mortar and at least a dozen boxes of shells. Next, Reggie brought out his .50 caliber machine gun, and last but not least, his 150-millimeter cannon.

Again, "Wow!" was all Lars could say. He had no idea Reggie was so well armed; well, he did, but not with such large weapons.

Reggie just smiled. "I have one more item to show you," he laughed. "These are homemade." Reggie dug out a box of spheres, each about the size of a volleyball with a rope hanging out the side. "I have more outside, painted green and hanging in trees along the perimeter of my meadow. I can shoot these with a rifle from various positions around the house. They explode when hit and will kill anything within fifty feet. They will also immobilize anything within a hundred feet." Lars was amazed. "I also made a tunnel from the bunker to the house," Reggie added, "just in case we're invaded." Lars again was in awe.

Reggie led Lars over to a back room in the bunker, inserted a key and opened the door to a room literally filled with boxes. The room had to be fifteen feet by twenty feet, and the boxes were stacked in rows all the way to the ceiling. "You know what these are?" Reggie asked.

"No," replied Lars.

"You know the non-perishable emergency food packets I used to sell?" Lars nodded yes. "Well, this is what I bought for myself and Emily," Reggie added. Lars was astounded. He had to have enough to last a hundred years. "If you ever need some food, you know where to come," said Reggie.

"How long will this last?" Lars asked.

"Just me and Emily, about sixty years. The stuff is only good for about half that time, so don't hesitate if you need a little extra food or want something a little different than what you usually eat. In fact, I'm going to send some back with you anyway," he added. Reggie began to pack a sack with some assorted meals, as well as powdered milk. "If you need more, just come on over, but be sure you bring a jar of beets," Reggie said with a smile.

"I won't forget the beets," grinned Lars.

"The chocolate is really nice," Reggie said. "I bet Eileen will like some of that. Not something you will find in the woods."

After about an hour, Reggie picked up two volleyballs and handed them to Lars to go with the sack of food, and they walked out and locked the bunker. Reggie instructed Lars to place the bombs in trees within shooting range. "If you're in trouble, just fire one off. These things are loud." Reggie added. "I'll easily hear it if you shoot one off." Lars noticed the closing mechanism and lock on the bunker, which looked impenetrable. Reggie assured Lars it was. Their conversation reverted back to Eileen, as they walked back to the house.

"When are you two going to get married?" Reggie asked.

"We're not," Lars answered.

"Are you crazy?" Reggie asserted. "She's hot, old man!"

"Am I going to have to smack you, Reggie?" Lars said. "Get your mind off Eileen."

"You needed a woman and now this hot chick falls into your lap and you're not interested? You're nuts!"

"I didn't say I wasn't interested," Lars replied. "I'm just not rushing anything. Keep your mouth shut around Eileen or I'll have to smack you," Lars said laughing.

"Okay, old man," Reggie said, "but don't put the inevitable off too long."

The men went inside and found Emily and Eileen working away at dinner and talking about various subjects. Reggie and Lars sat at the table. Eileen brought them glasses of tea with ice, and walked back to continue her task and conversation with Emily. Lars held up his glass and looked at the tea, then took a sip and smiled. *I wish I had a fridge with a freezer,* he thought. *If I had a wind turbine to produce enough electricity, I could have ice whenever I wanted. But I don't! And I won't!*

Lars and Reggie continued to talk, but Lars was not paying a lot of attention to Reggie. His thoughts turned to Eileen and he was watching her. She was facing the other direction and not noticing Lars' attention, which was good. Lars' mind was wandering to places where maybe it should not be wandering.

"We're about ready here, guys," Emily said. Eileen set the table and then refreshed everyone's glasses as Emily set out the food. The ladies joined the guys. "Dig in," Emily said.

"Where in the world did you get beef, Reggie?" questioned Lars.

"Just something I've been saving for a special occasion. I believe this qualifies," replied Reggie.

"This is just so good," Lars said between bites of mouth-watering meat. The table got very quiet as they all enjoyed their perfectly cooked steaks.

After the meal was finished, the men got up first and began to clear the table.

"I'll do the dishes tomorrow," said Emily, "just put them in the sink." The men gladly complied.

"How about a board game?" Reggie suggested. "We have Dominion, Monopoly, Risk…"

"Anything but Monopoly!" both Emily and Lars cried.

Many years ago, way before Reggie had gray hair, he had been fortunate enough to earn the title of United States Monopoly Champion in a tournament in Las Vegas. He never let them forget it whenever the game was played. As Emily and Lars explained this to Eileen, she diplomatically suggested a game of Dominion.

"Dominion it is then," Emily said. Reggie went to the linen closet and pulled out the game. As the women set the game up, Reggie and Lars fixed a fresh pot of tea and topped off everyone's glass. Eileen knew the game of Risk and didn't much care for it. She had never heard of Dominion, but the name sounded intriguing. Emily explained the rules to Eileen as they set up the game.

The game was fun and lively, with no talk of past events or the impending disaster they all may be facing tomorrow, next week, or next year. They laughed and played the game, paying more attention to conversation than to the game itself. The game took over two hours, with a close finish. Eileen came in first, Emily second, followed by Reggie and then Lars. Lars, Emily, and Reggie congratulated Eileen on the win and the game was put away for another day.

"Next time we're playing Monopoly," grumbled Reggie.

Lars had been so consumed with Eileen most of the day, he almost forgot to ask about his kids. "Reggie, have you heard anything about James and Georgia?"

"I'm sorry to say, no," Reggie replied. "Don't you worry, I'll keep after the radio, and you'll be the first one to know if I hear anything." Lars was a little sad Reggie hadn't found out anything; but after all, it has only been a few days since they last spoke.

"I appreciate anything you can find out," Lars added.

Lars was concerned about his daughter, Georgia. At the same time, he knew her and Dean could take care of themselves. Dean Fenwick was an ex-army Ranger, and Lars had taught his daughter as much as he could about taking care of herself. Their two kids, his grandsons, Paul and Ricky were just barely old enough to handle a gun. Lars knew Dean would make certain they could hit something, though, without hurting themselves. Lars really missed seeing and playing with his grand kids. They lived in the deep woods outside of Gonzales, and just maybe, they would be safe there. Lars could only hope at this point.

"You guys can share a bed, right?" Emily asked Lars and Eileen. "We have only one spare bed," Emily added. "Unless one of you want to sleep on the couch."

Eileen looked at Lars and then turned to Emily and said, "We are all adults here; I believe we can share a bed."

"You guys have a seat," said Emily, pointing to the sofa. Emily then went into the spare bedroom to check to see if it was presentable for her guests. She lit a scented candle in a glass jar and returned to the living room.

The conversation continued for another hour until everyone began to feel the effects of the long day. It was Reggie who suggested they should all retire for the evening, as there was a lot to do tomorrow. Eileen and Lars thanked their hosts for the delicious meal and their fine hospitality; then they adjourned to the bedroom. Emily and Reggie did the same.

Eileen went immediately into the adjoining bathroom. Directly, she came out wearing a negligee Emily had given her. Lars' eyes got nearly as big as the volley-balls Reggie had given him. Eileen looked stunning. Actually, she looked better than stunning; she was a knockout. Eileen crawled into bed and Lars went into the bathroom. Lars just had to pee, which didn't take very long, but he also looked into the mirror and found a toothbrush had been laid out for him on the counter. Lars brushed his teeth as he thought about what might or what was going to happen when he crawled into bed. *We are guests in my best friend's house. Nothing can happen, could it?*

Lars returned to the bedroom and walked around the bed to his side. He took off his clothes and climbed into bed. As he turned to face Eileen, he was greeted by a big smile.

"What do you have on your mind?" he whispered.

"Whatever," murmured Eileen.

"We can't here. This is my best friend's home, and the walls are thin!" Lars nervously replied. Eileen leaned over and blew the candle out. Then she turned away from Lars. She scooted back against him, reached back and grabbed his right arm and pulled him up against her. She then took his hand and moved it over her breast. She squeezed his hand onto her mound. Lars felt himself strain-ing against his briefs, and though he tried not to, he couldn't help but poke Eileen a little.

She feels and smells so damn good, Lars thought. This was as close as he had been to a woman for a long, long time, and it really felt good.

"How do you like the perfume?" Eileen asked.

"I like it just fine," he replied.

"It's called Unbridled Passion," Eileen said.

Lars didn't say a word, but his mind was spinning.

"Good night," Lars said.

"Good night, big boy," Eileen whispered.

Although it took a long time, he finally fell asleep. Lars awoke a couple hours later, though, and went into the bathroom to pee. He awoke from a dream. He couldn't get Eileen out of his head. She was the center of attention in his dream.

The two of them were on a deserted island. They were stranded and had no food, no clothes and were totally alone. They could do whatever they wanted. They were both doing what came naturally, but Lars woke up just before the dream got really good. Lars returned to bed without waking Eileen and fell back to sleep a short time later.

Lars and Eileen woke up about the same time. They were facing in opposite directions, so Lars turned to face Eileen. Eileen did the same, and she was smiling, as was Lars.

"Good morning, Mr. Lindgren," she said.

"Good morning, Ms. Branson," he responded. They both smiled and then crawled out of bed. Lars quickly dressed in his cleaned clothes. Eileen went into the bathroom with her own clothes but did not shut the door. She had her back to Lars when she slipped out of her negligee. *She left the door open on purpose*, Lars thought. *She is inviting me to look.* Lars looked away but then he turned back. He watched as she slipped her panties on and saw her turn to the side facing the mirror. She didn't look at Lars as she put on her bra. But Lars got another look at her breasts. This time in a much brighter light. Her nipples were hard and Lars again felt the stretching fabric of his briefs. He reluctantly turned away and went into the living room with Eileen soon following behind. They each had brought out their borrowed clothes and Emily told them to pile the clothes near the door to the spare bedroom. "I'll take care of those later," she added.

Reggie and Emily had only been up for a short time, but coffee was soon ready. Emily set out coffee mugs and grabbed the coffee pot off the stove. She poured each of them a full cup of coffee. Sugar, artificial sweetener, honey, and powdered creamer were on the table. Emily and Eileen took artificial sweetener and faux cream, while Reggie and Lars took theirs black with sugar.

"How did you guys sleep?" asked Reggie.

Eileen and Lars responded simultaneously, "Great!"

Lars didn't sleep all that well, but he couldn't deny that the dream was great even though it never reached its climax. Lars then drifted off into the dream trying to imagine what the remainder would have been like.

"Lars," Reggie said in a raised voice.

"What?" Lars asked.

"You seem to be a little distracted," Reggie said.

"No," Lars replied, "What do you want?"

Reggie reminded Lars to hang the volleyballs as soon as he returned home as they drank their coffee. "Those things will hang out there for at least ten years without harm. If you have a problem, I'm coming over loaded for bear," Reggie said. "When you shoot one of those things, you'll know why I said I would hear it. I hope you don't ever need to shoot one, but don't hesitate if the need arises, okay?" Lars said he would.

Eileen and Emily were whispering and Lars and Reggie weren't listening to what they were talking about, as they were talking to each other. But Lars heard something that caught his attention and he began paying more attention to the girls' conversation. Soon he realized they were talking about him. Lars turned a little red in the face, not even knowing what they had said.

Lars knew he and Eileen needed to get home soon, but he also knew they all needed to have a conversation they had avoided up to this point. "It is getting very dangerous around here," Lars said.

"Yes, it is," Reggie agreed.

"Our very survival is at stake. If things keep going as they have been recently, we may all soon be dead," Lars added.

"Maybe we need to take a more proactive approach to our security," Reggie said. "If we just sit around and react to what comes our way, we could get caught off guard and end up like the Westons," he added.

"You may be right," Lars responded. "It's hard enough to survive when you have to deal with Mother Nature, snakes, and too little time to do too many chores. Our newest threat will definitely make things much more difficult."

"I know I'm right," said Reggie.

"How do you suppose we remedy this problem?" Lars asked.

"I don't know yet," Reggie responded, "but we'll need to figure something out. We have been fairly lucky so far. Sooner or later our luck will run out, just like it did for the Westons."

Emily and Eileen didn't have any answers either, but they brought up more problems. "Now that we no longer have stores to shop at for all the items we will certainly deplete, life will become increasingly more difficult unless we find alternatives," Eileen brought up.

"We will certainly run out of coffee, tea, sugar, fuel, fertilizer, and more before long," Emily added.

"Our vehicles, and especially our tractors, will not last forever," Lars included.

"I know," said Reggie, "but I don't have any solutions just yet."

"Well," Emily inserted, "we had better come up with some solutions soon."

"Yes, we had," they all agreed.

"There are several families across the highway," Reggie said. "The Tuckers have been such a nuisance over the years, I don't know if contacting them could or would help our situation. There is also the Gómez family and the Johnston family. I don't know them well at all. They were always too far from here to visit and get to know."

"Maybe we need to take a field trip soon," Lars inserted.

"Maybe so," Reggie added, "but we need to talk to the Lins first and get some input from them."

"It's probably best if we think this new adventure over a bit more first anyway," Lars included. "If we go off half-cocked, we could get into more trouble than we bargained for."

"I guess we should let this simmer a bit more," Reggie agreed.

Emily and Eileen had no more to offer but listened to every word of Lars and Reggie's conversation. The conversation brought them back to the reality of their security problem. The ladies realized their lives were in great jeopardy. A few minutes ago, their thoughts had been on the idea of Eileen and Lars becoming a couple. Now their thoughts turned to whether or not they would live another day. The ladies' fears surfaced, and though they had confidence the guys could and would take care of them, they could not shake the uncertainty of the situation.

"I'll talk to the Lins in a few days," Lars promised, "and when we get together again, we'll have a planning session."

"Sounds good," said Reggie.

"We had better get going," Lars said, "before we wear out our welcome."

"That's not going to happen, bro," Reggie replied. "You and Eileen are welcome here anytime, and for as long as you wish."

"Thank you," Lars said, "that really means a lot."

"Thank you," Eileen added.

Eileen and Lars thanked their hosts for the use of their clothes, the great meal, and especially their hospitality. There were hugs, handshakes and appropriate kisses all around. Then Lars and Eileen headed home.

Chapter 10

On the trip home, Lars described Reggie's food locker to Eileen and told her about his toys.

"You really need to see his bunker," Lars said. "You will not believe some of the stuff he has stored in there. Maybe on the next trip, Reggie will show you around."

Eileen had really liked Emily, and she thought they had a lot in common. While she did not have to work due to Reggie's successes, she was a whiz on the computer and had worked in the accounting department of a large hospital. She too, like Eileen, had been a regular customer at Starbucks. Emily also read a lot of books. She really loved the *Game of Thrones* series. She didn't watch television much, but was dying to see the movie version of the series; she never got around to watching it before the grid shut down. Emily missed many things the city offered, but loved Reggie enough to follow him to the ends of the earth. Where they lived now was apparently the end of the earth with no road out.

Emily was happy though. She had grown accustomed to the peace and quiet she could never get in the city. She would miss the country life now if she moved elsewhere. Emily worked much harder than she ever did while in the city, but she didn't mind. These days Emily had a new reason for loving the country life. If she still lived in the city, she would likely be dead.

Lars and Eileen had plenty to talk about on their way home. However, since they stayed closer to the tree line where the ground was drier but the brush was thicker, much of the talk was about avoiding the thorns, nettles, and poison ivy.

"I guess you noticed they have a much better setup than I have," Lars stated. "Reggie made good money as a salesman but got rich later as an army contractor," Lars added. "About twenty years ago, he made a long list of all the things he would need to make life easy when he and Emily moved to the woods. Their wind turbine in addition to the solar grid makes it possible for them to have numerous luxury appliances we don't have, like a washer and dryer, a refrigerator and a pump on their water well. He even has a backup generator, but it takes fuel to run that thing so it's not used much. I couldn't afford a turbine when I moved here. Our grid will only do so much."

"We'll do just fine with the solar panels," she assured him.

"Emily was originally a city gal too, just like you. She didn't have to adjust quite as much as you will need to, but she did adapt pretty well didn't she?"

Eileen agreed, as they carefully worked their way through the briars and brambles.

"Dammit," Lars heard behind him. Lars turned to see Eileen bent over grabbing her leg. Eileen had a thorny vine wrapped around her ankle. Lars knelt to help her get the vine off. Lars didn't know the name of this vine, but it was common in the woods. It was really tough with nasty thorns. Eileen's ankle was bleeding badly as Lars removed the vine, getting stuck a few times himself in the process.

Lars examined the cuts, and while they were bleeding freely, they were not all that deep. The wounds should heal quickly. Lars took out his handkerchief and wrapped it around her ankle. This should do until we get home." Eventually they made it home without any further damage. The trip, however, took nearly two hours.

Everything looked fine as they walked around the house and grounds. It looked as though no intruders had been there while they were out. They arrived home about lunch time. Lars found some alcohol and bandages, and then cleaned and wrapped up Eileen's ankle. The bleeding had stopped and as long as it didn't get infected, it would be okay in a few days. Lars made a quick meal, and they ate it on the porch.

After they finished lunch, Lars asked Eileen to accompany him to the tree line to hang up the volleyballs Reggie had given them.

"Sure," Eileen said. Lars hung the balls just above the bottom limbs, first in the sycamore tree where the last intruder was seen and where Eileen had spent some time. The other, Lars placed in the tree line toward the Weston's place alongside the trail Lars had established on numerous trips there. When they returned to the house, Lars was satisfied that the balls were easily visible from there.

"How are we going to spend the rest of the day?" Eileen asked.

"I don't know," Lars replied. "How do you want to spend it?"

"Maybe we should have a long talk about us," Eileen suggested.

"Okay, I'm good with that," Lars replied.

Eileen went in and fixed two glasses of tea and returned to Lars on the porch.

"I don't see the economy changing anytime soon," Eileen began. "I don't have any place to go, and I don't see this situation changing," she continued. "I like you a lot. You're a very handsome man, and I feel very safe and comfortable here with you. I think you like me as well—going by your reactions to me lately! I want you to know I am not trying to force you into having sex with me; I'm only letting you know I care for you, and if it leads to sex—or even if it doesn't—I'm here for you."

Lars thought for a minute and then began, "I haven't been with a woman in a very long time, and maybe I don't know how to act with a lady anymore, but I do know I like you. I like you a lot. Sex? I don't know yet, but I guarantee you one thing, you will be the first one to know. It looks like we're going to be together for a while. If we mess up and cause a rift between us, or one of us gets hurt, which is likely to be you, then neither of us is going to be happy. I just want us to be happy and to work together for our common good. We both may die tomorrow, and this is constantly on my mind. If you and I begin fighting, we may increase the likelihood of that happening." Lars paused to give Eileen a chance to respond.

After a long pause herself, she finally said, "I agree." Eileen and Lars stood up, and Lars gave Eileen a big bear hug, followed by a long kiss.

"I know it's a little late in the season to be planting a garden," Lars said, "but we have a few hours of daylight left. Why don't we plant some greens and maybe some carrots and radishes?"

"Okay," Eileen said with a smile.

Lars went to the pantry and picked out some packets of seeds. Once outside, he grabbed a hoe. When he and Eileen reached the garden, Lars opened the gate and walked over to the end of a row at the side of the garden. Lars used the hoe to break through the hardened surface of the twenty-foot row, revealing the soft and moist soil below the crust. Lars then instructed Eileen on how he wanted the seeds planted.

"I know," said Eileen, "I've been planting a garden for years. Not on this scale, but I do know how to plant."

"I'm sorry," Lars replied," I assumed you didn't know how to plant a garden."

"That's alright", Eileen said, "I wouldn't expect you to know."

Lars continued to prepare several rows for planting without saying another word, but keeping an eye on Eileen's technique. When they had finished, Lars said again, "I'm sorry I underestimated your abilities." She just smiled.

The next morning, Lars and Eileen made a quick trip to the Lins. Lars informed Sam and Sally of recent events and invited them to a security meeting in a few days. The meeting would be held at Lars' place. Sam and Sally said they would be there.

The next couple days were rather quiet around the Lindgren place. There were no unwanted intruders, no visits from neighbors, no trips to the neighbors. There was just peace and quiet except the chirps of birds and the rustle of tree leaves. The weather had warmed and the temperature was in the eighties with a persistent breeze out of the southeast. Lars worked hard cutting wood and hunting along the tree line of the property, always making sure he didn't stray too far from the house. He shot a few squirrels and rabbits, which he salted and dried in the smokehouse. Lars and Eileen spent a couple hours each evening watching the sunset as they sipped on a glass of refreshing tea.

"It is certainly peaceful out here much of the time," Eileen said.

"You getting to like the country now?" Lars asked.

"Yes, I am," she replied. "You know, just a couple weeks ago I was sitting behind a desk working on the computer and now I am out in the middle of the woods with a strange man playing farmer, shooting at cans, and tramping around in the swamp. It's crazy."

"Strange man?" Lars inquired with a smile.

"You are a bit on the strange side, honey," Eileen replied, "but don't get me wrong, I have my quirks too."

"Yes you do," Lars inserted, again with a smile.

Eileen twisted her face a bit and gave Lars the evil eye, and then they both began laughing. "Maybe we're both a little strange; maybe that's why we get along so well together"

"Maybe so," Lars agreed. *I just love how she calls me honey*, Lars thought. Lars was getting that fuzzy feeling inside again.

During one hunting trip, Lars heard a rifle shot nearby, maybe a half-mile or so away, and quickly returned to the house and took Eileen with him to investigate.

Lars and Eileen quickly made their way toward the direction of the shot. After they had gone about a quarter-mile, they slowed their pace and then quietly and carefully made their way through the brush, Lars leading the way. It wasn't long until Lars heard voices. He and Eileen then slowly made their way in the direction of the voices, stopping from time to time to listen. Lars saw some movement. He then instructed Eileen to stay behind while he moved in the direction of the voices. As Lars got closer, he determined there were two boys. They did not notice Lars approaching. They were busy with their task of field dressing a deer. When Lars got within a hundred feet of the boys, he recognized the two as a couple of the Tuckers. They were not on Lars property, but were too close nevertheless. And the deer they had killed appeared to be a doe.

There were thousands and thousands of acres mostly uninhabited in the area. *Why do they need to hunt this close to my place?* Lars thought. *There had to be deer elsewhere.* Lars decided to back off and not approach the boys. He returned to Eileen unseen and the two of them headed home. Lars explained the situation to Eileen when they got out of earshot of the two boys—poachers in Lars' mind. Although he didn't like the poachers, there really wasn't much he could do about it.

Lars and Eileen had numerous conversations about long-term future needs and what-ifs in preparation for their upcoming security meeting. What if one of them was killed? What if someone were to approach their place? What if one of them was hurt? They had a lot to think about. Where would they get tea, coffee, and sugar? They would certainly need more fuel at some point. Where would they get this valuable commodity? When they talked on other subjects, it was mostly about chores.

When Lars was physically working, Eileen could tell he was constantly thinking and highly stressed by their current situation. He would pause from time to time as he rested his arms with a pensive look on his face. Lars thought about Eileen often, but his thoughts always returned to their security problems. Lars still had no solutions.

One afternoon, Lars decided it was high time he and Eileen went fishing. Fishing not only provided Lars with one of his favorite foods, but it was also one of his favorite pastimes. He grabbed two fishing poles and led Eileen to the barn. Alongside the building were two half-barrels filled with dirt. Lars dug his hand into one barrel and scraped the dirt aside. He pulled out a dozen or so red, squirmy earthworms and put them in his pocket. Lars then dug into the other container and came up with a few yellow grub worms, which he also put into his pocket. He made another grab for the yellow worms and came up with a few more. He added these to the first. Lars then led Eileen down to the river with fishing poles and bait.

One of the first things Lars built when he moved here was a small pier. There was a cleaning table with knives and an old, worn, but still useable, whetstone. A bucket with an attached rope sat under the cleaning table. Lars used this to dip water from the river into the sink. There were also two chairs on the pier. One had been there since the pier was first built, but the other Lars had recently made for Eileen. Lars demonstrated to Eileen how to attach hooks and sinkers to the end of the line and how to bait the hook. He also instructed her on the art of luring, catching and landing fish. They tossed their baited lines into the water and sat back and waited for the fish to bite. It was all up to the fish now.

It didn't take long for Eileen to have a fish on the end of her line. "Beginner's luck," laughed Lars. It wasn't a large fish but big enough to give Eileen a struggle to get it landed. As she swung the fish onto the pier, it almost hit Lars. Eileen then learned another valuable new lesson from Lars. The fish was a catfish. A catfish has three barbed fins that can stick and cut you. The barbed fins contain a poison which can make the cut or puncture hurt even more than just the wound itself. As Lars slowly took the fish off the hook, Eileen watched and listened as he explained how to remove the hook without getting finned. Eileen was a little squeamish when she re-baited her hook, but with Lars' urging, she got the worm on and dropped her line back into the water. Close to an hour later, they had caught a total of five fish between them. Eileen had caught three. It was a good catch.

Lars cleaned and prepped two of the fish for their dinner while the other three were made ready for smoking and drying. They would go straight to the smokehouse and hang next to the squirrels and rabbits. The heads and guts made good feed for the chickens.

Eileen took the two fish Lars had prepped for dinner and returned to the house to start cooking. When Lars joined her in the kitchen after cleaning up their mess on the pier, Eileen said, "If you want to enjoy the fish, you'll have to do the baking, frying, grilling, or whatever you do with fish, because I've never made fresh catfish. I can do potatoes and candied beets, but no way will I ruin the very first fish I ever caught!" Lars looked at her and laughed as he took the fish outside and started the grill. He was still grinning when he brought the grilled fish to the table.

They both sat down at the table and began to eat. Eileen was the first to speak. "Wow! I've never had such good fish. It must be one of the fish I caught," she laughed.

Lars didn't disagree. "I'm certainly enjoying it," he said as he smiled at her. They settled down to a comfortable silence as they finished their meal.

After the kitchen cleanup was completed, Lars and Eileen automatically went to the sofa. They had already started a habit of retreating there after the evening meal. Tonight they spent an hour in companionable silence, as Eileen read a novel and Lars read from his gardening book.

Eileen was the first to get up. She left the comfort of the sofa to take her shower. Then she went to bed. Not long after, Lars got up and took his shower. Instead of going to his bedroom, he went to Eileen's bed. Lars crawled under the bed covers. He leaned toward Eileen and she turned and faced Lars.

"I have been thinking a lot the past few days," Lars said. "I want you to stay with me permanently." Eileen started to speak, but Lars put two fingers over her mouth to prevent her from doing so. Lars continued, "I don't know if I love you, but my feelings for you are growing stronger every day. I will provide for you the best I can. I will protect you the best I can. I haven't had a partner for a long time, and I miss the closeness only a woman can provide. I want this, and I need this. I want this from you." Finally, Lars let Eileen speak.

She smiled and said, "I want this too."

Lars pulled Eileen close and touched his lips to hers. He ran his hand under her nightshirt and touched her breasts. He fondled the nipples and Eileen responded immediately. Lars slowly removed Eileen's nightshirt and began kissing and licking her breasts and nipples. He again pulled Eileen close to him and kissed her neck. Then he worked his way down to her navel, leaving soft kisses along the way. Lars continued kissing downward until he reached her soft and tender area. He gently pulled her panties aside, working his tongue over, around, and into the tenderness. Eileen let out a gasp of pleasure. "Yes, baby! Yes!" she moaned. Then he removed the panties entirely and moved between Eileen's legs. At the same time, he grabbed her buttocks and buried his face into her sweet juices. Lars quickly slipped his briefs off as he continued his loving nudges into her softness. He slowly worked his way back up to her breasts—the kissing continuing without interruption. Lars leaned in close to Eileen's soft lips and gave her a long and passionate kiss.

She reached down and touched him. Lars had been firm for a while, but when Eileen began to caress him, the firmness turned into hardness. Eileen guided Lars into her softness, which was flowing by this time. He slid in easily due to Eileen's abundance of natural lubricant. She was warm and inviting, and Lars pushed until he was consumed by her body. He began the natural rhythm he had not performed for such a long time. Lars pressed harder and harder against Eileen's clitoris, urging her to orgasm. Eileen could not remember when she last had an orgasm and she came quickly. Eileen jerked, squealed a little, and then gasped as she squeezed Lars with her arms wrapped around his mid-section. Lars squeezed back, forcing himself completely inside her. He kept up this force until he began to feel Eileen relaxing. Eileen became limp. Lars kissed her and looked into her beautiful eyes.

Lars was not done—he could not get enough of Eileen. He began his rhythm again, returning to Eileen's breasts, which he fondled with his tongue. Lars had softened a bit after Eileen finished her orgasm, but it didn't take long to reach his previous hardness as the rhythm continued. Lars was close to orgasm when Eileen exploded again. It didn't take long for Lars to feel his juices flowing outward into multiple eruptions, adding to Eileen's juices to fill her cavity with his love. Spent, he lay on top of Eileen for a moment and then rolled off to her side. "You're the best," Lars muttered. Lars grabbed her hand, turned his face toward hers, and gave her a tender kiss and a big smile as he squeezed her hand.

They both lay there for a while, not saying a word. Each knew how the other felt. Their feelings were exactly the same. Lars turned toward Eileen and put his arm around her waist; she leaned toward him. "We are going to have a good life together," Lars said.

"Yes, we are," Eileen replied. Totally satisfied, it didn't take long for both to fall asleep.

Lars and Eileen awoke early but did not immediately get out of bed. They snuggled together, each with thoughts of the previous night. After a while, Lars rolled out of bed, got dressed and headed for the kitchen. He started breakfast while Eileen went into the bathroom. She brushed her teeth, peed, and brushed her hair. She walked back into the bedroom and got dressed. Then she followed Lars' footsteps into the kitchen.

Coffee was ready. Lars soon had the bacon, eggs, and toast on the table. He was wearing his smile again, and this morning Eileen had a big smile on her face too. They finished their meal with a little small talk but made no mention of last night.

"Let's go for a walk," Lars said.

"Sure," Eileen replied. They put on their holsters and Lars grabbed his rifle on the way out.

They walked to the garden to check their plantings and then down to the river, until they finally came to the sycamore tree where Eileen had hidden when she first came to Lars' place. They made a full round of the meadow, but this time it was different. This time Lars held Eileen's hand as they walked. They had made a connection last night, and this was Lars' way to continue the connection today. Eileen liked holding hands and walking with Lars.

When she first came to Lars' home, Eileen had been confused, lost, and directionless, but now things were much different. She felt serene. She felt she had come home. Yes, there was still the threat from intruders. But Eileen no longer cared about the economy, the home she had left so abruptly, and the miseries she had suffered finding this place. She felt calm and unafraid. Eileen knew there was a future—a happy future here with Lars. He had been a stranger to her, but as of last night, Lars had become her best friend and her lover.

When Lars and Eileen returned to the porch, he asked Eileen to sit and offered to get them both a glass of tea. He leaned his rifle against the rail of the porch and went inside. Lars was almost finished making the tea when he heard Eileen.

"Lars, we have company."

Lars rushed out the door and grabbed his rifle. He saw two people walking down the road near the old sycamore tree. Lars raised his gun in their direction and put his finger on the trigger and his thumb on the hammer. He stood on the porch and waited, never taking his eyes off the two intruders. Unlike the previous intruder, these two just walked toward the house, not trying to conceal themselves. It was a man and a woman, both probably in their mid-thirties. They walked up to the porch.

"Stop! That's close enough," Lars warned.

The couple stopped. "I'm Jack and this is my wife, Jean. We don't mean to intrude, but we're tired, hungry, thirsty, and lost."

The couple were dirty, their clothes ragged and they looked like they were starving. But they appeared to be non-threatening. Lars eyed the couple for a minute. Without taking his eyes off the couple, he told Eileen, "Why don't you go in and get some tea; it's almost finished."

Eileen went inside and retrieved four glasses of tea on a tray and brought it out to the porch. Lars took a glass and handed it to Jean, and then handed another glass to Jack. All the while, Lars continued to hold his rifle in the other hand and kept it pointed in their direction. They drank the tea and thanked Lars.

Meanwhile, Lars had backed up to where Eileen was standing and they were whispering back and forth. Eileen wanted to let them stay the night. "We can send them on their way tomorrow, after we feed them and they get a good night sleep." Lars walked over to the two and looked inside Jack's coat for weapons. He then checked Jean's purse. They had no weapons. Lars walked back to where Eileen was standing, and they whispered some more.

Lars looked at Jack and Jean, "Alright," he said, "we will feed you, you can stay the night, and we'll feed you again in the morning, but then you'll have to leave." The couple gave a sigh of relief and smiled and thanked both Eileen and Lars for their hospitality.

Lars didn't like the increasing number of intruders coming around his property. While these two seemed harmless, others would not be. The Westons proved that. Lars moved out here to get away from people. Harmless or not, he just wanted them to go away. He didn't like Eileen inviting Jack and Jean to stay, but it was getting tougher each passing day to tell her no. Lars was a grizzly bear when Eileen showed up at his place. From that day on, he began turning into a teddy bear.

Eileen asked Jean to come inside to help make a meal. "I'm getting a little hungry myself," Eileen said. The ladies went inside. Lars looked at Jack for a moment and invited him to have a chair on the porch. He took the round out of the chamber of his 30-30, put it in his pocket, and leaned the rifle against the railing. They both sat down. Lars patted his pistol on his hip and said to Jack, "I'm pretty good with this side arm, so don't even think of trying anything funny around here." Jack eyed the pistol and nodded to Lars.

"Where are you from?" Lars asked.

"We're from Midland," Jack responded.

"Now tell me, what's going on out on the highway," Lars asked.

Jack told Lars, "The highway is mostly void of cars and people. Jean and I stick mostly to the back roads to avoid the few people who are wandering around. There are some pretty rough characters out there." Jack added, "Food is damn scarce. Most people out and about just take what they need. Many of them have guns." He continued, "Most of our family is dead. They were killed for either food or guns. Jean and I are fairly safe because we have neither. It's really tough on us, especially the lack of food."

"Have you heard anything from the big cities?" Lars asked.

"No," was the reply.

"More tea?" Lars asked as he took the last sip out of his glass.

"Yes, thank you."

Lars got up, took Jack's glass and, grabbing his rifle first, went in to refill their glasses.

Lars leaned his gun against the inside of the door frame, and then asked about dinner as he refilled the glasses. "Another thirty minutes," Eileen replied. Lars returned to the porch and handed Jack his glass. Lars continued to ask questions, with a little small talk in between.

"What brought you down our road?" Lars asked.

"We weren't making any progress on the highway or side roads, so we just took a chance," Jack said. "We figured we were going to die soon anyway, so we decided to take our chances in the woods. I thought maybe I could set some snares to catch some food, or maybe we could find a fruit tree. We weren't thinking rationally, I guess, but we were dying on the roads."

"There is nothing for you out here in the woods either," Lars said. "There's nothing but woods out back; I have neighbors on both sides. They'll shoot you," Lars continued. "When you leave in the morning, I suggest you go right back down the road you came in on, make your way to the highway, and just keep going. If you come back, I'll shoot the both of you. I know this may seem mean and cruel, but these are tough times for everyone. I will protect our interests. You understand?"

"Yes, sir," was Jack's response.

"You will get no more warnings," Lars added.

Eileen called Lars and Jack in to eat. They went in and sat at the table. Eileen had taken her gun belt off and hung it in the usual place in the bedroom. Normally Lars would take his gun off too for dinner, but this time was different. He was not certain he could trust Jack or Jean, so he kept his gun close. Jack and Jean ate like they hadn't eaten in a week, which may very well have been the truth. They were not pigs though; they had decent manners. There was little talk during dinner, as Jack and Jean didn't slow down eating long enough to talk.

When they finished dinner, Jean helped Eileen with the dishes. Lars directed Jack to the sofa, and Lars got his rifle and took it into the bedroom. While there, he also took off his gun belt and hung it on the wall hook by his side of the bed. Lars then got some string and a few cans. He strung cans on two lengths of string. "These will be hung on the outside of the bedroom door," Lars said. "You must stay in your room all night. If you open the door before I open it in the morning, there will be a big mess to clean up," Lars added. "Don't make me have to clean up a mess." When Eileen and Jean were finished with the dishes, they joined Jack and Lars.

"I'm sorry, but you guys stink to high heaven," Eileen stated. "You two need a shower."

Eileen took Jean to the shower and found her some clothes. Jean's clothes were rags, so she tossed them out the back door. She would dispose of them tomorrow. When Jean had finished with her shower, Eileen gave her some clean clothes to wear. They didn't fit perfectly but almost anything would have been better than what she was wearing. Eileen admired Jean's young body as she got dressed. Though she was a bit thin from lack of food, her breasts were full and perky. Eileen wished her breasts were a bit larger. Jean's nakedness also turned Eileen on a little. She liked the beauty of the female body as well as all that men had to offer.

When Jean and Eileen returned, Lars took Jack into the bathroom and found him some clean clothes to wear as well. Lars knew his clothes would be too large for Jack and the pants wouldn't stay up without a belt. Lars couldn't find a belt on Jack's old clothes, but he did find a length of rope to use instead. When Jack finished his shower and was dressed, he and Lars joined Eileen and Jean. They sat on the sofa and chatted for another couple of hours. All the time Lars pressed for more information about the outside world. He also mentioned several people's names, hoping to find information about people he knew but hadn't heard from. Unfortunately, neither Jack nor Jean knew any of the people Lars asked about. Soon Lars suggested it was time to retire for the night, confident there was little else to be learned from their guests.

The night passed quickly and without incident. Lars and Eileen got up early, and Lars strapped on his pistol. Eileen got started on breakfast, while Lars took the booby traps down and got their guests up. Jean went to help Eileen while Lars took Jack out to the smokehouse. While there, he fixed up a small bag of jerky, ham and potatoes. He handed the bag to Jack. "This is all you will get around here," Lars said. "You remember what I told you last night?"

"Yes, sir," Jack replied. They went back inside and ate a hearty breakfast. When the dishes were done, Lars and Eileen urged the couple on their way. They thanked Lars and Eileen for their hospitality and headed back up the road, retracing their steps back the way they had come. Lars went back inside, grabbed his rifle, and then sat on the porch for a while. Eileen joined him shortly with a couple glasses of tea. They sat and talked mainly about their guests.

Soon Lars said, "How about a shooting session?" Eileen took Lars' glass and went inside. She came back with her pistol strapped to her hip.

"I'm ready," Eileen said.

Lars and Eileen walked back to the woodshed where they had been shooting on a regular basis. Lars set the cans up and Eileen proceeded to hit four out of six cans in her first round. She finished off the other two the second round. Lars smiled and they walked back to the front porch, where Eileen cleaned her gun and Lars cleaned his rifle and pistol. Lars then went inside and brought out another rifle and a shotgun. He handed the shotgun to Eileen for her to clean while Lars cleaned the obviously high powered rifle she had not seen before. This rifle had a scope and a magazine which held twenty cartridges. Lars told Eileen, "This is a sniper rifle. It kicks like a mule," he added. "You probably won't shoot this one. I believe it is a little more than you can handle," he said. Lars handed the rifle to Eileen to feel its weight.

"Yes, it's probably a little too heavy for me," she commented and handed it back to Lars. Lars said he would be keeping this gun a little handier in the future, as there were too many intruders coming around. Of course, other than Eileen, one other intruder would have been one too many for Lars.

Lars went out back and found a short plank of wood suitable for a sign. He found a small paint brush and a can of red paint, opened the can, and made a sign with the words *Trespassers Will Be Shot!* Lars set the sign aside and went back to the wood shed and chopped wood for a couple hours. Eileen went back inside and curled up on the sofa with her novel. After stacking his wood in the shed, Lars checked the root cellar for rotting vegetables and checked the meat he had smoking. Lars got a quick drink out of the well, and then went inside to take a shower. When he had finished and gotten dressed, he went to the sofa to talk to Eileen. Lars did not think he had enough meat or vegetables for the both of them, now that Eileen was staying indefinitely.

"I think we need some more fish and a deer," Lars said.

"It's still early enough," Eileen said. "Let's go try to catch some fish." Eileen got up and got the bait while Lars grabbed the rods and they walked down to the pier. After an hour and a half, they had caught only three fish, and though one was pretty big, they still needed more meat.

"I'll get up early in the morning and see if I can get a deer," Lars said. "I won't go far. I'll make a big circle around the place, just outside the tree line. You need to get up too, Eileen," Lars added. "You will need to keep a watch around the place, and if you see anyone, fire a shot into the air," he instructed.

"Okay, I can do that," said Eileen.

The next morning, Lars got up early and dressed for the hunt. It was a little cooler this morning, so Lars put on his camouflage jacket. He made certain Eileen was awake and then headed out the door. Eileen got up and dressed, adding the gun holster and pistol. She went into the kitchen and made coffee. She would have breakfast with Lars when he returned. Eileen put on a light coat, and took her coffee to the porch and sat down. She watched the tree line as she sipped her coffee. After about an hour, Eileen went in to get another cup of coffee and returned to the porch. It was nearly two hours she imagined before Lars returned empty-handed.

"What will we do for food?" she asked

"I saw several does, but no bucks," Lars said. He assured Eileen they would not go hungry, as he had plenty of emergency rations, and of course he always had Reggie to fall back on. "There are plenty of deer around, and I will get one." Lars explained he only liked to kill bucks, to insure a good deer population, but if it were absolutely necessary, he would kill a doe or yearling—but not unless it was their last resort.

Lars then asked Eileen if she was up for a long walk. "Sure," she replied, "where are we going?"

"I made a sign to help keep people away, and I want to put it up near the tree I chopped down across the road. It will take us most of the rest of the day to make the trek, but if we keep up a good pace, we'll make it back well before dark."

"Okay," said Eileen. "Why don't you get some jerky, and I'll get us some water. This should keep us going today."

Soon they met at the front steps. Eileen had her pistol strapped to her hip and wore a heavy coat to ensure she wouldn't get cold. At the fast pace Lars insisted they maintain, the trip to the downed tree took less than three hours. Lars nailed the sign to a nearby tree, walked up the road a bit to check its visibility, and then walked back to Eileen. "It's good," Lars said, and they headed home.

They each took a sip of water, and divided the remaining jerky. The trip home was a little slower, as they now had plenty of time to make it home before dark. The fast pace Lars had insisted they keep up on the trip there gave them a little extra time to get back home. Lars pointed out the different types of trees to Eileen and told her about some of the different kinds of animals living in the woods. "Most of the trees and brush are mesquite when you get away from the river. It is thorny, but it is a good wood for firewood and cooking. Closer to the river, there are mostly willow, elm, ash, and cypress. Poison ivy is a nasty little vine and it is everywhere, but mostly near the river. The three glossy leaves make it very noticeable if you know what you are looking for. And it will burn you even if the plant is dead and dried out."

"There is the occasional bobcat that can hurt you, but they generally stay away from people," Lars continued. "There are too many gophers. They play hell with my garden. You've already seen that," he stated. "There are raccoons and opossum and you will see them mostly around the river. The main thing you need to be concerned with out here is snakes. We have four poisonous snakes: rattlesnake, water moccasin, copperhead, and coral snakes. The water moccasins are a constant threat near the river."

Since they kept their minds off the long trip home with idle chat and discussions, the trek seemed to pass quickly and they made it home just as the sun touched the horizon. They went inside, showered, and as tomorrow was the day of their planned security meeting and would likely be a long day, they decided to go to bed early.

Chapter 11

The next morning, Lars and Eileen were up early. They prepared and ate breakfast, and then waited for their neighbors on the front porch. "Are you alright?" Eileen asked, as she noticed Lars wrenching his hands.

"Yeah, I'll be okay. My arthritis is acting up a little with the cooler weather. It does every year around this time. It's just my body reminding me I'm not as young as I used to be."

Lars heard Samuel Lin's off-key wolf howl toward the back of the house and he got up and returned the wolf howl. Lars then stepped off the side of the porch to welcome Sam and Sally, with Sean in tow and Debra in Sally's arms. Eileen also got up and immediately took Debra from Sally when they made it to the front of the house.

Eileen and Sally went inside. Lars heard Reggie's familiar wolf howl a short time later and quickly returned the signal. Sally and Eileen returned with glasses and a pitcher of tea as Emily and Reggie made their way to the porch. Lars grabbed some extra chairs from inside. Hugs and kisses were shared all around and they sat down to start the meeting.

Reggie was anxious to start the meeting. He started by sharing news he had gotten on the ham radio. "I've been talking to my buddies from all over the country and some nearby. There is no real government anywhere that I can tell. Washington D.C. basically doesn't exist anymore. Everything that could burn was burned to the ground. The National Guard functioned for a few weeks after the grid went down, but lack of fuel shut them down too. The only remaining government is newly created within small groups, but national or state governments are non-existent."

"What about locally?" Lars asked.

"Gangs and vigilante groups mostly," Reggie replied. "These are mostly around the cities."

"And in the outlying areas?" Eileen asked.

"A lot of small communities much like us," Reggie responded. "Up to a dozen or so families and prepper groups working together to survive."

"Is it going to get better?" Sally asked.

"Doesn't look like it," Reggie answered. "Without adequate fuel, there is little anyone can do to work and trade with other communities. It's all about proximity."

"Can we survive?" Eileen inquired.

"Yes, we can, but we will need things," Lars replied. "Maybe we do not need much now, but we will run out of supplies and stuff will break or wear out."

"We are better prepared than most people though," Reggie added. "The vast majority of people had no preparations. They had few of the primary skills they needed to survive. Most couldn't even build a fire to cook a meal and had no hunting skills."

"The real question is not **if** we can survive, but **how** we will survive," Lars said. "I don't think I just want to survive. Any animal can do that. I want to live better than an animal."

"You know the saying *it takes money to make money?*" Reggie asked. "Well, it takes fuel to make fuel. Sufficient fuel production may take years if not decades. This country was totally dependent on fuel. If this country is going to get moving again, it will take fuel. Without it, things will only get worse Lars." Everyone just sat there staring at each other in dismay.

"In the short term, we will run out of tea, coffee, gasoline, sugar, soap, toothpaste, vinegar, salt, and gun powder," Eileen brought up.

"Don't worry about gun powder," Reggie said, "I've got enough to last a lifetime."

"Okay," Eileen said, relieved.

"In the long term, things will break," Lars added. "My tractor, solar panels, batteries, and many tools, will need parts or we will do without. Life will get very tough without some of these."

"We will need to find sources for the things we need," Reggie said. "We are on our own here and we will not find these things in our valley."

"Sooner or later, we are going to need to find out what's out there," Lars said.

"Yes, we are," Reggie agreed.

"Not to change the subject," Lars said, "but we had a couple more intruders."

"They were harmless," Eileen inserted, "just a starving couple."

"Maybe they were harmless," Lars added, "but they were intruders nevertheless. And intruders will not always be harmless."

Eileen looked over at Lars and gave him a hard glare.

"Yes, these two were harmless," Lars repeated smiling, realizing he belittled Eileen's comment. He did not want to cause friction between himself and Eileen. "Alright, I'll take my foot out of my mouth now," he added with a smile.

Everyone laughed.

"A couple of the Tucker boys were on this side of the highway hunting again," Lars said. "We need to do something about that too. If they kill too many deer around here, they are going to cause problems for all of us who depend on the deer for our food. And they don't care if they kill a buck, doe, or fawn as long as it's edible. I'm reasonably certain they have been stealing stuff out of my garden too. I've seen footprints and they weren't mine. They don't take much, like rats, but over time it adds up. If not for the footprints, I probably wouldn't have noticed."

"Just like the rats they are," Reggie said. "Damn those boys! What's it going to take to keep them on their side of the highway?"

"Maybe we need to take a little trip," Lars added. "We need to see if they are going to be an asset or a liability."

"Do you think they can be reasoned with?" Reggie asked with a smile, knowing they couldn't.

"We can only try," Lars responded.

"Many things are not likely to be available out there to be found," Eileen brought up. "In the immediate future, we will need tea, coffee, salt, and sugar. We will likely need to find alternatives for these products or do without. Probably the only thing we cannot find an alternative for among these is salt. There are alternatives for tea—mint or chamomile, for example. We can produce honey to sweeten things. We can make many things like vinegar and soap."

"Okay," Reggie said, "we need to find salt then."

"And we need to start looking around in the woods for alternatives for tea and coffee," Lars added. "I am addicted to these almost as much as I am to bacon."

Eileen chuckled.

"There is wild mint in some of the swampy areas," Sam said. "Mint tea is good."

"We don't drink coffee," Sally added.

"Maybe I can get used to mint tea," Lars added, "but what about coffee?"

"I don't know," Emily replied.

"After these," Reggie included, "we need fuel."

"Agreed," Lars said. "I must have fuel to prepare my garden and plant my crops. I will have enough for several seasons if I use it sparingly, but if there is no more fuel and we start taking side trips here and there, I will run out quickly. My crops can still be planted, but it will take a lot of backbreaking work and production will fall off drastically."

"We are fairly self-sufficient now," Sam included. "We don't have many needs. We are primarily concerned about intruders."

"Okay," Lars said.

"I think our first task is to take a trip across the highway to talk with the Tuckers, Gómezes, and Johnstons," Reggie stated.

"Will you stay with the ladies?" Lars asked Sam.

"Of course," Sam replied.

"Where are we going to get salt?" Emily asked.

"I don't have a clue," Reggie replied.

"I don't either," Lars added.

They all sat quietly for a while.

"Anything else?" Lars asked.

No one said a word.

"Care to join me in a trip across the highway, Reggie?" Lars asked.

"When?" Reggie responded.

"How about this afternoon, if that is okay with you, Sam?" Lars queried looking over at Sam.

"Yes," Sam said.

"Thank you, Sam," Reggie and Lars said.

The men checked out Lars' truck as the ladies continued to chat on the porch. The truck started easily and Lars checked all the fluids. Lars added a few gallons of gas to the tank to make certain they had more than enough. The truck was ready.

"What kind of seeds do you have?" Lars asked Reggie.

"All that were available," he replied. "I know I have a lot, but they are mostly vegetables and herbs. I don't think I have any to grow coffee and tea plants. It is going to be difficult to replace some things, especially coffee. I know you can't seem to go long without your morning java, but you just may have to."

Lars frowned.

"If we get beehives started, it is going to take a lot of hives to take care of our needs," Lars said. "I don't have any experience with bees. Does anyone?"

"I'm allergic to bees," Eileen stated.

"I've tended to bees before," Sally said. "I don't know if I can handle a lot of hives though. I guess I could try."

"Shall we get started on some lunch?" Eileen asked.

"Yes," Emily replied.

"I'll help," Sally added.

The ladies went inside and left the men to continue their discussions. Sam reiterated his intruder concerns. Lars stressed his long-term concerns about food and repair parts, especially tractor parts. Reggie had the least concerns of anyone. He had only one intruder thus far and he had all the food he and Emily needed. He would need salt, sugar, coffee, and tea soon, but besides a little fuel, this was the extent of his needs. The survival food packets he had cases of were already seasoned and only needed water. He felt safe and secure but was highly concerned for his neighbors. Reggie was smart and he knew that if his neighbors were to disappear, his safety and security would be in grave jeopardy; bunker or no bunker. For this reason, their concerns were also Reggie's concerns. They were friends too. Lars was Reggie's best friend and visa versa.

The ladies decided to bring lunch out to the porch. It was such a lovely day. The porch table was small, so the men held their plates to give the ladies more room for their plates on the table. The group was quiet as they ate. When they finished, the men gathered up the dishes and Sam and Lars took them inside. Lars quickly washed the dishes while Sam dried and stacked them on the countertop. They then returned to the porch.

Reggie brought the subject of salt up again. "Where in the hell are we going to get salt?"

"We can get salt in two ways," Lars said, "sea water and salt deposits. We have neither around here."

"Can't we do without salt?" Eileen asked.

"No," Lars replied. "We need salt to cure our meats, preserve our animal hides, and for cooking."

"Maybe we can use less," Reggie added, "but I don't think we can do without it. I have maybe a year's supply left. How about you, Lars?"

"Maybe six months," he replied.

"Sam?" asked Reggie.

"A year or so," he replied.

"That does it," Lars said. "We need salt."

"How much can we cut down on salt?" Eileen asked.

"A lot," Lars answered, "but it won't be pretty. With no refrigeration, we need salt to cure our meat. I need a little salt on my meals too. We can live like animals and do without many things, but I don't want to live like an animal as I have said before."

"I'm with you, bro," said Reggie.

"If we are going to be taking trips out of the valley," Lars said, "we're going to need more fuel. I must have fuel for my tractor."

"I understand," Reggie said. "I have fuel needs too. You probably have more gas than I do, but I don't use as much as you. I still need a little fuel though."

"Well then, we will need to find a fuel source soon," Lars added.

"And not use any more than absolutely necessary for road trips," Reggie added.

Everyone knew what they needed. They all knew they were going to have to work even harder now to ensure they not only survived but also thrived. Thriving would be the tricky part and possibly very dangerous. The conversation turned to idle chat. After another hour, the conversation seemed to die completely.

"I guess we had better get going," Reggie said.

"I'll take good care of the ladies," Sam said.

Reggie and Lars loaded the truck with some jerky and their guns and ammunition. The men walked over to the porch and kissed their respective ladies goodbye and then returned to the truck. Lars cranked up the engine as Reggie got into the passenger side. Lars backed the truck up and then turned toward the sycamore tree and up the road.

"What's the plan?" Reggie asked.

"The Tuckers are the closest," Lars said. "Why don't we just drive up and announce ourselves with the horn? I don't know after that."

"Doesn't sound like much of a plan," Reggie said.

"If you have any better ideas," Lars said, "I'm open to suggestions."

Reggie didn't say a word.

"Well?" Lars inquired.

"Well, what?" Reggie asked.

"You're supposed to be the smart one. Are you going to come up with a better plan or not?" Lars queried.

"I wish I could," Reggie said. "I don't have anything better to offer."

They were quiet until they reach the tree across Lars road. It only took a minute to move and replace the tree and then the men made quick time to the highway. They didn't see anyone on the highway and proceeded down the road a ways to the Tucker's road. Lars thought it was about a mile down the dirt road to the house. The road was rough and brushy and took a while, but the men finally made it to within a hundred yards of the home. Lars and Reggie both thought it best if they didn't show guns on the trip, so they laid their rifles between them pointed at the floorboard. They had their pistols, however, on their laps.

Lars honked his horn several times and then yelled out, "Tuckers!"

Lars waited a few seconds and yelled again, "Tuckers! Lars Lindgren here!"

Lars drove up to within fifty feet of the house and hit the horn again and yelled "Tuckers!"

As Lars and Reggie sat and waited, they looked about the place. There was trash everywhere. The house appeared to have been painted about thirty years ago but not since. They were not even certain of the color.

"Are you sure this is the right place?" Reggie asked.

"It doesn't look like anyone lives here, does it?" Lars asked.

The place was rundown and looked like it had been abandoned for years. Brush had grown up around the house and there was a lot of rotten wood around the windows and eaves. The asphalt shingles no longer looked waterproof.

"If anyone lives here," Lars said, "they have to be living like animals."

Suddenly the front door opened and a large man stepped out onto the porch, which was littered with junk and trash.

"Lars Lindgren here!" Lars yelled.

The man just stood there with a rifle across his arm but not pointing it toward their truck.

"Don't look to your right, Reggie, but there is someone in the brush. There is also someone in the brush on my side," Lars said quietly.

Finally, the man on the porch yelled back, "I'm Tucker."

Lars opened his door and stepped out, laying his pistol on the seat beside him. "Richard Tucker?" Lars inquired.

"Yep."

"Lars Lindgren and Reggie Carston here. I'm Lars. I would like to have a little talk," Lars said in a loud voice but not yelling anymore.

"Well, well, well, if it ain't the rich neighbors from across the way."

Lars didn't say anything.

"What you wanna talk about?" Richard said.

"Food. And intruders," Lars replied.

"We have plenty food," Richard said.

"That's good to hear," Lars replied. "How about intruders?"

"We don't got intruders. We send them all over to yore place," Richard responded.

"That might explain things then," Lars said. "We seem to be having a lot of intruders, including your boys," Lars stated. "Your boys seem to be doing a little poaching on our side of the highway."

"My boys' hunt where the food is," Richard said. "It ain't poaching."

Lars leaned over so he could see Reggie's face. "Any ideas?" Lars asked.

"None," Reggie said.

Lars looked back at Richard. "Don't you have deer around here?" Lars asked.

"Maybe we'd have more if you don't plant so much damn corn," Richard replied.

"How do you know how much corn I plant?" Lars inquired.

"We know," was the response.

"This doesn't seem to be going very well," Reggie noted.

"No, it's not, Reggie."

"Okay, Richard, we are going to leave now. Try to keep your boys on your side of the highway, will you?" Lars said. There was no answer and Lars climbed into the truck and started the engine. Lars backed the truck up, turned around, and headed toward the highway.

"That went well, don't you think?" Lars said almost laughing when they were well away from the house.

"Splendidly," Reggie responded.

Lars got on the highway and headed toward their next destination. The next road was not far.

"Same plan?" Reggie inquired.

"Same plan," Lars replied. "Maybe I should try some different questions this time. The last ones didn't seem to work."

"You're definitely no diplomat," Reggie added.

Lars grinned.

Lars turned down the road he thought led to the Johnston's homestead. This house was less than four hundred yards off the highway. Lars drove up and honked and yelled as before, but it appeared no one was at home. The front door was wide open and after fifteen minutes no one came out.

"Shall we investigate?" Lars asked.

"May as well," Reggie replied.

Lars got out first with his rifle ready. Reggie did the same. Lars headed toward the house first while Reggie covered him. There was no one inside. Lars checked out the kitchen and bathroom. Lars was looking for anything they could use. All he came up with was a couple used bars of soap. Lars came back out and joined Reggie.

The two then walked around to the back of the house and checked out the shed. There was some steel and old lumber they may find useful later, but nothing to meet their immediate needs. The Johnston family must have been ill-prepared to survive out here and left. There was no sign of mayhem, so they must have left on their own accord.

"Well, let's go," Lars said. "There's nothing for us here."

Lars drove to the highway and headed toward their third destination. Lars drove nearly a mile and turned down the dirt road to their third stop. It was nearly another mile down the overgrown road to the residence. When Lars approached and honked his horn, there were immediately three shots through the front windshield instantly followed by the reports of the guns.

Reggie screamed as Lars crammed the gearshift into reverse, "Get the hell out of here!"

Lars gunned the engine, propelling them backward and into some brush. Reggie stuck his pistol out of the window and fired a full clip in the direction of the house before the brush forced him to pull his arm back inside the truck. Lars forced the gearshift into forward and hit the gas while turning the steering wheel away from the residence. The rear tires spun a bit in the grass and dirt, but then grabbed enough to propel the truck quickly back towards the highway. There were several more shots, which hit the back of the truck and the side mirror on Reggie's side.

The trip back to the highway was fast and rough, brush slapping the fenders of the truck all the way out. Lars wanted to get out of there as fast as he could. When they made it to the highway, he sped on toward his road and made quick time to the log across his path before he stopped. Lars didn't say much to Reggie on the trip back. He couldn't have gotten a word in edgewise if he had wanted to. He knew Reggie was okay, though, because he didn't shut up the entire trip. Lars heard every curse word Reggie knew at least ten times each.

When they finally stopped, Lars put the gearshift into PARK and looked at Reggie. "You okay, man?" Lars asked. Lars didn't see any blood.

"I know I don't have to piss anymore," Reggie replied.

Lars laughed. "Looks like the Gómez family is home," Lars finally said.

"You think!" Reggie exclaimed.

Both men checked for damage to themselves and to the truck. Lars had a little blood on his right ear. Must be a glass cut from when the bullets went through the windshield. Lars could find no more injuries.

With all the excitement and Reggie's adrenalin level spiking higher than it had been his entire life, Reggie hadn't noticed the pain in his left arm. He had been screaming obscenities all the way here. Now that he had settled down some, he began to notice the ache in his arm. Reggie pulled his jacket off and saw the blood on his shirt near the source of the pain. Reggie's arm was beginning to hurt badly now. Lars went around to Reggie's side of the truck and helped him get his shirt off, revealing a neat little hole just below the shoulder. There was no exit hole. The slug had to be a small caliber and the windshield also slowed its velocity.

"We're going to have to dig that thing out," Lars said.

"I know," Reggie answered.

"Let me wrap it up and we'll take care of it when we get home," Lars added and proceeded to wrap the wound. Lars then made a quick inspection under the hood of the truck and nothing appeared damaged. At least the truck was running. Lars moved the tree off the road with Reggie insisting on helping. Lars pulled up, they moved the tree back across the road, and then they headed to Lars' house.

"I'm going to kill those sons-a-bitches," Reggie kept saying over and over.

Lars kept driving until he reached the meadow, honking his horn, and then pulling up to the side of the house. Sam, Sally, Emily, and Eileen were sitting on the porch. They got up to welcome the men home.

Sam noticed the bullet holes in the windshield first and ran over to the truck. "You guys okay?" Sam questioned.

"We're alright," Lars said, "but Reggie took a bullet in the arm."

When Reggie came around the truck and Emily saw the blood running down his arm, Emily screamed and ran over to him.

"You're hurt," she said with tears forming in her eyes.

"I'll be just fine," he said. "It's just a flesh wound."

"It's a little more than that," Lars added. "We'll need to dig the bullet out."

"Surgery?" Eileen questioned.

"Yes," Lars replied.

Lars looked at Eileen, "We'll need alcohol, an ice pick, a sharp knife, and sterile dressings."

Lars then ran out to his shop inside the warehouse. He found a pair of needle nose pliers, cut a short piece of garden hose and headed back to the front porch. Eileen returned to the porch with all but the dressings and put her items on the porch table.

"This is all the alcohol we have," Eileen said.

"That will do," Lars said.

"Who is going to perform the surgery?" Eileen asked.

"I am," Lars said.

Lars poured alcohol on the pliers, ice pick, and knife while Eileen went back inside to get the dressings. He hoped he would not need the knife.

"Okay, Reggie, get over here," Lars ordered with a smile.

Sally carried Debra to a nice grassy area in the yard and told Sean to sit with her. "Uncle Reggie is hurt and he may scream a little when we try to fix him. He will be okay though. Do you understand, Sean?" Sally inquired.

"Yes, Mommy," Sean replied.

"You're really going to like this, aren't you, Lars?" Reggie asserted.

"You know it, buddy," Lars said with a big grin on his face.

Reggie lay on his side near the porch steps. The sun was still bright and the light was much better outside than they could make inside. Lars pulled the porch table close while Emily scooted under Reggie's head and gently held it in her lap. Sam straddled Reggie's mid-section and held onto his hurt arm. Eileen returned with the dressings and she and Sally each straddled a leg and held on tight.

Lars picked up the piece of garden hose and stuck it in Reggie's mouth; then he reached for the ice pick.

"This shouldn't hurt much," Lars said as he gently slid the point into the wound. Lars was only into the wound an inch when he hit the slug, or at least what he thought was the slug. Reggie moaned a bit. Lars used the point of the ice pick to wiggle the bullet a little, and he knew what he had was the slug. Lars withdrew the ice pick and reached for the pliers.

"That hurt more than just a little," Reggie alleged.

"This will hurt a little more," Lars said. "Hold him tight."

Lars eased the pliers into the wound to very near what Lars estimated to be the bullet. Lars then spread the jaws of the pliers and pushed. Reggie screamed and struggled. Lars knew this hurt a lot as Reggie struggled, but everyone held on to him as tight as they could so Lars could do his job. Lars was steady and made a grab at the slug. He latched onto something. He hoped it was the slug. Lars gripped the pliers hard and pulled in one swift motion. Reggie really strained hard as the pain shot through his body which reacted violently. Reggie also screamed as loud as he could with the hose in his mouth.

Lars looked at the item he pulled from Reggie's arm. It looked like a .22 caliber slug. It was distorted from hitting the windshield and then Reggie's arm, but appeared to be all there. Lars was relieved. He really didn't like hurting his best friend, but he had no choice. At least he got the slug on the first try.

"This looks good," Lars said. "The bullet appears to be intact. Now we need to clean the hole."

There was a steady stream of blood oozing from the wound. "We'll let it bleed a bit to wash out the hole," Lars said.

Lars got up and went into the house. He came back with a small plastic squirt bottle. Lars poured some alcohol into the squirt bottle and slowly squirted a stream into the bullet hole. When the bottle was empty, Lars repeated the procedure. This hurt and Reggie protested with a few foul words you could just understand with the hose in his mouth. Lars then poured some alcohol over the wound.

"Let's get it wrapped up," Lars said. This was good news to Reggie. Eileen handed Lars some gauze. Lars covered the hole with a pad about a half-inch thick, and then wrapped cloth strips around the arm several times. Eileen made a sling for his arm.

"Thanks bro," Reggie said.

"My pleasure," Lars said with a smile.

"I'm certain of that," Reggie replied, also with a smile.

Sally had finished her task and she got up and went to Debra who was now crying. Sally picked Debra up and she immediately stopped crying.

"Uncle Reggie is okay now," Sally said to Sean. *Uncle* was an honorary title.

"Eileen, Reggie and Emily need to stay the night," Lars said. "His arm will need some intensive care the next day or so."

"It's just my arm," Reggie said.

"I won't take no for an answer," Lars replied. Emily nodded her agreement.

"I'll help you with the bedroom," Emily offered.

"No need," Eileen replied. "Everything is prepared."

"We need to get home," Sam said, "now that you are going to live, Reggie."

"Thanks, good friend," Reggie said.

"Are you going to call another meeting?" Sam asked.

"I'm sure we will," Lars replied. "As soon as Reggie is able, I'll let you know."

"We'll keep you informed," Reggie added.

Sam and Sally said their goodbyes, grabbed up Sean and Debra, and headed home.

"We'll see you soon," Lars said.

"Thanks for coming over," Eileen added.

Sam and Sally walked around to the back of the house and disappeared into the woods.

"You guys hungry?" Emily asked. "Eileen and I cooked while you were out."

"I can eat," Lars said.

"I'm feeling better," Reggie said. "I'll try to eat a little too."

Emily set the table while Eileen brought the food over. Lars ate hearty as he always did, but Reggie only nibbled a bit and began to feel weak. "I think I need to lie down," Reggie said.

Emily got up and helped Reggie to the bedroom. Eileen got a few ibuprofen tablets for Reggie before he went to bed.

"We'll talk tomorrow," Reggie said.

"Good night Reggie," Lars said.

Emily returned and then asked to be excused. "I need to stay with Reggie."

"Absolutely," Eileen said, "we'll talk more tomorrow. Good night."

Lars took a shower when he finished eating, and he and Eileen went to bed but neither was sleepy.

"This little incident has really opened my eyes," Lars said.

"How so?" Eileen asked.

"We definitely need to make some serious changes," Lars replied. "If we don't, we may soon end up just like the Westons."

"What are we going to do?" Eileen asked.

"I don't know yet. We definitely need to discuss the situation with Reggie and Emily in the morning. If we don't stop the poaching, we may run out of wild game as well," Lars added.

Lars and Eileen snuggled up. "Don't worry," Lars whispered, "we'll come up with a solution. We'll be okay."

Eileen kissed Lars on the cheek and they both soon dozed off.

Lars and Eileen were up early, having had a restless night's sleep. Emily was up shortly thereafter. Reggie was still asleep. "He didn't get to sleep for quite a long time," Emily said.

Lars fixed coffee as Eileen and Emily sat at the table whispering about what had happened yesterday. Lars dug out coffee mugs and set four on the table. Coffee was soon ready and Lars poured each a full cup. They were on their second cup when Reggie emerged from the bedroom.

"Come on in, bro," Lars said as he poured a cup of coffee for Reggie. "How's the arm?"

"It hurts like hell!" was the response.

"Let's have a look," Lars said.

Eileen got up and got a couple more ibuprofen tablets for Reggie.

"Thanks," Reggie said.

As Reggie began working on his coffee, Lars got up and began to remove the bandages from his arm. The gauze was almost completely saturated with dried blood. The last bit of gauze was stuck to the wound.

Lars went into the bathroom and drew some hot water. He soaked a wash-cloth with the hot water and squeezed just enough out so it wouldn't drip much. Lars then went to Reggie and pressed the warm wet cloth to the gauze over the wound. After a few minutes, the gauze came off easily, revealing the wound. Lars cleaned up the area with the wet cloth and then wiped the area with alcohol.

"It's a little red," Lars said, "but it doesn't look infected yet."

Lars went back into the bathroom and retrieved some more gauze and anti-biotic ointment. He placed a little ointment on the gauze and placed it onto the hole; then he covered the wound with more gauze and wrapped it back up with cloth strips.

"Thank you," Reggie said.

"You're very welcome," Lars replied.

"It feels a little better now," Reggie added.

"If you can keep it from getting infected, it will heal in a few weeks. The last thing you want is an infection," Lars said.

"This one incident used up all but what you see here of our alcohol, gauze, and ointment," Eileen said. "If you guys keep going out and getting shot, we are going to need more stuff to fix you up with."

"We don't have a lot of medications at home either," Emily responded. "We have some but not enough if you guys keep getting hurt."

"I guess I just never thought we'd need a lot of medications when I was planning our escape from the city," Reggie said. "I brought pain pills and a few salves and ointments but never really considered we would be going to war."

"The question is what are we going to do about it?" Emily asked.

"We are not going to find anything across the highway," Lars inserted. "The Tuckers and Gómezes are going to be nothing but thorns in our sides as long as they live. They will never change."

"We need to kill them all and take everything they have, as little as that may be," Reggie said.

"We can't do that!" Eileen exclaimed.

"No we can't," Emily asserted.

"Yes, we can," Reggie said in a raised voice, "and mark my word, it will hap-pen one day. They will give us no choice. Maybe not right now, but one day those sons-a-bitches will need to die."

The room got real quiet. You could have heard a pin drop. After a few minutes, Lars got up and walked over to his bookshelf. After a bit of searching, he walked back to the kitchen table. "I thought I had a book on healing herbs," Lars said. "I guess I was mistaken."

"Looks like we need to add healing herbs to our growing list of needs," Reggie said.

"I may have a book on herbs at home," Emily said.

"And I'll look through my seeds," Reggie added.

"If you'll bring me the herbs, Eileen and I will get some started here in the house. We can then transplant them outside in the spring," Lars said.

"Sounds good," Reggie said.

"And we need to keep sterile bandages and operating tools stored in a handy location," Lars added.

"Do you really think we'll need them?" Eileen asked with a troubled look on her face.

"If we are going to war, which it appears is exactly what we have in store for us, then we may very well need more than we have," Lars said.

Eileen and Emily got up and began to prepare some bacon and eggs. After a light breakfast, Reggie and Emily headed home.

"Take care of that arm," Lars instructed. "We'll talk soon."

"Will do," Reggie said.

"Thank you for everything," Emily said.

"It was our pleasure," Eileen replied.

Chapter 12

A week went by and there were no further problems with intruders. Lars and Eileen were growing closer each day. They often took walks just for the sake of the walk itself. One walk to the Carston's found Reggie's arm healing steadily. Emily did have a book on herbs with photos of some medicinal plants they might find in their area. Lars and Eileen kept their eyes open for the plants as they walked. They were not certain they would know if they spotted one, but they looked anyway.

Lars continued to examine Eileen's body in great detail while she did the same with him. Eileen loved how Lars made her feel in bed. She had never felt so safe, so comforted, and yet so excited. Lars acknowledged to himself that he would have been physically satisfied to have an orgasm with a woman. But, he admitted, with Eileen it was so much more. She really knew how to please him. It was as if she instinctively knew how to satisfy him. More importantly, he sensed Eileen really wanted the intimacy with him. Lars smiled as he thought about how proactive Eileen was in executing their intimacies. He remembered back at how Rachel would just lie there, like a piece of meat.

Up until now, the cold fronts blowing in from the north had not been too cold and didn't last long. This morning, however, Lars woke up cold. The wind had been howling since the middle of the night, but still Lars was surprised it had turned so cold so soon after the front blew in. Lars quickly got up and dressed, being careful not to disturb Eileen. Then he stoked the fireplace and fired up the stove. The house was soon warm and Eileen got up and dressed.

Eileen prepared breakfast while Lars carried more firewood into the house. He filled all the bins and cut extra kindling. As the day wore on, the air outside got progressively colder, forcing him and Eileen to spend much of it indoors. Lars went outside briefly to check on the garden. Everything they had planted was beginning to come up. The lettuce was about three inches tall, while the beets and carrots were just beginning to sprout. He spread some mulch around the tender plants to help protect them against the cold, and quickly returned to the house.

The rest of the day Lars and Eileen spent reading. Every now and then, Lars would get up to stoke the fires while Eileen made sure there was always a warm pot of coffee ready. The day was gone before they knew it, and they showered and went to bed. Lars threw an old but heavy comforter on the bed before he crawled in.

Even with the comforter to help ward off the cold, Eileen snuggled against Lars. His body was always warm and she liked the feel of his hard body against her softer skin. Soon she was caressing Lars while at the same time giving him little love bites. Lars could not resist and soon he began to return the caresses and bites. Eileen's response was spontaneous. Lars smiled as Eileen's body began to quiver and shake. Then he heard her cries of release and her deep sighs of contentment.

As Eileen began to drift off to sleep, Lars smiled to himself. He acknowledged that he certainly did love her touch, but he also realized what a feeling it was to know his touch could have such an effect on her. And he was surprised. Never before had he felt such power and satisfaction. Lars snuggled closer to Eileen and held her as she slept.

Lars got up first the next morning and stoked the fires. The house warmed quickly, and Eileen came in and wrapped her arms around Lars. She gave him a big passionate kiss and thanked him for last night.

"Just doing my job, ma'am," Lars said with a big smile. Eileen smiled back and got to work on some coffee.

Lars dug out a heavy coat and went outside. The morning was really cold. There was no frost due to the wind blowing in hard from the north. Frost forms when the wind is light. Lars checked around for standing water. What little he found was frozen solid. Lars guessed the temperature had to be around twenty-five degrees Fahrenheit. Soon he went back inside and took off his coat. "Looks like winter time is finally here with a vengeance. What do you say we stay home today, darlin'?" As if they hadn't been staying home most of the time. Eileen smiled and handed Lars a cup of coffee.

Another quiet week went by. There were no intruders, no visitors, and no drama. Lars and Eileen spent most of their time inside. They read and cleaned the house. Each day they got to know each other a little better—both in bed and out of bed. Lars did manage to get out a couple of mornings and finally got the buck he was after. He cleaned the deer as Eileen watched through the back door window. After removing the deer's heart and liver for dinner, Lars finished removing the skin and entrails. He then hoisted the carcass high in the tree to prevent other animals from getting to the meat. The air was plenty cold enough to ensure the meat would keep for days, if not longer, just hanging outside. It would cut up better if it were well chilled. The cold night ahead would chill the meat perfectly.

Next, Lars took the heart and liver and gave them to Eileen, who was still standing at the back door. "Dinner," he said. Lars returned to the entrails and removed the small intestines to use as casings for sausage. He pumped water from the well into a pan. Then Lars began to clean. He cleaned the intestines better than he cleaned his own body when he took a shower. Lars salted the casings and stored them in the smokehouse. He noticed his barrel of salt was now less than half-full. This was less than four months' supply, he imagined, at current usage—less than he had originally thought. Then Lars ran some water into a barrel by the barn near his worm farm and mixed in a bucket of ash. The deer hide went into the mixture to soak for a couple weeks. This way the hair would be easier to remove and the skin could be tanned. He cleaned the blood from his hands and arms and went inside to warm up.

Lars informed Eileen he didn't care for liver much, but he really loved heart.

"Perfect," Eileen laughed, "I like liver better. Just another reason we fit together so well; we don't compete with each other for food," she added with a smile.

Lars continued to stoke the fire to make sure Eileen stayed warm. In the meantime, she had found some old plastic ice trays and filled them with water. She asked Lars to put them in a safe place outside.

"We'll have iced tea tomorrow. Just like we did at Reggie's."

Her enthusiasm caused Lars to grin as he did as she asked. When Lars came back in, he found Eileen on the sofa reading her novel. Lars joined her and continued with his gardening book. He soon dozed off and it was Eileen who kept a watchful eye on the fireplace. It was also Eileen who got up from time to time to take a look outside to scan the tree line for intruders. Close to two hours later, Lars awoke to Eileen's smiling face from the other end of the sofa. He yawned and looked around. First, his eyes went to the fireplace, then around the room and back to Eileen.

"You taking care of things?" he asked.

"Sure am. Don't worry. I've got you covered," she laughed.

The next day, Lars began to butcher the deer hanging in the back of the house. Then he fired up the smoker and about half the venison went there. He cut up the remainder into small chunks to grind into sausage. He retrieved the casings and a couple chunks of salted pork out of the smokehouse. Lars had Eileen wash the salt out of the casings while he processed the pork for grinding. Lars then began to grind the meat with his old crank grinder. He started with a

couple of pieces of fattier pork to lubricate the grinder. Then he alternated between chunks of pork and venison. After the meat was ground, Lars washed his
hands and dug out garlic powder, cumin, sage, red and black pepper, salt, celery
powder, and onion powder. Lars added the spices to the meat, using his eyes to
measure. Experience had taught him the best method of mixing was using his big
hands. Then Lars began to mix the meat and soon the sausage mixture was ready
for stuffing. Lars ran the meat through the grinder one more time to more thoroughly mix the spices into the meat. Once again, Lars washed his hands and removed the cutting blades from the grinder. The sausage stuffing tube replaced
the blades. He slid the casings Eileen had prepared onto the tube, and put the
seasoned meat into the grinder again. This time, Eileen helped Lars by turning
the hand crank to force the meat into the casings, as Lars guided the filled casings
onto the table, stopping from time to time to tie two pieces of twine about an
inch apart at about two feet intervals. When they were finished stuffing the sausage, Lars cut the sausage between each pair of strings to make links, and tied the
ends together with the strings on each end of each link. Lars then hung the links
by the strings onto metal rods to smoke.

After washing his hands again, Lars stood back to admire the two dozen or
so links hanging from the two rods, ready to be smoked. Lars walked around the
table to give Eileen a big hug and kiss. "This should take care of our sausage
needs for a while," he said.

"It will be nice to have some sausage for a change for breakfast," Eileen
added.

Lars really liked bacon, but sausage ran a close second. He turned to pick up
the first rack of sausage and took it to the smoker. He then returned for the
second rack, hung it alongside the first and added more wood chips to the
smoker. After he was done, he returned to the kitchen to help Eileen clean up
their mess.

Afterward, they decided to relax for a while. "How about a glass of iced tea?"
Eileen asked.

"Sounds good," Lars said and he stepped outside to get a tray of ice while
Eileen prepared the tea. Lars returned and dumped the cubes into a bowl. Lars
didn't re-fill the tray. This early cold spell won't last long this early in the season
and though it would stay cold for a couple more days, the tray would not re-
freeze.

Eileen poured the tea into a couple large tumblers and then Lars added the
ice to each. They took a sip and smiled at each other. Lars really liked his iced tea.
Too bad he could only have it regularly during freezing weather. Lars didn't have
a freezer. *Maybe I need to work on this,* Lars thought. They then walked to the sofa
and continued their reading.

The next couple days the sky began to cloud over and the air began to warm up a bit as the wind returned out of the southeast. They lost about a third of the more tender plants in the garden due to the hard freeze, but the remainder seemed healthy enough. The next few days would be critical.

Lars moved his tractor into the metal storage building. He would not need it for a while. He also rummaged around in the building looking for something, but he just didn't know for what. As he searched, Lars organized this and that, trying to make a little more walking room in the building now that the tractor had been moved inside. Lars also went down to the river to check the water level; it was nearly bank full and a little muddy due to moderate rains upstream. There was a deer—a doe—across the way drinking from the stream as Lars walked up, but she got spooked and trotted off. She had nothing to fear from Lars, but she really didn't know this. Lars wandered back to the house, not really having any chores pressing. When he went in through the back door, he asked Eileen if she would like to go for a walk. He already knew the answer, as Eileen loved to take walks with him. She got up and strapped her gun belt on, which she did instinctively at this point, each time she was going outside. Lars opened the door and then shut it behind them and took her by the hand.

This little walk was a leisurely perimeter stroll along the tree line. Lars and Eileen were beginning to make a trail, as they took this walk often. Lars turned to Eileen, "Shhh." He turned back and pointed to a doe and her twin yearlings. They just stood there and watched for a few minutes. The deer did not seem to see the humans and showed no fear. They just grazed on willow leaves that had fallen due to the cold weather, which also had turned them yellow. As Eileen and Lars began to walk again, the doe's ears perked up and she spotted them immediately. It took only a second for the doe to sense danger, and she trotted off with the two yearlings in tow.

Lars pointed to birds, squirrels, and a rabbit along the route. Eileen paused each time to take in the critters that seemed to be enjoying the fine day. Lars and Eileen were enjoying the day as well, and Lars finally led Eileen up to the house. He asked her to have a seat on the porch, and he would get them another glass of tea to sip as they watch the evening sky. Lars came back out shortly and joined Eileen with the glasses. They discussed the day's events and future plans. Future plans included another trip to the Lin homestead. Lars also tossed around the possibility of enlarging his woodshed and smokehouse, to include a larger root cellar. If this were to be accomplished, it would need to be done in the late spring when it would likely be mostly empty, and then finished by harvest time to store their fresh crop of vegetables.

Lars also asked Eileen if she had any needs. She shrugged her shoulders, not being able to think of anything off the top of her head. "If I do think of something, you'll be the first one to know," she said after a short pause. Lars then suggested they go to bed, as the last little bit of light in the horizon slowly disappeared. Eileen got up and led Lars into the house; they showered and went to bed.

About mid-morning the next day, Lars heard the sound of a chainsaw in the distance. He walked out onto the front porch, with his rifle and pistol on his hip as usual. He leaned the rifle against the railing in its customary position and sat and listened for a while. The noise was coming from the direction of Reggie's home, but Lars could not imagine Reggie out there with a chainsaw. The chainsaw would buzz for a while and then stop. This repeated over and over for the next thirty minutes or so. At first, he had decided he would just sit and wait, as the noise kept getting closer and closer, but finally upon second thought, his curiosity got the best of him and he decided to go investigate. Lars grabbed his rifle and stepped back inside to inform Eileen of his intentions. He asked her to come along, and they walked out the door towards the direction of the noise.

Their pace was pretty fast until they reached the tree line, where they slowed dramatically. Lars worked the lever on his rifle and then eased the gun onto his arm with his finger on the trigger and his thumb on the hammer. Lars lowered the hammer but kept his finger in place on the trigger and his thumb on the hammer, ready to cock it again, if necessary. They eased on through the edge of the woods, keeping a close eye out for intruders. It wasn't long before Lars spotted some movement. He stopped and held his arm out to stop Eileen. They stood there motionless until Lars heard the chainsaw start up again. Lars told Eileen to stay there, and he moved forward, stopping behind a tree about a hundred feet from the noise. Lars peeked around the tree and recognized Emily Carston standing off to the side. Lars waited for the buzz of the chainsaw to stop, and then let out a wolf howl. Reggie turned to spot Lars beside the tree.

Lars called for Eileen and the two walked toward their intruders. "What the hell are you doing, Reggie?" Lars asked.

"Well, you guys had such trouble getting to our place last time around, I thought I'd clear a better path for you city folks," Reggie responded with a laugh.

"I guess the arm is doing well?" Lars inquired.

"Yes," Reggie replied. "It gets a little sore if I overwork it. If it starts to hurt, I just stop what I'm doing and it feels just fine in no time."

"Good to hear," Lars added.

Lars smiled, as did Eileen. "You guys come on up to the house and we'll have a drink and some lunch," Lars instructed. Reggie and Lars led the way, stopping a few more times to remove some brush, with Emily and Eileen following close behind. It didn't take long to finish the trail, and the crew walked up to the house.

Reggie set his chainsaw down on the porch, and Lars invited their guests to sit while he went inside to prepare some tea. Lars asked Eileen to keep them company. He returned shortly with four glasses of tea. Reggie began the conversation, telling Lars he had news of his daughter Georgia. "It seems one of my regular ham radio friends lives close to her, outside of Gonzales," Reggie said. "I asked him to check in on your family, which he did readily. Seems like Georgia and Dean are doing just fine, as are your two grandsons."

"I guess they are buried in the woods so far, they have not had any problems," Lars said.

"They said to tell you they are all good, love you, and hope to see you when the economy improves," said Reggie. Eileen smiled, gave Lars a big hug, and told him she was so happy for him.

"And what about my son and daughter-in-law?" Lars asked.

"No word on James and Ruby," Reggie responded. "They will be fine," Reggie added. "James is tough just like his old man."

Lars agreed.

Eileen asked Lars to get a couple of links of sausage, and she and Emily would begin lunch. Lars complied and then continued his conversation with Reggie while Emily and Eileen went inside.

Lars thanked Reggie for the news about his kids.

"I'll keep checking on James and Ruby," Reggie said.

"Thank you," Lars said, "I appreciate that. I really appreciate you and Emily cutting the trail up here. That was above and beyond the call of duty."

"Nothing you wouldn't have done for me and Emily, if you had thought of it," Reggie said with a smile. "Looks like you and Eileen are really getting along good."

"Yep," Lars said, "she's a dream come true. She works hard, has maybe a little more passion than I can handle at times, and she learns fast. I think we will be just fine around here. She's getting really good with her shooting too."

"Good," said Reggie, "you two look great together."

Lars told Reggie he was trying to get a few late vegetables to grow in the garden and they walked out to check the progress. "The veggies didn't grow much the past few days, but they should do better if the weather warms back up just a little bit," Lars said.

"I hope it does stay warmer," Reggie said. "It was a little too cold for my taste the other night."

"Me too," agreed Lars. "We did have iced tea though," Lars added with a big smile.

It wasn't long before Eileen and Emily called the guys in to eat. The ladies served the smoked sausage cut up and sautéed with onions. Eileen opened a fresh jar of pickled beets because she knew Emily loved them, and some canned green beans which she stir-fried with potatoes.

"Sorry guys," Eileen said, "no ice for the tea; our ice melted."

"A meal like this and you're worried about a little ice?" Reggie replied. "Don't worry, the last thing we are concerned about is ice. Besides, the tea is plenty cold."

Eileen smiled and said thank you.

This was a good amount of food for four people, but when the meal was finished, every pan and plate was completely empty. "That was absolutely the best meal I can recall ever having. Great food and great company," Lars said sincerely.

"I agree wholeheartedly," Reggie added.

"You ladies go relax on the sofa," Lars said. "After a meal like that, you cannot do the dishes." Lars got up and started gathering the dishes and Reggie joined in. The guys washed, dried, and put up the dishes, and then joined the ladies.

Lars grabbed the pitcher of tea on the way over and refreshed all the glasses. They chatted for a while and Lars invited Reggie and Emily to stay the night.

"Nah, we need to get back home," Reggie said. "I really appreciate the offer, and we will stay next time, but we really do need to get back home today."

Lars and Eileen understood, and Eileen added, "Yes, you two can plan to stay over next time."

Lars agreed.

"Have you figured out a source for salt yet?" Lars asked Reggie.

"Possibly," Reggie replied, "but it may be dangerous."

"What's that?" Lars asked.

"It's fifty or sixty miles to the nearest large town with a Wal-Mart or HEB store," Reggie said. "If we can get there, and if the store is vacant, salt and a few other items may have been overlooked by scavengers."

"That is a long way," Eileen stated, "and it may be too dangerous."

"Yes," Emily agreed.

"Maybe so," Lars said, "but it may get to the point where we have no choice." Reggie nodded agreement.

Emily and Reggie got up to go. But before they could leave, Lars went to the smokehouse and retrieved a couple links of sausage while Eileen brought out a jar of pickled beets for them to take home. They hugged and kissed on the way out, and Lars told them he and Eileen would go look in on the Lins the next day or so and swing by the Weston place on the way back if the Lins didn't hold them up too long.

"Good," said Reggie, "we need to keep in pretty close touch with each other in these trying times. And we need to have another meeting."

Lars and Eileen agreed, and Reggie grabbed his chainsaw; then he and Emily walked away. They turned back at the tree line and gave a big wave to Lars and Eileen still standing on the porch. They returned the waves.

"That really was a fine meal," Lars said to Eileen as he turned toward her and gave her a big kiss. "You are an amazing lady," he added. Eileen blushed a little and returned the kiss.

As she turned to go back inside, Lars gave her a little pat on the butt. She turned and gave him a little smile. "It's still early in the day," she said.

"Does the time of day matter?" he responded.

"Not to me," she said. "Do you want to try the table, couch, or just go for it on the floor?"

"No," Lars said, "the bedroom is more comfortable. Don't get me wrong, because I really like how you've spiced up my sex life, but I've been an old-fashioned guy for a long time, not to mention that I've gone without for a few years. It's going to take me a while to get comfortable with your ways; not to mention the fact that I'm not as limber as I once was."

"Alright old man," Eileen smiled, then headed into the bedroom and Lars followed. Eileen went into the bathroom while Lars slipped his clothes off and crawled into bed. Eileen returned shortly and slid into her side of the bed. Lars snuggled against her and began to kiss her neck. Then he whispered into her ear, "I may be old, but I can still make you squeal." By the time he finished, he had kissed every square inch of her body, finishing with the soft, warm, and sensitive place he liked so much. Lars worked his tongue into her sweetness as he reached up and played with her breasts. It wasn't long until Eileen's body became tense and she began to jerk and moan into an explosion of ecstasy, which lasted much longer than any of the previous events. Eileen's body finally relaxed and she was unable to speak coherently. Lars understood this feeling, and he lay beside her until she recovered from the experience. After a couple minutes lying there, Lars holding one of her hands and his other hand on her breast, Eileen recovered and turned to give Lars a kiss he would not soon forget. Then she whispered in his ear, "Yes honey, you can still make me squeal!"

Eileen began to fondle Lars' soft toy and it didn't take long for it to change into a rock-hard weapon of mass destruction. Lars rolled and took a position above Eileen and paused a second to look over the terrain he was about to destroy. His weapon was ready; Lars took careful aim and then hit his target. Lars had been a little timid during their last sessions, but this time Lars showed Eileen what a real weapon could do. He was not rough with her, but he destroyed her tenderness with an explosion, which made her ooze in defeat like never before.

Lars leaned down and gave her a tender kiss and a big hug; then Lars rolled over to lie beside her. "Wow," she said and then smiled, giggled, and retreated to the bathroom.

Lars just lay there for a while until he recuperated a bit, and then got up and went into the living room. He got a drink and waited for Eileen on the sofa. When Eileen finally returned, Lars snuggled up to her and they sat and talked a while. "You up for a trip to the Lins tomorrow if the weather is good?" Lars asked.

"I'm fine with that," she replied. "Should we take a gift along?" Eileen queried. "Maybe some sausage?"

"I think sausage will make a nice gift," Lars said agreeably.

Lars and Eileen then headed outside and walked around the house a couple times, looking at this and that. Lars checked his smoker and wood supply; then they walked around back to the cistern, which was about half full. Lars stepped back and eyed the solar panels on the roof; then he opened up the hot water heater closet and gave it a quick check. Everything seemed fine. On the second round around the house, Lars checked the root cellar and included a trip around his barn. Not finding any problems, he suggested they might as well go inside, unless she wanted to walk a little longer.

"No, we will get a good walk tomorrow," she said. "We should get a good night's sleep."

Lars agreed and they retired early.

Lars and Eileen got up a little earlier than usual, since they had gone to bed so early. Lars checked the setting moon and estimated the sun would be up in about an hour, more or less. Lars didn't need a watch or clock. He had grown accustomed to watching the sun and moon rise and set years ago and could estimate the time by their position in the sky. Lars never needed to know the exact time here in the woods, so the approximation was good enough. Lars fixed breakfast while Eileen finished up her beauty work in the bathroom. Eileen really didn't need much beauty routine but always insisted she do at least a minimal amount of maintenance. This was fine with Lars as she looked gorgeous each and every morning when she came out to join him. This morning was no exception.

When they finished breakfast, Lars stepped out onto the porch to look around a bit and to check out the weather. The sun would be up shortly just as he had expected and it appeared a warm front had moved through during the night. With the warmer air there was no fog, which had been persistent during the cold spell. There were very few clouds up high as well. It would warm up a little more and would be a fine day, Lars estimated. He was a pretty decent weatherman. He went back inside and shared the good news with Eileen. They packed up water, jerky, sausage for their neighbors, and a few pounds of nails, which Sam indicated he needed last time he was over for a project he was planning. As Lars led the way, Eileen followed talking about this and that the entire trip. Most men would think she talked too much, but Lars savored every word that came from her mouth, whether it was important or not. He had basically been alone for three years before Eileen came into his life. There was no such thing as talking too much.

When they reached the Lin place, Lars let out his usual wolf howl and watched for permission to enter the property. Sam walked around from the back of the house and gave out a howl in return. Sam's howl seemed a little foreign to Lars, but this just seemed reasonable to him, and Eileen really didn't know the difference. Lars knew the howl didn't have a snowball's chance in hell of fooling a real wolf, but Lars would never tell Sam this.

Lars and Eileen strolled up towards Sam, and Sally emerged from within the house about the same time, little Sean hanging onto Sally's dress and Debra in her arms. They all met where Sam was waiting for their guests. Lars handed the nails to Sam and Eileen handed the sausage to Sally, taking Debra in the process. They shook hands then hugged and kissed, which seemed to be the normal ritual to Eileen.

Eileen and Sally went inside while the guys stayed outside. Lars told Sam they came by just to check up on them. Sam said they had not seen anyone coming around. Lars said he ran a couple off but put up a sign down the road which might deter other visitors. Lars added that Reggie and Emily didn't seem to be having any further problems with intruders and that he was happy to see he and Sally also had no problems. Shortly, Eileen and Sally returned and joined the guys. Eileen was carrying a small pouch.

"What do you have there?" Lars asked.

"Cheese," Eileen replied.

"You didn't have to," said Lars. "We didn't come here for stuff, only to give you guys some things and check to see if you were alright."

Sally responded, "This is a new cheese recipe. I need to try it out on you guys. We will check on you guys in a week or so to see if you're still alive," she said with a chuckle. Lars had never known Sally to have much of a sense of humor. The only thing she ever seemed to do was work and she was very serious about it. Now he knew differently.

Lars smiled.

Lars and Eileen thanked their friends for the cheese while Sam thanked Lars for the nails. Sally thanked Eileen for the sausage, and then the couple headed out in the direction of the Weston homestead.

Chapter 13

Lars and Eileen made quick time getting to the Weston place. They stopped just inside the tree line and watched and listened for a while; then Lars signaled with his wolf howl. They waited a few minutes longer, and seeing no activity in or around the house, he and Eileen strolled up, keeping their guns ready and pointed toward the house at all times. Lars opened the back door and peeked into the house, and when he was certain there were no intruders, Lars and Eileen checked the outhouses to make certain everything was still as they had left it last time they were here. Lars especially checked the guns he had hidden. Everything was as it should have been. The intruder's bodies were still where Lars had left them. There was not a lot left, as the vultures and coyotes had mostly taken care of the remains, leaving only the clothes and white bones, which were scattered around.

Eileen was a little distraught over the decimated bodies and steered well around what was left of the men. As she was walking around the bones and looking well to her right at the scattered remains and not watching where she was walking, Eileen stepped on a mostly intact set of hand bones. When the bones crunched, she looked down to see what she had stepped on. When she saw the hand, she screamed at the top of her lungs. Lars turned to see what was the matter, and about that time Eileen ran into him, nearly knocking him down. Lars wrapped his arms around her and held on tight.

"Maybe that will teach you to watch where you're walking," Lars said, unable to control his laughter. "Experience is, after all, the best teacher," Lars added with a smile. Lars didn't know if it was what he had said that made Eileen so mad, or that he had laughed so hard at her. Whatever it was, she was certainly mad at him. Eileen stopped just short of hitting him. Yep, he was in trouble all right. He didn't say another word and walked off.

"Dammit, don't walk away from me when I'm hurt," Eileen scolded.

"You're not hurt; you're mad," Lars stated turning back around. "Do you expect me to stand around and get slapped?"

"If you say something for which you should be slapped," Eileen responded.

"That's not going to happen," he replied. "Look, I'm sorry I said what I did. Well, not what I said, but how I said it. I really didn't mean for it to come out like that. And I'm sorry I laughed so hard." Lars paused a few seconds and said again, "I'm sorry!"

Eileen calmed down enough to accept his apology, but she was still mad. She didn't say another word to Lars and walked around the side of the house to look for flowers. The freezing weather had knocked back all but a few roses, which are a little hardier than most flowers that grow here in the south. Eileen picked two roses and took them to the graves. Lars joined her and Eileen handed one rose to him to put on Ronald's grave while Eileen put the second one on Sara's grave. They were both speechless as they stood and stared at the graves. Eileen wasn't ready to speak to Lars anyway. Lars could sense Eileen was still a bit upset over the incident with the hand and thought he had better keep his mouth shut for a while. After a few minutes, they both turned and headed for home, still quiet for most of the return trip.

Eileen and Lars didn't talk much, but Lars was thinking all the way home. Why did these guys have to kill his friends and neighbors? He wished it had not happened, but it did happen, and he knew why. The men had two sacks of food packed up, taking mostly smoked meats and potatoes. They had also gone through the pantry and took spices and some cooking oil. They were eating when Lars shot them. Though he pretended not to understand, in the back of his mind he did understand, and he did know why; they were hungry. With the state of the economy, men were desperate, and desperate men will do whatever they needed to do, just like he would do whatever he needed to do to protect himself, Eileen, and his property. *It just isn't right though*, he thought. No, it wasn't right, but this was the reality of life now. Lars thought of Ron's face, in pain from the agony of being shot—not once, but three times. Lars also thought of Sara, how it must have been a huge relief when she was shot and killed. Her body had been so bruised, she must have put up a terrible fight, but the men were just too much for her, as one by one they pawed and poked her body. This was not right. These days, this was something which had to be dealt with, but Lars was not dealing with it very well.

What would I do to protect Eileen? Lars thought. The answer was whatever he had to do, no matter how cruel or how mean he might seem to be. He would do whatever it took. Eileen would never be mean and cruel, he knew this, but she could help defend the both of them and their property. Maybe she could not do this very well now, but soon she could. With Lars' help and encouragement, she would become a competent shot, and the two of them would be a force to be reckoned with. This sounded good to Lars, but in the back of his mind, he still had his doubts. *We can do this*, he kept telling himself as they reached their home.

Are we home already? Lars thought to himself. It seemed as though they had just left the Weston place. He was so engrossed in his thoughts that the trip seemed to take only minutes, instead of the hour it actually took. At the edge of his meadow, Lars and Eileen stopped as Lars let out his wolf howl and then waited and looked around. They saw nothing at the house or the perimeter of the property, so they worked their way to their home.

It was still a couple hours before sundown when they arrived. Lars went inside first, with Eileen following close behind. Lars went to his bedroom closet and pulled out another gun—a short rifle he had not shown to Eileen before. He also looked through the ammunition he kept in the closet and pulled out the appropriate caliber. Lars spotted a pair of earplugs and picked those up as well. Eileen has been handling her pistol safely and has continued to improve with her accuracy, but considering their continuing threat from intruders, Lars thought it was time she had more fire power. Lars took the cartridge magazine out of the underside of the gun, pulled the bolt back to make certain it was empty, and then walked back into the living room where Eileen was. Lars told her he was sorry and asked for her forgiveness once again. She had settled down now and walked over and gave him a kiss on the cheek.

Lars then handed Eileen the .30 caliber M-1 carbine. He led her out to their shooting range, telling her about the gun on the way. When they reached the shooting area, Lars took one of the cartridges out of the magazine and showed it to Eileen. "This is a fierce little gun," he said. "Every time you pull the trigger, it will fire and then reload automatically. This gun is light and easy to handle and there is little kick. It's much louder than anything you have been shooting, but you don't have anything to be afraid of. It won't hurt you. Just pretend you're shooting the .22 rifle."

Eileen looked the gun over and Lars showed her the safety. He then pulled the sliding hammer mechanism back a few times, showing her how the gun worked. Lars pulled a couple of earplugs from his pocket and handed them to Eileen. "These will help you get used to the gun before you have to deal with the loud noise," he said. He then put the magazine clip back into the underside of the gun and handed it to her.

Lars positioned the cans on the log and walked back over to Eileen. She was standing there with the gun pointing into the air as Lars had reminded her to do. He did not have to say a word to Eileen about this important safety practice. "When you're ready, pull the hammer back just like I showed you, and the gun will be ready to shoot," Lars said.

Eileen did exactly as Lars instructed; then she aimed and pulled the trigger one time. She missed the can but looked over to Lars and smiled. "I like this gun," she said.

"Pull the trigger three or four times. Don't worry about hitting the cans, just get used to shooting several times in a row."

Eileen raised the gun to her shoulder and pulled the trigger again and again. *She does not fire the shots fast, but at least she is firing multiple times*, Lars thought. *She even hit a can.* Lars told Eileen to put the safety on as he reset the cans.

Lars walked back to Eileen and instructed her to hold the gun alongside her hip. "Now look at the angle of the gun," he instructed. "Try to line up the gun with the cans. Let's see how you do with a hip shot. Remember, have fun. Don't think about shooting; just think about the cans," Lars continued.

Eileen flipped the safety off, checked the rifle alignment and squeezed off four quick shots.

"Much better," Lars said. "Again,"

Again, Eileen fired four shots, hitting two cans this time. "Fantastic," Lars said with a smile. "You're doing great," he added.

Eileen smiled and said, "Thank you, dear. Why can't I stay mad at you?"

"Because though I mean what I say, they don't always come out so nice," Lars said. "My timing may not be all that good either, but I do mean well," he added. "And I'm good in bed."

Eileen smiled and Lars smiled back as he took the gun from Eileen, removed the cartridge magazine, pulled the hammer back to eject the round in the barrel chamber, and then flipped the safety on. He opened the box of shells and showed Eileen how to fill the clip. He let her put the last few cartridges into the clip, which she did quickly and perfectly. He told her to put the magazine back in, which she did but with a little trouble.

"It's a tight fit," she said.

Lars agreed. He told Eileen to put another round into the barrel. "That's good," he said, "but pull the hammer back fast all the way, and then let it go quickly. This will insure the cartridge goes into the chamber correctly."

Eileen said, "Okay."

"You have six cans," Lars said. "Aim and keep shooting until you knock all the cans off."

"You sure?" Eileen asked.

"Yes, and try to do it as fast as you can."

Eileen raised the gun and aimed. She squeezed the trigger one, two, three... When she stopped firing and all the cans were down, she had fired fourteen times."

"Very good," Lars said.

He instructed her to reload the gun again while he set the cans back up, keeping an eye on her progress. She did it perfectly and with less trouble with the clip this time. Lars walked back and Eileen flipped the safety off and aimed again. It only took twelve shots this time to knock all the cans off.

"Very good," he said.

Lars took the gun and told her that was enough for this lesson. This will be your new gun to carry along with the pistol," Lars said. "If we have intruders, this will be the first gun you get," Lars added. "Keep this gun nearby at all times, just like I do with my rifle."

"Alright," Eileen said.

Lars continued to instruct Eileen on what she should do when dealing with intruders. "You keep firing at one intruder until he goes down; then go to the next intruder, just like you did with the cans. Don't hesitate either. Our lives depend upon us killing all of them before they get one or both of us," he continued. "Aim for their chest. That is your biggest target," Lars added. "I really hope you never have to kill anyone," Lars said. "This is not a very good feeling and one which will haunt you the rest of your life, but if necessary, the life you save may be mine," Lars said. Lars could see Eileen was thinking about what he was telling her. Lars said no more. She had enough to think about. He could never be certain she could handle a situation until the time came for her to do so. At least he would be better off with her at his side than alone, but Lars also had Eileen to protect as well. Lars had feelings for Eileen now and he was not sure he could handle her getting shot. Hopefully they would never have to find out.

Lars and Eileen went inside and prepared dinner; then they read a little on the sofa and went to bed.

It rained much of the following day, so they cleaned house and talked more about strategies for dealing with intruders. There was a double set of windows to the left of the front door and a single window to the right of the door. The only other windows were the single in the bedroom and the one in the back door. There was a large and very thorny cactus growing just outside the bedroom window to deter anyone from entering the house through that access point. In addition to the deadbolt locks on the front and back doors, Lars had made brackets to hold a two by six board across the door to prevent anyone from busting them in. All the main entry points were well protected except the front windows and the back door window. Lars needed to come up with a plan to better protect these windows. There were storm shutters on the front windows, but these could only be closed from the outside, which would not be possible when intruders were out there.

Lars went outside and looked around in his barn. After a while, he found several steel bars about two inches wide. He grabbed a tape measure and went to the front windows to measure their dimensions. He also measured the window in the back door. Back in the barn, Lars cut three lengths for the back door with a hacksaw, whose blade had seen better days. His cordless drill was dead, so he took the charger inside and plugged it in to charge the removable battery for a while. He then went back out and measured and cut lengths of the steel bars for the front windows.

As Eileen watched the progress of Lars' project, she thought about San Antonio—where she used to call home. *It would be nice to see a concert or play,* she imagined. *Lars hadn't had his computer on all the time I have been here,* she thought. "Honey, do you have any music on your computer?" she asked. "It would be nice to listen to a little music for a change. I miss music."

"I think there might be something on there somewhere," he replied.

"Do you mind if I look around on it a little?" she asked.

"No, not at all."

"I'll turn it on after lunch. Lunch is about ready," she announced. Lars laid his tools down and ate with Eileen. He then discussed the progress of the project with her to give his battery a little more time to charge. After lunch, Lars took the charged battery from the charger and inserted the spare battery to charge. Lars put the fresh battery into the drill and drilled holes in each end of the cut bars. He finished the holes and found some lag bolts to fasten the bars onto the window frames. Lars found a drill bit just slightly smaller than the size of the lag bolts to drill pilot holes and a wrench to screw the bolts in. He installed four bars across each of the front windows, and then took the shorter bars to the back door. The lag bolts were too long for the thickness of the door, so he rummaged around in a few boxes of bolts in a corner of his barn until he found six bolts, washers, and nuts for the three bars he would install over this window.

Directly, Lars heard some music playing. He paused to listen to the familiar song. "I see you found some music," he said.

"Yes, and that is not all I found," she said with a laugh.

"Oh," Lars said. "What else did you find?" he queried, peeking around the corner of the open rear door.

"How about Marsha, Tina, and bombshell Bambi?" Eileen posed.

"I guess I should have deleted a few files after you decided to drop in on my life," Lars said.

"A few!" Eileen exclaimed. "There are a lot more than just a few. Some quite nice, in fact."

"What?" Lars asked peeking back around the corner.

"You've got good taste in women. Well, some anyway. I'm not so sure about Bambi."

"That's enough," Lars demanded. "I'll delete those files when I get finished with this project."

"That's not necessary," Eileen said. "Really, it's not necessary."

Lars' entire project took most of the day, and by the time the task was completed, the sun was well down in the evening sky. Lars showed Eileen the finished project. She approved. They took a couple glasses of tea out to the porch and talked, mostly about further security options, but also how nice it was going to be to have music to listen to. Lars thought they were reasonably secure now and Eileen was pleased he continued to work on their safety. Lars continued to reinforce her feeling of safety in spite of recent events.

Several cool but sunny days went by and Eileen practiced shooting the carbine a couple more times, getting better each time. She really liked the gun. It did not kick much and when she hit the cans, they didn't just fall but went flying. If she kept hitting the cans, she would soon need some new ones. The carbine was not too heavy, and with the shoulder sling, she could carry the gun easily over her shoulder. She was also getting used to its loudness.

After she had finished her target practice, her mind drifted off to her past life, as she cleaned her guns. Her life was so routine—her life seldom changed. *I went to work, went home, jogged and puttered in my garden. The only thing I did that was really interesting was to go on an occasional tropical vacation. I did enjoy my work though. Now look at me, I look like a farmer, I'm out here in the woods shooting guns and learning how to kill people. I haven't a clue what tomorrow will bring. I may be dead tomorrow, but I'm having so much fun. It's tough, but yes, it is fun! My how things have changed.*

The carrots, beets, and lettuce began to grow a little now that the weather had warmed up a bit, and Lars hoed a little more dirt around the still tender plants. It would not be long before the plants would toughen up a bit and the cold weather would not harm them. Lars knew the plants might not make it when they planted the seeds, but nothing ventured nothing gained. They just might make a small crop now that the plants had started to grow. Most winters were mild here in south Texas and Lars hoped this year would be no different. The temperature in the mid-twenties last week was actually very cold for this area. Maybe they would not see this low a temperature again for a while. Winters in this area are usually really crazy. You can have summer temperatures in mid-winter. Then a few days later it can be freezing and back to spring the following week. As the saying goes down here, if you don't like the weather, just wait a little while. What will the weather be like next week? Only time will tell.

A couple days later, about mid-morning, a stray dog showed up on the place. Lars spotted the dog eying his chickens. The chickens had never seen a dog before and didn't seem to be overly concerned as they continued pecking at the ground. Lars walked over near the chickens. In a stern voice, Lars said, "Don't get any ideas about my chickens, buster."

The dog, a mix of some sort, maybe Golden Labrador and German Shepherd, was not more than two or three years old, Lars guessed. He backed off a bit and just stood there watching Lars, but still eying the chickens. The dog was thin and looked to be starving. Eileen walked out the front door and saw Lars confronting the dog; then she went back in and retrieved some leftover potatoes and sausage. She walked over to Lars, the dog backing off a bit more with the two of them standing there. Lars saw the food Eileen had brought out and backed off a little as well. Eileen stepped forward a bit, knelt down, and held out the food. She could see the dog sniff the air as he picked up the scent of it. Slowly, a step or two at a time, the dog finally closed the distance between himself and the food. He reached out and snatched a morsel and backed off. Two bites and he swallowed the piece of sausage and came back for more. After he had taken another bite and again backed off to eat it, Eileen laid the rest on the grass and stepped back so he could eat. As the dog finished the remainder of the food, he wagged his tail and looked as if he wanted more. He would not get more though, as Eileen knew in his condition he should not eat too much at one time. Eileen and Lars walked back to the porch to sit and watch the dog for a while. The dog again eyed the chickens and Lars growled, "Don't even think about my chickens." The dog looked back at Lars and Eileen; then he laid down.

"If we can get this guy fattened up a bit, and if he'll stay around, you know he is the answer to our remaining security problems," Eileen said.

"I know," Lars responded.

After a little while, the dog got up and began to wander around, Lars and Eileen keeping a close eye on him. He ignored the chickens now as he made his way to the back of the house and then down to the river. After he drank his fill, he wandered back around to the front of the house and laid down near the porch.

"How about Buster for a name?" Eileen said directly.

Lars didn't care what she named the dog, only that the name suited her. "Sounds good to me," Lars replied.

Eileen called at Buster with a little whistle. Buster got up and came to the edge of the porch but would not come up onto the porch. Eileen got up and walked to the edge of the porch near the steps and put her hand out, making a smooching sound with her lips. Slowly, Buster made his way to her hand and allowed Eileen to pet him a bit. "Good boy," she said. Buster wagged his tail, and then backed off and laid down again.

Over the next few days, Buster became more accustomed to his hosts, letting Eileen pet him whenever she wanted, which she did often. Lars petted him a bit too, but Buster acted as if he remembered this was the one who had growled at him a few days earlier and would continue to talk sternly toward him every time he caught him eying the chickens.

Buster was a friendly dog and didn't bark much, but did on occasion when something scared him—like the coyotes he would hear howling in the distance sometimes. Buster fattened up quickly. He didn't care for vegetables much but ate them anyway. He never left the bowl empty. Eileen had picked it out for him as his personal food container.

After Buster seemed to settle in and decide this was his new home, Lars told Eileen they needed to see how he did with guns. Lars instructed Eileen to shoot some cans with her .22 rifle first, as it didn't make as much noise. Eileen set up to shoot the cans while Lars took Buster a fair distance back and petted him some before Eileen shot. Eileen shot once and Buster jumped but did not run away from Lars. On Lars' signal, Eileen shot again, and again Lars petted Buster. Eileen fired several times more and Buster sat still, watching Eileen and her noisemaker.

Then Lars instructed Eileen to try her pistol. She leaned her rifle against the house, drew and fired her .32 once then looking back at Lars and Buster. Buster seemed to accept the gunshots as not harmful, and after several more shots, Buster did not seem bothered by the guns. "Now let's try the carbine," Lars said.

Eileen took the .22 back inside and returned with the carbine. With the first shot, Buster jumped and started to run away from this very loud noise, but Lars managed to call him back and gave him a good petting and told him it was alright. After Buster had settled down, Eileen fired again, and again Buster jumped but did not run. Lars continued to pet Buster and Eileen continued to fire the gun. Buster never settled down completely.

Lars said, "Maybe this is enough for his first lesson."

Eileen agreed.

The following day, Eileen and Lars had another shooting session with Buster and he did much better this time. Buster was fed well, and while he continued to eye the chickens, he made no attempt to harm them. For the first time, Lars and Eileen felt they had a new member of their family.

It had been a while since they had visited with Reggie and Emily, so Lars proposed another trip to the Carston's. "We can check out the new trail and introduce our neighbors to Buster," Lars said. Eileen agreed. Early the next morning, Lars and Eileen packed their gear and headed up the trail.

Reaching the edge of Reggie's place about mid-morning, Lars let out his usual howl, and when he saw Reggie, they moved forward. Buster followed, stopping here and there to sniff something which would catch his nose. He was constantly making side trips and often lagged behind.

As Eileen and Lars greeted their friends, Buster finally showed up to take a sniff of Reggie and then Emily.

"What do you have here?" questioned Reggie.

"Our new addition to the family," replied Eileen, "and the newest member of our security team."

"Looks like a fine dog," Emily added.

"We've only had him a few days," Lars inserted, "but he seems to like his new home. So far, he hasn't caused any problems. We're still keeping a close eye on him when he is around the chickens though."

"The new trail is lovely," Eileen said, "much better than our old path."

"Glad you like it," said Reggie.

"How about some iced tea?" Emily asked.

"We never turn down iced tea," Lars said.

Eileen agreed.

They went inside and Eileen helped Emily with the tea, and when the glasses were poured, Reggie said, "We'll let you ladies talk a while," and Lars and Reggie went out to the bunker.

Reggie pulled out boxes of brass, primers, gunpowder and projectiles, then carefully reloaded a hundred rounds of ammunition for one of his assault rifles, while Lars looked on and assisted when he could. Reggie had this task down pat and didn't need any help, but Lars insisted on doing what he could. Then Reggie grabbed a flashlight and showed Lars the tunnel to the house.

"This is a fine tunnel," Lars said.

The fact that Lars could walk upright without fear of bumping his head was the major qualification making it a fine tunnel. It looked well braced and the doors into the tunnel, as well as the stairway and door into the house, were well designed and constructed.

"You do this all by yourself?" Lars asked.

"Yes," Reggie said with a big grin. "You're not the only one who can build things around here."

"I approve," Lars said. "You did a fantastic job."

"Thank you very much," Reggie said with a smile.

Lars and Reggie went back outside, first to check on Buster, who was napping by the front porch, and then on inside to refill their glasses. Lars complimented Emily on her superb tea.

"Thank you very much, dear sir," Emily said with a smile.

"I trust you ladies had a nice talk?" said Reggie.

"Yes we did, better than you can imagine," Emily said looking at Lars.

"Thank you both for your hospitality, my dear friends," Lars said, "but we must go now. I want to thank you again for the nice path to your place."

"Was nothing," Reggie replied. "You know we haven't had that meeting we really need to have."

"I know," Lars replied. "It just seems like there is so much to do these days. We will have the meeting though."

Eileen gave Emily a big hug and thanked her for everything while Lars gave Reggie the usual handshake and hug; then they swapped and finished their good-byes. Lars gave a sharp whistle and Buster leaped to his feet, and then followed his new owners toward the new trail with his tail wagging. Buster then darted on ahead, now knowing his owners' intentions.

That night, Lars awoke to Buster barking. He got up, grabbed his gun, and looked out the windows for a while. Lars did not light a lamp, which could give any intruders a distinct advantage over him. He moved from window to window, but after about thirty minutes did not see a thing. Buster finally settled down and Lars went back to bed. "I guess we are going to have regular false alarms like this from now on," Lars whispered to Eileen.

"It goes with the territory, honey," she replied.

Eileen snuggled up against Lars and they both soon fell fast asleep.

Eileen was up before Lars the next morning. She got up and fixed coffee, and then decided to wait until she heard Lars stirring before she cooked eggs with the last of their bacon. While she waited, she mixed up a batch of cornbread and also put on a pot of pinto beans with salt pork. The pinto beans would be ready for dinner.

Eileen finished her cup of coffee and had begun another before she heard Lars stirring in the bedroom. Eileen started the bacon. Finally, Lars emerged and Eileen took the bacon out and began the eggs.

"Did you get your beauty rest?" she asked.

"Yes," Lars replied as he walked over and gave her a kiss and her morning bear hug.

Eileen turned back to the stove to stir the eggs, and then handed Lars a cup of coffee. She put plates and silverware on the table before turning back to retrieve the eggs. Eileen and Lars finished their meal; then they sat and chatted while they finished their coffee.

"You better get out and feed Buster," Eileen said. "We don't want him going after the chickens."

Lars walked outside and got Buster's bowl. Next, he went out to the smoke-house and cut some older slices off his smoked and salted venison and pork. He then went into the root cellar and found some older potatoes. He took these back inside and cut everything up into a skillet. He let the meat and potatoes simmer in bacon grease a while with some leftover corn. Lars dumped the meal into Buster's bowl, let it cool and took the meal out to Buster.

"How you doing this morning, boy?" he said to Buster, giving him a pat on the back of the head and setting the bowl on the ground. Lars went back inside.

"If we are going to keep a dog," Lars said, "I'm going to hunt some opossum and raccoon." Lars explained, "I don't normally hunt these as there are much better animals to eat," Lars explained, "but they will be just fine for Buster. I'll make a wire trap to catch the raccoons down by the river, and I'll make another trap to put up here near the house for the opossum."

Eileen agreed.

"I'll get after it," Lars said and headed out to the barn.

Chapter 14

Finally, a night without barking, Lars said to himself as he got up earlier this morning than he did most of the past week. This was the first day he had gotten up before the sun came up since Buster showed up. Lars felt good to have gotten a full night sleep, but he also felt thankful he and Eileen had Buster. Buster could possibly save their lives as their first line of defense against intruders. Buster was also eating much more food than Lars expected; he needed to go hunting again. The sun had already been up for a while by the time they finished breakfast, but Lars decided to take a stroll around the tree line anyway, keeping the house visible at all times to see if he could get another buck. Lars told Eileen his intentions and stepped out the front door with his rifle.

Lars took Buster along and worked on training him a little during the hunt. He brought some small treats and worked on keeping Buster close to his side and quiet. Lars was gone about an hour and came back empty handed. Buster, on the other hand, did very well. He had some training at some point in his life, or he was a very smart dog; maybe it was a little of both. When they got back to the house, Lars played with Buster a bit and found he really liked his belly scratched.

Having been unsuccessful with his hunt, Lars then asked Eileen if she would like to join him on a fishing trip. "The river is up a little and the extra current tends to congregate the fish along the banks out of the swifter water," he said. Eileen liked fishing, especially after having caught more fish than Lars on the two previous trips, so she didn't hesitate to join him. They got their poles and made a trip by the bait barrels. After he had retrieved a sufficient quantity of worms, Lars stirred the coffee and tea grounds that had accumulated on top of the barrel into the soil. He then picked up a few dead sticks and stuck them into the barrel containing the grubs. He and Eileen then headed down to the pier. "Fish just out of the stronger current," Lars suggested. Eileen got her line into the water first and was the first to catch a fish. She snickered a little as she brought up the first fish. It didn't take Lars long to catch a fish and they were even, but neither of them was really thinking this was a competition. The fish were really biting today and so they continued to fish. *There must be a really big school of fish passing through this morning,* Lars thought, as they fished for nearly two hours before the fish finally quit biting. All in all, they did really well, catching twenty-seven fish, but neither could tell who caught the most. They were having so much fun catching the fish that they lost count of how many each had caught. Eileen, however, insisted she had caught more.

"I always catch more," she said with a laugh.

Lars didn't argue the point.

Lars generally processed all the fish, but he let Eileen help him with such a large catch. She had watched Lars clean the fish before, but if she was going to help, she needed more instruction, so Lars showed her how to clip the fins off. As she was working on this task, Lars gutted the fish, showing her how to perform this task as well. When Eileen had finished clipping the last of the fins, Lars let her gut the last two fish to see if she could handle this chore. Having successfully gutted the fish to Lars' satisfaction, Lars further instructed her on how to cut off the fish heads, being careful not to cut herself on the ragged ends of the bone where the barbs were cut. Lars did about half the fish and left the rest to Eileen.

"Snake!" Eileen yelled.

Lars looked behind Eileen in the water just below her. A cottonmouth was swimming in the water next to the pier.

"He smells the blood. He's not going to bother you," Lars said.

"But he's bothering me now by his presence," Eileen stated. "Kill it," she insisted. "I don't like snakes."

Lars tossed a piece of fish guts into the water near the snake and the snake swam over and grabbed the guts. The snake then drifted downstream with the current and its meal.

"I want you to kill it and you're feeding it like a pet!" Eileen exclaimed.

"Living out here means knowing when you need to kill something and when you do not," Lars said. "He's just hungry. If he gets into the house, we'll kill him. I don't think this will happen, though, as they like to stay around the water."

When Eileen calmed down a bit as the snake drifted downstream and didn't come back, Lars showed her how to wash the fish and as she washed, keeping a close eye on the moccasin, Lars split the fish to hang on rods for the smokehouse. He went to the smokehouse to retrieve some rods and loaded them up with fish; then he carried them to the smokehouse and hung them up with the sausages.

As Lars came out of the smokehouse, Eileen yelled, "Lars!" Lars came running over and Eileen had backed away from the pier. She pointed to an alligator in the water when he reached her.

Lars laughed. "I'd like to introduce you to Charlie."

Eileen frowned at Lars as he reached into the bucket of guts and tossed a morsel to the reptile. Charlie eased over and grabbed the fish guts.

"A little blood brings out the critters," Lars said. "Charlie is about six feet long. He is a pet now, but when he reaches eight feet, we will eat him. They get dangerous if they get too big. They also eat too many fish and aren't good for the habitat. If we need food sooner, then we'll eat him sooner."

"What does alligator taste like?"

"Fishy pork or whatever else you want it to taste like. It is a mild white meat and you can season it to make it taste however you want," Lars said.

Eileen stood watching the gator, not certain as to whether anything which looked so vicious could possibly taste good.

Lars got back to the business at hand; he put most of the fish heads on a rod as well and hung them in the smokehouse. A few went to the chickens to peck on. Buster apparently had decided the chickens didn't need all the heads they were given and took one for himself. The guts went into a pot and Lars added a little river water. Then he asked Eileen to put the pot on the stove to boil while Lars cleaned up the fishy mess. When Lars finished, he joined Eileen in the house, and they sat and had a nice glass of tea as they discussed their fishing trip. "Not only did we get a lot of food for us," Lars said, "we also got enough food to feed Buster for a few days." When the pot reached a rolling boil, Lars took it off the stove and went out to get Buster's bowl. Lars dipped some of the guts into the bowl and then poured some of the broth on top. He let it cool a bit before taking the bowl back out to Buster. Lars whistled and Buster came running. He set Buster's bowl on the ground. "This will taste better than the head you were chewing on, old boy," Lars said giving him a pat on the back.

As Lars turned to head back into the house, Eileen stepped through the doorway with two glasses of tea. He stepped up onto the porch, reached for a glass, and put it up to his lips. As he took a sip, a loud but muffled boom rang out from the direction of Reggie's place. Lars' heart sank, as he knew this noise had to be one of Reggie's homemade bombs. He listened closely for a minute and there followed the faint yet distinct sound of auto and semi-automatic gunfire. Lars went for his rifle and instructed Eileen to get her carbine. He grabbed a box of cartridges while she got several fully loaded magazine clips for her gun. They also picked up some extra ammo for their pistols then headed toward Reggie's at a half-run. Lars let out a couple short but sharp whistles and called Buster. Buster, already on his feet and a little anxious due to the activity, immediately followed along.

It took Lars and Eileen about twenty-five minutes to arrive at the edge of the property at their hurried pace, and Lars could hear the shots were fairly close now. The gunfire was more intermittent, but still definitely something bad was going on. Lars and Eileen slowed to a crawl, keeping a close eye all around. "We had better get off this trail," Lars said. "If the men noticed the trail, they may be watching it." Lars then led Eileen into the brush and told her to keep Buster close.

As they got closer, Lars could tell there were two distinctive areas of shooting. Reggie and Emily were shooting from slightly to the right, while the remainder of the shots were coming from slightly to the left. Lars crept slowly now, with

Eileen following closely, trying to sneak up on the suspected intruders before they spotted them. Buster stayed at Eileen's heels. Buster, still not totally used to gunshots, did not venture ahead.

Lars finally got close enough that he could see some movement. He then eased up behind a large elm tree and peeked around. He could see several men, none of whom he recognized. Lars just sat and watched and listened for a while, keeping a close eye all around. Eileen looked terrified, but her senses were keen as she kept her eyes on their surroundings, especially behind her. She also petted Buster, as he was doing exactly what he should have, helping Eileen watch for intruders. There was a small bush directly between Lars and these men, close enough to Lars that he could easily see the men, but it also helped to conceal Lars and Eileen from them. The bush also prevented Lars from taking a good shot at the men, as it would likely deflect any bullet he shot. Lars determined there were six men left. He assumed Reggie had taken out some with his bomb. *This is quite a gang*, Lars thought. *What were they doing this deep into the woods, and how did they find Reggie's place? It could just as easily have been my place*, Lars thought.

Suddenly another very loud shot rang out and one of the men dropped. This had to be Reggie's sniper rifle. Lars suddenly realized Buster had not barked, and he turned around to see if he was still around. Buster was sitting by Eileen like a guard dog, quiet but very alert. *Good dog*, Lars thought. The remaining men launched another volley of shots towards Reggie's house. These men really had to be desperate to take Reggie on. Several had to be dead, yet they still attacked. *There is nothing worse than desperate men*, Lars thought.

Lars pointed out two large trees to Eileen. "Let's back off a little and then sneak up behind those trees," Lars whispered.

Lars and Eileen eased back about fifty feet; then the two began to sneak up behind the trees Lars had pointed out. "Be ready when I shoot," Lars quietly told Eileen. "We're shooting at cans, remember. You shoot the left two and I'll take the rest," he added.

Lars and Eileen crept forward, keeping their respective trees between themselves and the men. As they inched their way toward the intruders, Eileen noticed her hands beginning to shake. *Dammit girl, get a hold of yourself,* she thought. *Cans, cans, they are just cans,* she kept saying to herself. *Big Goddamn cans!* She gripped her carbine tighter and the trembling lessened. Now they were about fifty yards from the men and had a clear line of sight. Lars peeked around the tree and saw the five remaining men clearly. They were focused on the house and didn't see Lars or Eileen. Lars looked over to Eileen and gave her a nod. She got ready and he quietly pulled the hammer back on his rifle and took sight. Lars took out his first man and Eileen immediately began firing. Lars sighted in on his second man and hit him in the chest while Reggie almost simultaneously took out another man with his sniper rifle. Eileen took out her first man, but before she got sighted on the second, he turned and spotted her and sprayed machine gun fire in her direction. Eileen felt a tug at her side but squeezed off three rounds into the man's chest. He buckled and fell to the ground. Eileen screamed and fell to the ground as well.

A seventh man stood quickly and screamed, "Don't shoot! Don't shoot!" as he threw down his gun. Lars had not seen this man, who was completely concealed well past the other men. He was young and much smaller than the men he and Eileen had shot. His voice crackled as he screamed again, "Don't shoot!"

"You the only one left?" Lars yelled.

"Yes," was the response.

"You better be telling the truth," Lars said. "If not, I'll shoot you where you stand."

"I'm not lying," the man said.

Lars looked around, and not seeing anyone else, gave out a big wolf howl. Reggie returned the howl and walked out the front door with Emily at his side. Lars called for Eileen to come over, but as he turned and looked in her direction, he saw her lying on the ground crying and holding her side. Lars yelled to Reggie to hurry, tears forming in his eyes. Buster who was alongside Eileen the entire time, lay at her side.

Reggie hurried and left Emily behind, but she ran as well.

"I'm shot!" Eileen screamed.

Lars could not take his gun off his prisoner though. "I'm coming," he said to Eileen. It didn't take long for Reggie to reach him to watch over the prisoner. Lars then ran over to Eileen.

Lars opened her coat and looked inside. He pulled at her blouse looking for blood. There was no blood. "Where are you shot?" he asked.

"Right here," she said as she reached for her side.

"I don't see anything," Lars responded.

"I know I was shot; I felt it hit me."

"I'm sorry, but I don't see any blood."

Lars helped Eileen up to her feet. Lars then examined her thoroughly. There was no wound. Lars looked at her coat. He found two holes where a bullet had apparently just missed her.

"You are not shot. It looks like a bullet caught your coat," Lars said.

Eileen examined her coat. Then she smiled and let out a sigh of relief.

"What?" Eileen said looking at Lars looking at her.

He smiled. "Nothing," he replied.

"Well I've never been shot!" Eileen exclaimed. "I don't know what it feels like. I thought I was shot, dammit!"

"Okay," Lars said and gave her a big hug. "I'm glad you're okay."

Emily arrived by this time and Lars and Eileen walked over to where she and Reggie were guarding the prisoner. Their prisoner heard every word about Eileen thinking she was shot and was grinning when they walked up.

"I can make that smile go away in a heartbeat," Lars said harshly, pointing his rifle at the man's nose. The smile was gone in an instant.

Lars instructed Eileen to move up to within fifteen feet of the last intruder and to point her carbine at the man's gut. "If he moves, shoot him," Lars added.

Reggie brought out a pair of handcuffs to secure the hands of their prisoner. He clamped one side to the man's right hand; then pulled both hands to the middle of his stomach and clamped the cuff on the other hand. Reggie instructed Emily to keep her gun up and keep an eye out around them while Lars and Reggie checked the bodies. They poked all the bodies with their rifles and checked to see if they were breathing. They were all dead. Lars walked over to take a look at the two Eileen had shot. Eileen could not have done better. Both men were shot in the chest; not square in the chest, as one was not facing her, but excellent shots nevertheless. Lars and Reggie returned to their prisoner and relieved the ladies from their duty.

Reggie poked the prisoner in the back with his rifle. "Go on down toward the house," he instructed. Lars motioned for the ladies to follow Reggie while Lars took up the rear, keeping an eye to their six o'clock throughout the short trek. When they reached the house, Reggie pushed the prisoner toward the ground and asked his name.

"Jesse," was the reply.

Lars told the ladies to take a position on the porch, keeping their rifles pointed at Jesse. "If he moves, shoot him," Lars added.

"I know these ladies very well," said Reggie. "They will shoot your balls off first, if you get any wrong ideas."

"We'll be back in a little bit," said Reggie as he and Lars turned and headed up to the site of all the mayhem. When they reached the bodies, Lars turned to look back at the ladies. Jesse was still where they had left him and the ladies looked alert with their guns pointing at their prisoner. Buster took a position beside Eileen. Lars poked at the bodies again before he touched them with his hands. Lars noticed two bodies which had virtually no heads. The bullets had entered their faces and splattered blood, brains and bone all over the ground and bushes. He looked up at Reggie, "This what your sniper rifle does?"

"Yep," Reggie replied.

"Sweet," Lars said. Lars then walked over to where the bomb had exploded and looked at those bodies. They were burned badly, as was the entire area around them, and their clothes were mostly burned off. The area was still smoking, as were the charred bodies. A small fire was burning off into the woods. The odor of burned bodies was strong and horrible.

"What did you make these bombs with?" asked Lars.

"Don't tell anyone," Reggie said with a laugh. "A fairly stable nitroglycerin mixture."

"Define *fairly*," Lars responded.

Reggie just smiled.

Lars and Reggie dug through the pockets of the unburned men but found very little they wanted or needed. Information in their billfolds indicated they were from Harlingen. They all had tattoos of different sorts, but they all had one particular tattoo on their left arm which indicated they were a gang.

"Guess they weren't a big enough gang to survive in the city," Lars said.

Most of the guns were inferior to those Lars and Reggie had, so they unloaded them and let them lay. They also gathered up all the loose ammunition they could find. It wasn't much as they had spent most of their ammo at Reggie's house, but it was largely a common caliber and they could always use extra ammunition. They found some old food the men had in a sack as well. It wasn't much for such a large group of men, and it was getting stale. Then they headed back to the house.

When the guys got back to Jesse, Reggie asked, "Can you think of any reason why we shouldn't kill you right now?"

"I don't want to die, man," Jesse replied.

Lars laid the food sack the men had on the porch, glancing toward Eileen and Emily. Lars could tell Eileen was very upset, but there were no tears and she was focused on Jesse. Lars then turned to Reggie and Jesse. "What are we going to do, brother?"

"I want to know how you guys found my place?" Reggie asked.

"Just lucky I guess," Jesse replied.

Lars hit Jesse in the head with the butt of his gun, Jesse falling to the ground. "Don't get smart," Lars said.

"Get up," Reggie demanded.

Jesse got up and wiped the blood trickling down the side of his face. "We were following the river downstream and just came upon your place. We had to have food and your place looked like an easy target. Let me go and I won't come back."

"That's what the last guy said and he came back," Reggie stated. "He's buried over there," pointing to a big mesquite tree.

"Have you run into anyone else roaming around?" Lars asked.

"No, you're the first people we've seen in weeks," Jessie replied. "That's why we knew this was our last chance for food. There doesn't seem to be much game around here."

"There's plenty of game if you know how to hunt it," Lars said.

"I can't think of a single scenario that will allow Jesse to live," Reggie said.

Lars pulled Reggie aside to discuss the situation. Neither could think of a way to let Jesse live which would not jeopardize their future. Reggie instructed Lars to take Jesse back to the dead bodies, and Reggie would get his small backhoe to bury the men. They agreed and walked back over to Jesse. Lars instructed the ladies to go inside, which they both did immediately.

Lars pointed his gun at Jesse and then pointed it toward his dead buddies. Jesse got up and headed in that direction with Lars following. Jesse began pleading for mercy. "Please don't kill me," he insisted over and over again.

"You sorry bastard! You and your men come around here to kill us and now that your plan has gone awry, you expect us to be merciful. You stupid son-of-a-bitch!"

Reggie and Lars arrived at the bodies at the same time and Reggie began digging a deep hole. Lars and Jesse stood and watched.

"Please don't kill me," Jesse continued begging. "You're good God fearing people; you don't want to shoot me."

The hole finished, Reggie took the cuffs off Jesse and told him to drag his buddies into the hole. One by one, Jesse dragged the bodies into the hole.

"Please don't kill me," Jesse continued to beg. "I can help you. You need things, right? I can help you find them."

"Do you know where we can get salt?" Reggie asked.

"No," Jesse replied.

"How about fuel?" Lars inquired.

Again, Jesse answered, "no."

Lars and Reggie didn't say another word as they stood and watched Jesse. Jesse wouldn't shut up though, but nothing he said could help Lars and Reggie.

Emily prepared tea and poured a glass for herself and Eileen. They could not talk about anything but today's event. Eileen picked up her glass and realized she was shaking badly. She grasped the glass with both hands to keep from spilling the drink. Emily was touching Eileen's arm, trying to soothe her, when they heard a gunshot. Eileen jumped and dropped her glass; then she began to cry. Eileen apologized as Emily got up to clean the mess.

"I understand," Emily said.

"I'm sorry," Eileen said, "I know you are probably just as upset as I am, maybe more. This is your home that was invaded."

"I am upset," replied Emily, "but I have confidence in Reggie and good neighbors. Reggie gives me strength as do you and Lars. In time, Lars will give you the strength you need to live out here. You will also draw strength from

Reggie and me. We are family and we will all support each other."

Eileen smiled and thanked Emily, but her sobbing continued. Eileen had seen prisoners executed on television before and could imagine Jesse's brains splattered all over the ground. She couldn't shake the vision. Emily fixed Eileen another glass of tea and they continued their conversation, but now steered the talk away from the incident.

When the guys came in, they saw the ladies sitting and sipping tea. They appeared cool, calm, and collected, but upon closer examination, Lars could tell they both were visibly upset. Eileen got up and gave Lars a big hug. She squeezed him tight and wouldn't let go. Lars could feel Eileen was trembling. Reggie set the bag they had taken from the men on the floor by the door and joined Emily who poured two more glasses of tea. Eileen could not let go of Lars and the two just stood there locked in a bear hug.

It took a few minutes, but Eileen finally calmed down and they joined Emily and Reggie at the table. They were quiet for a bit before Reggie finally spoke. "Emily, it's getting too late for Lars and Eileen to go back home. Don't you think they should stay the night?"

Emily agreed and she got up to prepare their room. Reggie followed to give Lars and Eileen a few minutes alone.

"You're gonna be fine, baby," Lars said. "You did great today."

"Those were not cans I was shooting at," Eileen said. "They were men. I killed two human beings today. And Jesse…" She could not finish her sentence. "I am not going to be fine; I'll never be fine!" And the tears continued. Lars wrapped his arms around Eileen and gave her another bear hug and a kiss on the cheek.

"You did exactly what you needed to do and as a result you are alive, I am alive, and our friends and neighbors are alive and well."

"I know," Eileen said, "but today was terrible. How can these men come here and try to kill us?"

"They are just trying to survive," said Lars. "They do not have the skills to hunt and survive on their own, so they kill and take what they need from those who do have the skills. We have the skills. We worked a lifetime to learn the skills we needed. We thought, planned, and worked hard, so in the face of adversity, we not only could but would prevail."

Emily and Reggie came back in to inform their guests their room was ready. "You guys hungry?" inquired Emily.

"I don't think I can eat this evening," replied Eileen.

"Maybe something light," Lars said.

"I could use something light too," Reggie added.

Emily got up and walked over to the kitchen. She heated up some water and pulled a couple packets of survival food from the pantry. "How about a little beef Stroganoff?" she asked.

"Sounds good, sweetness," Reggie responded.

Emily pulled four bowls out of the cabinet and four spoons, setting them on the table. As the pot began to boil, Emily added the packets and stirred until it was well mixed. She kept it on the fire a bit longer until it began to boil again; then she set the pot off the stove to sit and let the mix soak up the water. After a few minutes, she set the pot in the middle of the table and told the guys to dig in. Eileen, after smelling the aroma of the food, decided to have a little as well.

"I knew you would," Emily said with a smile. "I make the best Stroganoff in the valley," she chuckled.

Lars finished his food and looked inside the bag lying on the floor. He found enough food to make a meal for Buster and took it outside. "You did good today, Buster," Lars said as he scratched him behind the ears and then laid the food at his feet. Buster dug in and Lars returned inside.

Emily refilled the glasses all around and they retired to the living room. Most of the conversation was about how well everyone had performed in the midst of their crisis, but they just couldn't stay entirely away from the more gruesome aspects of today's events. Eileen tried to hold back the tears, which she did for the most part, but she was not completely successful. After a short while, she decided she needed a shower and bed. Emily retrieved the same nightie she had let Eileen wear during their last stay and Eileen said good night and retired to the bedroom and the adjoining bathroom.

Lars chatted a bit longer until he heard Eileen turn the water off; then he retired himself. "I'm really glad you were here, brother," Reggie said.

"Wouldn't be any place else," Lars replied. "Good night friends," Lars added.

Reggie and Emily said goodnight and went to bed a short time later.

It was a long night for Eileen, as she tossed and turned constantly. Lars didn't sleep so well either, partly because of the day's events but also because of Eileen's persistent turning and kicking him.

The sun came up and Eileen was ready to get up. She went into the bathroom and Lars figured he would get up as well; he got dressed and went into the living room. Their hosts were not up yet, so Lars went outside to check on Buster, who was lying on the porch eying a few hens walking around pecking on the ground. "Don't get any ideas," Lars said as he walked to the end of the porch to take a pee.

After Lars finished relieving himself, he walked back inside and started a pot of coffee. He put four cups on the table and waited for the coffee to boil. Eileen came in dressed and composed as the coffee was beginning to boil, and Lars poured her a cup and then filled his. Reggie and Emily followed a few minutes later and Lars poured their cups. There was dead silence as they sipped their coffee. It didn't take long to finish.

"How about some breakfast?" Emily asked.

"I just want to go home," Eileen said. Eileen wanted to go and try to put yesterday's events behind her.

"Alright," Lars said, "I think we will head back to the house."

"Don't rush off," Reggie said.

"I think we need to go," Lars said and Eileen got up. Lars followed her cue.

"Well, old friend, I can't say it was a blast, but I'm glad we could help out," Lars said.

"Glad you were here, brother," Reggie added.

"Thanks for your hospitality," Lars told Emily.

After the usual hugs and kisses, Lars and Eileen headed back home. A quick whistle from Lars, and Buster tagged along.

Chapter 15

When Eileen and Lars reached home, Lars took a good look around while Eileen went inside. Lars checked the woodshed, smokehouse, garden, and worm bins. He strolled down to the river and checked his raccoon trap; it was still empty. Everything seemed fine and after about thirty minutes, Lars went inside to find Eileen fast asleep on the sofa. Lars stepped back outside without waking her and went out to the barn. Eileen had had a rough day and night and she needed the sleep. Lars rummaged around in the barn for a while. He then sat on the back porch and rolled a cigar. He smoked the stogie and thought about what else he needed to do. Nothing else needed his immediate attention. Lars finished his smoke and went back inside.

Lars fixed himself a glass of tea and then sat down in the recliner as Eileen was still stretched out on the sofa. Lars read a little in his gardening book and directly Eileen began to stir. She awoke to Lars smiling at her. "Feel better now?" he asked.

Eileen yawned and said, "Much better."

"How about a glass of tea?" Lars inquired.

"A glass of tea would be lovely," Eileen said.

Lars brought her a glass and sat down beside her and gave her a little time to wake up. He leaned over and gave Eileen a little kiss on the cheek. "How about a walk?" Lars asked.

"A walk will help me wake up," Eileen said.

Lars decided he and Eileen should stroll up the road. He grabbed his rifle leaning against the front door frame and Eileen slung her carbine sling over her shoulder, then adjusted the rifle to a comfortable position. They headed across the meadow and up the road. Buster tagged along, darting ahead from time to time and venturing into the brush. He then ended up behind them again. Buster came alongside Eileen and begged for a scratch on the back, which she readily supplied. Buster licked her on the hand in appreciation of the scratch, but maybe a little because he could tell she needed some attention as well.

As they strolled along, Lars spotted a few does with their yearlings, which he stopped and pointed out to Eileen. She just didn't seem to have the eye for spotting critters in the woods. They came across a few squirrels jumping around in the tree tops, but they didn't kill any. Lars was after larger game, so while he pointed out the smaller game to Eileen, they were allowed to live another day. Along the way, Lars spotted a snake lying in the middle of their route. Lars didn't point the snake out to Eileen to see if she would see the reptile. She walked right up to the snake without seeing it, so he stopped her and pointed down. Eileen then saw the snake and squealed as she jumped back.

"I thought you would have learned this lesson after what happened at the Weston place," Lars said. Lars warned her again that she always needed to watch where she was walking. This was not a lethal snake, but the next time it could be a rattlesnake or copperhead.

Eileen was mad again, but this time she was not mad at Lars. She was mad at herself. She had to remember her lessons. *Dammit, I'm smart. I should be able to remember these things. I must pay more attention. I will learn*, she thought to herself.

Directly, Lars stopped Eileen in her tracks and he stood without moving a muscle. "See the buck," Lars whispered to Eileen. "I'm going to shoot," Lars said as he raised his rifle. The deer stood about thirty yards into the woods and didn't seem to be afraid of Lars and Eileen walking along the road. Sometimes, when deer think they are well hidden, or not seen, they will stand still rather than running. Lars eased the hammer back, aimed and squeezed the trigger. The deer fell where it stood. Lars threw another shell into the chamber of the rifle and stood for a moment watching for movement in the deer. Buster had been in the brush on the other side of the road but, hearing the shot, came over to Lars and Eileen. Buster caught the scent of the deer and ran over and sniffed the carcass. Buster barked and there was no movement, so Lars led Eileen to the kill. The deer lay motionless and Lars pulled out his knife. He began to gut the buck, putting the heart and liver into his pocket. He then cleaned out the small intestines and stuffed them with the heart and liver. The antlers were not very large, the deer having only four points, but Lars told Eileen he didn't hunt for antlers; they are not edible was the reason. The antlers are to help hunters to distinguish between the males and females, and to help judge the age of the deer. The antlers also make it easier to drag the animal. They make good hat and gun racks, Lars told her, but he didn't have enough hats to need a big buck.

When he finished field dressing the deer, Lars told Eileen, "Looks like you are carrying the guns home," as Lars threw the carcass over his shoulder and they headed home. At about eighty pounds field dressed, Lars could easily carry him on his shoulders. Luckily for Lars, they were only about a half mile from home when they spotted the deer.

On the walk back to the house, Eileen thought about Lars, how alert he was. He spotted every creature long before Eileen did. This made her feel safe and she felt confident that should they run across an intruder on their property, he would spot them first and take care of the threat. *But what if it was a large group of men like the ones at Reggie and Emily's*, she thought? *Could he handle them; could we handle them?*

Lars could hunt, garden, and fish and seemed to always know exactly what to do no matter what needed to be done. She really admired him for his many skills and still felt safe with him at her side, but the incident at the Carston's gave her reason for concern.

"Are we going to be alright?" Eileen asked.

"What do you mean?" Lars responded.

"Are we going to die?" Eileen probed.

"Not in the near future," Lars answered. "We will be just fine," he added. In the back of his mind, though, there was uncertainty. The conflict at Reggie's added greatly to his uneasiness.

"Reggie and I are working on some solutions," Lars added. "It may take a while to solve all our problems, but in time we will take care of everything. Don't you worry."

Eileen stopped in her tracks. Lars stopped as well and turned to Eileen.

"What's the matter?" he asked.

"I need a hug."

Lars smiled. "I promise you will get the biggest hug I can deliver if you can wait until we get home."

Eileen smiled, then walked on.

It wasn't long until they reached home and Lars hung the deer. He handed the heart, liver and intestines to Eileen. Eileen took these inside to clean up while Lars began to skin the animal. When she finished with her chore, Eileen went back outside to help Lars just about the time he finished skinning the animal.

"Where's that hug?" Eileen asked.

Lars dropped what he was doing and grabbed Eileen into his arms. He wrapped his arms around her and squeezed tightly. He then moved his hands down to her buttocks and gave a squeeze as he rubbed his manhood into her femininity. Lars also pressed his chest into her breasts as he moved up and down a little. Then he planted a passionate kiss, tongue and all, onto her waiting lips.

Lars finished up his bear hug and stepped back.

Eileen was a bit dazed from the monster hug, but then looked down at her clothes. "Now look at all the blood you got on me!" Eileen exclaimed.

"Bitch, bitch, bitch!" Lars responded.

They paused a second and both smiled. Then their smiles turned into laughs.

"We better get back to work," Lars said.

"Yes, we had," Eileen replied, "but we need to resume this a little later."

"Of course," Lars said with a smile.

As the weather was a little too warm now to let the carcass hang, Eileen helped Lars cut up the meat to hang in the smokehouse. A couple hours later, having finished the task, Lars and Eileen went inside to shower and change clothes. Eileen showered first, and then began dinner as Lars showered. They had heart and liver stir fried with onions, with cornbread and pickled beets. They also finished off the pinto beans Eileen had made a few days earlier.

Eileen suggested they go to bed early this evening and so they crawled into bed. Eileen snuggled up to Lars' backside and after they had both warmed up from each other's body heat, Eileen reached around Lars and eased her hand into his briefs. She fondled him and he reacted quickly. Lars squirmed a bit and Eileen could tell he liked the attention. She pulled Lars onto his back and moved her head under the covers until she found his firmness with her lips. She kissed and licked, as she moved her arms around both sides of his body. She moved her lips over his manhood and began to massage it; up and down she moved. Eileen used her tongue to manipulate Lars inside her mouth, teasing and exciting him, causing Lars to thrust deeper and deeper into Eileen's mouth. At just the right time, Eileen began to pull Lars' entirety into her mouth, slowly increasing the speed to a regular and steady stroke. Lars took Eileen by the head with his strong hands and gently guided her up and down, as he began to breathe heavily. His body began to tremble and he felt his fluid begin to gush. Lars let out a gasp as he exploded into Eileen's mouth; his body jerked wildly with no control, and continued to do so until all the fluid had exited his body.

Lar's rigid body relaxed and he lay there unable to speak or move. Eileen swallowed his juices and then lay there on his stomach for a moment. She then moved upward until they were face to face. Eileen could see the ecstasy in his face and the smile on his lips. Eileen kissed him on the cheek and when Lars finally emerged from his state of limbo, he looked into her eyes and pulled her close to kiss her on the lips.

"You are an amazing woman," Lars said, when he eventually returned to the real world.

"Yes, I am," Eileen said with a big smile. "And don't you forget it." They kissed for a while longer, and then Eileen turned away from Lars and he snuggled up against her. Eileen said, "I just wanted to thank you in a way you would never forget for giving me a place to stay, for feeding me and protecting me, and also just for being the man you are."

"Thank you, darlin'," Lars said, "but I'm just doing my job."

"And you do your job very well, sir," she added. They laughed. Both soon fell asleep.

The next morning, Lars was up early and took care of feeding Buster and put coffee on. Eileen came in when she finished up in the bathroom and Lars was preparing breakfast. Eileen noticed he had a little livelier step this morning and a big smile. He grabbed her as she walked into the kitchen and gave her a morning bear hug and kiss. He also thanked her again for last night.

"It was nothing," she said.

"If that was *nothing*," he replied, "I don't think I can handle *something*."

Chapter 16

Over at the Carston homestead…

After Reggie and Emily had finished breakfast, Reggie walked out onto the porch to look around. Suddenly, he saw some movement near the tree line. He stepped back inside and picked up his sniper rifle; then he scrutinized the area he had seen the movement. He saw some color—red, green, and a little white. He raised up his rifle and eyed the area with his scope. There was someone sitting by a tree looking toward the house.

When will it all stop? Reggie thought to himself. *How many people do we need to kill? What do we have to do to keep the intruders out?* Reggie could feel his blood pressure rising with the sudden shot of adrenalin his body began churning out.

Reggie looked around the area to see if he could spot more intruders. He could see only one person. He moved back to this person and turned the zoom up, and then adjusted the focus until he could see the intruder more clearly. This was a woman, but what was she doing out there alone? Reggie moved his rifle up a little and spotted a green volleyball directly above her. He moved his finger onto the trigger. *An easy fix*, he thought.

For some unknown reason, Reggie moved his scope back down until he could see her face again. She stood up, having spotted Reggie on the porch, and then began to move toward the house.

"What the hell?" Reggie muttered to himself, keeping his rifle pointed at her.

When she got a little closer, she raised her hands and yelled, "Don't shoot." She continued forward as Reggie stood there with his gun pointed in her direction and his finger on the trigger. She got closer and said, "I don't mean you any harm."

Then she got close enough Reggie could see her clearly and he recognized this woman. A tear ran down his cheek. He lowered his gun and set it against the porch railing. Reggie called to Emily as he hurried toward the woman and wrapped his arms around her, giving her a long hug.

Emily walked out and squealed, "Melissa!"

Emily ran over and gave her a big hug, tears already running down her cheek. Emily kissed Melissa and continued to hug her. It had been so long since she had seen her daughter. Melissa began to cry as well.

"Come inside," Reggie said as he moved toward the door.

Melissa took her backpack off and laid it by the door. Emily immediately went to the kitchen to fix some iced tea, not even asking if she wanted some, knowing she had to be thirsty.

"How about something to eat?" Reggie asked.

"I could use a little to eat," Melissa replied.

Reggie fixed some sausage while Melissa and Emily went to the sofa to begin years of catching up.

Reggie could not remember how long it had been since they last saw Melissa. It had been years, but he could not remember how many. They certainly had a lot to catch up on. Melissa told her parents she had been living in Waco when all hell broke loose. She was working in a pharmacy, and after the second armed robbery, she headed out of town fast, grabbing a backpack, a map and as many food items she could stuff into her backpack. Everywhere she went, there was killing and robbing and she knew she had to hurry and get out of the city.

When she finally made it out of the city, she stayed off the roads and followed along the tree lines whenever possible. When there were open spaces, she moved well off the road, moving closer only when there were again trees to conceal herself.

She found some food along the way but mostly did without, rationing the food she took with her at near starvation level. One night she broke into an old country store. She was scared to death she would get caught, but managed to get away with some salami and nutrition bars. She hated robbing the store but saw only two options: rob the store or die. Water was a constant problem. She had only a couple plastic bottles she found to take water with her. Walking, it was a long way between water holes and streams.

To Reggie and Emily, Melissa was a baby when she left home, but now she was all grown up. A little on the skinny side, but still a woman.

"I'm sorry I ran away from home," Melissa said, unable to control her tears. Reggie and Emily accepted her apology, of course.

When Reggie and Emily had moved to the woods, Melissa was only twelve years old and she just loved the woods and river for the first few years, but as she grew older and the hormones kicked in, she felt alone. There was no one to play with—only adults, and especially no boys.

Melissa explained she had been married for a short while, but the guy turned out to be a real asshole. Luckily, they had no kids. The remainder of the time, she worked and took care of herself the best she could. She had written from time to time and Reggie and Emily thanked her for writing, but it had been two years since the last letter. Melissa explained why the wilderness life had been so terrible for her, but now that her world had fallen to pieces and with all she had seen the past few weeks getting here, the wilderness looked pretty damn good now.

"Are you looking to stay here?" Reggie asked.

"Yes," Melissa replied.

Emily began crying again, and for her there were no conditions Melissa had to satisfy. However, Reggie, while he would never have turned her down, said, "If you are going to stay here, you are going to carry your own weight. You work, you stay; you don't, you go. It's as simple as that."

Melissa agreed wholeheartedly.

"We'll see," said Reggie.

Emily squinted a hard glare at Reggie. Melissa didn't see the little wink he gave Emily, after which Emily calmed down a bit.

"Well, we'll need to get your room ready," said Emily as she got up and headed toward the spare bedroom. Melissa got up to follow. The room didn't need a lot of work as Lars and Eileen had stayed there a couple times so Emily kept it mostly prepared for guests. When Melissa and Emily finished preparing the room, they returned to the living room.

Reggie joined the two and said, "How about we go outside and I'll give you a tour of the place? It's changed quite a bit since you were last here." Reggie led the way, with Melissa and Emily following arm in arm. The girls had big smiles on their faces, both forgetting about all the troubles in the world.

Reggie pointed out a few chores Melissa could easily handle but mostly instructed her on water and electricity usage. Reggie asked Melissa how she was with guns. She liked to shoot before she left so many years ago, but hadn't shot a gun since. Reggie led the ladies into the bunker.

"Do you have a gun?" Reggie asked.

Melissa said, "No."

Reggie took Melissa to his gun racks, showing her the pistols first. Melissa handled the guns trying to find one which was not too heavy but had plenty of knockdown power. She settled on a 9mm. Reggie found her a matching holster and she tried it on. "This will do just fine," Melissa said. Reggie handed her a box of ammunition.

Next, Melissa went to the rifles. "Damn, Daddy! You have a lot of guns," she said. Melissa didn't know Reggie had two more gun vaults hidden in the back of the bunker. He didn't tell her.

Reggie suggested the AR-15, telling her that the rifle is not overly heavy, has good distance and knockdown power. "I also have probably more ammunition for the AR-15 than for anything else."

Melissa said she liked the gun and decided it would work for her. Reggie put a shoulder strap on the rifle, handed her a box of ammo, and Melissa was set.

"A gun is worthless if you can't hit anything," Reggie added.

"I'll practice," Melissa said.

"Good," said Reggie, "self-defense has become a top priority around here."

"We've had some really bad incidents here lately," Emily said.

"It seems like this area has become a war zone," Reggie added. "I won't go into details, but believe me, you really need to be careful around here. I very nearly blew you to kingdom come."

Melissa assured Reggie and Emily she would not be a burden. It might take her a while to get up to speed, but she would work hard to make her parents proud of her.

Reggie showed Melissa the tunnel into the house, and then they went back outside through the bunker. Reggie showed Melissa the volleyballs hung around the perimeter, pointing out she had been sitting under one when Reggie first spotted her. "You don't want to be anywhere close to one of those things when they go off," Reggie said. Reggie told Melissa that with another mouth to feed, she would have to do some hunting and also should be able to clean what she killed.

This couldn't be farther from the truth, as Reggie and Emily would never need to kill another animal again with all their survival foods, but that was just Reggie. She really didn't have to know this yet.

Chapter 17

Lars put coffee on and began breakfast. He then gave Eileen her morning bear hug and poured her a mug of coffee while he continued to work on the meal. "I hope you got a good rest," Lars said.

"Yes I did, sir. Thank you for letting me sleep in this morning."

"You are very welcome, ma'am," Lars replied.

Lars finished breakfast and served Eileen eggs, sausage, and potatoes. When they finished their meal, Lars went outside while Eileen cleaned up the kitchen and table. He gave her a peck on the cheek and headed out the back door.

Lars went over to the barn and when he opened the door, he heard a squeal around the back of the shed. He peered around the corner of the building and saw a sow rooting around the outside of the barn with a half-dozen little piglets. She did not see him. Lars hurried back to the house and grabbed his .22 magnum leaning just inside the back door. He told Eileen to stay inside. Lars then eased back to the corner of the barn and took sight on the hog. The piglets jumped when he dropped the mama hog, but they did not run, just as he had hoped. The little pigs were not old enough to fear the gunshot. Lars leaned the gun against the barn, got down on all fours, and grunted a little. The little pigs, just about weaning age, calmed down a bit; since mama didn't run, they did not sense any danger. They were not old enough to realize mama was dead.

As Lars continued to grunt and crawl around, the little pigs rooted around in the dirt as they had been taught by their mama. The little pigs accepted Lars as another hog and showed no fear. He managed to crawl around the far side of the little critters and herded them into the open door of the barn, the swinging door helping guide them inside. Lars shut the door. *Dumb little bastards*, Lars thought, *but mighty tasty*.

Lars immediately pulled some wire out of the barn, being careful not to let the little pigs out, and began constructing a small hog pen. It didn't take long to finish the pen and Lars drug the mama hog around the barn to begin processing her. The sow weighed around 200 pounds and would provide many tasty meals. The little pigs would grow up quickly and be mighty fine eating for months to come.

Lars hung and gutted the sow, then let her hang a while to let the blood drain while Lars went in to get Eileen. Eileen admired the fresh meat as Lars led her to the barn to help him get the little pigs into the newly constructed pen. One of the little pigs managed to get away from Lars and Eileen, but they got five of the little porkers safely into the new pen. The escapee would not go far alone, so Lars was not concerned. He would catch it later and put it into the pen. Lars found a couple metal pans to feed and water the piglets. *I'll make some proper troughs tomorrow,* he thought. Then he got back to the task of processing their mama.

Eileen was a little sad for the baby pigs losing their mama but was really happy to have the extra meat.

"The little dumb shits won't know the difference," Lars said.

"That's a little crude, don't you think?" Eileen asserted.

"You want me to talk like a city girl?" Lars queried.

"No," Eileen replied, "I just thought you might be a little more sensitive and a little less crude."

"Like a city girl?" Lars reiterated.

"Dammit, old man!" Eileen said raising her voice.

"So now I'm an old man, am I?" Lars inquired. "You're no spring chicken, lady!"

Eileen paused for a minute and then she laughed. She could see the smile forming on Lars' face. *Men can't be changed,* she thought. *Well, they can, but only slightly and over a long period of time.* Eileen loved Lars for the man he was, but at times like this, he was so exasperating.

Lars gave Eileen one of his famous bear hugs and she gave him a peck on the cheek.

"You had better get at your hog," she said.

Lars gave her a little kiss and walked back over to the hog. He cut the heart out of the pile of guts he had removed earlier and then removed the small intestines to use for sausage casings. He took these in to Eileen and then got back after the task of skinning and quartering the pig. *This is going to be some mighty fine eating,* he thought.

Once Lars finished up with the hog, he went over to the barn and pulled the deer hide he had been soaking in ash water a couple weeks, out of a barrel and began scraping the hair off the skin. A short time later, Eileen walked out to see what he was doing. She asked what he was going to do with the hide when he finished getting the hair off.

"I'll make a rectangular frame from saplings," Lars said. "Then I'll use strips of leather to tie the hide to the frame, stretching the hide tight. Then I'll salt, scrape, and dry the hide to make more cordage. Why do you ask?"

"I'm considering a new hobby," Eileen replied. "Do you have any paint?" Eileen inquired.

"Somewhere," Lars said. "When I built this place, the contractors brought a lot of paint. I didn't know what colors I would need, so I told them to bring an assortment. They had a lot left over and I told them to leave it here, that I would use it up sooner or later. Let me finish scraping the hair off this hide and I'll see if I can find where I stashed the cans."

"Thank you, baby" Eileen said as she continued to watch Lars.

When Lars finished, he said, "Let's go see what we can find in the barn," as he led Eileen in that direction. Lars scratched the back of his head a bit as he looked around. Not that his head needed scratching, but rather he was trying to titillate some memory cells inside, as to where the paint might be. He knew he had some paint somewhere.

The barn was literally full of more items than Eileen could imagine Lars could stuff into the allotted space. There were many items she didn't even recognize, which led to numerous questions. Lars diligently answered the questions as he continued to look for paint. After a bit of digging, Lars remembered he might have put some paint in the far left corner. It was going to take some doing to get to the far left corner of the building, but Eileen had a need so he was going to do his best to fill the need. It was a good thing Lars had a light breakfast, or he would never have made it under, around, and through the huge pile to the far corner. After a few minutes, Lars said he had good news. "I have red, brown, green, yellow, blue, white and one can with no label. Which ones do you want?"

"All of them," Eileen responded.

Lars rolled his eyes, but then thought he was glad Eileen couldn't see him roll them.

"Yes, dear," he responded.

Slowly and carefully, Lars worked his way back toward Eileen with seven one-gallon cans, pushing them ahead a few inches at a time until he reached open floor. When Lars emerged from the jungle, he looked up and into Eileen's smiling face.

"You are my hero," she said.

Lars smiled too.

He set the paint on his workbench and dusted off the top of the cans. Then, one by one, Lars shook the cans to see if there was still liquid inside; they were all good.

"Do you care to let me in on what you have in mind?" Lars asked.

"I found some old pencils the other day," Eileen said, "and I figured I could pull the erasers out and borrow a few tail hairs from Buster to make some small paint brushes. I thought I'd do a little painting. I used to love painting when I was in school, but my life got hectic later, and I never seemed to get back around to the hobby. Maybe I'll have enough time now. I can make an easel, but there is still one thing lacking. I need a canvas."

"You're in luck, if you can wait a few days until I get this hide dried," Lars said.

"That's what I had in mind," Eileen said with a wink.

"Alright," Lars said as he returned to his hide.

Lars stretched the deer skin out on the ground and estimated the length of saplings he would need for his frame; then he went back into the barn for a machete.

"Do you need some saplings for your easel?" Lars asked.

"Yes."

"Alright," he said, "let's go find some limbs." And with that they headed down to the river.

Lars cut four hefty limbs for the frame, two about eight feet long and two about six feet long. Lars then proceeded to cut several limbs to Eileen's specifications.

As Lars cut the limbs, he noticed an asp on one of them. "Come here, Eileen," Lars asked.

"What is it?" she questioned.

"See this little brown worm?" he asked pointing to a tiny critter on one of the twigs. "This little shit will sting the hell out of you if he gets on you. You don't see them often, but during certain times of the year, they come out in numbers. There are not many this time of year, but with the warm weather we've had lately, there is at least one around."

"He's really cute. Is it that bad?" Eileen inquired.

"Absolutely," Lars replied as he squished the critter. "The quills contain a neurotoxin and they really hurt. They will make you sick too. Keep an eye out for these little guys."

"I'll do my best," Eileen promised. "There is so much crap to watch out for around here."

"Yes, there is," Lars agreed. "We have stinging nettles, poison ivy, fire ants, and the list goes on and on. You already got a taste of our thorns and you have seen a few snakes and Charlie the gator. You will run into more," Lars assured her.

Another lesson on wilderness survival completed, Lars and Eileen got back to their task at hand. They carried the limbs back to where the deer hide was laying and Lars went into the barn to retrieve some leather cordage to tie the limbs together. Lars constructed his frame while Eileen worked on her easel, keeping an eye on him to see how he was tying the limbs together. Lars also kept an eye on her progress.

Lars finished his frame and began tying the hide to it, stretching the skin, but not so tight the hide would break the frame when the skin began to dry and shrink. After an hour, Lars had the hide stretched inside the frame, tying strings every two inches, all the way around. Eileen also had her easel completed. Lars leaned his frame against the barn where it would get the most sun during the day. He also scraped some excess fat off the hide; then he dusted some salt on one side and then the other.

Lars inspected Eileen's easel and showed his approval by giving her a big hug and kiss. "Do you have an idea what you want to paint?" Lars asked.

"Not yet," Eileen replied.

"Well, I guess we'll both know when you get there," Lars said.

"Do you mind if I look around in your barn?" Eileen asked.

"No, not at all," Lars replied. "My barn is your barn."

Eileen strolled over and Lars tagged along. Eileen looked up and down and all around.

"What are you looking for?" Lars asked.

"I don't know yet," Eileen replied. "I'll let you know when I see it."

The barn was literally stacked to the ceiling and there were things stuck in the rafters high above. It was bursting at the seams with lumber, metal, tools, rope, plastic, pipe, and probably anything else Lars would ever need to build just about anything he wanted to build.

"You certainly have a lot of stuff!" Eileen exclaimed.

"Yeah, the barn is almost full," said Lars, "and you haven't even seen my attic yet," he added chuckling.

"Next rainy day I guess we'll just have to take a look at the attic," Eileen said.

Maybe she'll find what she wants in there, Lars thought.

Buster didn't seem to mind the missing hairs and Eileen fashioned three paint brushes out of the pencils—large, medium and small. Eileen gave Buster a good rubdown and a belly scratch, which was his favorite. Buster showed her his appreciation by licking her in the face. "You're such a good boy!" Eileen exclaimed.

Eileen placed the easel near the left front window, where she could see outside while she painted. She placed a small table alongside, which she found in the barn. Eileen also found seven small glass containers with lids, into which she poured a few ounces of each paint; then she sealed the large cans up tightly. The unmarked can turned out to be black paint. She also found a cedar shingle, into which she cut a thumb hole to use as a palette. As all the paints were oil based, Eileen also poured a small amount of lamp oil into a larger eighth container with a lid, to clean her brushes. An old washcloth finished out her tools and all she needed was her canvas.

Lars asked Eileen again what she thought she might paint. She still wasn't certain but added it would most likely be a scene with him in the foreground. Lars blushed a little as he said, "I'm honored."

"I'm not sure I can do you justice, but I'll do my best," Eileen added.

"I'm sure you'll do just fine," Lars assured her.

"When can I get my canvas?" Eileen asked.

"If the weather stays dry and sunny, maybe in a week," Lars replied.

"I suppose that will give me plenty of time to think about what I want to paint," Eileen added.

Lars repositioned the deer skin daily and scraped both sides each day, adding more salt for the first three days. At the end of the third day, the skin had dried sufficiently and Lars scrubbed the hide with soap and water, scraping afterward to remove all the excess water; then he set it back up to continue drying. The weather stayed fair and at the end of a week, Lars cut as large a piece of canvas as he could get out of the hide. He found a piece of plywood and cut it to the exact size of the canvas. He then tacked the hide onto the plywood with small nails every few inches around the perimeter. Lars cut the scraps into cordage, which he stored in the barn.

Lars took the finished product inside to present to Eileen. She was ecstatic over the canvas; she now had a vision of what she wanted to paint and was ready to get started.

"Well," Lars said, "I guess I'd better get started on a frame for your master-piece."

Eileen smiled, "Yes, but I don't think you need to hurry."

The next morning, Lars finished his chores shortly before lunch, so he went inside to help Eileen prepare something to eat. After lunch, he went out to the barn and found some boards suitable for a picture frame. Lars measured out the required lengths and cut the ends at opposite forty-five degree angles. Then, he placed the boards on the floor into a rectangular frame. Satisfied the corners fit snugly together, Lars glued and nailed the ends together. Then he left the frame on the floor until the wood glue had time to dry and the frame was sturdy.

Lars went inside to find Eileen sitting at her easel making pencil marks on her canvas to mark the locations of items she wanted to include in the painting. Lars couldn't make much sense of what she was doing at this point, so he lost interest and fixed a pitcher of tea. He poured two glasses and took one over to Eileen. Lars watched for a few minutes, as Eileen took a sip of tea and then continued her pencil strokes. Directly, Lars decided to go back outside, giving her a kiss on the cheek before he headed towards the back door.

Lars went back into the barn, and satisfied the wood glue had dried suffi-ciently, began working on the picture frame. Lars moved the frame onto the workbench and clamped it securely to the table. He dug around in a toolbox for a few minutes until he came up with a small box, which he took back to the frame. Lars opened the box to reveal seven wooden-handled woodworking tools. The wood working tools had belonged to his dad. His dad would never let him touch them. He had watched his dad use the tools for hours at a time. Now it was his chance to see if he could use them properly and create a wonderful frame for Eileen's upcoming masterpiece.

He studied the tools for a minute before he pulled out a large gouge and began working on what would eventually become an intricate design. The design began with simple cuts at regular intervals around the frame. Over time, various tools would cut different connecting designs to create a work of art Lars could not even imagine at this point. He hoped he could create a frame that could do justice to Eileen's creation. He would give it his best effort.

Several days passed by and there were no intruders. Eileen had made some progress with her painting, but Lars still could not tell what she was painting. There was a stick figure of a man near the center of the landscape, but all the work thus far was on the background.

The weather had remained fairly warm well into December and the garden was progressing nicely. Eileen even harvested some of the lettuce and beet greens. Buster had fattened up nicely and had even warmed up to Lars a little more, in spite of Lars reminding him to leave the chickens alone occasionally. Lars was, after all, feeding him the majority of the time. Buster certainly seemed to take a lot of interest in the chickens. He would lie near the porch for hours at a time staring at the hens walking around pecking at the ground. He never once made an aggressive move towards them though. Maybe he understood what Lars was saying when he reminded Buster that the chickens were off limits. Maybe he was just trying to figure out why the chickens were always pawing and pecking at the ground. Who knows?

Lars eventually caught two raccoons and one opossum in his traps. These were a considerable amount of trouble for Lars to clean, but Buster seemed to like the meat and Lars tanned the raccoon hides.

One night, Buster started barking and wouldn't let up. Lars got up to check on him but couldn't see anyone outside. He grabbed his rifle and stepped out onto the front porch and sat down in one of the chairs. The moon was getting close to the full stage and Lars could see fairly well but couldn't see Buster. He was off towards the edge of the meadow somewhere.

Suddenly, Lars heard a shot from the direction Buster was barking. Buster stopped barking, but soon Lars saw Buster running toward the house. Lars whistled at Buster and he came up onto the porch and sat down beside Lars. He checked Buster for injuries, but there were none. "Good boy, Buster," Lars said as he scratched and petted him.

Lars spent the remainder of the night on the porch. When the sun came up, Lars went out to the garden. Then he walked around the house. Everything seemed fine. There were intruders, but when they shot at Buster, they must have feared the shot had woken someone up and left.

Lars and Eileen hung around the house most of the day. Lars didn't get enough sleep and was angry that intruders were now coming around at night. Maybe they had always been around at night and he only knew about them now because of Buster. *It's probably the Tucker boys*, he thought. Lars took a nap in the afternoon while Eileen kept a sharp eye out and worked on her painting, which she did most of the day.

Lars and Eileen made a couple of trips—one to see Reggie and Emily, and the other to see the Lins, with a stop on the return trip to check on the Weston farm. Lars reminded his neighbors that Christmas would be here soon and they were invited over for a big feast. Lars didn't know exactly what day Christmas was, as he did not have a calendar and judged the months by the cycles of the moon, but Reggie whipped out his iPhone and brought up the calendar. He informed them Christmas would be in eight days.

"Good," said Lars, "we'll expect you guys in eight days. I guess that phone is good for something after all." Lars had seen Reggie's phone a time or two, but thought it was a waste of time keeping it charged all the time when he couldn't call anyone.

"I use it all the time," Reggie said. "The calculator gets the most use these days, but I used to use the compass a lot when I first moved here. I have several apps on here which are quite handy, and schematics which I use to build stuff and repair some of my equipment. It won't last much longer. The battery won't stay charged long."

"Now I wish I had one," Lars said with a frown. "I'd probably lose it or break it though."

Reggie introduced Lars and Eileen to Melissa, which was a pleasant surprise, as Reggie had never mentioned they had a daughter. Of course, they made sure Melissa knew she was also welcome at their Christmas party.

Lars and Reggie spent a couple hours in the bunker. The main topic of discussion was the Tucker and Gómez clans. Lars told Reggie he had another visit from someone. He didn't know who they were but suspected one of the neighbors across the highway.

"You know they will never leave us alone," Reggie said.

"I know," replied Lars. "But we can't just go over there and murder them. That's not right."

"It may not be right, but it may be necessary," Reggie stated. "You saw what the Gómez bunch did to us and without provocation. The bastards shot me!"

"I know, Reggie, but we can't just go kill them. We would be no better than them," Lars explained.

"I'd go over there and kill them right now," Reggie asserted. "That's what we need to do and we may as well take the Tuckers out in the process."

Reggie was getting too riled up as he always did. *Reggie is going to have a stroke if he keeps it up*, Lars thought. He decided to change the subject.

"Let's go see what the ladies are up to," Lars suggested.

"Okay," Reggie agreed after a short pause.

Lars led the way toward the house as Reggie locked the bunker and followed along. Just before Lars got to the house, he noticed the large burned area at the edge of the meadow from their earlier battle. He stopped for a minute as Reggie caught up with him.

"There's been a lot of killing around here," Reggie said as he walked up.

"Too much," Lars added.

"There will be more, you know," Reggie included.

"I know," Lars agreed somberly.

The guys walked into the house and found the ladies on the sofa engrossed in conversation. They fixed glasses of iced tea for themselves and refreshed the ladies" glasses.

"You ladies having fun?" Lars asked.

"Just catching up on Melissa's life," Emily said.

"Are you about ready to go?" Eileen asked.

"No big hurry," Lars replied.

Eileen turned back to the ladies and they continued their conversation. Reggie and Lars sat at the table.

"We gotta kill those bastards," Reggie said, still hung up on their previous conversation.

Lars didn't agree with Reggie, but the problem was Lars could think of no other solution. The Tuckers would never change. It was highly likely they would only get worse. The deer and hog populations would go down. Squirrels and rabbits would also become scarce and Lars' garden would get raided on a regular basis. They might even get bold enough to raid his root cellar and smoke house. Lars knew this problem would not go away on its own, but he could not condone killing them either. The Gómez clan already showed their aggressiveness. They knew Lars and Reggie had much more than they had and they know where they lived. *Sooner or later, they will be coming after us,* Lars thought. Lars didn't like it, but Reggie was right.

"We'll discuss this more at Christmas," Lars said. "I think it's about time we headed home," he announced as he finished his tea.

Eileen overheard Lars and got up. "We'll see you guys in eight days," Eileen said.

Hugs and kisses were shared all around. "It was very nice to meet you, Melissa," Eileen said.

"Likewise," Melissa said.

Lars led Eileen out the door and after taking a look around the perimeter of the meadow, they headed off in the direction of their home.

Chapter 18

Two hundred miles away near Conroe…

James Lindgren sat at his guard post on the roof of Fort Williams. His AR-15 lay across his lap and James nibbled on some jerky, washing it down at regular intervals with a warm can of soda. A few months earlier, James and his wife Ruby lived in their comfortable suburban home, not far from here. James had a good job as a structural engineer, while Ruby worked in medical research at a local hospital complex. James and Ruby did not seem to have a trouble in the world and had even considered having kids. They could not have imagined their world would be turned upside down. The two were happy and optimistic about their future.

James got in with a prepper group that had worked out an ingenious plan. They all lived within a mile of Bubba Williams Truck Stop on Interstate 45, just outside the Conroe city limit sign. The prepper group collected guns, ammunition, plywood, bedding, and a few tools which they packed into a storage facility they had rented next to the truck stop. The plan, should there be a major disaster, was that the men and their families would infiltrate the truck stop and take over the place. The well-armed prepper group would block all the entrances with trucks and force out all the occupants; then they would prevent anyone else from entering the truck stop. They would have all the fuel, food, and drinks they needed for a month or so, if they could successfully accomplish this. The group would bring all the guns and ammunition they needed to take and hold Bubba Williams Truck Stop. They all hoped they would never need to implement the plan, but nearly two months ago—suddenly and without warning—the need presented itself. The plan worked perfectly, well, nearly perfectly.

The group, James and Ruby included, kept in constant contact with each other via hand held radios. When the grid shut down, three of the men from the group made their way to the truck stop and took up positions around the perimeter of the parking lot. Their primary purpose was to sit and watch—to monitor the activity around the business. When the electricity went down, which happened about mid-morning, the fuel pumps quit working, and since they were unable to get fuel, many of the customers began leaving.

With no electricity, the business could not function and most of the customers inside the store left immediately. After a few hours had passed, the store clerks decided the electricity was not coming back on. Since they weren't able to contact the owner, they closed and locked the building and then left the facility. The members of the group monitoring the truck stop contacted the remainder of the team and alerted them the service station had shut down and closed its doors. The group was convinced the situation had reached dire proportions and they made the unanimous decision to act. Within minutes, the remainder of the team converged upon the service station to put their plan of action into effect. The wives and children remained in their vehicles while the armed men routed the drivers from the few eighteen wheelers that remained on the lot. The trucks were then commandeered and used to block all the entrances. The truck drivers were instructed to leave and not return. The few remaining cars and their occupants at the store were simultaneously forced to leave with similar instructions.

Once secure, armed men were posted around the perimeter of the truck stop. They broke one window out of the store to gain access, and the women and children entered the security of the building. A few abandoned vehicles and the prepper group's vehicles were used to block weak areas in their barricade.

James and a couple of his buddies had brought their motorcycles. They immediately unloaded these from the back of their trucks and took them inside the building for safety. Their trucks were also added to the barricade. Three men went to their storage unit next door and retrieved the plywood, one standing guard while the other two loaded the sheets. They grabbed a couple of cordless drills with chargers, a large bucket of screws, and a generator, before heading back to the truck stop. They fastened the plywood over all the glass windows and doors. The ladies rearranged the inside of the store as the men secured the plywood to the outside of the building. As the last few sheets of plywood were going up, the women lit lanterns.

When the plywood was secure, the three men returned to retrieve the beds and bedding. This task took two trips, and by the time the men returned on the second trip, the women had the first set of beds ready for occupancy. The ladies continued their rearrangement of the interior while the men assembled the remaining beds. From start to finish, the crew took six hours to secure their new fort and make the interior habitable. They all agreed to name their new fort 'Fort Williams'. The ladies then made a meal for the group and finally they were able to relax for a while. The sentries were relieved of their duties and they ate as well. Their chore now was to hold the fort.

After six hours had passed, virtually all the traffic on the freeway had stopped. There were a few stragglers and a few tried to get into Fort Williams, but they were quickly deterred with a few shots into the air. The concern now turned to invaders, armed groups which might want to take the fort, but the night and following day were reasonably quiet. This gave the men and women a little time to think and there were discussions about possible security breaches and how they were to be handled. A complete inventory of their resources was made and all were reasonably satisfied about their stock of goods. The plan they were never certain could or would succeed, thus far went fairly well. So far it was a good plan—if they were able to defend their fort, which they now thought they could, it would be a great plan.

Their inventory found an extension ladder in a storage shed at the back of the building and the men decided that if they would post sentries on the roof of the building, it would only take two men to keep an eye out for intruders. A couple of chairs were placed on the roof, which had a three-foot parapet wall all around that helped conceal the sentries. One of the men came up with the idea to cut a hole into the roof, as it had no hatch, and then extend the ladder up to the roof from the inside. This would avoid the need to go outside to change sentry shifts. The men decided this was a good idea and the improvement was quickly implemented. The men made makeshift sandbags to place around the opening they cut into the roof to prevent water from pouring into the building should it rain. An umbrella was also placed near the ladder to cover the top of the ladder if it started to rain.

The following morning, a shot was heard from above and James and Wesley quickly headed up the ladder. Robert and Chip were on sentry duty. Robert was pointing his gun toward the freeway, but all the action was over by the time the reinforcements arrived.

"A pickup stopped and was eying Fort Williams," Robert said, "but I skipped a round off the pavement beside them and they sped off."

James and Wesley relieved Robert and Chip of their sentry duties and they went below. They explained what had happened to the remainder of the team. Robert and Chip ate a bite and after about an hour, having become bored with the idle chat, they grabbed a few sodas and returned to the roof.

Shortly thereafter, a pickup stopped on the freeway again—this time on the other side of the concrete median. There were a couple of men in the back, as well as two inside the vehicle. "It looks like the same truck that was here earlier," said Robert, "except there are two men in the back now."

Robert told Wesley to skip a round off the roof of the truck this time. When he did, the men in back jumped out and got behind the concrete median. The man on the passenger side hopped out as well and hid behind the concrete wall. The truck driver got out and used the truck to shield himself. They leveled their semi-automatic rifles toward Fort Williams and returned fire.

Chip moved into position from the opposite side of the roof and all four sentries returned fire. Reinforcements were up the ladder quickly and there was a flurry of gunfire from both sides. The intruders may have thought they were good shots and well prepared, but they were no match for the highly trained men of Fort Williams. The two men who were in the rear of the truck were shot and went down quickly. The intruder who had been in the passenger side of the truck eluded the flurry of bullets much better and managed to send his own flurry of lead toward the fort. After a few more seconds, however, he too was hit and dropped his gun and fell over the concrete median. The truck driver crawled back into the vehicle and sped away, leaving three bodies behind. Robert and Chip shot a few rounds into the man lying over the median, and seeing no movement, they were certain this man was dead. They could not see the other two men but were certain they were dead as well. But they had to be checked out. James volunteered for this duty.

Chip asked if everyone was alright. Wesley said he took a bullet in the arm, but it missed the bone. There was a scream from below and the reinforcements, including James, went back down the ladder leaving Robert and Chip to take sentry positions. Wesley went down first saying he needed some first aid.

When James made it to the floor, he turned to see Charlene kneeling at the end of the counter, her eyes focused on him. He saw she had tears in her eyes. James walked over to see Ruby's lifeless body lying on the floor behind the counter in a puddle of blood. James knelt down beside Ruby and pulled her toward him, not able to hold back the tears. Ruby had taken a wayward bullet just above her left eye; she died immediately.

Mark went outside to check the bodies on the freeway. The men were all dead. On the return trip, he rummaged around in the adjoining storage building. He found a shovel and leaned it against the outside of the building, knowing this tool would be needed soon. Mark then returned inside but did not mention the shovel.

The group gave James all the time he needed to mourn his loss. Charlene and Ruby had been very good friends and she mourned Ruby's death alongside James. Finally, Charlene told James it was time to let her go and she gave him a long hug. Mark said he would help bury Ruby if James would pick out a good place for the grave. James and Mark went outside to look around for an acceptable spot. James saw a large mesquite tree and told Mark near that tree would be a good place. Ruby liked barbecue cooked with mesquite wood and so being buried under this tree would be fitting for her. Mark agreed and went to retrieve the shovel. When he returned, James said he wanted to dig the hole.

"She was my friend too," Mark said and asked if they could share the task.

James agreed. James began digging the hole and then the two shared the digging until the hole was finished.

Charlene had been watching the progress of the grave and when it was completed, she passed the word along to the inside crew who had carefully wrapped

Ruby's body in a tarp from the store's shelves. They took the body outside and carried it over to the hole. James knelt over her body and kissed the bundle good-bye. Three lengths of rope, which were found on the store racks, were used to lower the body into the hole. When Ruby was at the bottom of the hole, the ropes were removed and James tossed in the first scoop of dirt, saying a few words under his breath. Unable to contain himself, James began to tremble and cry, and Mark and Chip finished the chore while Charlene, also in tears, consoled James. With the grave finished, one of the less distraught ladies said a few kind words.

Chapter 19

The next few days were mostly uneventful, but very stressful, for James. James was a tough man, but from time to time he would burst into tears. Then his tears would dry up and his feelings turned to rage. He thought about the man who had escaped in the truck. James wanted to make him suffer. The remaining three intruders had already paid the ultimate price. The shooter, who remained lying across the median on the interstate, though he would never suffer again, received a round of bullets from James' AR-15. "Take that, you sorry son-of-a-bitch!" There was a flurry of action from the men below and the team hurried onto the roof. James apologized for the incident.

After a couple of weeks, some members of the group became concerned about the food supply. Most of the frozen and chilled foods were consumed or had spoiled. They still had a good stockpile of non-perishable foods, but these would not last with such a large group. Three of the men went out to take a look into the eighteen wheelers. One, a refrigerated truck, was running when they took over the place but had stopped shortly thereafter and had not run since. The men could smell the container as they walked up to it and the lock seal was left untouched. Three trucks contained nothing useful, while two were empty. One truck contained bottled water and this was a good find. The contents of this truck would keep until they needed it. They then found two more empty containers, but the last truck—a grocery delivery truck—contained tons of canned goods. This was very good news for the group and they vowed to concentrate their efforts to protect this truck. This truck would supply them for months.

James continued to pull his weight over the next several weeks, volunteering for sentry duty every chance he got. He felt too confined inside the building and it was not safe to be constantly walking around the property. Besides, he grew tired of the solemn looks from the rest of the group. He knew they meant well, but he felt they were whispering about him or Ruby when he was around. When James was on the roof, he had time to ponder his options. He didn't want to abandon the group, which had been so good to him, but the need to leave kept growing within him.

James continued to weigh his options. He knew his mom and dad had gone their separate ways and his dad built a place in the woods. He thought he knew where this place was located, but since he had never been there, he could not be absolutely certain. Would his dad have room for him? How was his dad doing without electricity and modern conveniences? Was his dad even alive? How long would it take him to get there even if he could find the place? There were a lot of unanswered questions, but there was only one way to find out.

Finally, James decided it was time for him to leave and he informed the rest of the group. "We've held this place for two months now and there have been few incidents with intruders. You guys can hold this place without me, and there will be one less mouth to feed."

"We're going to miss you," said Charlene.

"I'm going to miss you guys too," he responded. "I'm going to see if I can find my dad's place out west. It will be Christmas soon and I'd like to be with my family."

James got up early the following morning and checked his motorcycle over from end to end. He filled the gas tank to the brim and also filled a couple thermoses with gas and packed them into his saddlebags. He packed some jerky and cans of potted meat from the container truck. Bottled water and sodas finished out the load. He tied a small tarp and blanket roll to the outside of the saddlebags and his cycle was ready. Before James could leave, there was another small incident with a couple of armed men, and by the time this incident was thwarted and the fort secured once again, it was afternoon. James decided to stay one last night and get an early start the following morning. Before retiring for the night, he hugged everyone and told them he would be out early. Bright and early the next morning, James peed, ate a bite, stuck a couple bottles of water into his coat pockets and pushed his cycle out the door. Wesley handed him his AR-15, which James stuck into his rifle holster strapped to his bike. James checked his .45 auto strapped across his chest, cranked his cycle and was off, not taking another look back.

James, not seeing any vehicles on the interstate, climbed onto the freeway and headed north. He turned off onto the loop, and then got off at the exit to Navasota and headed west. James wanted to stay off the freeways as best he could. He worked his way toward Navasota, running about half speed. His off-road cycle was a bit noisy at high speeds and he wanted to attract as little attention as possible. The cycle would also get better mileage at a slower speed. He drove on the edge of the pavement, and at the slower speed he could safely and quickly vacate the road, should he come upon someone.

James wasted a lot of time ducking into the brush here and there, but thus far, there had been no altercations. It was a slow trip to and around Navasota, James sitting for hours stopped in the brush, watching and listening to the surroundings. Once he made it around Navasota, however, he made better time, but it got dark before he could make it to Brenham. James made camp in the brush well off the road.

There were few cars and no incidents, as he neared Brenham mid-morning the next day, but it seemed to take forever to get around the town. It felt like he spent more time parked in the brush than he did driving. There were a few trucks driving around with armed men inside. James did not want to tangle with these men. There were several armed groups at a few of the service stations around the outskirts of town. It seemed others had the same plan as James' group at Fort Williams. To try to avoid these heavily fortified positions, James took some side roads to get farther away from town. He ended up getting lost and this side trip cost him an extra day and some precious fuel, but at least he finally made it around Brenham.

As he continued on toward La Grange, he came upon a pickup headed in his direction. James quickly diverted his cycle off the road and into a clump of trees. He parked behind a large tree and kept his motor running in case he was spotted. James saw the larger vehicle quickly and thought he had hidden before he was spotted. The truck approached with three men in back with guns. They were talking to each other and not paying much attention to anything but the road ahead. They passed him by and James continued to watch as they sped away and shortly disappeared. They did not see him.

As James approached the outskirts of La Grange, he spotted several vehicles on the road and wasted hours hiding in the brush or down the occasional side road. At one stop, he heard a couple flurries of automatic and semi-automatic gunfire. As he made his way around La Grange, he also noticed several plumes of smoke rising high into the air from within the city. It seemed he would never get around the city, but finally he made his way to the south side of town and headed south toward Cuero.

It was getting late toward the end of yet another day by the time James had put a little distance between himself and La Grange. James was a bit tired from riding his cycle, which rode rougher than a street bike. No doubt the tension and adrenalin flowing through his veins added to his fatigue, so he decided to stop for the day. James drove over to the fence along the road and made a hole through the fence to get his cycle through, just as he did the day before. He then rode well into the brush and found a nice place to camp. James put the last of his gas into the tank. He had half a tank and two empty thermoses. The thermoses went back into the saddlebags and James ate a little jerky with a warm can of soda. He walked around in the brush near his campsite for a while to stretch his legs and get his circulation going again. As the sun sank below the horizon, James unrolled his bedroll and tried to get a good night's sleep. He awoke a couple times during the night to the howl of coyotes, but they were a good distance away and not a threat. James arose early the next morning, took a pee, and then made his way to just outside Cuero.

James made good progress at times, but at other times it seemed to take forever to get anywhere. He didn't know how many hours he spent sitting in the brush watching and listening. Safety was, however, more important than forward progress. Though James was heavily armed, if he came across a group of marauders, he might find himself in more trouble than he could handle. All in all, it took him nearly a week to make the trek to Cuero and he was about out of gas. He was glad he had an off road cycle, but the disadvantages were an undersized fuel tank and less fuel efficiency. James guessed he was about halfway to his destination and would need another tank of gas, as well as a couple spare thermoses. He was out of food too, but this was not as important as the gas.

Just outside of Cuero, James came upon a shootout. There were two groups of vehicles about a hundred yards apart with dead bodies strewn around each group. Two of the cars were on fire and the black smoke from the tires was rising high into the air, creating a huge black cloud in the sky. There were still a half dozen or so men left in each group. James sat and watched for a while. They would yell at each other and then exchange another round of gunfire. James watched for an hour and every so often another man would go down.

Finally, the remaining men in the group nearest James got into two vehicles and headed straight toward him. He hid the best he could, but James was spotted. The two vehicles stopped and the men started shooting at James. James immediately shot one of them. The men in the group down the road saw them shooting at James, and rained bullets toward the vehicles, taking out one more man. The remaining men climbed into the first car and this vehicle sped away. James fired a few more shots but only hit metal.

The remaining group now knew where James was. James was not certain what he should do. If he were to come out of his hiding spot, the men may shoot at him. He decided to wait where he was and let the men come to him if that was their intention. After a few minutes, the men got into their vehicle and drove away. They apparently were not interested in James.

James breathed a sigh of relief and after a few more minutes, made his way past the burning vehicles and dead bodies and a little closer to town. It wasn't long before he found an apartment complex which bordered a brushy pasture. James took his cycle into the brush. He hid his motorcycle and then hid his AR-15 in a tree some distance away, taking only his pistol and two thermoses on a scouting trip to the apartments. About halfway to the apartments, James sat down for a little while. He was still breathing heavily from the ordeal he had just gone through and needed a short break. After about fifteen minutes, James felt he could continue and headed toward the apartments.

There were numerous cars around the complex and James hoped most people were staying inside, afraid to venture out and had little use for their vehicles. If this was the case, there would be gas in their tanks. It didn't take James long to spot some likely vehicles, but did they have gas in the tanks and would he get caught stealing the gas?

Luckily for James, there was no security fence and the vehicles were close to the brush line on this side of the apartment complex. James sat inside the brush for a while to check out the activity around the cars and to come up with a plan of action. After twenty minutes and not seeing a soul nearby, James crept between two vehicles and crawled underneath near the gas tank. He spotted the return line to the tank and cut it with his knife. Immediately, there was liquid and the smell of gas. James quickly filled his thermoses and then plugged the hose. James made it back to the brush without being seen and quickly made his way back to his motorcycle and poured the fuel into the tank.

On his second trip to the apartments, James procured enough gas to fill the tank, and then he headed back for a third round. James paused at the brush line again, but this time he spotted a stranger near one of the cars. He was digging around inside the car. James had no idea what the man was looking for and didn't care—only that he would leave. The man finally finished whatever he was doing and backed out of the car. He stood and looked around a bit. James noticed he had a pistol strapped to his hip. He looked straight at James—or at least he thought he did—for a few seconds and James was certain he had been spotted. James was prepared to reach for his pistol but squatted perfectly still. The man pulled out a pack of cigarettes and lit one, continuing to stare in James' direction. James could hear his heart beating in his chest and felt the adrenalin pumping through his veins. It seemed like an eternity had passed before the man finally turned away and headed toward the apartments and disappeared around the corner of the building. James wiped the sweat from his brow and breathed a sigh of relief.

All the while he squatted in the brush, there was gunfire in the distance, some a good deal away and some fairly close. As soon as the man disappeared, James hurried to the car and retrieved the last of the gas he needed. James again plugged the line and headed back to the brush, continuing back to where he hid his cycle. Now he had all the gas he needed. James retrieved his AR-15 from the tree while he waited for dark and then bedded down.

At first light, James awoke to a heavy rain shower. He quickly rolled up his bedroll before it got wet. James hadn't had a shower in a week and he was really beginning to stink. Even though it was quite cold, he decided to take advantage of the rain. He took off all his clothes and washed them as best he could without soap and hung them over his cycle. He then scrubbed his body and put his briefs back on. The rain felt especially cold on his bare body, but he needed the shower badly. *Maybe this isn't such a good idea,* James thought shortly after he took all his clothes off, *but I guess I should have thought of that earlier.* The rain only lasted about thirty minutes then the sun came out brightly. James squatted against a tree on the downwind side in the sunlight to keep warm. He was shivering a bit, but he was tough. It took another hour before his clothes were dry and he got dressed. He started to warm up and the shivering stopped. James hopped on his motorcycle and was again on his way.

Once James had gotten past Kenedy, the population became a little more sparse and the trip became a little more safe and less stressful, but James needed food badly now. There was also less water in this arid area of the state. He finally found a spring coming out of one of the hills near a creek bed, but he still needed food. He found some cacti, which provided some nourishment, but wasted a couple travel days searching for more food. James spent hours along trails through the brush, hoping a critter would find him. Late the second day, James spotted a snake. He was hoping for something a little more substantial, but snake had to provide more calories than cacti. It would certainly taste better. If he could kill the snake, it would have to do. The snake was only about three feet long, so he figured a stick to hold it down and the butt of his gun to kill the critter would be sufficient. He was right. James waited until dark so no one would spot his smoke and built a small fire. He ate half the snake and saved the remainder for breakfast. It was definitely better than cactus pulp. After breakfast, James headed on down the road. James rode a while and then rested. He was exhausted and weak due to the lack of food. He made three stops during the day and bedded down early near one of the few streams he had seen in the area.

Early the next morning, James was fortunate enough to find a javelina getting a drink from a pool in the rock stream. One shot from his AR-15 and James had all the meat he needed. He again built a small fire, but this time in the morning. He didn't want to build a fire where someone might see the smoke, but he had to eat. James quickly nixed the possibility of eating the meat raw. The raw meat would also spoil quickly.

James dressed the pig and roasted it whole over his fire. He ate off the carcass as it cooked and was full by the time the critter finished cooking. The meat would last several days having been cooked, that is, if he took that long to eat it. He had been living pretty lean lately and it may not take three days to eat all the meat. Since someone might have heard his shot and then would be able to find his location from the rising smoke, James decided he had better vacate the area as quickly as possible, so when the meat was finished cooking, James headed on his way.

The next couple days, James made good time, not having to worry about food. He had also filled his water bottles at the waterhole where he got the javelina. At the end of the second day, James imagined he was reasonably close to his dad's place. He pulled his map out the following morning as soon as it was light enough to see. He couldn't figure out exactly where he was on the map, so he didn't know whether he was five miles or fifty miles from his dad's place. He was, however, reasonably certain the distance was somewhere within that range.

Chapter 20

Meanwhile, back at the Lindgren homestead…

The eighth day finally rolled around. It was Christmas Day and Lars and Eileen were up early. After taking care of a few small chores, Lars went out to the garden to pick some greens. Lars pulled a few baby carrots to snack on. Lars took the greens and carrots inside, and then asked Eileen what they should have for their Christmas dinner.

"A pork roast from our newly acquired pig would be nice," she replied.

"A pork roast it is," Lars responded and headed out to the smokehouse. Lars also grabbed a little jerky to replenish the snack jar in the house and some potatoes. *You can't have a roast without potatoes*, he thought. Lars returned to the house with his load and got busy helping Eileen prepare the feast. When they finished preparing the roast, Lars slid it into the oven. He told Eileen he had to do a few things in the barn and stepped out the back door.

Lars found some paper and twine to wrap the gift he made for Eileen. He then went around to the back of the barn and found a four-foot cedar shrub for a Christmas tree and chopped it down with his machete. He stuck the tree into a pot and packed the pot with dirt and rocks to hold it upright. Lars took the pot into the house and found a place for it near the double window at the front of the house. Eileen looked over to see what he was doing, having not paid any attention when he came in through the back door. Eileen saw the tree and went over to give Lars a big hug and kiss.

"This is so sweet," Eileen said. "You're so thoughtful," she added.

Having finished with the tree, Lars ventured back out to the barn to retrieve the gift he had wrapped and placed it under the tree. Eileen looked on with a smile.

Eileen finished the tea she was working on and poured glasses for herself and Lars. They sat together on the sofa and discussed gifts for their guests, who would be arriving in a couple hours. Lars went back to the barn to retrieve some paper and twine for the gifts they intended to wrap. They both wrapped gifts and when they finished, Lars placed the presents under the tree.

After finishing their teas, they returned to the kitchen to continue with their dinner preparations. Buster began to bark at the rear of the house. Lars grabbed his rifle and walked over to the rear door window and peered out toward the river. Two adults and two children were working their way toward the house. Lars immediately recognized the couple as Samuel and Sally Lin. He opened the door and gave a yell to his neighbors, "Come on up, friends. Don't mind Buster; he won't hurt you."

Sam and Sally continued toward the house and when they reached the back steps, Lars gave Sam a handshake and leaned over to give Sally a little hug. Lars bent over to give Buster a pat on the back and a 'good boy' for alerting him to his neighbors.

Lars took the package Sally was carrying and motioned the couple to go inside the house. Lars took Sean by the hand and led him inside. Sally walked in and gave Eileen a big hug.

"Welcome neighbors," Eileen said, "and Merry Christmas."

Eileen took one of Sam's packages, set it on the table, and gave Sam a big hug. Eileen then took Debra from Sally. Sam took three smaller packages out of his remaining bag and put them by the Christmas tree.

"What do we have here?" Lars said, looking at the packages. Sally's package contained two loaves of freshly baked bread, one loaf was white bread and there was a darker second loaf, which smelled like whole wheat. "Very nice," Lars said. Lars took a whiff of the remaining items in Sam's bag and knew immediately what this was—bacon. "You certainly know what I like, don't you, Sam?" he said with a big grin on his face.

Buster began barking again, out front this time. Lars grabbed his gun again and opened the front door. Then Lars heard the familiar wolf howl, which could only be Reggie's signal. Lars returned the howl, spotting Reggie, Emily, and Melissa near the tree line. Lars leaned his rifle just inside the door and walked out onto the porch. As the trio reached the porch, Lars walked down the steps and took some of the packages they were carrying. He pointed to the front door and followed his neighbors into the house. Reggie put some packages under the tree and the remainder on the table.

"Look here," Lars said to Eileen.

Eileen turned to see Lars holding a pie. She smiled. Hugs and kisses were exchanged all around and Lars said, "make yourselves at home, my good friends."

"Merry Christmas," said Eileen and Lars simultaneously.

Lars found several bottles of wine Reggie and Emily brought and held them up for Eileen to see. Wine was a luxury Eileen had given up the past couple months, as Lars did not care for the drink and kept none in the house. But on this special occasion, he would have a small amount. Eileen enjoyed a glass on occasion when she finished her walks after work, but since coming to Lars' this was something she was very willing to give up for her new life and her new man. Now that there was wine available, though, she would enjoy a glass or two. Eileen found seven similar glasses in the cabinet for the wine and fortunately Reggie brought a corkscrew, as this was not in Lars' arsenal of kitchen utensils. Lars opened a bottle, poured a little in each of the seven glasses, and made a toast.

"To good friends; to good neighbors; to peace and safety; and to love," Lars said as he held out his glass.

Everyone held out their glasses. Clink, clink, clink. All took a sip and continued to mingle.

Buster began barking again at the front of the house. Lars walked over and opened the front door as he grabbed his rifle and stood in the doorway. Buster was looking toward the old sycamore, but Lars saw nothing. Directly, Lars spotted some movement out past the tree.

"We have company," Lars said, and Reggie and Sam went for their rifles and joined Lars. Lars stepped to the side so Sam and Reggie could join him on the porch. Buster continued to bark. Lars, Sam, and Reggie walked forward to the edge of the porch and each took up positions behind the posts holding up the porch roof.

Lars worked the lever on his rifle, throwing a cartridge into the chamber, and fired into the air.

Suddenly they heard, "Don't shoot!"

"Step out so we can see you," Lars yelled back.

A dark figure stepped out from behind the sycamore with his arms in the air.

"You alone?" Lars asked.

"Yes," was the response.

"Keep your arms in the air and come on down," Lars yelled again.

The dark figure began to move toward the house, his hands remaining in the air. As the figure moved toward them, Reggie and Sam moved to each end of the porch and scanned the tree line for more intruders. They saw none.

As the man got closer, Buster stopped barking and began to growl and the man stopped, not certain what Buster would do.

"James?" Lars queried.

"Yes," the man replied.

"Put your guns down," Lars said. "I almost didn't recognize you with the beard," Lars said as he walked forward. "I didn't know you were even alive," Lars added.

Lars stepped off the porch and gave his son a big hug, tears beginning to stream down his cheeks. Lars introduced James to Sam and Reggie, and then led his son inside to introduce him to the rest. Lars introduced James to Emily, Sally, and Melissa, and then took him over to Eileen. Eileen gave James a big hug.

"You caught us at the perfect time," Lars said. "We are gathered for a Christmas feast. I trust you will join us," he added.

"My pleasure," James replied.

Lars gave James another big hug. "I'm really glad to see you, son." Lars then realized someone was missing.

"Where's Ruby?" Lars asked.

A tear ran down James' cheek. "She didn't make it," he replied.

"I'm sorry," Lars said.

"My motorcycle and rifle are out past the big tree," James said.

"Let's go get them," Lars said, and the two excused themselves.

On the walk up to the sycamore, James told his dad the story about Ruby. Lars was really saddened by the loss of his daughter-in-law, but the return of his son was the best Christmas present he could ever have received.

By the time the two had returned to the house, the table was set and the meal was ready. Lars retrieved another chair from the barn while Eileen set another place at the table. Everyone sat down to a meal of roast pork with potatoes and a rich brown gravy. Samuel and Sally had brought barbecued pork ribs and, of course, the bread. Reggie and Emily brought fruit salad and creamed corn. Eileen also fixed a nice salad and—for everyone, but especially for Emily—a couple jars of pickled beets. Reggie had also brought a small cooler with enough ice so they could all have iced tea.

The group had been pretty lively, but since the arrival of James and the answers to the queries from Sam, Reggie, and Lars, the tone turned more solemn. James talked about Fort Williams and all the chaos. He also shared the difficulty over the past couple weeks making the trek from Conroe. The world was pretty messed up—something the group already knew and the news didn't cheer anyone up. It did, however, reinforce the need for Lars and his neighbors to stay alert for intruders. The horror stories slacked off, and for much of the remainder of the meal, the talk cheered up again. After all, this was supposed to be a celebration—a day for love and camaraderie. The feast had to have lasted for two hours as everyone filled their stomachs, and then even longer when the pie was served. They were all stuffed when the meal was finished, but they were also happy and glad for good friends and neighbors.

After dinner, Emily prepared coffee while Eileen opened a bottle of wine. All except Melissa and James gathered at the sofa. Eileen turned Lars computer on and set some music to play. Lars and Eileen danced while Reggie took the recliner as he proclaimed he was going to die, having eaten way more than he should. James, feeling a little nauseated from the overabundance of rich food, decided to go out onto the porch and Melissa joined him. James told Melissa a little more about his ordeal over the past few weeks while Melissa shared her story as well. She was also a newcomer to her dad's place after having left when she was a teenager. It seemed James and Melissa had a lot in common and both ended up back at home with their parents—one parent anyway for James. Melissa told James she didn't know much about Eileen, but she seemed good for Lars. She asked what he was going to do, but James had no idea. Melissa also shared she didn't have anywhere else to go but wasn't especially happy back at her parent's home. "They are just too old," as she put it; not exactly what she meant, but she let the description stand.

Before they realized it, they had been talking for a couple hours and decided it was time to go back inside to be sociable. James informed everyone he was feeling better. The food seemed to be a little more than his system could handle.

James and Melissa danced as did Reggie and Emily. Reggie didn't die from eating too much after all. He claimed the wine had cured his bellyache. The set of songs Eileen had selected in the playlist had played three times and was about to start a fourth cycle, and Eileen turned the computer off.

"Well, what do you say we open some gifts?" Lars queried.

"Good idea," replied Eileen and Reggie.

Melissa said she would hand out the gifts, not expecting any for herself. Melissa handed the first gifts to Sean. This was Sean's second Christmas and he could now enjoy his handmade toys. The toys kept him busy while everyone else opened their gifts. Sally announced that Debra was wearing her Christmas gift from them, a knitted body suit. Then Melissa handed a gift to Reggie. It was a coonskin hat from Lars and Eileen, which he said he would wear proudly. Emily was happy and thankful for her two jars of pickled beets and gave their hosts a big hug and kiss. Lars and Eileen gave the Lins an assortment of jerky and smoked sausage and they reciprocated with a smoked ham and bacon. Again, hugs and kisses were exchanged. The Lins gave the Carstons a smoked ham and bacon as well and they gave the Lins a box of assorted emergency ration entrees.

Melissa handed Eileen a gift from Lars. She opened the package to reveal a knife Lars made especially for her, along with a leather sheath. She pulled at the carved deer antler handle, removing the shiny and perfectly honed blade from its case.

"A country gal always needs a good knife," he said.

Eileen leaned over and gave Lars a big kiss and hug that was maybe a little more appropriate for the bedroom.

"Yeeehaa!" Reggie exclaimed. "You guys want to take it into the bedroom?"

"That's enough, Reggie," Lars scolded.

"What!" Reggie exclaimed, and took another sip of his wine.

Lars knew Reggie had had a little too much to drink. Maybe Eileen had a little more than she needed as well, judging from the kiss she gave him in front of everyone.

"Maybe we need to perform a wedding," Reggie stated.

"Shut the hell up, Reggie," Lars demanded, "or am I going to have to smack you? A good ass-kicking would probably do you some good."

"And who's going to whip my ass?" Reggie growled, "you, old man?"

James and Melissa looked at each other, then at Emily with a quizzical look.

"Don't pay any attention to them," she said. "They are always like that—their manly way of showing their love and admiration for each other, I guess."

Reggie got up to pour himself some more wine. "Care for some more, Eileen?" he asked.

"No thank you," she replied. "I think I've embarrassed myself enough for one day."

"Maybe you've had enough too, Reggie," Lars said.

"Kiss my ass, Lars," Reggie replied. "I've had enough when I think I've had enough."

Lars went into the kitchen and got a cup of coffee for Eileen, then walked over and sat down beside her and handed her the cup.

Emily explained to James and Melissa, that Lars and Reggie were best friends. They don't mean anything by what they are saying.

After things settled down, Melissa found one more gift under the tree. "Who is this last gift for?" Melissa asked.

"It is for you, Melissa," Eileen said.

Melissa opened the gift to reveal a tube of lipstick.

"This is all I could think of on such short notice," Eileen said.

"It's wonderful," Melissa replied.

Melissa went to the bathroom and returned a short time later with rosy red lips.

"Thank you so much," she said as she hugged Eileen and Lars.

Eileen remained standing and announced one final gift. "This is for Lars," she said, walking over to her easel. Eileen had kept her painting covered with a cloth the past week and gave Lars strict instructions not to touch the easel. Eileen removed the cloth to reveal her painting. "It's not finished," she added as she stepped aside to show her artwork to their guests. The painting was an amazing likeness of Lars standing on the porch with his trusty rifle across his arm. The group got up and gathered around the painting, all smiling and commenting on her ability. Lars took Eileen into his arms and kissed her maybe a little more tenderly than he should have in front of their guests, especially after the incident with Reggie. Lars looked over to Reggie. "Don't even think of saying what you are thinking, Reggie." Then he turned to Eileen and said, "I've said this before and I'll say it again, you are an amazing woman."

The Lins and Carstons got up, announcing it was getting late as the days are at their shortest this time of year.

"If we are going to make it home by dark, we better get going," Reggie said.

Lars would have loved for all of them to stay the night, but they all knew there simply was not enough room, especially now that James had returned home. Lars and Eileen thanked them for coming and for bringing all the wonderful food and gifts. Then they exchanged hugs and kisses. Melissa told James to look her up when he got settled. Their guests gathered their gifts and empty containers and headed out the doors.

"Merry Christmas," was wished from all as they parted.

Lars and Eileen apologized to James for not having a gift for him, especially after receiving such a wonderful gift from him by his presence.

"I know you must be tired," Eileen said, looking at James. "Lars, help me with the spare room."

As Lars and Eileen retreated to the spare room, James stretched out on the sofa. Eileen also laid out towels in the bathroom. Eileen and Lars weren't gone long before returning to the living room.

"Whenever you get ready, you can take a shower and go to bed," Eileen said.

"Thank you," James replied.

Eileen told Lars to join James, as they had a lot to talk about. "I'll clean up in the kitchen." Lars felt bad leaving all the cleaning up to Eileen, but he did have a lot of questions for James.

James and Lars chatted for about an hour, first about Ruby and the prepper group, and then about his trip from Conroe and the condition of the surrounding towns, especially those nearest the Lindgren place. Eileen said good night and retired to the bathroom for a shower while James and Lars were talking. Having heard Eileen turn the water off and move into the bedroom, Lars told James to go take his shower and get some sleep and Lars got up to join Eileen. James told his dad he really needed a good night's sleep and they hugged; Lars said they would talk more tomorrow. Lars joined Eileen, and James went into the bathroom. He apologized for not helping Eileen clean up in the kitchen. Eileen told him this wasn't a problem. When James finished his shower, Lars showered and joined Eileen in bed.

Chapter 21

The following morning, Lars and Eileen got up quietly so as not to wake James. They fixed coffee and quietly discussed their new situation. Lars was happy to have James home. Eileen hadn't felt she had been here long enough to make any decisions, but Lars wanted her input anyway. She was half the family now, regardless of how long she had been here. Certainly, James would stay with them, at least temporarily, but for the long term there would be inconveniences. Eileen told Lars she would deal with whatever decision he made and was very pleased Lars considered her view on the situation.

Eileen poured a second cup of coffee and Lars his third. There were certainly pros to James being here, the main one being security. James was definitely a strong man and young too. He could do at least as much work as Lars and probably much more. On the downside, the first Eileen could think of was the one bathroom, not just time spent there but sufficient water, particularly hot water. Privacy could also be a minor problem. The walls in the house were thin and Eileen tended to be a little noisy in the bedroom.

They could hear James stirring in his room and Eileen decided she better brew another pot of coffee. Directly, James came out and sat at the table. Eileen poured James a half cup of coffee, the last in the pot, and then Eileen started the second pot.

"Feeling better?" Lars asked James.

"Much," James replied.

"Good! You have any plans?" Lars asked.

"I would like to stay here a while," James replied. "I don't have any other place to go."

"I didn't think you had anywhere to go," Lars said, "and I assumed you would stay here. I just thought I'd ask."

"Yesterday, I was talking to Melissa," James added, "and she has been in pretty much the same situation as I would be if I stayed here. While she loves her parents, the situation gets a little sticky at times."

"Things will certainly change some," Lars said.

"Ideally, I'd like to stay here just long enough to find another place to live. Maybe I can build a place around here. You have any ideas?"

Suddenly, a light went on in Lars' head. "There's the Weston place a couple miles downstream from here," Lars said. "It's in good shape," Lars added. "They were killed a while back. If you don't mind that, I'm certain the Westons had no family around to object."

Eileen poured another cup of coffee for James and filled Lars' cup. James pondered the idea as he changed the subject. "Where did you meet Eileen, Dad?" James asked.

"She just showed up at my doorstep a couple months back," Lars responded. "She's not going anywhere," Lars added.

Eileen smiled.

"You two look good together," James said.

"Thank you," Lars acknowledged. "She's a good fisherman too," Lars said with a smile. Lars got up. "I've got a few chores to do outside."

"I'll tag along, if you don't mind," James said.

"Not at all." Lars kissed Eileen and then the men went outside. James asked a few questions about Melissa, not letting on he could be interested in her. He also asked a few more questions about Eileen and reasserted his opinion that she was exquisite. There were a couple questions about Rachel, James' mom, but Lars had no information about her. Lars showed James around the place and shared his intention of rebuilding the root cellar and smokehouse. When they were finished with their tour, James and Lars swapped off on the axe for a couple hours and put a couple more cords of wood in the shed. They quenched their thirst at the wellhead, then went inside for lunch. James asked if Lars would show him the Weston place.

"I don't see why not," Lars said, "but I'll need to see if Eileen has any objection." Lars explained that due to the security problems, he and Eileen never ventured far from each other.

James understood. "What kind of security problems are you having?" James asked.

"We've had intruder after intruder. Some have been harmless, but we had a fierce little war over at Reggie Carstons not long ago."

"I'm glad you didn't shoot me," James inserted.

"Me too, son," Lars said. "We have had some discussions but have not found a solution yet."

"Maybe I can help," James said.

"We have some neighbors across the highway too. The Tuckers mostly are just poachers, but the Gómez clan shot at us when we went over there. Reggie wants to kill them all," Lars added.

"If they are that bad," James included, "that may be your only solution. I've learned from the prepper group I was in, that problems are best taken care of quickly and permanently."

"Now you sound like Reggie," Lars said.

"I don't know what Reggie sounds like, Dad," James added. "I'm just making a statement."

Eileen had finished her chores and lunch was almost ready. Lars asked if she objected to a trip to the Weston place. She was hesitant, but when Lars explained why, she agreed.

They ate a light lunch of smoked ham and a few leftovers from the day before. When they finished their lunch, the guys went back outside and into the barn for a while. Lars showed James a few projects he was working on and they made a place for James to park his motorcycle. The men then went to the side of the barn and Lars showed James his worm and grub farm. Lars said he wanted to take James to the river to see if they could catch a few fish. James was agreeable. Lars stepped into the back door and told Eileen his intentions.

"Maybe I can catch more fish if I change fishing partners," Lars chuckled.

"Yes, you guys go fishing. I'm going to work on my painting."

Lars gave Eileen a little kiss and he and James grabbed the fishing rods and a few worms before heading down to the river.

Lars and James had been gone three hours and, tiring of painting, Eileen decided to stroll down to the river. She found that James and Lars had caught only two fish—both of which James caught—and were still sitting and holding their rods, but were more interested in the conversation.

"How are you guys doing?" Eileen asked.

The guys turned around smiling. "Just fine," Lars said.

"Not catching much," James added, "but the conversation and company are great. I haven't had anyone to talk to for several weeks."

"Good," Eileen said. "You guys need anything?" she asked.

"No, not really," Lars said. He didn't tell her that James caught both fish. He would have heard about that for a week for sure.

"Well, if you do, you know where to find me," and with that Eileen strolled back to the house.

Eileen felt she needed a little attention and didn't get it. Lars was consumed by his son and the stories he had to tell. James had information about the outside world. Eileen didn't want to butt in on Lars and James, but she felt a little left out by Lars' inattention to her. Eileen was no longer the new kid on the block and she felt a little hurt. *But then again this was his son,* she thought. *They needed to talk man to man and they cannot do this with me around.* Eileen went inside and found a little wine left over from the Christmas party on the cabinet top and popped the cork. There was only half a bottle, but that was more than enough to give her a little buzz. It didn't take long until the alcohol kicked in, and she began to feel better about James and Lars. Eileen was not out of his life; she just needed to share him now.

James and Lars fished for another hour but didn't catch any more fish. Lars cleaned the fish and sliced them up into fillets. He used the guts and heads to bait his raccoon and opossum traps. He cut up the fish for dinner and they walked to the house. Lars gave Eileen a big hug and kiss, feeling she was a little cold when he and James came into the house. Lars and James also offered to cook dinner, which Eileen readily accepted.

"I'll take a glass of tea first," Eileen insisted.

Lars put the tea on and when he finished he took Eileen a glass with a big smile.

Lars and James then got after dinner. James cut onions, which went first into their intended one-pot dinner with a little bacon grease, followed by potatoes shortly thereafter. When the potatoes were soft, Lars added the fish, which James had cut up into small chunks. It didn't take long for the fish to cook. Lars gave the mixture an occasional stir and as soon as the fish began to crumble, he took the pot off the heat. "It's ready," he announced.

James set the table and Lars put the pot on a hot pad in the center of the table. Lars then poured tea, refreshing Eileen's glass first, and the men sat down. The meal was really quiet, but when finished, Eileen gave the men a big, "Bravo; well done!" The men smiled. Fish was fast becoming Eileen's favorite food.

Chapter 22

The following morning, Lars was up first. He put a pot of coffee on and took breakfast to Buster. He walked back in to greet Eileen and James, who were finished dressing and had already started packing their gear. Lars poured coffee all around, and anxious to get started, they quickly downed their coffee and the trio headed out the door.

Lars led the way with James bringing up the rear. When the group reached the edge of the clearing at the Weston place, they stopped to look around for a few minutes; then Lars let out a loud wolf howl. Immediately, two boys walked around the corner of the house. Lars, Eileen, and James quickly ducked down. The boys didn't see them. The boys looked around for a second and then called at someone inside the house. A third boy came out with a cloth sack in his hand. Lars recognized the boys as Joe, Sonny, and Ernest Tucker.

Lars lowered his rifle at the boys and threw a shell in the chamber of his 30-30, while James instinctively flipped the safety off his AR-15. Eileen pulled the bolt back on her carbine as well. When she did, the boys heard her and raised their guns to a ready position.

Lars didn't want to start a fight, so he yelled out "Tuckers!" The boys looked in their direction and Lars yelled again, "I don't want to hurt you boys."

The boys froze and did not try to conceal themselves.

"You boys are on the wrong side of the highway," Lars yelled. "You come back over here again and I'm going to kill you. This is your final warning."

The boys stood there and Lars stood up, as did James. "You are outgunned. Drop the sack and get home as fast as your legs will carry you." Then Lars fired a shot into the air and quickly reloaded. The boys immediately dropped the sack and took off in the direction of their home. James fired five shots in rapid succession into the air as well. The boys then reached their full speed and quickly disappeared up the road.

Lars let out a sigh of relief and turned to Eileen. She had an intense look on her face. Lars wasn't certain what she was feeling, but she was definitely on the edge.

"You see what I mean?" Lars said to James. "Every time we turn around, there is an intruder to deal with. This time it was just the Tucker boys, but quite regularly there are armed men and women to deal with."

"I see what you mean," James acknowledged.

"I'm getting mighty tired of it all," Lars added. "One day one of us may get seriously hurt or killed."

Lars and James walked out into the meadow constantly keeping an eye in the direction the Tuckers ran. Eileen followed slowly. After a few minutes, they assumed the boys had kept going. Lars went ahead and checked the house while James and Eileen stayed behind. Lars signaled the house was empty. Eileen and James followed Lars' path to the house, James eying the scattered bones as they approached the structure. James looked at his dad and pointed at the bones. "The intruders that got the Westons," Lars said.

"Your work?" James queried.

"Yes," Lars responded.

Eileen walked over and picked up the sack the Tuckers had dropped, then waited on the porch watching the road where they had escaped, while James and Lars went inside the house. Eileen didn't feel comfortable going in after what happened to Sara. Though the intruders had made a mess, there was food, spices, dishes, and the like still here. The bathroom appeared untouched. The furniture was not damaged. The Tuckers only wanted food. The first intruders only wanted food—and Ron's wife. There was still a little blood in the bedroom, but Lars had the good sense to bury Sara in the bloody sheet and placed the remaining bedclothes into the hole with her.

The men went back outside and Eileen handed them the sack. It contained spices mostly. James set the sack inside the door then Eileen followed the men to the woodshed. There was still plenty of firewood and meat in the smokehouse. The Westons were not big on vegetables, but the root cellar did have a few potatoes stored and in fair condition.

The barn did not appear to be touched by the intruders. There was plenty of lumber, metal roofing, and a small tractor that appeared in good condition. There was a nice workbench and all the tools needed to perform most any task. There were numerous power tools, but the Westons did not have the electricity to run all the tools unless there was a generator, which Lars had not seen around the place. Lars looked around the back side of the barn and, to his surprise, there was in fact a generator between the Weston truck and barn. The truck was a few years older than Lars' truck. There were several solar panels on the roof of the house, which provided minimal electricity to the house and hot water system. The generator may have been on the backside of the barn because it did not run. Time would tell.

Lars, James, and Eileen then went down to the river. There was a small but sturdy pier, and while it needed a little attention, it was basically in sound condition. The river was a little wider here than it was at his dad's place, James noticed, but it did not appear to be as deep. The Westons had a small aluminum boat as well. There were also a few more fruit trees than Lars had expected were on their place.

"I didn't realize the Westons had this many fruit trees," Lars said. "Maybe we can dig up a few saplings coming up underneath the larger trees and get them started at our place. I really like fruit," Lars added.

"I do too," Eileen confirmed. "That sounds like a good idea."

There was a nice sized garden, but it appeared the Westons did not utilize all the available space.

"It may take a little work to get the garden up to speed, but it will be worth the effort," Lars stated.

James liked the place. This was a big farm, though, and would be a lot for him to take care of. He would have to think on it a bit. Lars again took the lead on the trip back home. James and Lars discussed the Tuckers in greater detail on the walk back. *James seems to be leaning toward Reggie's solution*, Lars thought. He didn't like the solution but knew in the back of his head that may be the only remedy for their raids.

They arrived home mid-afternoon, Eileen going in to fix some tea, while James and Lars sat on the porch. Lars pointed out the green ball hanging in the sycamore tree. James had a little trouble spotting the sphere at first, but when he finally located it, it was obvious. "Don't shoot at that tree unless you want to kill someone," Lars said. "I got it from Reggie, and there is another over near the trail we came here on. It is highly explosive and will kill anyone within fifty feet, if you shoot it with a rifle."

"Cool," James said.

"Reggie said it was a fairly stable nitroglycerin compound. When I asked him to define *fairly*, he shrugged his shoulders. He told me not to drop them," Lars continued. "Reggie used one last week and I'll tell you, the result was very impressive."

Eileen came out with the tea and the guys changed the subject to something a little less gruesome.

"Thank you," the guys said simultaneously as Eileen handed them their teas. Eileen smiled.

Lars explained he decided to plant some cold weather vegetables in his garden at Eileen's urging, a little late, but he has managed to harvest a few very sweet carrots and lettuce. The beets were doing well and they hoped to get a bushel of fresh beets soon. In the spring, he would plant the entire garden, and with a little rain and luck, they would get a better harvest than he did the past couple years.

Lars went on to explain their water and electricity issues and asked James to limit water usage in particular. James asked his dad if he could spare a little gasoline for his motorcycle, but Lars explained he reserved all the gas for his tractor and that he didn't even use his truck unless it was absolutely necessary. The only time he used it the past few months was to retrieve Eileen's car and to go to the Tuckers and Gómezes. Eileen had gas in her tank and the visit across the highway was necessary.

"Unless you can add to our gas supply, I need to say no," Lars said.

James understood.

Eileen brought up the food supply and Lars explained their current food stocks. They estimated they only had enough food for themselves, and this was provided they caught a few more fish and they would need at least one more deer. The wild hog helped a bit, but it would be a while before the little pigs would provide any amount of additional meat. And they needed to be fed too, along with Buster. With James in the mix, they would definitely need even more. James suggested they rob the Weston place and this was certainly an option Lars would consider.

It was starting to get a little dark, but it was still very early; however, James felt he needed another really long night's sleep and excused himself. Before he left, though, James informed Lars and Eileen he would take a trip to see Melissa, if they would point out the way. Also, by tomorrow afternoon, James promised to offer some solutions to their current predicament. James then made his way to the bedroom.

Eileen and Lars continued to discuss the situation, coming to no conclusions, thinking it best to wait until tomorrow afternoon to see what James came up with. They decided they had no more to discuss and so they might as well get a good night sleep. They retired to the bedroom.

Chapter 23

James was up early the next morning, as were Lars and Eileen, but James beat his hosts to the kitchen and got coffee started. Lars was second out and Eileen emerged shortly thereafter when she finished in the bathroom. The coffee was ready by the time Eileen made her way to the kitchen and James poured coffee all around. Lars told James to be sure to give out a loud wolf howl when he reached the third clearing where the Carston house was located. "You fail to give out the proper warning and you may not make it to the house. Reggie has an impressive arsenal and can probably take on a mid-sized army single-handedly. He seems to be a little trigger happy lately too and would have no trouble taking you out."

James finished his coffee and asked for directions. Lars got up and followed James to the door and pointed out the path. James picked up his rifle and headed out. Lars watched as James disappeared into the woods, turned to Eileen and locked the door. "How do you feel about morning sex?" he asked.

"I prefer it," she responded with a smile.

James followed the path as instructed, stopping here and there to check out the scenery. James came upon a few deer, noting two were bucks, but did not shoot them or even consider taking one. James had issues to settle and the primary reason for his trek was to think about what he intended to do in order to resolve his problems. If Ruby had been with him, he would not hesitate moving into the Weston residence, but Ruby was not with him and he missed her terribly.

Melissa and James hit it off pretty good at the Christmas party, he thought, but they had just met. James liked Melissa, but he did not know her. He had absolutely no idea who she was or what kind a woman she was. *At least she is mature*, he thought, *and maybe she is a reasonable person.* Was he absolutely crazy to think a woman would move into a strange home with him, both of them being basically complete strangers to the other?

James stopped for a while and ate some of the jerky his dad packed for him, almost turning around and going back to his dad's place. He was crazy to even think about doing what he was thinking. *Melissa said she was uncomfortable staying at her dad's place*, he thought, *but is she going to jump from uncomfortable to crazy?* There was only one way to find out. *She is a gorgeous gal*, he thought. She seemed smart and if she wasn't entirely nutty, this could be a lady he could eventually fall in love with. *Man, now I'm putting the cart ahead of the horse*, he thought. He began to think she definitely would think he was totally crazy. *Maybe I should just talk to her for a while. Yeah, that's it, I'll just talk to her a while; just ease into the living together arrangement if the conversation goes well.* James just shook his head at how bad his idea sounded, as he mulled it over and over in his head. *I better get going*, he thought, *I'm just wasting time.*

James reached the edge of the third clearing and spotted the Carston house, a small column of smoke rising out of the chimney. James let out a loud wolf howl and then waited. Reggie walked out onto the porch, rifle in hand, and James headed in his direction. A few seconds later, James gave out another wolf howl and saw Reggie look his way. James then waved his arm in the air and Reggie gave a wave back. James then made his way to the porch.

"Sorry to barge in, but I'd like to see Melissa, if I may," James said with a smile.

Reggie stuck his head back inside, "Melissa, you have a visitor."

"Melissa is in the bathroom," Emily said. "I'll send her out when she's finished."

Reggie shut the door.

"Well, what brings you up this way?" Reggie said.

"I think Melissa and I hit it off at the Christmas party and I just thought I'd like to see her again. Oh, by the way, we ran into the Tucker boys at the Weston homestead."

"You kill any of them?" Reggie asked, hoping they had.

"No, we just ran them off," James replied.

A disappointed frown appeared on Reggie's face. "What are you going to do?" Reggie inquired. "You going to stay with your dad?"

"I don't know," James replied. "That's what I'd like to discuss with Melissa."

Melissa came out and greeted James with a smile. "I'd like to take a walk and talk with you for a while," James said.

"Alright," Melissa said.

"You guys stay in the meadow and keep your eyes out for intruders, alright?"

"Yes, Dad."

James and Melissa strolled off across the meadow, Reggie watching until he could no longer hear what they were saying. James piqued his interest saying he wanted to talk to Melissa about his living arrangements.

James asked how she was doing and Melissa said she was doing good. James told Melissa how much he liked the river valley. There were a lot of animals on the trip here. He told her about the two bucks he saw.

Melissa told James she had been living in Waco and worked at a pharmacy. Two armed robberies in as many days sent her scampering away. This was the only place she could think of, where she might be safe.

James couldn't believe she made the entire trip on foot. *This gal is tough*, he thought. They talked about the weather, their likes and dislikes and plans for the future. There were no plans for the future and Melissa indicated she was not overly happy staying with her mom and dad, but she really didn't have any other options.

Then James told Melissa about the trip to the Weston farm. He told Melissa he was considering moving there, but it would be an awful chore for him to manage the place on his own. He did not tell Melissa he considered asking her to move to the place with him but hoped she was smart enough and interested enough to come up with the idea on her own. James described the layout of the place with an emphasis on the fine garden and orchard. He then described the house in detail as the two made a complete trip around the meadow.

James thought Melissa was really hot. She was certainly very smart, but could she cook? James suggested another trip around the meadow and she agreed. Melissa said she loved to cook and gardening was alright, but she really didn't like to hunt and didn't know anything about fishing. She really liked the spring and swimming in the summer, but fall was her favorite time of year. "Right after the first cool spell and the trees start to change colors. Just about the time you get tired of the summer heat, the refreshing north winds come in and changes everything," Melissa said. James really hadn't thought of it that way, but agreed with Melissa.

About halfway through their second trip around the meadow, James asked Melissa if she would like to take a trip to the Weston farm. She was listening but didn't say a word. James explained they could stay the night with his dad and Eileen, and then they could get up bright and early the next morning and make the trek. Melissa kept walking and still kept quiet. James shut up for a while and gave Melissa a little time to think about the proposition. Finally, when they were just about back to the house, Melissa said she would love to see the Weston place. They walked up onto the porch and Melissa told James to wait outside while she packed a bag. Melissa went in and informed her parents of her intentions. While she was packing, Reggie came out onto the porch to talk to James. Emily followed Melissa into her bedroom and had a little talk with her. It wasn't long, and Melissa and Emily soon walked out to the porch.

"You two know what you're doing?" Reggie asked.

"I think so," replied Melissa.

"Yes," replied James, though maybe he wasn't 100% sure; nevertheless, they headed back down river. Melissa and James didn't talk much on the walk back. James didn't want to say anything which might screw up his plan and they had run out of small talk. There were no big issues to discuss, though issues were definitely churning in James' head. These issues would certainly come up once they made the trek to the Weston place.

James let out a loud wolf howl when he reached his dad's place. Then, seeing his dad on the porch, he and Melissa headed toward the house. Eileen strolled out before the kids reached the porch. Lars and Eileen were surprised to see Melissa with James. James explained they were going to the Weston place in the morning and also apologized for bringing Melissa along to stay the night without asking.

"I don't see a problem," said Eileen.

"None here," replied Lars.

"Good," said Eileen.

"You guys may as well come in; dinner will be ready soon," Lars said, and James and Melissa followed them inside.

"I guess you're sleeping on the couch tonight?" Lars said to James, Eileen eying James and awaiting his answer.

"Yes sir," James replied.

Perfect answer, Eileen thought.

They all sat down for dinner and immediately Lars began to ask James about the trip. James said he just thought Melissa might like to see the place, and then James quickly changed the subject to the two bucks he spotted on the trip to the Carston's place.

"Nice bucks, huh?" Lars asked.

"Yes, mature bucks," James replied.

"We need to get one of them. We are pretty low on meat now. Don't pass one up again," Lars said. Then his attention returned to the food on his plate.

When they finished the meal, Lars asked Eileen and Melissa to go on over to the sofa and get better acquainted; he and James would clean up the table and dishes. James and Lars cleaned up, filled their glasses, and joined the ladies. After a little chitchat, they decided it was time to go to bed and Melissa and Eileen readied the spare bedroom while Lars and James got the sofa ready. Eileen shut the door to Melissa's room, and when she saw James was making his way to the sofa, she went into her bedroom followed closely by Lars.

Chapter 24

Melissa and Eileen were up first the next morning. Eileen put a pot of coffee on the stove while Melissa got out four coffee mugs. James woke up to the noise the ladies were making, though they were being as quiet as possible. James had slept in his clothes and he got up to put his boots on. He joined Melissa and Eileen for a cup of coffee and Lars finally made it in as they finished their first cup. "Good morning," they all said as Lars came in. Melissa poured coffee for Lars and refreshed the remaining cups.

"We should be back about mid-afternoon," James said.

"When we get back, I'll head straight home," Melissa added. "I won't intrude on you a second night."

"It's no intrusion," Lars said with a smile.

Finishing their coffee, Melissa and James loaded up and headed out the door. James told Melissa the trip should take about forty-five minutes, if they had no problems. There were no problems and they arrived at the edge of the meadow. They knelt down behind a tree for a while, watching the house and the perimeter of the meadow. James let out a wolf howl and they waited. Seeing no movement, they headed for the house.

Melissa noticed the bones and shredded clothes on the way to the house but said nothing. James opened the front door and peered into the house. The barrel of the AR-15 led the way as James walked to the center of the main room. Melissa followed and looked around. She checked out the kitchen to find that the home had running water. The stove looked good and there was food in the pantry, though it was in disarray and there were food containers scattered around and on the floor. Some spices were on the floor as well as scraps of food. There were a few ants and a roach or two, but no serious pest problems.

The bathroom seemed alright and it had running water too. She checked the hot water and after a few moments, the water warmed up and then got hot. She turned the faucet off. The bedrooms were a bit messy, but there were plenty of sheets, blankets, and pillows. The fireplace needed cleaning out, but otherwise it was in good shape as was most of the furniture. James led Melissa outside and showed her the woodshed, root cellar, smokehouse, and barn. When they walked out of the barn, James pointed out the solar panels and the cistern. James checked the gas tanks on the Weston tractor and truck. The tractor was almost full and the truck was half-full.

"Yes!" he exclaimed.

"What?" Melissa inquired.

"There's gas in the vehicles," he replied.

The generator was empty and so James siphoned a little fuel out of the truck and poured it into the generator. He checked the oil level, which was okay, and then set the choke and gave it a crank. The generator fired on the fourth pull and James opened the choke and pulled the cord again. The generator fired up and ran smoothly. This was good news to James. He then shut it off.

"A little cleaning here and there and this place would be ready for someone to move in," said Melissa.

"That was my thought," James replied.

"You going to move in?" she queried.

"I would love to," James replied, "but I don't think I can move here alone. There is just too much to take care of for one person."

Melissa paused for a minute as she stared at James. James didn't say a word.

"You scoundrel you! Did you bring me up here to try to get me to shack up with you?" Melissa asked.

"That's a little crude, don't you think, Melissa? I wouldn't have put it quite like that."

"How would you have put it?" Melissa inquired.

"You said you didn't feel comfortable staying with your parents. I don't feel good about disrupting my dad's household. This place could be a good solution for both of us if we can come to some sort of agreement."

"An agreement, huh?" Melissa repeated.

Melissa walked outside and was quiet for a few minutes. James followed.

"Let's walk down to the river," she said and strolled in that direction. James didn't say a word, but followed. There was a small pier with a couple chairs on the deck and Melissa sat down in one of them. James stood for a minute and then sat in the second chair. He just watched her as he could tell she was thinking about the proposition. *James is a good looking guy*, she thought, *and he seems nice enough. If he was bad, I could just tell his dad and he would deal with him.* She could not think of any reasons why this wouldn't work. There would need to be some rules though.

Melissa finally turned to James and looked him in the eyes. He started to say something, but she stopped him, putting her hand over his mouth. James kept quiet and patiently waited for Melissa to say something—anything. *My, she has beautiful blue eyes!* James hoped he wasn't drooling. Melissa started to speak but stopped herself and continued to stare at James.

Finally, Melissa said, "There must be strict rules. If you violate the rules, there will be severe consequences."

"Of course," James replied.

Nothing more to do here, James and Melissa headed back upstream. Melissa told James the relationship would be platonic. They would work for their mutual benefit, James doing all the heavy work. She would take care of what she was physically able to do. They would maintain separate bedrooms and share the bathroom. They would respect each other's privacy and any interaction would be as if they were brother and sister, only hopefully without the sibling squabbles.

By the time they reached the Lindgren place, they had worked out a plan.

"When do we get started?" James asked.

"I'll inform my parents tonight and I'll be back here first thing in the morning," Melissa replied.

"You can't go home and back alone," James said.

"I've been taking care of myself for a long time," Melissa replied. "I'll be just fine."

James let out a big wolf howl and when his dad came out, Melissa continued on toward her parent's place while James headed up to the porch.

"Where is she going?" Lars asked.

"She's headed home," James replied, "but she'll be back in the morning."

"She shouldn't be traveling alone," Lars said.

"I told her that, but she said she would be alright," James replied. "We are going to move into the Weston place tomorrow," James informed his dad.

James and his dad went inside to find Eileen working on her painting. James walked over.

"You have really done an excellent job capturing my dad," he said.

"Thank you, I think so," Eileen replied.

"Melissa and I are going to move into the Weston place tomorrow."

"Oh!" Eileen said, turning toward James.

"Yes, she will be back here in the morning and we will head on over immediately."

"Something going on between you two?" Lars asked.

"No," James replied. "She doesn't feel comfortable staying with her parents and I am not comfortable disturbing your household. This will be a purely platonic relationship for our mutual benefit. That's all."

"Is there anything we can do?" Lars asked.

"I don't think so," James replied. "I think we need to do this ourselves. If I do think of something, though, I know where you live."

"Yes, you do, son," Lars said with a smile.

"I wish you guys luck," said Eileen, giving James a kiss on the cheek.

"Do you have any gas in your motorcycle?" Lars inquired.

"Yes, some," James replied. "At least enough to get to the Weston place. There is gas in their tractor and truck, but I guess I'll be learning to use my feet a lot more like you have. The gas is more important for the tractor."

Lars smiled.

"Oh, I put some gas in the generator and it runs good," James added.

"How about something to eat?" Eileen asked.

"A bite to eat would be good," James replied.

"Let's have an early dinner then," she said.

Lars agreed and they all got busy preparing dinner, James helping as well. As they worked on dinner, Lars told James where he had hidden the Weston's rifles, and then went into the bedroom to retrieve a few boxes of ammunition, as he had confiscated it all.

"Thanks," James said.

When dinner was ready, they sat and talked while they ate. When they finished eating, they again all helped with washing the dishes and cleaning up the mess they made. Then, each with a glass of tea, they retired to the sofa and recliner and continued their conversation. Lars reminded James of the demise of Ron and Sara and that it was not a good idea for him to stray too far from Melissa, and visa versa. "Safety has to be a top priority," he stated. He had not told James before that Sara was tortured and raped, but included this additional information now in their conversation, hoping the severity of her fate would drive home the importance of their need to always be concerned for their safety and security.

It had been a long day for James and tomorrow would be a much longer day, so James decided he wanted to retire early. Lars and Eileen agreed and they all went to bed early.

Melissa arrived home an hour or so before dark and gave a loud, though quite feminine, wolf howl before entering the meadow. Seeing her dad come to the door and hearing him immediately return the call, she proceeded to the house. She noticed her dad always seemed to have a rifle in his hands when he came to the door.

Reggie was a bit upset she was alone. "It's not safe for you to be out alone," he scolded.

"I had no choice," she replied.

"Well, come on in," he instructed.

"I'm going to be staying at the Weston place starting tomorrow," she blurted out.

Emily was in the kitchen, but she heard and came over. "You're what?" she questioned.

"James and I are going to clean up the Weston place tomorrow and that is where we will live."

"You don't even know James," Emily said.

"I know, but he is a nice guy and he does come from good stock," Melissa said.

Reggie could not deny this.

"I can't stay here," Melissa added.

"So you're leaving again," Reggie let slip out.

"Maybe so," Melissa replied, "but at least you'll know where I am. You can check up on me anytime you want," Melissa added, though she was hurt by her dad's accusation. "The decision has been made," Melissa asserted, "and I'll be leaving early in the morning. There is nothing to discuss."

"Can we at least escort you to the Lindgrens?" Reggie asked.

"Of course," Melissa replied.

Reggie left and went out back to his bunker to retrieve a couple volleyballs and took them into the house. "You'll be needing these," he said.

"Explosives?"

"Yes," Reggie said.

"How about something to eat?" Emily asked.

"No, I'm fine. I think I'll just go to bed. Tomorrow is going to be a long day." She kissed her mom and dad good night and retired to her bedroom.

They were all up very early the next morning; a fresh norther having blown in during the night. Lars peeked outside and then stepped out to take a look around. *Well, at least it's dry*, he thought. Lars rolled a cigar and sat on the porch a bit while he finished his smoke, then went back inside. Eileen had coffee ready. After a cup of coffee, James packed a few items in the saddlebags on his motorcycle. It wasn't long before Lars heard a familiar wolf howl, and after grabbing his rifle, he walked onto the front porch and returned the howl. Then he saw Melissa and Emily coming out of the woods with Reggie in tow.

After the greetings were exchanged, Reggie went to James and handed him the two volleyballs he brought, telling him how to use them. "The main road into the place in a large tree will be a good place," Reggie said. He also told him not to drop them as this could shatter his plans, along with every bone in his body.

"I can attest to the effectiveness of those things," Lars added.

James took the balls and tied them securely to the handlebars of his motor-cycle. "I think we're ready," James said, and climbed onto the bike. He steadied the bike while Melissa crawled on, then cranked the motor.

"Don't be a stranger around here," Lars added, and they were off.

Melissa held James tightly around the waist as they worked their way down the trail to the Weston place. James thought it felt good to be held tightly, though he knew there was not an ounce of emotion in her clinch. Though the trail was a bit rough, the motorcycle made the trip much shorter. It was no time at all before they reached the homestead. James stopped for a minute at the edge of the meadow and gunned his motor a couple times, then watched the house and perimeter. Seeing no sign of life, he then proceeded to the house. James pulled around to the rear and parked the bike next to the barn. He and Melissa went inside through the back door. The cycle was too loud to have a decent conversation on the trip over, but as soon as they went into the house, Melissa reminded James there were no man's chores and no woman's chores. As long as you are physically capable of doing something, it is your job. This includes all kitchen chores. James acknowledged and agreed.

James suggested they each name a task as top priority, then they would choose between the two as their first job. Then they would do this with the remainder of the chores. Melissa agreed. James named cleaning the house, bedrooms first. Melissa said, "I need to pee." Peeing wasn't a chore but won two votes. James said he would go off the front porch while Melissa went into the bathroom. James returned to the living room and when Melissa returned, James named cleaning again. Melissa named starting a fire in the fireplace. The fireplace won two votes again. When they finished with the fire and the house began to warm up a bit, they both decided on cleaning. They chose to do the living area first and opened the room doors to allow the remainder of the house to warm.

"So far, so good," Melissa said.

"Seems like we work pretty well together," James said.

Melissa agreed.

It was mid-afternoon before the bedrooms were finished and they voted to take a little break and have some tea. Melissa said she would make the tea, if James would get the glasses and check if there was ice or a way to make ice. There was no ice and no way James could find to make it.

They voted again after the break and decided to take an inventory of all their assets. James agreed to check outside items while Melissa went through the inside. James went outside and took a look at the water heater, which seemed to be in good shape. Then he stood back to check the solar array on the roof. There were a dozen large panels, which was more than his dad had, so he assumed they were sufficient. James then found the woodshed to be nearly full. He checked the root cellar where he found a few vegetables, but not in abundance. The good news was there was about fifty pounds of potatoes. The smokehouse was alongside the wood shed and contained one ham, six fish, and two rabbits. The fish and rabbits looked like they should be thrown out and the ham was probably still good, but some would need to be trimmed off and thrown out. *The ham will not last long*, James thought.

James went back inside and gave Melissa a full report. Melissa reported an abundance of tea and coffee plus numerous spices, particularly salt and black pepper. Melissa also reported a large bag of beans and another of rice, several jars of honey, lots of corn meal, a huge sack of dried fruit and a half dozen jars each of corn, beets and okra. As far as liquids, there were several jugs of soap and three bottles of white vinegar. Melissa also reported plenty of bed clothes and bath towels.

"Seems like we're in pretty good shape," James said, "with the exception of meat. One deer will remedy this shortfall."

James had forgotten about the volleyballs and chose this as the next priority. Melissa agreed, but James could do this alone, so Melissa said she would start dinner if he would hang the balls.

"I'm on my way," James said as he went out the back door to the balls hanging on his bike. He hung one ball near the main trail and another near the river. On the return trip, James remembered the guns in the woodshed and brought them in as well. Then he went back once more to retrieve some items from his saddlebags, particularly the ammunition.

When James returned to the house, dinner was already smelling good. He walked over to see what they were having and asked how long it would be and if he could help. Melissa instructed him to fix more tea and set the table, which James did promptly. Having a little more time before the meal was ready and receiving no more instructions from Melissa, James made a couple trips to the woodshed for wood. He then stoked the fire. When he finished, Melissa called him over to the table.

"We have worked one day," said Melissa, "and look what we have accomplished. You are terrific."

"You were just as good and I truly cannot believe how hard you worked today," James replied, "and this meal; excellent!"

"Thank you," Melissa said.

"Tomorrow I think we should check out the barn for more assets," James suggested. "Tomorrow morning is going to be really cold due to the norther, so maybe I should go deer hunting first thing," James added.

"Two good suggestions," Melissa said. "Shall I go hunting with you in the morning?"

"No, stay in and stay warm. I won't stray far, just outside the tree line but where I can still see the house," James said. "When I get back, we can check out the barn. Or if you want to venture out on your own, feel free to do so," he added.

"Sounds like we have a plan," Melissa said.

"Yes, we do," James said with a smile.

James was up early the next morning, but after a couple hours he had no luck with the deer. He did see a few doe and yearlings, but no bucks. *At least there are deer here*, he thought.

When he got back, he found Melissa had been cleaning a little more in the house and had kept the fire well stoked in the fireplace. James and Melissa walked out to the barn and they found pretty much what they expected. There were all kinds of building materials and tools, a nice workbench, and a lot of stuff stuck up in the rafters like pipe and wire. As they worked their way to the rear of the building, they found a storage vault which appeared to be fifteen feet by fifteen feet. The vault was locked with a very heavy lock and hasp. They had no idea where the key might be.

They both stood back and looked around. James said, "Look for some drawers, ledges or nails where it might be likely someone would hide a key." They looked up, down, and around and checked many places but could not find a key. They finally decided to go inside the house and maybe one of their dads could help them out.

Inside, they prepared lunch and warmed up. James stoked the fire again while Melissa worked on lunch.

"Is there any salt pork in the smokehouse?" Melissa asked.

He didn't know but said he would go check. James ran outside and back, but informed Melissa there was none. She then sent him back out for a chunk of the ham. "The fatty stuff," she said, as she wanted to put it into a pot of beans. James brought the ham back and she started the beans. She then served up some potatoes and pickled okra for lunch.

James heard a wolf howl and headed to the front door, stepped out and returned the howl. He was surprised to see his dad and Eileen coming out of the woods. "I'm really surprised to see you guys so soon," James said. "Come on inside; its cold out here."

They went inside and Eileen gave Melissa a big hug and handed her a package.

"What do we have here?" she said.

"Open it up and see."

Melissa opened the package to find three links of sausage and some bacon.

Melissa gave her a big hug and thank you and turned to Lars and thanked him as well. "We seem to have a lot of food but are short on meat. This will really come in handy until we can get a deer."

"Well, how are you two lovebirds doing?" Lars asked. "Looks like you guys got the place cleaned up really nicely," he added before they had time to answer the question.

Melissa looked at Lars and said, "We are not lovebirds—I am a lesbian and we will not be lovebirds." James looked at her with a surprised look, as did Lars. She wasn't a lesbian, but *they don't need to know that,* she thought. The room did get really quiet though.

A lesbian, James thought. *I don't think I've met a lesbian before, but how can you tell. A hot gal like Melissa and she's a lesbian! Just my luck.*

"Tea or coffee?" Melissa inquired.

"Tea will be fine," Lars said.

"Hot or cold?"

"Hot will be fine," Lars replied. "Assuming you don't have ice."

"Your assumption is correct," said Melissa as she put on a fresh pot of tea.

Lars said they couldn't stay long; they just wanted to see if they were getting along and to bring them a house warming gift. James asked his dad to take a look at the lock in the barn and the men went outside. Lars told James the lock would be impossible to pick and the best thing to do would be to wait and see if they could find the key. If not, it could be cut and then replaced with another lock, if there was one around. Or maybe Melissa's dad would have one. The men went back inside and drank a mug of hot tea, after which Lars said they better get headed back home.

"It was good to see you guys," Eileen said. They exchanged hugs and kisses, and then Lars and Eileen headed back home.

When they were saying their goodbyes, James noticed the bones again. He meant to do something about them but had been too busy and forgot about them. He asked Melissa if it would be alright with her if he put the skulls on some sticks around the place. He knew it would be a little horrific, but it just might deter intruders. He said he would put them around the tree line and they would not be overly visible from the house. James having explained this, Melissa agreed and went back into the house.

James gathered the skulls and took them into the barn. He found a can of paint, a small paint brush and a couple of scraps of plywood, and then painted a little sign to hang under each skull. He wrote: *Go away or end up on a stick* on one; *Trespasser's Fate* on the second; and *Death awaits you here* on the third. He then found an axe in the barn and went out to the tree line. He put one near both of the locations where the volleyballs were placed and the third near the trail to his dad's house. Having completed this task, James went back to the barn and exchanged the axe for a shovel, which he used to bury the remaining bones and shredded clothes. It was nearly dark when he completed the work, returned the shovel to the barn and went inside.

When he got in, Melissa already had dinner ready. After dinner, James took his shower and then drank another glass of tea while Melissa took her shower. When she returned to the room, they relaxed and discussed the day and their plans for tomorrow. Having no more to say, they secured the doors and went to bed.

Chapter 25

On the trip home, Eileen mentioned that James and Melissa made a good couple. "It's too bad she's a lesbian. Maybe she will come around after a while if she and James have enough in common and they get along well. It's hard to be a lesbian when there are no women around."

Lars didn't say much. He really didn't have anything to say on the subject and had a difficult time understanding lesbianism. After a while, not getting much of a response from Lars, Eileen dropped the subject. When Lars and Eileen got back home, they had just enough time to fix dinner and relax a little bit before showering and going to bed. The cooler weather made Eileen a little frisky again and Lars was ready to oblige.

A week went by and Lars had not seen his son and Melissa. He assumed they must be doing well. He decided they should give the kids a little more time on their own. *They must be adjusting*, he thought. If they were not, they would have heard from them by now.

Lars approached Eileen about another visit to the Carstons. Eileen was always ready and willing to visit with Emily. They got up early in the morning and geared up before heading up to Reggie's; but there was one little change. Lars wanted to see if Buster would stay home and guard the homestead while they were gone. Lars made Buster sit and told him to stay. As they walked away, Lars continued to tell Buster to stay. After they had disappeared into the woods and they didn't see him following, Lars figured he stayed but wouldn't know for certain until they got back home.

Lars told Eileen a little more about Reggie on the trip over. He was basically crazy, which for Lars, was an easy description of Reggie. "Actually, it's difficult to explain Reggie," Lars said. "He's eccentric." Reggie was extremely smart, but he was damn peculiar if she hadn't already noticed. He hadn't been all that weird around Eileen so far, though. Maybe he was on his best behavior because she was new to the place. "After a while, you kind of get used to him being strange and don't think twice about it," Lars added. "Emily, on the other hand, is the sweetest gal you would ever want to meet. She is thoughtful and caring. She's a little on the quiet side, but you and her seem to have been getting along good so far," he told her. "You really need to see Reggie's bunker. Then maybe you can see how weird he is. But he is also a very good neighbor to have. Reggie has a lot of good points, otherwise he would not have Emily. Am I rambling on too much?" Lars asked.

"No, not at all," Eileen replied with a smile.

Having reached the Carston's, Lars signaled with a howl and after receiving a response, they headed down to the house.

When they reached the house, they exchanged hugs and went inside where Emily greeted them. Emily immediately had a lot of questions. She asked first about James and Melissa. Eileen said they hadn't seen them in a week, but they were doing fine after a couple days together. Apparently everything was okay; otherwise, they would have heard from them by now. Emily offered the choice between iced tea and hot tea. Lars chose iced tea, as did Eileen. It didn't matter how cold it was outside, Lars always preferred iced tea.

"Well, to what do we owe the honor of this visit?" Reggie asked.

"Just lucky, I guess," Lars replied with a chuckle.

They had really just wanted to get out of the house. They hadn't seen Reggie and Emily in a while and thought this was good enough an excuse to make the trip.

"Well, we're really glad you guys came," Emily said.

Lars asked if Eileen could see their bunker and Reggie led Lars and Eileen to it, with Emily following close behind. Eileen looked around in amazement at all the stored stuff, but she was equally amazed at the construction of the bunker and the tunnel. The place looked like a bomb shelter. The bunker was neatly organized and every square inch was utilized. Eileen was really impressed with the emergency food stock. It was impressive, but after only a few minutes, Eileen had seen all she needed to see and lost interest.

Eileen and Emily went back into the house and left the guys to their man talk in the bunker.

"I guess you can't really appreciate a bunker like this without a full load of testosterone," Lars said.

"Yeah, Emily's the same way. She appreciates the bunker, but to her, most of my toys are a waste of space."

"Nonsense," Lars added.

"That's what I told her," Reggie said. "These are all basic necessities."

Lars asked Reggie about the state of the nation which was customary every time he came to visit. Reggie informed him he lost touch with several more of his radio buddies and assumed they had been killed. "They're dropping like flies. It seems the country has not improved, but the decline has leveled out a bit. The population in all the large cities is down anywhere from sixty to ninety percent," Reggie said.

The people who survived were well stocked prepper groups, gangs, and vigilante groups, which were formed for their common good after the grid shut down. Most people had no stored food, no guns and no plan. Millions froze to death up north, starved or were killed in robberies. They didn't last long. It seems country people fared much better, especially those who lived farther away from the big cities. Marauders got a lot of the people on the outskirts of the cities, but a little farther out they were fairly safe due to the lack of gasoline. "Country boys can survive, right Lars?" he said.

"Yes, sir," Lars said. "Few will starve to death. If they die, it will be much like the Westons," Lars added.

Ronald and Sara Weston were well prepared and they had weapons and ammunition, but died because they were caught off guard by their intruders. Lars and Reggie were always on their guard. They hoped James and Melissa would learn the same lesson from the Weston's fate. No one can be on guard all the time, but they did the best they could. Lars was glad they had Buster.

"I'm going to miss some of my buddies on the radio," Reggie said. "We'd gotten to be good friends over the years."

"I'm sure," Lars responded.

"The rest, the world is much better off without them," Reggie added.

Lars didn't say anything. It appeared Reggie was going to get off on one of his rants.

"You know, Lars," Reggie continued, "the only creature on this planet that has no purpose is man. Every other animal has a reason for being here. The world would be much better off if man did not exist."

"You're probably right, but I'm glad we're here," Lars said.

"Me too, but these days there are way too many people. Well, there were anyway. Man infests and destroys!" Reggie exclaimed.

Lars could see Reggie was getting all worked up as he always did.

"We need to go over and take out the Tuckers and Gómezes," Reggie declared.

After a short pause, Lars changed the subject. Lars told Reggie about the lock on the storeroom that James and Melissa could not get into. Reggie suggested cutting the lock and gave Lars a replacement to give to them on their next visit. Lars said they would see the kids next week, and if they hadn't found a key by then, he would pass the instructions along as well as the new lock and key. Reggie and Lars finally finished their talk and returned to the house to visit with Eileen and Emily.

Eileen and Lars stayed long enough for another glass of tea and then shared hugs and farewells before making their way back home. Eileen and Lars talked more about Reggie's bunker on the trip home, or more correctly, Lars talked about Reggie's bunker. Reggie seemed to have every conceivable need covered as he meticulously gathered and stored items in his bunker. All the way down to the construction of the bunker, Reggie had a well laid plan. "He had to be a little crazy to come up with and implement his plan," Lars said, "but was this crazy, or was it smart?" It really didn't matter; he and Emily were relatively safe and secure.

"If anything was crazy," Eileen said, "it is what I did when I left San Antonio."

Lars didn't comment.

When they reached the edge of their meadow, Lars gave out a big wolf howl and to his surprise Buster jumped up from the front porch and ran to Lars and Eileen. Buster sat at their feet, his tail wagging, awaiting a treat. Lars had taken a few chunks of smoked fish in his pocket at the outside chance Buster performed as Lars hoped, which he then took out of his pocket and fed him along with a good scratching and some gentle words of approval.

Lars and Eileen made their way to the house. Lars picked up a stick and gave it a toss. Buster immediately took off after the stick. He brought it back and Lars took it from his mouth and gave him another treat and a scratch on the back. Buster ran around a bit and barked a couple times. He was getting more used to his new home every day and was getting more playful.

Eileen knelt down and Buster immediately came to her. She scratched his belly and Buster gave her a lick in the face. Lars didn't like Buster licking him in the face, but Eileen loved it. "A dog's mouth is cleaner than yours," she said.

"I don't care," Lars said, "I don't like it. You can let him lick you in the mouth, but don't come kissing on me afterward."

"I won't," Eileen promised.

Lars liked Buster almost as much as Eileen did, just not the face licking. After all, he would most definitely save their lives one day if he had not already done so without their knowing it.

Meanwhile, back at the Weston homestead, James and Melissa not only survived two weeks together, they thrived. The house and grounds were clean and the two were getting along very well. They had interesting and lively conversations, mostly about their pasts but also about their future. They were developing a plan for their mutual survival and happiness. They both worked very hard and their hard work paid off.

One evening, James and Melissa finished dinner and were relaxing on the sofa discussing their daily accomplishments and plans for the following day. James had worked hard physically that day hauling rocks to the house. His dad told him about the lack of rain the past couple years and how it affected his garden. James decided to build a storage tank to catch water to irrigate his garden, having found some mortar mix in the barn and plenty of plastic pipe for the task. Planting season would be here soon. The cistern collected water from the rear of the roof, but the rain off the front side of the roof went to waste. Their garden was not nearly as large as his dad's, so in order to produce enough food for himself and Melissa, they would need a good harvest; for this, adequate water was essential.

James went into the bathroom to take his shower. He was tired and wanted to go to bed early. James got into the shower and had finished washing his hair when Melissa pulled the shower curtain back and got into the shower behind James. She told him to not turn around. Melissa grabbed the soap and began to wash James' body, rubbing her breasts against his back. James began to feel an erection coming and when Melissa began to clean his manhood, he became incredibly hard. James reached around to touch Melissa, but she cautioned him not to do this and he stopped. Melissa asked James to rinse and forced him out of the shower, telling him to dry and go to his bed. James followed her instructions to the letter. Melissa cleaned herself and then turned the water off and stepped out to dry herself.

Melissa peeked around the corner to see if James followed her instructions, which he had. James was in bed facing the other direction, only his head out of the covers. Melissa walked into James' bedroom and crawled under the covers, snuggling up to James' backside. She reached around him and began to fondle his manhood, which jumped to its full hardness. "Alright, big boy, it's your turn," Melissa whispered into James' ear.

James turned over and climbed on top of Melissa.

"Be gentle," she said and James kissed her voluptuous breasts as he teased her tenderness with his manhood. It didn't take long until he could feel her wetness and he gently slipped inside her. She felt so warm and soft and her breasts tasted better than honey. James pressed hard onto Melissa's tenderness as he thrust deep inside her and she burst into climax quickly. James followed suit quickly as well, having had pent up energy which had been stored for longer than he could remember. James' orgasm was strong and seemed to last for minutes, though it was actually only seconds, as he emptied his reservoir completely into Melissa. After a few moments, Melissa said, "This is your reward for all your hard work and not pestering me with your sexual needs." Melissa then climbed out of bed and went back to her own room. She went to sleep almost immediately.

James tossed and turned for nearly an hour before he could fall to sleep. Melissa's breasts were as sweet as he had imagined. Her skin was so soft, especially her tenderness, which warmed his heart as well as his body. *Are all lesbians this hot in bed?* he asked himself. If so, his view toward lesbians would definitely change. Melissa's tongue teased his mouth when they kissed and James imagined all lesbians must have wonderful tongues. *Maybe I should have dated a few more lesbians when I was younger*, he thought. Finally, James dozed off and slept better than he had in months.

The next morning over breakfast, Melissa told James not to get any ideas. They both had needs, but this did not change their living arrangement. James said he understood. He asked her about her lesbianism to which she replied, "I just thought that might help you keep your mind on the main task at hand, which it seems it has." James was ecstatic she was not a lesbian, though he did not show it. Melissa told James if he were a good boy maybe they could repeat the performance next month. The remainder of the day, James had a little vigor in his step as he worked on the storage tank. A couple hours before dark, he spotted a buck near the tree line. He sneaked inside and got his AR-15 and shot the deer from the front porch.

Chapter 26

A few days later, Eileen and Lars paid Melissa and James a visit. "Well, you guys haven't killed each other yet," Lars said with a smile.

"Actually, we are doing quite well," Melissa replied. Eileen helped Melissa prepare some tea while Lars and James chatted on the sofa.

"You guys have really cleaned this place up," Lars said.

James smiled as he told his dad about the new storage tank to irrigate the garden.

"Maybe you can help me with one when you get finished with yours," Lars said.

"Maybe so," James said.

Lars asked James if he found the key to the storage room, to which James said he had not. Lars produced the lock and key Reggie gave him to give to James. Lars said he liked what James did with the skulls and James informed him he had been diligent in keeping an eye out for intruders.

"Good," Lars said, "you just never know who might wander through."

James agreed.

"How about we go check out your storeroom?" Lars asked. Melissa and Eileen were also curious about what might be in the room and followed James and Lars out to the barn.

James found a hacksaw and began to cut on the shank of the lock. It didn't take but a few seconds to see this was a hardened lock and the men looked around to find something else to cut it with. They finally decided that inserting a pry bar into the shanks of the lock and twisting to break the lock was the only viable option. James inserted the bar and twisted one way and then the other, being careful not to damage the hasp. After several twists back and forth, it was clear the lock was not going to break. Lars found a grinder with an abrasive wheel, but they needed electricity. James went and got the generator and pulled it into the barn. The generator started easily and Lars cut the lock open. As the generator was smoking up the barn, James cut it off as soon as the task was finished. He decided the generator was best left inside if he wanted it to last and pulled it over near his motorcycle.

Lars pulled the lock out of the hasp and opened the door to reveal row after row of shelving. James and Lars walked down one aisle while Eileen and Melissa took another. They found boxes and boxes of emergency food packets down one aisle. The Westons had apparently been in cahoots with the Carstons in the accumulation of these items. There were canisters of seeds of all sorts, neatly organized and labeled. James and Lars found some pistols, holsters, a few more rifles, numerous boxes of ammunition, and several large canisters of gun powder. He also found a loader, slugs, primers, and shell casings.

The guns reminded James to tell his dad about the deer he shot a few days earlier. They now had plenty of meat in the smokehouse. Lars asked what he did with the hide. James didn't know what to do with the skin, so he buried it so it would not stink and attract varmints. Lars instructed James on the art of tanning and told him the leather would come in handy, as would good leather cordage. Lars told him the hide will still be good since the cold ground would not allow the skin to spoil for a week or more. James told him he would get an empty barrel and some ashes, which they had been dumping into the garden, and would get to tanning the hide.

Melissa found a huge supply of spices, teas, coffee, and canning jars with lids. A big find was a large plastic barrel of salt and a couple barrels of commercial fertilizer. There were more containers of vinegar, as well as pots and other utensils, obviously for canning. There were spare electric motors, electrical connectors and a wide assortment of hose, wiring, and tubing. Another important find was several large barrels of mortar mix. "Looks like we have plenty of mortar mix to build your water storage tank," James told Lars.

"Thanks, son," Lars said.

They all left the storage area very pleased with what they had found. James locked the room and then placed the key in an inconspicuous place, making certain everyone knew where it was hidden. They went back inside and Melissa poured glasses of tea all around, as they discussed the contents of the storage room further.

James instructed his dad to gather enough large rocks to construct a storage tank and to let him know when he wanted to get started on his irrigation system. "I'll be happy to help you with the project," James said. Lars said he would.

"And James," Lars said.

"Yes?" he replied.

"Reggie will be over in a couple days. Why don't you and Melissa come over? Reggie wants to discuss our intruder problems."

"I think we can do that," James replied.

"Good," Lars said, "I'll see you day after tomorrow."

Not wanting to wear out their welcome, Lars and Eileen got up and said their goodbyes, sharing hugs and kisses. He and Eileen headed back home. Lars and

Eileen were really happy James and Melissa were getting along so well, and especially with their hoard of supplies. They were certain the kids would have no trouble providing for themselves.

As soon as his dad and Eileen left, James proceeded to dig up the deer hide and began preparing the empty barrel with an ash solution. He stuffed the deer hide into the solution, poking it down into the liquid; then he placed a large rock on top of the skin to hold it down. He then covered the barrel with a piece of plywood and put a rock on top. Having finished this task, James filled the hole where the hide had been buried and went inside to join Melissa and help her with dinner.

A couple days later, Melissa and James made their way over to Lars and Eileen's. Reggie and Emily were already there and just finishing up their cups of coffee on the porch. The ladies went inside while the men made their way to the pier.

"Well, Reggie, what's up?" Lars asked.

"I've been hearing gunshots around the place," Reggie responded.

"Me too," James added.

"Yeah, I've been hearing them too," Lars said.

"We need to do something about our neighbors across the highway," Reggie asserted. "If we don't, we will never be safe around here. And they are going to kill all the deer."

"What do you have in mind?" Lars asked.

"I think we need to kill all of them," Reggie asserted.

"We can't do that," Lars replied.

"Why not?" Reggie asked.

"We just can't," Lars responded. "That's not right. We would be no better than them."

"I'm with you, Reggie," James added.

"Who's to say we have any more right to this land than anyone else?" Lars asked. "What gives us the right to murder our neighbors just because we do not see eye to eye?"

"Those son-of-a-bitches shot me without provocation. I say they die," Reggie asserted. "Now that my arm has healed, I say we go over and kill them. If we want to be safe and secure here, that is what we have to do. You know this, Lars. Maybe you don't think so, but in the back of your mind, you know this."

Lars knew Reggie was right. In the back of his mind he knew they had to get rid of their neighbors. They were nothing but trash and would always be trash. Killing someone in self-defense was one thing, but to just go out and kill someone pre-meditated was a struggle for Lars. Lars killed the Weston's murderers. He was their judge, jury, and executioner, but that was different. He had to kill them, though in the eyes of some, what he did was murder. Lars could easily justify killing these intruders in his mind, but going across the highway to judge and execute these neighbors was a stretch for Lars' conscience.

"We should have invited the Lins to this meeting," James said.

"Yes, we should have," Lars added.

"I think we need to have another meeting," Reggie said, "and we need to create a local government—a government where we can make decisions and act on those decisions."

"Are we going to legalize murder?" Lars asked.

"Dammit, Lars!" Reggie exclaimed. "We are going to create a system whereby we can protect ourselves," Reggie stated. "We are going to implement a system whereby we can survive—a system where when we are dead and gone, our families will live on."

"I want to live and I want Melissa to live," James added. "I don't want to sit around worrying about which day someone will come around and kill me and Melissa, or you and Eileen, Dad," James said. "I want this to be a peaceful valley where we can live, work, and enjoy life.

"I do too," Lars said, "but do we need to go out and kill everyone else?" Lars asked.

"I think we do," Reggie replied.

"I do too," James added.

"I'm not so sure," Lars concluded.

"If Eileen gets killed, will that change your mind?" Reggie asked. "I think it will."

"Are you going to wait until Eileen gets killed before you are willing to act?" James asked.

James and Reggie could see Lars was wrestling with his conscience. Lars would eventually come around to their point of view. They knew this, but would it be before or after Eileen or someone else got killed?

"I guess we'll have to give you a little more time to think about it," Reggie said.

"It will be planting time soon," James said. "Maybe we should have another meeting after we get our crops planted."

"Yes," Reggie stated.

"And the next meeting must include the Lins," James added.

"And the ladies," Reggie included.

"Alright then," Lars said, "let's get our crops planted and we'll have another meeting."

Chapter 27

It's hard to believe it's been two months since Christmas, Lars thought as he got up and went outside. *Finally, some warmer weather. Maybe my arthritis will quit acting up now,* he thought.

He walked back inside and gave Eileen her morning bear hug. "It's time to get the garden planted while there is good moisture," he said.

The weather had warmed and there was a more persistent wind out of the south. Lars knew it was time. Lars and Eileen gathered up their tools and seeds and ventured into the garden. Fortunately for them, there was sufficient moisture for planting. The winter rains were good to them, though this was normally the dry time of the year. This was a good start, but Lars had seen years before when the garden quickly dried out as the rains were not forthcoming during the critical time for good plant growth. Lars decided he would contact James for help with the irrigation system as soon as planting was finished.

Lars cranked up the tractor and plowed the rows. As soon as he made two passes down the garden, Eileen began planting in the freshly turned soil. Lars continued plowing for another hour. Then he returned the tractor to its proper place and walked back to the garden to help Eileen. Eileen planted beans, beets, carrots, squash, cucumbers, and cabbage, being careful not to plant the beets and carrots in the same place where the two were previously planted. Lars checked her progress and techniques. Eileen stood to stretch her back, which was aching by this time. Lars gave her a big hug and complimented her on her work. He then helped Eileen plant onions and peppers; then Lars planted some tobacco, which Eileen refused to help with. Lars understood.

Lars went to the root cellar and returned with a large basket of partly sprouting potatoes. He dumped the contents of the basket onto the ground and then began cutting the potatoes into chunks, placing the pieces back into the basket. Lars explained to Eileen that they needed to leave at least two eyes on each piece, as Eileen helped with the task.

As they cut up the potatoes, Lars began talking about Reggie and James' solution to their intruder problems. "Reggie and James want to go across the highway and murder the neighbors," he stated.

"What did you tell them?" she asked.

"I told them we couldn't do that, but they seem to think that is our only solution. The more I think about it and wrestle with the idea; I fear they may be right. I don't want to be a party to murder, but for the life of me, I can't think of another solution. What do you think?"

"You keep telling me I need to change if I want to live out here," Eileen responded. "And I have changed. In order to survive, I have changed."

"Yes you have," Lars admitted, "but must I resort to murder in order for us to live on? I just don't know."

"I'm not saying I agree with James and Reggie," Eileen continued, "but change is inevitable for all of us. The world has given us no choice."

When they finished cutting all the spuds, he directed Eileen to the area where he wanted the potatoes and he began digging the trenches with a hoe while Eileen placed the sets along the trench about a foot and a half apart. When they reached the end of each row, Lars went back and covered the sets with his hoe, while Eileen walked down the row to compact the dirt. About a quarter-way through the basket of potato sets, the two went in for lunch, but soon returned to get the task completed, which took the rest of the day. "Tomorrow, we will finish planting the potatoes," Lars said, and they retired for the evening.

The next day, after breakfast and an extra cup of coffee, Lars retrieved another basket of seed potatoes from the root cellar and cut them up as he had the day before. They then resumed the potato planting. They took their usual lunch break and then completed the planting by late afternoon. Eileen was extremely tired, not ever having worked this hard in her life, but she never complained.

The next day, they began planting the corn. Lars retrieved the corn seed from the root cellar and carried the large sack on his shoulder to the garden. He returned to the barn to get a gallon pail, which he filled with seeds from the sack. He handed it to Eileen. Lars took the hoe, as he had with planting the potatoes, and began making a trench down the middle of the first row. Eileen followed, dropping kernels of corn into the trench approximately six inches apart.

Eileen brought up the problem with the neighbors across the highway again. "I am not certain I can condone murdering our neighbors."

"Do you have another solution?" Lars asked.

"No, but I will come up with one," she replied.

"That's what I thought, but I have not thus far," Lars said.

"Well, we have to think of something," she replied.

The first row completed, Lars covered the kernels with about an inch of soil. Lars took a rake and handed it to Eileen. "If you'll tamp the soil over the seeds, I'll continue covering the row." They continued this process row after row until lunchtime. They took a break and then continued with the planting. At the end of each row, they would straighten their backs to give their muscles a short break and looked at each other. Each could see the other wrestling with the problem with the neighbors, but neither said a word.

By late afternoon, Lars could see Eileen was straining to keep up with her chore. They had planted about half the corn and Lars decided it was time to call it a day. He waited as Eileen finished tamping the row to the end. Lars took the rake and set it against the fence and then took Eileen into his arms and gave her a big hug. "I am so proud of you," he said. She managed a weak smile. "I think we can finish the remainder of the corn tomorrow," he added and they strolled to the house, both ready for a hot shower.

Eileen went into the bedroom first and began taking off her dirty and sweaty clothes. Lars followed and began undressing as Eileen went into the bathroom and turned on the water. When she got into the shower, Lars followed her in and grabbed the bar of soap and began soaping her up. Face to face, he worked the soap up and down her back, massaging her shoulders and lower back as he pressed against her breasts. He then turned her around and ran the bar up and down her front side. He lathered up his hands and began to massage her breasts, working down to her tenderness. Eileen's legs became weak when Lars reached her special place and she started to slump a bit. Lars kissed her on the neck and she turned and planted a big kiss on his lips. Eileen felt his firmness inching up between her spread legs and when it reached the end of the road, he backed up a little to let his fullness point upward. Lars then pressed into Eileen and massaged his boys against her tenderness. "Maybe we should take this into the bedroom," he said.

"Or just go for it here," Eileen said. "You seem to be ready."

Lars was ready and hard as a rock. He smiled and pulled Eileen upward while she wrapped her legs around his body. He then let her slide down onto his awaiting manhood. Lars slipped into her wetness and he began to work his magic. Eileen wriggled around as if she had done this before and it didn't take long for both of them to burst into orgasm. They then rinsed each other off, both with that stupid grin on their faces, which seemed to be so common these days. It seems neither was as tired as they let on. They then went to bed and fell asleep, forgetting they had not eaten dinner.

The next morning, Lars and Eileen returned to the garden and began where they left off the day before. The planting seemed to go a little faster and all the corn was planted by mid-afternoon. Lars suggested to Eileen that she go inside and take it easy for a while. He also complimented her on her fine work and her amazing stamina. Lars put up the gardening tools, basket, bag, and a few leftover corn seeds. He then retrieved his wheelbarrow and parked it near the front porch.

Lars then stood back from the house and peered up toward the roof. The single downspout from the gutter was on the wrong side. If he were to put his new water collection tank where he wanted, the downspout needed to be moved. Lars could see no advantage of having the tank on the side with the downspout and decided to move the spout to the opposite end.

Lars rolled the wheelbarrow around the pasture, mostly around the perimeter of the garden, gathering rocks here and there. He dumped them near the location he chose for the tank. Lars hauled several loads, but not nearly enough, so completing the task would have to wait until tomorrow as it was beginning to get dark. Lars parked the wheelbarrow near his growing pile of rocks and went inside. Eileen had dinner ready. They were both happy the planting was finished but were too tired to celebrate. Guess what they did that night? They both went to bed and got some much needed sleep.

Lars got up early the next morning and began breakfast. By the time Eileen got ready, the table was set, coffee was ready and the sausage was done. As soon as Eileen stepped through the door, Lars put the eggs on and poured Eileen a cup of coffee. He gave the eggs a stir, turned to give Eileen her morning bear hug, and then returned to the eggs. He split the eggs between the two and added equal shares of the sausage to their plates. Lars told Eileen he was going to continue to gather rocks, and then maybe after lunch they could take a walk to see James and Melissa. Lars needed some of his mortar mix and help building the tank.

"Sounds like a plan," Eileen said, and Lars walked out the front door.

Eileen was really sore and had a tough time getting out of bed. She did not let on to Lars though. She was happy that they had finished the planting, but she was equally happy that she had a few hours to relax for a while. *Damn Lars is tough*, she thought. Eileen stretched out on the sofa and started a new novel. After a couple of chapters, she got up and painted for a while.

Lars returned four hours later when his task was finished, he had piled up enough rocks to complete the tank. As Lars entered the door, Eileen made her way toward him and led him over to her painting. The cloth covering the painting was gone now. Eileen announced the painting was finished. Lars' mouth dropped open in awe. He saw the painting at Christmas and it was taking shape then, but what he saw now was magnificent. He gave her a big hug and kiss and thanked her for such a wonderful gift. Eileen could tell she did well by the tears in Lars' eyes.

The painting was of Lars standing on the front steps of their rustic wood frame home. Lars was all dressed up in his leather pants and jacket with his 30-30 across his arm. He had his coonskin cap and moccasins on as well. He was looking across his meadow with a stern look on his face. He was the perfect model of a mountain man. The house and outbuildings were shown in great detail.

Lars went to the barn to retrieve the frame, hammer, and nails. He laid the frame face down on the kitchen table and then carefully placed the painting face down onto the frame. He secured the edges of the canvas with its plywood backing to the frame with six small nails. He then attached some leather cordage to the sides of the frame. When he turned the frame upright, the painting sat perfectly in it. Eileen complimented Lars on his artwork.

"Where do you want to hang it?" Lars asked.

Eileen pointed to the partition wall between the bedroom and living room. "This way it will be visible when you walk through the front door," she added.

Eileen directed Lars to the center of the wall and Lars drove a nail. He hung the portrait and leveled the frame at Eileen's direction. They both stood back and admired each other's artwork. They turned to each other, hugged and kissed.

Lars pushed Eileen back a little and looked into her eyes. "You know, you are the most beautiful woman I have ever met, inside and out. I don't think I could live without you. I thought I might have loved you quite some time ago, but now I am positive, I love you more than life itself. I don't want you to ever leave."

"I've loved you for a while," Eileen confessed.

"Also, I'm sorry," he continued, "I should have told you this a long time ago."

"Yes you should have," she replied with a smile followed by the best kiss she could deliver. Lars did the same.

They both wiped the tears from their eyes and Eileen asked, "Do we still have time to make a quick trip to see James and Melissa?"

"Yes, we do," Lars responded, "if you are up to it."

"I made it through planting," Eileen said. "The trip should be a walk in the park, no pun intended."

"Well, let's get going," Lars said. They packed up and headed out the door. A quick whistle and Buster tagged along.

Lars and Eileen paused at the edge of the new Lindgren place and gave the signal. As they waited for the return signal, they admired how good the place looked. It was clean and had started to green up. There was an inviting column of smoke rising out of the fireplace chimney. James returned the howl and Eileen and Lars headed on over.

Eileen gave James a kiss on the cheek and then headed towards Melissa, who was waiting in the doorway. Lars informed James that he had finished gathering rocks for his water tank, and now that planting was completed, he was ready to begin construction on the tank. Lars and James headed back to the barn to retrieve a barrel of cement mortar mix. James rolled the very heavy barrel out to the barn door and asked Lars how they were going to get the barrel to his place. Lars had no plan.

Lars didn't think a truck would make it up their walking trail. They could take it up the river with the aluminum boat, but with no boat motor and the trip upstream with a moderate current, this would be a difficult task with only paddles. James said a platform to drag the load behind the motorcycle might work, but the cycle was a mid-size machine and he wasn't certain this would work either. The guys went inside to have a glass of tea and inform the ladies of their dilemma.

Eileen's solution was to divide the mortar into small buckets. They could all carry a couple buckets with about fifteen pounds per bucket—maybe a little less for the ladies and a little more for the guys. "That's 120 pounds a trip," Lars said. "This will be four roundtrips and will take all day."

James agreed, but at least the task was possible.

"We can roll the barrel all the way over," Lars suggested. The men decided this was possible as well, but also would take all day. When the men decided Eileen's solution was the best option, James and Lars went to the barn to see if they could find eight buckets.

As they were looking for the buckets, they found a couple wheels slightly larger than a bicycle tire. The guys then changed the plan. They could make a two-wheel buggy, which could easily be pulled with the motorcycle. It was getting late and they didn't have time to build the cart today, but Lars consulted with Eileen and decided they could come back tomorrow to build their cart.

"Or you guys can stay the night," Melissa suggested. "This will give you time to work on the cart this evening and you can finish it up in the morning," Melissa added.

They all agreed and James and Lars went back outside while Melissa and Eileen started dinner and prepared the guest bedroom.

James cut a three-foot length of pipe for an axle and it took a little ingenuity, but they got the wheels mounted securely. James cut two lengths of pipe for the frame and tongue and got them bent to the correct configuration, but it was now getting too dark to see what they were doing, so the guys went inside. They washed up. Melissa and Eileen had prepared a wonderful meal. Lars and James both complimented the ladies on the grub.

The next morning, Lars and James were up at sunrise. After a quick cup of coffee, they got back after their cart. A couple more hours and the cart was finished. They then loaded the barrel onto the cart. James siphoned some gas from the truck and poured it into his motorcycle. Then he cranked it up and backed it up to the cart. They fastened the cart securely to the cycle and finally they were ready to go. They went back inside and informed the ladies. Breakfast was ready and the ladies insisted they eat first. They had bacon, ham, potatoes and beets.

"Where did you get bacon?" Lars asked. "You been sneaking over to the Lins and stealing my bacon?" Lars questioned with a smile.

"Of course," James said smiling. "We needed bacon, so Melissa baked a couple fruit cobblers and we took one to the Lins to trade. You can have some of the one we kept, when you're ready."

Lars quickly cleaned his plate and Melissa scooped out a generous serving for him.

He took a bite and a big smile developed on his face. "This is absolutely delicious, Melissa."

"Thank you," she said.

Lars estimated the tank would be a two-day job, so he asked the kids to prepare to stay the night. They said they would. Everyone finished their coffee and they headed out the door.

James cranked up his cycle and ran the cycle in low gear, so the terrain would not tear up the fragile cart with its heavy load, but also so they could all make the trip together. Slowly but surely, the trip went well, and though it took just over an hour to make the trek, the mortar mix was safe and sound at the Lindgren place. The guys unloaded the barrel and began work on the storage tank.

Lars took his shovel and wheelbarrow to the river and shoveled a load of sand from the riverbank. He dumped the wheelbarrow and headed back for a second load, James following this time. James shoveled the second load and hauled it to where Lars dumped the first, and dumped some of the sand onto the first pile, but leaving about a third of the load in the wheelbarrow. Lars opened the mortar barrel and shoveled some of the hardener into the sand and mixed it a little. James retrieved a bucket of water from the well and began to pour as Lars stirred the mixture. James added water at Lars' direction and Lars stirred until he achieved the perfect cement mix. They then began laying the rocks for the bottom of the tank.

A second wheelbarrow of cement mix was prepared, and after a couple hours, the bottom was completed. The ladies called the men in for lunch and they cleaned up and went inside to eat. After lunch, the guys went back outside and continued their task. By late afternoon, the men had built a wall all the way around and three feet high. They installed a one-inch pipe at the bottom of the tank with a cutoff valve on the end. They decided to call it a day, as they could easily finish the tank by early afternoon tomorrow. The guys cleaned up again and went inside. Melissa and Eileen were just getting started on dinner and asked the guys to take a shower. Lars insisted James go first, but asked James to save him some hot water.

James and Lars were up again at daylight and immediately began working on the tank. They came in briefly for breakfast and a cup of coffee and then went straight back to work. As planned, they finished the tank just after noon. Lars was really pleased with the completed water tank, not just for the quality of the work but also for the time he spent with his son, whom he hadn't seen for so long, and the man talk they shared during the course of the project. His son had turned out to be the man he hoped for so many years ago.

Their wonderful ladies had lunch ready and again called the men in to eat. Having finished the project in good time, James suggested he and Melissa run up to see her dad to let them know they were alive and doing well. It had been a while since she last saw her parents and this was the least Melissa could do. Lars asked James to check to see if Reggie had a pail of waterproofing coating suitable for the inside of the new tank. James said he would ask.

They finished lunch and James and Melissa headed upstream immediately, Lars thanking James again for all his help. They said they wouldn't stay long and would stop back by briefly on the way home.

Emily and Reggie were happy to see the kids and to hear they were doing well. James told Reggie about the tanks he and Lars built to water their gardens and asked Reggie about the coating to seal the inside of the tanks. Reggie produced a gallon of suitable sealer from his bunker. James and Melissa then stayed only long enough to have a glass of iced tea and chit chat a bit.

Reggie asked James to tell his dad to invite the Lins over for another security meeting day after tomorrow and that he and Emily would be there early. "You and Melissa be there early too," Reggie added. James said he would inform his dad and then he and Melissa were on their way.

James and Melissa stopped by Lars and Eileen's only long enough to deliver the pail of coating and Reggie's message to Lars; then they said their goodbyes. Lars thanked his son for his help and the mortar and gave him a big hug. "I'll have a few more vegetables this year," he said, "and we'll share to pay you guys back for the labor and mortar."

James thanked Lars and Eileen for everything, gave Buster a pat on the back and he and Melissa were on their way. "We'll see you in a couple days," James added.

The following day, Lars painted the inside of his new tank with the waterproofing coating. He then got after moving the downspout and plugging the hole where he removed the spout. This was an easy task and took only an hour or so. All he needed now was some rain and to connect the irrigation lines.

Lars went inside and he and Eileen talked on the sofa for a while. Lars told her a little about the meeting they were having tomorrow and asked if she would like to accompany him to the Lins to invite them to it.

"Of course, darling," she said with a smile and gave him a little kiss.

They got up, grabbed their guns, and headed out the back door. Buster heard the door shut around back and immediately came around the corner of the house to join them, tail wagging. Lars leaned over to give Buster a pat on the back and Eileen did the same with some sweet words.

"Okay boy, you can come along," Lars said.

Lars and Eileen headed toward the river and down the bank a ways to a shallow place they could easily cross the stream. Buster stopped for a quick drink and followed on toward the Lins'.

Lars let out a big wolf howl when they reached the Lin homestead; he waited for Sam to return the howl. Sam walked onto their porch and returned the signal. Sally stepped out onto the porch as well and invited Eileen into the house while Lars and Sam stayed on the porch.

Lars informed Sam about the meeting, and then the men walked around back to the hog pen. Lars was amazed at the size of some of the hogs. The biggest had to weigh five hundred pounds, in Lars' estimation. Sam informed him it was closer to six hundred. *Wow! If I can fatten up one or two of my little piglets like that, I could make my own bacon*, Lars thought. *That is probably a little too much to ask for from wild pigs, though.* They then wandered into the workshop for a while and finally back into the house. Lars was ready to head home. Eileen showed Lars her little gift of cheese from Sally with a smile, and then the two headed home.

Reggie and Emily showed up for the meeting bright and early. James and

Melissa were not far behind and the Lins showed up a short time later. Eileen had coffee ready when Reggie and Emily showed up. By the time the Lins showed up, she had a second pot brewing.

"Everyone is here," Lars said, "so we may as well get the meeting started."

"The purpose of the meeting is to decide whether or not we will take out our neighbors across the highway," Reggie stated. "The Tucker and Gómez families continually hunt our side of the highway and the Gómezes tried to kill me and Lars. The Tuckers were unwilling to get along with us when we talked to them. We will never be safe as long as they are alive and they will jeopardize all of our major food sources, particularly deer and feral hogs."

"I have struggled with the thought of killing our neighbors ever since Reggie and I confronted them," Lars added. "I had hoped we could all get along and benefit from each other, but I have now come to the same conclusion as Reggie has," Lars added. "We cannot trust them and they will deplete the deer, hog, rabbit, and squirrel in the area. I truly believe they have been responsible for raiding our garden, though Buster has now helped in this respect. In time, I believe they will confront us to try to take food from us and someone will die. That someone may mean one of us."

"Problems are best taken care of as soon as possible," James inserted. "This problem has gone on long enough."

Eileen, Melissa, Sam, and Sally sat and listened intently. None said a word, but you could see the distress in their faces.

"I think the sooner we take care of this problem, the sooner we will be more secure around here," Reggie said.

"We'll let you guys think about it for a bit," Lars said. "There are some other things we need to talk about. We need a name for our little community. I think *Peaceful Valley* would be a fine name for this place, though it has been anything but peaceful around here for some time. I hope we can change that though."

"There are eight adults and each should have an equal vote," Reggie added.

"I agree," said Eileen.

Everyone else voiced their concurrence.

"Shall we take a vote on the name?" James asked and held up his hand.

Everyone raised their hands.

"Then it's settled," Reggie said, "*Peaceful Valley* it is."

"Shall we take a vote on the fate of our neighbors across the highway?" James asked.

Reggie and James immediately held up their hands. After a short pause, Lars also held up his hand.

"I cannot be a part to murder," Sam stated.

Sally agreed. "I don't care what you say, I cannot be a part of killing them,"

Sally said.

"Okay, what about you Emily?" Reggie asked.

"I love you Reggie and I'm sorry, but I cannot vote with you," Emily replied.

"That's your prerogative," Reggie said. "Melissa?"

"While I don't totally agree with you," Melissa said, "I don't feel safe here. I have to vote with you," and she raised her hand in the affirmative.

Everyone looked toward Eileen. She would be the deciding vote. If she were to vote 'no', they would be at a stalemate.

"Why do I have to be the deciding vote, dammit?" Eileen exclaimed, tears forming in her eyes.

"Just lucky I guess," Lars said, unable to stop himself from blurting out.

Eileen glared at Lars with tears beginning to flow freely.

"I'm sorry, darlin'," Lars said. "Tough decisions must be made out here."

"I could use a *cafe latte* about now," Eileen said.

"Me too," Emily concurred.

"I just meant that we are on our own out here," Lars added. "There is no one to help us. If we do not help ourselves, then we are doomed. We may not like a lot of the things we need to do, but to do nothing is not an option."

"But must we become animals?" Eileen queried.

"If we are to survive," Reggie inserted, "we may not have a choice."

"Are we going to live, or are we going to die?" James added.

"Will you hate me if I vote *no*, Lars?" Eileen asked.

"No baby," Lars answered. "Your vote is yours to make. I don't want to kill our neighbors either and I have struggled with that for a long time now, but I believe our safety and security are at stake. That is why I voted how I did."

"Will you hold me tight and love me when I wake up in the middle of the night crying and screaming about what we did?" Eileen asked.

"Of course I will," Lars answered.

"Then I vote *yes*," Eileen said raising her hand; then she immediately broke down and started bawling.

Lars gave Eileen a big hug and kissed her wet and salty lips. Lars held on to Eileen for a couple minutes before she could compose herself.

"Sam, will you watch over the ladies?" Reggie asked.

Sam and Sally were whispering back and forth. "I'm sorry Reggie, but Sally and I cannot be a party to murder," he responded.

"We voted and you **are** a part of it," Reggie stated.

"The hell we are!" Sam exclaimed and got up. Sally got up as well. "You do whatever you have to do," he said in a raised voice, "but we're going home." And with that, he and Sally got up, grabbed the kids and headed home.

"Kiss my ass!" Reggie yelled as they headed toward the river.

"Well," Lars said, "what are we going to do now?"

"We will be alright by ourselves," Eileen said.

"You sure?" Lars asked.

"Yes," Melissa said. "We can take care of ourselves."

"Okay then, we'll leave here just before dark this evening," Lars added. "We may not be back before daylight."

"That's not a problem," Eileen said.

"Sounds like a plan to me," Reggie said.

Chapter 28

"We'd best get started," Lars said.

Reggie, Lars, and James began preparations for their assault. They began by preparing the truck for the trip. Reggie and James ran over to Reggie's place for a few rocket propelled grenades (RPGs), on which Reggie gave James some additional instructions. Reggie also picked up some night vision goggles and laser sights for each of their rifles, flak jackets and a machine gun for Lars.

Reggie and James returned to Lars' by lunchtime. The men ate a hearty lunch, which Eileen, Emily, and Melissa had prepared while the men were busy. After lunch, the men went back out to the porch to continue their preparations.

They added the laser sights to the guns and went around back to practice and verify the sights. Satisfied, the men returned to the porch to clean and reload the guns.

The ladies did not want to be involved in any of their plans or discussions. They wanted to distance themselves from any talk about what was to happen this evening. But, they could not entirely avoid discussing the impending mayhem. Their major concern and topic of discussion, however, was about the safety of their men.

By mid-afternoon, the men had finished their preparations and worked out their plan of attack. The plan was simple and straightforward. They would take out the Tuckers first and then the Gómez clan. James would hit the house with a couple of RPGs while Lars and Reggie took positions where they could see anyone trying to escape out of the back of the house, Lars on one side of the building and Reggie on the other. The attack would begin after dark but before the men went to bed. They would all likely be in the living area and maybe the RPGs would take all of them out.

About an hour before dark, the men headed for the highway. They reached the road to the Tuckers' at dark. Lars drove about a third of the way to the house and the men got out and geared up. They walked the remainder of the way. The night vision goggles made the trip easy. James took his position while Lars and Reggie made their way to opposite sides of the house and got ready.

The lights were on inside the house and James could see some shadows of the men moving around inside through the windows. James sighted on the left window and fired. There was a huge explosion. All the windows were blown out and the interior of the house immediately burst into flames. James reloaded and fired a second shell into the right window. Again there was a big explosion and the interior of the house became engulfed in flames. James laid the RPG launcher down and aimed his rifle at the house. Lars and Reggie had their guns aimed as well, waiting for a target to exit the building.

After fifteen minutes, the house was totally consumed by the fire and began to crumble. No one exited the house, there were no screams and everyone was dead. The shock of the initial explosion had likely killed everyone inside. Reggie and Lars joined James and they watched the house burn for another thirty minutes. Satisfied no one escaped and no one would escape, the men headed back to their truck while the house continued to burn.

Lars cranked the truck up and they headed toward the highway. They made their way to the road leading to the Gómez homestead, drove a ways down the dirt road and parked. The men again donned their night vision goggles and headed toward the Gómez house.

James took up his position, just as he had at the Tuckers', while Reggie and Lars took similar positions as before. Just like at the Tucker house, James could see lights inside and shadows from the occupants inside the building. James aimed and fired. The inside of the house burst into flames just as before at the Tuckers'. James fired another RPG into the house with the same effect.

As the house began to burn, Lars spotted someone at the back of the house. He had come out of the outhouse crapper when James blew up the main house. As he turned his gun in that direction, Lars could see the red laser line shine across the man's body. Lars steadied the light on his chest and squeezed the trigger. The machine gun launched a volley of slugs into the man and Lars could see the bullets tearing at the man's clothing. The man crumpled and fell face down into the dirt. The main house was totally consumed by flames a short while later, and Lars and Reggie joined James at his position. They watched for thirty minutes and satisfied their task was complete, the men headed back to the truck.

Lars started up the truck and headed back to the Tucker's, this time driving all the way to the house. As the men pulled up to what was left of the structure, all seemed quiet. All that remained was a smoldering pile of ash and embers. The men got out and began examining the remains. They found four black charred bodies. The destruction was total and their task here was complete.

The men got back into the truck and headed back over to the Gómezes house. By the time the men arrived, the house had burned to the ground. Lars walked over to where the man lay at the back of the house. He poked the body with the end of his gun. The man was dead. Lars could see six exit wounds on the man's back and his gray shirt was soaked with blood.

Lars walked over to where James and Reggie were poking around in the ashes of the main house. They found five charred and smoldering bodies.

"There are supposed to be only four bodies," Reggie stated.

"We have six bodies, including two women and a baby" Lars added. "Where do you suppose they came from?"

"I don't know" Reggie replied, "but I bet we got the bastard that shot me."

"Likely," Lars added, "but we killed some innocent people."

"Innocent my ass!" Reggie exclaimed.

"Yes, innocent," Lars said. "The baby was innocent for certain."

"Sometimes collateral damage happens," James said.

"Collateral damage?" Lars questioned. "This is a baby!"

There was nothing that could be done now. What happened couldn't be helped. They all knew this, but Lars was definitely going to have some problems with his conscience in the coming days.

"We better not tell the ladies about the baby for a while," James said. They all agreed.

Reggie raised his AR-15 and pointed at one of the bodies. He squeezed the trigger four or five times, and then pointed at another body and squeezed off a few more rounds.

"What the hell are you doing?" James asked.

"I can't go on a raid and not fire a shot," Reggie replied.

James and Lars chuckled.

"Well, men, I think our work is done here," Lars said.

"Yes, it is," Reggie replied.

"Yes, sir," James said.

The men got back into the truck and headed home. As they pulled up to the house, Lars honked his horn. The men got out of the truck and Lars saw Eileen on the porch alert with her rifle across her lap. She got up as Lars made his way up the steps. Emily and Melissa came out onto the porch as well.

"You're back early," Eileen stated. "Did everything go alright?"

"Yes," Lars replied.

"Those RPG's really pack a wallop," James said. "They didn't know what hit them."

"One did," Lars said, reminding them of the guy in the outhouse.

Lars gave Eileen a big hug. Reggie and James also hugged and kissed their ladies. The girls were happy to see their men back home safe and sound. Eileen went back inside and retrieved some snacks, and a pot of coffee and cups for Lars, James, and Reggie. They then sat on the porch and sipped their drinks and ate while they discussed the trip in detail. It would be a couple hours before it got light enough for the neighbors to go home. When they finished their second pot of coffee, the eastern sky began to lighten up. Their adrenalin levels were now dropping and they were getting tired. Everyone got up and got ready to head home.

"I'm definitely going to need a nap today," Reggie said.

"Me too," James stated.

"Well, good friends and neighbors," Lars said, "we'll talk in a few days. You guys get rested and then let's have another meeting."

"Okay," Reggie said.

"See you in a few days," James added.

Hugs and kisses were exchanged and everyone headed home. Lars gave Eileen a big bear hug and wet kiss before heading for the recliner. He was fast asleep in minutes. Eileen sat and read while she kept a sharp eye out of the window, and she took a stroll on the porch occasionally. She also gave Buster a loving pat on the back each time she went outside.

The next several days there was a persistent light rain and Lars caught up on his sleep. When the sun finally emerged, it came out bright and warmed up the crisp air to a comfortable temperature. The rain only put a few inches in Lars' new storage tank, but the light rain was very beneficial for the spring garden; the potatoes, corn, and other vegetables Lars and Eileen planted, came up quickly and grew like weeds. Lars and Eileen had worked hard on their plot and as a result the garden flourished. Lars completed their new irrigation system and though the root cellar was nearly empty, this would change soon and the smokehouse was already well supplied. The new crops destined for the root cellar would not be in for another couple of months. The current crops would be out of the root cellar in a week. This would give Lars plenty of time to rebuild the new and bigger root cellar, but for the next month or so—other than tending to the crops—there would be little to do. Lars suggested they just relax for a while and enjoy each other's company and do some of the things they liked to do. Among these, walking in the woods and visiting the neighbors. Lars struggled with killing a baby and this bothered him every day. Eileen was struggling with the ordeal too, and Lars never told her about the child. Their leisurely walks and trips to the neighbors helped. Time would heal their wounds. Lars also thought about the Lins and wondered if he had lost his source of bacon.

Lars had been hearing a few turkeys in the woods and told Eileen if he could get a big tom, maybe they could have another feast with turkey and dressing. They didn't have much of a Thanksgiving, and though it was now springtime, maybe this would be a good time to celebrate the holiday.

Eileen agreed wholeheartedly.

The families had another meeting, but the only thing they decided was to have another meeting. The Lins showed up, but were quiet and distant from the rest. They were certainly safer now with the neighbors across the highway gone, but there were still serious challenges to be met and foes to be dealt with. They all felt more secure now, but no one could let their guards down. To do so could be deadly. No matter what they did to increase their safety, they would need to stay on guard the rest of their lives.

The next few days, instead of carrying his trusty 30-30, Lars carried his twelve-gauge shotgun with buckshot. He and Eileen took morning and late afternoon walks every day but they failed to bag a turkey. They heard a few but were unable to sneak up on them. Lars wasn't concerned though. Persistence always pays off and Lars was persistent. Lars also carried some bird shot for his shotgun and one day was able to bag five white-wing doves. Lars roasted the birds over an open fire. Eileen had never eaten dove before but was very pleased with the taste of the birds and insisted that they have them more often.

The following week, Lars awoke early one morning to the sound of a turkey gobbling nearby. Lars dressed quickly as he kept his ears tuned to the sound of the bird. He grabbed his shotgun and peered through the windows. He spotted the turkey between the house and barn. He sneaked out the front door, eased over to the end of the porch and peeked around the corner. He leveled his gun, took bead on the turkey and fired. The turkey flounced around a little and then lay still. Buster heard the shot and came running out of the woods near the trail to Reggie's place. He ran up to Lars, then noticed the turkey and walked over and took a sniff of the bird.

Lars went over and picked the turkey up and walked back over to the door. The shot got Eileen up quickly and she was pleasantly surprised to see Lars standing in the doorway with a big tom turkey.

He walked all over the woods with Eileen and no turkey, and then the feast shows up on his doorstep. You just never know how things are going to turn out.

"Guess we need to send out invitations," she said.

"Yes, ma'am," Lars replied. "Let me get this bird cleaned up and we'll make a round to the neighbors," he said.

"I'll be ready soon," Eileen replied.

Lars cleaned the turkey and hung him in the smokehouse. He then cleaned his hands and went back inside. Eileen was already ready and it didn't take Lars long either. They decided to leave Buster home for this trip and Lars told him to stay. Lars and Eileen ventured to the Carston place first and informed them, that if they were available, they were going to prepare a Thanksgiving feast for tomorrow, having bagged a turkey.

"Of course we are available," Reggie said.

"Good," Lars said, "then we'll expect you tomorrow. Alright, now we're off to pay a little visit to the Lins." The Lins were hesitant, but said they would join in on the feast, asking what they could bring. Lars suggested bacon. Lars and Eileen then made quick time to James and Melissa's place. Melissa and James were always happy to see Lars and Eileen, and they both agreed wholeheartedly they wouldn't miss the feast. Eileen noticed Melissa was acting a little strange. She also noticed that she and James seemed to be getting along better than ever. Lars, as usual, didn't notice a thing. "What's going on?" Eileen asked.

"Nothing," Melissa said with a smile.

James walked over to Melissa and put his arm around her. Eileen then knew something was different about them and gave Melissa a quizzical look.

"You'll find out tomorrow," Melissa said.

Lars, knowing they had few vegetables, told them they didn't need to bring anything. He and Eileen would provide everything they needed. Lars and Eileen then headed home saying there were a lot of preparations necessary before the party. Eileen stopped about halfway to the tree line and looked back at James and Melissa standing in the doorway. *They certainly look happy,* Eileen thought. *Something definitely is going on around here.* Eileen gave a final wave as did Lars and the two continued on their way.

Eileen wanted to make a pie but told Lars she didn't have any fruit. She made a pitcher of tea and after a while, Lars reminded her there were some fresh beets in the root cellar from the winter crop.

"Can we make a pie out of beets?" she inquired.

"Sure you can," Lars said. "I'm not sure what it will taste like, but you can make the pie."

Eileen pondered the idea for a few minutes. She finally decided she'd give it a try and went into the kitchen. "Will you get me a few beets, honey?" She said.

Lars got up and headed to the root cellar. He returned and began to clean the beets while Eileen worked on the crust. When he finished with the beets, he turned the task over to Eileen. An hour later, she took the pie out of the oven and set it on the table. Lars came over to take a look.

"It looks good anyway," he said with a smile. "Guess we'll know tomorrow," he added. "I'll give it a try first," Lars said.

"Thanks, honey."

Eileen and Lars got up early, fired up the stove and put the turkey in the oven. She then began working on the dressing. Cornbread and giblet gravy were the next items on the main list; then Eileen pulled out pickled beets and creamed corn. Lars went out and fed Buster about the time Samuel and Sally Lin showed up. Sam had brought bacon. Lars breathed a sigh of relief that he hadn't lost his source of this precious meat. Melissa and James arrived a short time later, and to Eileen and Lars' surprise, she made a fruit cobbler, saying she found some canned peaches.

"I sure do like a good peach cobbler," Lars said.

"I hope it meets your expectations," Melissa added.

"It will," James included, "Melissa is a great cook, Dad."

Melissa smiled.

Reggie and Emily showed up fashionably late but not all that far behind James and Melissa. Everyone mingled while the finishing touches were made on the feast. Melissa and Emily set the table while the men socialized on the sofa. It wasn't long before the ladies called the men to the table. The spread was amazing and Eileen asked Lars to remove the turkey from the oven. He placed the bird on his end of the table. Eileen did a wonderful job with the turkey and as Lars carved the bird, he knew this was going to be a big hit with his and Eileen's guests. He had covered the bird with bacon and it was moist and juicy. Lars would have been happy just eating the bacon but would eat a little of the turkey as well.

When everyone had a generous helping of turkey, Lars asked them to dig into the rest of the meal. It was pretty quiet, as everyone was enjoying the meal and they were too busy eating to talk. When everyone was running out of room for more food, the talk started again, but they continued to nibble. This went on for quite a while, as no one could seem to turn away the splendid food. The beet pie was very good and Melissa exceeded Lars' expectations with her peach cobbler. It eventually got to the point where no one could eat another bite. Maybe they could have a little more after the first round settled a while.

When it appeared everyone was finished eating, Eileen suggested that, since this was a Thanksgiving feast, everyone take turns saying what they were thankful for. Eileen said she would go first.

"I am thankful first and foremost for Lars and his loving and caring nature, and for not killing me the day we met. I am also thankful for good neighbors."

Reggie said he would go next. "I am thankful for my wonderful wife, Emily; I am thankful for good friends and I am thankful for explosives."

Everyone chuckled.

Emily said, "I'm thankful first for my wonderful husband. I am thankful for good friends and good food, especially the pickled beets. I am particularly thankful that my baby daughter has returned home."

Lars said, "I am also thankful I did not kill Eileen the day she showed up on my doorstep." There were a few more chuckles. "I am thankful for good friends and neighbors and Sam's bacon. I am thankful for my son, our new irrigation system and for a good start for our crops."

Samuel said, "I am thankful for my wife and good friends and neighbors."

Sally cleared her throat. "I am thankful for my loving husband, two beautiful children, and for our wonderful valley."

James announced he was thankful for surviving the trip from Conroe and that his dad was alive and well. He was also thankful for Eileen and the good she had done for his dad. He also mentioned he was thankful for good friends, especially Melissa's hard work and companionship, and he looked forward to a long, happy life in this valley.

Melissa was a little hesitant when her turn came around. She was the only one to stand up. She held her stomach. "I want to thank the Westons for such a wonderful place to live, rest their souls, and Lars for such a wonderful and hardworking son. I want to thank all of you for all you have done for us, but most of all I want to thank James for the wonderful life he has placed inside of me."

You could have heard a pin drop as everyone stared at Melissa, all mouths open.

The ladies got up and crowded around Melissa all with tears in their eyes and smiles on their faces.

"So you're not a lesbian?" Reggie asked.

"No, Daddy!"

The men shook James' hand and gave him a hug. "Congratulations, son," Lars said.

When the hubbub had settled down a bit, Reggie said, "Emily, where is that bottle of wine we brought?" Reggie got up and Emily directed him to the proper sack. Reggie reached in to find the bottle and corkscrew. He opened the bottle while Lars retrieved some glasses. Reggie poured a glass for each, with the exception of Melissa, telling her babies do not drink wine. Melissa smiled and said she didn't care for wine anyway, that everyone else should enjoy their Pinot Grigio. "I'll toast with tea," she added.

Reggie held up his glass saying, "To a fine and healthy son."

"To a healthy baby," Emily added, as everyone held up their glasses. Clink, clink, clink.

It was getting late and the men expressed the need to get home before dark, so they washed the dishes and cleaned the table and everyone prepared to head home. Before they left, though, Reggie informed everyone that they should have another meeting soon to discuss a few things he had picked up on the ham radio. The men agreed they should all meet here in two days. Lars asked Eileen if she could handle hosting the meeting.

"Of course." She was interested in the outside world too and would be happy to have everyone back over.

Reggie instructed the women not to cook—that since they had just prepared such a wonderful feast, he, Sam, and James would take care of all the food. Eileen and Lars agreed, however, Lars said he could supply the greens knowing everyone else was short on fresh vegetables. Everyone else agreed.

Two days went by and everyone showed up about mid-morning. Eileen prepared coffee and after everyone had a cup, the meeting began.

"I have some good news and I have some bad news," Reggie started. "The good news is we have not seen any intruders around here for a while. The bad news is there is still a huge potential for problems. I have now lost contact with seven more of my ham friends. I have radio friends all over the country, and while losing touch does not absolutely mean they are dead, this possibility does exist. Another piece of good news is I am still in touch with my few local ham friends.

"My local friends say," Reggie continued, "the world is not so bad here locally as it is in most of the rest of the country. All the large Texas cities—San Antonio, Houston, and Dallas—are just as bad as big cities in the rest of the country, though, but the outlying areas seem to be faring much better. If the reason for this is well-organized and well-armed groups in the area—much like us—then we may be reasonably safe. If these outside groups are aggressive and just haven't found our valley yet, then we may very well have some really bad problems soon. If we are faring better because there simply is no one out there, then we may be in pretty good shape. I think we need to know which is the case."

"What are you suggesting, Reggie?" Lars asked.

'I'm suggesting a reconnaissance mission," Reggie said. "Regardless of what the mission turns up, I think you guys need to block your roads better. I do not have a road to my place, but Sam, your road joins James' road, which goes all the way to the highway. Lars, your road joins the main road about a half mile from where James' road joins the highway. This is where any intruders are likely to come in. There is nothing but miles and miles of heavy forest and brush everywhere else."

Everyone agreed, but if they were going to use fuel for scouting, this fuel needed to be replaced. "Where are we going to get this fuel?" Lars asked.

"It seems most, if not all, the oil fields in the area have completely shut down," Reggie added. "If this is the case, there must be tanks of distillate out there somewhere if we can find them. This can provide years of fuel. We may need to adjust the timing on our vehicles, but it will work. If we can get some crude, we can also distill our lube oil and crude byproducts."

The ladies went to the kitchen table and began their own discussion group. They were still interested in what the guys were saying but were concerned over the safety of the mission. Emily told the rest of the ladies Reggie had this all planned out. He did not know what they would run up against, but he did have a solution for most problems they might encounter.

The ladies returned to the men to hear Reggie say, "I fear the road to James' place may be wide open. This could be why the Westons were hit. If this is the case, James, you and Melissa are at high risk, as are you Sally and Sam." Sam and James had not thought of this, but Reggie might very well be right.

They decided to take a vote to see where everyone stood on the issue of the mission. The vote was unanimous for the mission.

The men then began their plans. Lars' truck would be used and Sam reluctantly agreed to watch over the ladies. It was also decided James and Reggie would take James' motorcycle to pick up the gear Reggie thought would be vital for the mission. The men also decided, regardless of what they found on their mission, the roads to the highway would be closed a little more permanently rather than just a few logs across the road. If someone was to come to their homesteads, they would really have to work at it. The final decision was when would they go? The men voted to complete all the preparations tomorrow and then head out early the following morning.

Having made their plan, everyone would meet at the Lindgren place tomorrow. They then decided it was time to go home, gather up their gear, and get a good night's sleep. There were hugs and kisses all around, especially for Melissa and her little gift, and then everyone headed home. Lars and Eileen sat chatting on the sofa for another hour. Lars gathered up a few items in the barn and loaded them into the truck. They then went to bed early.

The following morning, the neighbors began showing up shortly after sunrise. Immediately, James and Reggie went back to the Carston's place to pick up gear. The motorcycle would be faster and they had some heavy gear to haul. In the meantime, Sam and Lars began to prepare his truck—checked the oil, radiator, and topped off the gas tank with gas from the spare drum. He started the engine, checked the transmission fluid and kicked the tires. The truck was running good, so he shut it off. He and Sam then went to the porch, cleaned their rifles and pistols and gathered up enough ammunition for the trip.

Eileen brought them another cup of coffee and some jerky to nibble on, as they had pretty much worked their breakfast off by now. The men then went out to the barn and Lars grabbed an axe, machete, towing strap, and a chain to load into the truck. Lars also cleaned all the windows and mirrors, since he could not remember when they were last cleaned.

Finally, Reggie and James came riding up slowly with Reggie's gear. James and Sam were especially impressed with what Reggie brought, James not ever having seen his bunker and Sam having not paid enough attention the few times he had. James' saddlebags were literally filled to the brim. The first to unload were a couple rocket propelled grenade launchers, after which Reggie produced ten grenade rounds. Reggie brought bulletproof vests for all, wearing his with four fragmentation grenades and two smoke grenades attached to the chest. Reggie wore a pistol on each hip, plus his AR-15 and his sniper rifle. There was plenty ammunition for each. Reggie made the other guys feel under dressed, but they didn't mind this. They would be well enough armed for just about anything.

Reggie brought a canteen for each, as well as some ration bars. Reggie also informed the men when they were ready to close the roads, he had some *mine field* signs as well as ten mines to place in the roads. This was even a surprise to Lars. "Why didn't you bring your tank?" Lars said jokingly.

"It was past due on its oil change," Reggie replied quite serious. "I don't like to run it outside its scheduled maintenance."

Everyone laughed except Reggie and this got a queer look from everyone.

Early the next morning, Reggie, Lars, and James gave the gals a hug and kiss, and then told Sam to take good care of the ladies. The men loaded up in Lars' pickup and slowly made their way past the sycamore tree and up the road. Reggie rode shotgun while James took the back. It wasn't long before the pickup reached Lars' downed tree and James got out with the chain and hooked the tree to the truck. Lars pulled the tree away from the road. Then after going around the log, he hooked back up to the tree and pulled it back across the road. The guys made their way up the road slowly, keeping a keen eye out for anyone and anything.

Samuel, Sally, and Emily lingered around on the porch awhile after the guys left while Eileen and Melissa went inside to make another pot of coffee. When the coffee was ready, Eileen took the pot outside and refilled cups all around. They decided someone should remain on the porch at all times, as sentry, until the men returned. Sam took first sentry duty. He liked Buster, giving him a good scratching all over. He wished he had a watchdog to help keep an eye on his place.

As Lars' truck rolled up to the highway, he asked which direction they should go. Reggie immediately said to the left. Lars obliged easing out onto the pavement. A couple minutes later, they came to the dirt road to James' place. They decided to check out the road. They drove until they could see James' cabin. Reggie was right; there was nothing to stop intruders from driving all the way to James' place. They all agreed this security problem needed to be remedied. Lars turned the truck around and drove about two-thirds of the way back to the highway and stopped. Just for a temporary measure, the men got out and cut two trees down across the road. They would add more later. They then headed back to the highway.

Lars turned left and checked his odometer and drove for about twenty minutes, going about ten miles. There was no traffic. Lars rolled to a stop at the top of a hill where they could see an additional couple miles ahead. They sat for a while, and seeing no one, decided to go an additional five miles.

They reached the edge of a small town and stopped and watched for a while. Lars got out and Reggie did the same. James stayed in the back of the truck with his RPG launcher. Lars reached into the back of the truck and grabbed an old white tee shirt and a stick. He attached the shirt to the stick. Lars then got his rifle and fired a shot into the air. A short while later, a car pulled onto the highway and eased toward them. Lars began to wave his white flag in the air. The car crept forward and stopped about a hundred yards in front of Lars, Reggie, and James as Lars continued to wave his flag.

Lars leaned his rifle against the truck and began walking forward toward the car, continually waving his white flag.

"Keep me covered, guys," Lars said.

"Will do," Reggie answered.

Lars continued to walk forward and then stopped about a third of the distance to the car. Directly, a man got out of the car and began to walk forward. When he had walked about a third of the distance from his car, Lars again began to walk forward. They both stopped when they were ten feet apart.

"My name is Lars Lindgren. I am your neighbor to the south."

"I'm Marco Gonzales," the man replied.

"We are peaceful people," Lars said. "We want to secure our borders. If you are peaceful as well, we can secure your southern flank if you can do the same for us on our northern flank."

"There are not many of us here, but we are peaceful people as well," Marco said.

"We are becoming more self-sufficient every day and maybe we can do some trading as well if you like," Lars added.

"Same here," Marco said.

"Then we can be friends?" Lars queried.

"Yes, I think so," Marco replied.

The men shook hands. Lars waved to Reggie to pull the truck forward while Marco did the same with his associates. Reggie slowly pulled forward as did Marco's followers. Gingerly, Lars introduced James and Reggie to Marco, Ralph, Curtis, and Alfredo. Once the introductions were made, the tension seemed to let up a bit as the men discussed details of their new alliance.

Both groups were happy with the new security arrangement and the prospect of someone to trade with who wouldn't shoot first and ask questions later. Lars secured the deal with a handshake and Lars, Reggie, and James got back in their truck and headed back the other direction.

Lars drove until he passed, first James road then his. He checked the odometer again and drove for about twenty minutes, going about ten miles. Lars stopped at the top of another hill and asked Reggie what they should do now. Reggie reached into his jacket and pulled out a map. To Lars' surprise, Reggie had an aerial map of the area laminated with plastic. He showed the map to Lars, pointing out a couple side roads a few miles ahead. A mile or two down these side roads, the map showed some oilfield storage tanks. Reggie said they should check out the tanks.

Lars drove onward until he came to the first side road. There was a gate protecting the barely visible trail. Reggie got out and grabbed Lars' axe, and with one strike to the chain, the lock popped off and the chain fell loose. Reggie pulled the gate open and Lars drove through. Reggie got back into the truck and Lars continued forward. The brush had grown up around the road—it seemed to have been unused for quite a while. When they reached the tank battery, the area opened up to reveal a nice meadow with four large steel tanks.

They saw no one around—the area seemed to have been long abandoned. Lars opened the valves one at a time on each of the tanks. The first two were empty. The third contained a thin, clear liquid with a green tint. Lars smelled the liquid and it smelled like kerosene. The fourth tank was empty as well. Reggie found a stick and tied a piece of string to it. He then climbed the ladder to the top of the third tank and opened the roof hatch. He dropped the stick into the hatch and with the stick floating on top of the liquid, measured the distance to the top of the tank. It was eight feet to the liquid. The tank, however, was eighteen feet high. Reggie deduced there was ten feet of liquid in the tank.

Reggie went back down and took a small bottle out of a pocket. He cracked the valve and filled the bottle with the liquid. He held it up to the sun and studied his sample. This appeared to be exactly what they were looking for, but Reggie would perform some tests on the liquid when they returned home. Satisfied with their find, the guys loaded back into the truck and headed back to the highway. When they reached the gate, Lars drove past the opening and Reggie got out. He closed the gate and pulled a lock from his pocket. Reggie pulled the chain tight around the gate and post and inserted the lock. Lars was amazed at how Reggie always seemed to have everything he needed regardless of the situation.

As Reggie was locking the gate, James spotted someone coming down the road near the fence line. James alerted Lars and Reggie and Lars killed the engine. Lars pulled his 30-30 up and out his window and opened the door to use it as a gun rest. Reggie reached in and got his AR-15. The men just sat there for a few minutes, as it appeared they had not been spotted. It turned out there were two people coming their way on foot. The couple was coming from the same direction Lars had driven, but no one had seen them. The man and woman walked almost up to the truck before they spotted Lars' vehicle and the men watching them. The couple mostly kept their eyes on the ground ahead. When they did spot the truck, they turned and started to run.

Reggie yelled, "Stop!" and fired a shot into the air.

The couple froze in their tracks. Reggie quickly ran toward the two with his rifle pointed at them and told them to put their arms into the air. They dropped what appeared to be a bedroll and a small sack and threw their arms up. The man and woman appeared to be in their mid-twenties. Reggie got within twenty feet of the couple and they appeared unarmed.

"Do you have any weapons?" Reggie asked to make certain.

"No," was the response.

By this time, Lars started and eased the truck toward the couple and they could see James in the back of the truck with a loaded RPG launcher pointing at them. Reggie didn't see the couple as a threat and told them they could put their arms down, that he would not harm them. The couple lowered their arms and relaxed a little.

"What are you doing way out here?" Reggie asked.

"We're trying to find a better place to stay," the man said. "The shack we were at was old and caved in. We just want a good shelter and some food. We don't mean you any harm," he continued.

Reggie asked them if they had seen anyone else and the man said "No".

"We haven't seen anyone for weeks," the girl added.

Reggie, satisfied they were telling the truth, told the two there was nothing for them around here and they had best keep going down the highway. "If you don't, all you'll get is the business end of my AR-15."

"We'll keep going," the man assured Reggie.

"We'll be back through here a little later to check on you," Reggie said as he walked back over to the truck and got in.

James took a drink out of his canteen and tossed it to the couple. He then reached into a pocket, pulled out four emergency ration bars and gave them to the couple as well. They thanked James with a big smile on their faces. Lars turned the truck down the highway and the couple picked up their bedroll and sack. They each immediately opened a bar and began eating as Lars drove away.

Lars checked the couple in his rearview mirror. Then he drove a few miles until he reached another side road, which Reggie instructed him to turn onto. This road was also gated, and again Reggie took the axe and opened the gate. Lars drove through and Reggie got back in. They drove nearly two miles and came to another tank battery. The tanks contained no liquid in them, but Reggie opened the side hatch to one tank and noticed the smell of crude oil. Reggie pulled his flashlight off the Velcro strip on his belt and flipped it on. He pointed the light into the tank and though there was little liquid, the level appeared to be about a foot deep. Reggie grabbed a stick and dug it into the muck at the bottom of the tank. He pulled the stick out and looked at the goo on the end of it. Reggie took out another small glass bottle and raked some of the goo into the container. Then he reached back into the tank for another sample of the goo and used it to fill his small bottle.

Reggie walked back over to the truck where James and Lars were standing.

"What do you have?" Lars inquired.

"Looks to be paraffin," Reggie replied.

"Wax?" Lars asked.

"Yes, paraffin settles out of crude oil to the bottom of the tank."

"Cool," Lars added.

"Well, men," Reggie said, "looks like that's about it for this trip. There are no more tank batteries nearby."

Reggie got back into the truck as did Lars and James. When they got back to the highway, Lars turned south and continued farther down the road. About twelve miles down the road, Lars came upon a roadblock. Several old cars were parked end to end across the highway with a sign painted on the side: *Keep Out! Anyone past this point will be met with deadly force.*

"Looks like someone means business," Lars stated.

"Seems so," Reggie said.

"There doesn't appear to be anyone around though," James noted.

"Maybe there aren't enough people to post sentries," Lars inserted. "Maybe they are just trying to keep people away like we are with our signs."

"Could be," Reggie added.

Reggie pulled his map out again, but the map did not extend this far up the road.

"It's getting late," Lars said. "Maybe we should call it a day and save this dilemma for another day."

"That sounds good to me," Reggie agreed and the men headed back home.

Up the road a bit, they came across the couple again headed their way. They appeared to have taken their warning seriously and were continuing up the highway. Lars told them "good luck" and gave them a few more ration bars, again reminding the couple to keep going. "There is a blockade up the highway," James said. "You should probably steer clear of this area." The men continued on their way.

Lars drove to the road into James' and Sam's places and then a couple miles down the road where they had previously cut down the two trees. Lars turned his truck around and stopped. The men got out, walked down the road a ways and began chopping trees. They cut five more large trees across the road about thirty feet apart. Satisfied that this, along with the signs and mines they would add tomorrow, would deter intruders, the men got back into the truck and headed back to the highway and then down Lars' road. Again, they moved the tree Lars previously cut down and drove the truck past the tree, pausing to pull it back into its place. They moved the truck ahead a bit before cutting six more trees down across the road. Satisfied with their deterrent, the men drove to Lars' place. Lars honked the horn as he approached and Sam and the ladies greeted them as they drove up.

Reggie said he'd leave his RPG's with Lars and James if they had no objections, saying he had several more at home. They did not object. Reggie told James if he would follow him home on his cycle, they could load some mines into his saddlebags; then he and Emily would return the following morning and show them how to set the mines.

James agreed.

Reggie told the group he would test the samples he collected and let them know the results as soon as he had them. He and Emily then headed home with James in tow. Reggie loaded up the saddlebags with mines, and then James returned to Lars' and dropped off the explosives. Lars insisted James take one of the RPG launchers and half the grenades. James did not argue with the extra protection the launcher would give them and gladly took the weapons. He and Melissa then headed home.

Lars shared the story of their adventure with Sam, Sally, and Eileen. Then after a nice glass of tea, Sam and Sally headed home. Lars and Eileen played with Buster for a bit, checked out the garden and then headed inside for the evening. Eileen served Lars dinner as she, Sam, Sally, Melissa, and Emily had eaten shortly before the men returned home. Lars ate while Eileen kept him company. They talked a little more about the tank batteries and that if the tests Reggie were going to make proved acceptable, they would not have fuel worries for many years.

Bright and early the next morning, Reggie and Emily, and James and Melissa were on the Lars' doorstep. They decided they would all make the trek to the site where they wanted to bury the mines, each taking one mine, which were not very heavy to carry, even for the ladies. Reggie carried the signs, a shovel and his expertise. When they reached the location up James' road, Reggie instructed James on where and how to dig the holes. While James was digging, Reggie and Lars nailed up a sign to a sturdy tree on each side of the road. The signs made it appear the mine fields were in the woods on each side of the road rather than on the road. If anyone ignored the numerous trees which had been felled onto the road and the skull James brought with him and placed alongside the road, then they would be funneled into the mine field.

Reggie then took the first mine and placed it in the first hole while instructing the team on the proper placement of the mine. Lars, Eileen, Melissa, and James each then installed a mine with Reggie's close supervision. They then returned home for the other five mines and repeated the procedure up Lars' road. James took a second skull and placed it on a stick as a warning. Satisfied they were now well protected, the crew headed home. Melissa, James, Emily and Reggie followed Eileen and Lars to their place.

They didn't work very hard, but they all got a good bit of exercise just making the trek. Eileen and Emily fixed tea and the crew sat on the porch to enjoy it. They then discussed their successful excursion in detail.

"We still need to keep a close eye out for intruders," Reggie commented, "but it looks like we are much more secure now than we have ever been. There is always the chance someone could find their way here through the woods, or a group of marauders could ignore our warning and make it through our minefields. We let our guard down for one second and we could end up like the Westons. This will be a fact of life from now own."

"Be a little optimistic, Reggie," Lars said. "We have food, we have water, and we have each other."

"To good friends and to good neighbors," Reggie said as he held his glass up for a toast.

"Here! Here!" Lars said as they all held their glasses up toward each other. Clink, clink.

Reggie and Emily headed home in time to arrive before dark, as did James and Melissa, leaving Lars and Eileen to discuss the next day.

"I think I'll get started on the root cellar tomorrow," Lars announced.

"Good idea," Eileen said.

The two then showered and went to bed.

The next morning, Lars and Eileen finished breakfast and fed Buster; then the two went out to clean the remaining vegetables out of the root cellar. There were a few potatoes, carrots, and beets from the winter garden, but little else. They could finish these off in a few days. Lars then began to excavate the additional area to double the size of the cellar. He cut logs for the floor and walls, anchoring the new walls with some leather cordage. He then constructed bins and shelves for easy access to their new crop. The following day, Lars finished up the cellar construction, adding a new door. Eileen was pleased with the new root cellar.

Lars then expanded the smokehouse. The current smokehouse was probably big enough, but he decided a little more room would never hurt. Lars took two additional days on this project. Although he could have done it in one, he figured the garden needed a little attention as well during the course of the project. Lars hoed in the garden for several hours. The garden again in good shape, Lars returned his attention to the smokehouse, rebuilding the fire pit to finish off this project.

Chapter 29

It only seemed like weeks, but it had in fact been months since Lars and Eileen planted. Lars walked onto the porch and out to the garden. Lars and Eileen had been eating fresh cabbage, carrots, and beets for a month, but it was time to get the remainder of the crop out of the field. The tops on the potatoes had yellowed. Lars pulled a couple of the plants and dug around in the dirt to find a half dozen nice potatoes under each plant. There were also numerous small potatoes he would use for seed the following year.

Lars informed Eileen it was harvest time. He grabbed several baskets out of the smokehouse to put the vegetables into and headed back out to the garden. Lars began pulling onions, cabbage, carrots, and beets, Eileen joining him when he was half finished. Buster, who had seen Lars digging in the dirt, was busy digging his own holes here and there. After taking the first batch to the root cellar, he returned to help Eileen finish up. Lars hauled another batch to the root cellar and then returned to help Eileen with the potatoes.

As they dug the potatoes, Lars stopped from time to time to carry a few baskets to the root cellar. After he hauled ten bushels of potatoes to the cellar, he walked over to Eileen and gave her a big hug. "Thank you for all your help and attention to the garden. With your help and loving care, we have way more spuds than we need," Lars said. Lars massaged her back a little as he hugged her.

"Get back to work, big boy, we don't have time for this," she said with a smile and a peck on the cheek. Lars turned away and got back to work.

They took a break for a late lunch, but got back to work shortly thereafter and worked to nearly dark. They got all the eating potatoes dug and into the root cellar, except five bushels which were well in excess of what they needed. Lars put these potatoes onto the front porch to give to their neighbors. Lars also added a couple baskets of miscellaneous veggies for the neighbors. The following day, Lars and Eileen gathered up their baskets and collected all the small potatoes, which they stored for seed the following year. Having finished this task, Lars checked the corn.

He peeled back the shucks on a few brown and dry ears of corn. Lars twisted one of the ears in his hand and a few the kernels popped off the cob, but not enough for the corn to be ready. The corn needed to dry another week. About mid-afternoon, James and Melissa came around. Lars met them as they walked up to the porch. "Just in time, guys," Lars said with a smile, "now that all the work is finished."

Lars admired Melissa's tummy, which was beginning to stick out noticeably. Eileen walked out of the house with four glasses and a pitcher of tea, having grabbed a couple extra glasses when she heard their wolf howls and noticed Melissa and James coming up the way.

"We're so glad to see you," Eileen said.

Lars and their guests walked onto the porch. Eileen handed everyone a glass and poured the tea; then they sat and talked a spell.

"We have a couple bushels of potatoes for you," Lars said. "With Eileen's green thumb, we had a bumper crop. The new watering system helped as well. Thank you for your help with that, James."

"We'd love the potatoes. Thank you very much," Melissa said.

"Thank you," James added.

"Our pleasure," Eileen said.

"Come by next week and we'll have corn to harvest," Lars said. "Looks like we will have a bumper crop there too."

"I'll be here early," James said.

"I'll count on it," Lars responded with a smile.

Lars got a sack out of the root cellar and he and James sacked up a bushel of potatoes and tied the sack with some leather cordage.

"Next time you come over, you can get the other sack," Lars said.

Melissa and Eileen walked out to the garden as James and Lars sat and talked on the porch. Eileen grabbed a bucket by the gate and the ladies picked some green beans for her to take home.

"We have a good crop of green beans," Melissa said, "but they are very stringy and not very tasty. We need to plant a different variety next time."

"That happens when you are just getting started," Eileen said. "Throw all your seeds out and we'll give you some of our variety for next year."

"Everything else did well," Melissa added. "We just don't have enough garden space to produce the excess you guys seem to have."

"All you need is enough for your needs," Eileen stated. "If all goes well, we can supply the potatoes and corn. With a little luck, we will have an abundance every year thanks to the new watering system."

"Green beans, potatoes, and some sausage stir-fried together makes a mighty good and easy meal," Eileen said.

Melissa said she would give it a try.

"You do have sausage, right?" Eileen asked.

"Yes, we do."

The ladies joined the men and continued their conversation for another hour. Then it was time for James and Melissa to head back home. James hauled the sack onto his shoulder while Melissa carried the green beans in a small bag Eileen retrieved from the house.

"It is good to see you guys again, as always," Eileen said.

"See you next week, kids," Lars said.

Eileen and Lars watched Melissa and James fade into the distance before going inside to prepare dinner. "How are you holding up, sweetheart?" Lars asked.

"I'm alright," Eileen responded.

"You really look tired," Lars said.

"I am tired," Eileen said, "but if we are going to survive out here alone, then it is going to take everything we have in us to make it happen."

"That is certain, darlin'," Lars stated.

"How is your arthritis holding up?" she asked.

"Up and down as usual. Worse yesterday, but better today. I'll survive."

"There is one thing I'd like, if at all possible," Eileen added.

"What's that sweetheart?" Lars asked.

"A café latte," Eileen answered with a smile.

"I don't know if that is possible, but I'll see what I can do," Lars said.

Lars and Eileen continued to work on dinner. Finally, he said, "You'll have to tell me how to make your café latte."

Eileen then proceeded to give Lars the exact verbal instructions. With a strange look on his face, he said, "I can do that." He wasn't certain, but he was determined to give it his best effort.

Reggie and Emily came over the following day to give Lars and Eileen the test results for the samples he had taken from the tank batteries. "The distillate is nearly perfect to run in the vehicles. If you add a little paraffin, you can use it in your oil lamps," Reggie said. "The paraffin will need to be melted and filtered," Reggie added, "but this should keep all of us in candles for the rest of our lives."

"Excellent!" Lars exclaimed.

Lars then went into the kitchen and began to work on a special treat. He mixed up a packet of the powdered milk Reggie had given him a while back in a saucepan. He whisked the milk as he heated it until it was foamy. He then half-filled four mugs with the leftover coffee from the morning pot and added a little sweetener. Lars then stirred in the steamy and frothy milk into each mug. He handed a cup to Eileen and Emily first.

"Here is your café latte, ladies," Lars said with a big smile.

Lars then poured the milk into the remaining cups, handed one to Reggie and kept the fourth for himself. Eileen and Emily took a sip of their drinks.

"It's not Starbucks," Eileen said, "but you did very well, dear."

"I could get used to this," Emily said.

"I did the best I could with the ingredients I had," Lars stated.

"Yes you did, honey," Eileen said, "and I certainly appreciate the effort. You get an "A" for effort and I think I could get used to this too."

Eileen and Emily looked at each other and smiled. The latte was not the same as Starbucks, but it wasn't bad either. Eileen got up and gave Lars a big hug.

"Thank you, darlin'," she whispered into his ear.

Lars and Reggie took a sip of their drinks, and then looked at each other.

"I don't know what all the fuss is about over café latte," Lars said.

"I don't either," Reggie stated.

"Oh well, as long as the ladies are happy," Lars said.

"Yep," Reggie said.

"What now?" Lars asked.

"All we need to do is get Sam over here to keep an eye on the ladies while you, James, and I take your truck over with a few drums every so often to get some distillate and paraffin," Reggie said.

"One trip a year should take care of us, right?" Lars asked.

"If we don't take too many wild excursions," Reggie said.

"Speaking of excursions, you know we need to go back out to the barricade to the south?" Lars questioned.

"Yes, we do," Reggie agreed.

Lars informed Reggie and Emily that Melissa and James had come over the day before but would be back the following week. Reggie and Emily said they would visit again then. Lars went and grabbed another sack and Reggie helped him fill it with a bushel of potatoes, telling him he could pick up the other sack the following week.

"Great," Reggie said, "thank you very much."

"My pleasure," Lars said. "You can thank Eileen's green thumb for the spuds and James' help on the new water tank was beneficial as well."

Reggie and Emily only stayed a couple hours, so Lars decided he and Eileen could deliver the remaining bushel of potatoes to the Lins, if she was up for the trip. She was, and Lars sacked up the spuds and they were off to the Lin homestead.

The Lins were happy to see them when they arrived and were really surprised and thankful for the potatoes. Sally and Eileen sat on the porch and talked for a while as Lars and Sam went to his root cellar to deposit the potatoes. Sam then went inside the smokehouse to fetch a slab of bacon.

"You don't have to, Sam," Lars said. "I didn't come for a trade; the potatoes are a gift. But, of course, I can't turn down the bacon," Lars added, knowing Sam would insist he take the meat anyway.

"Thank you, Sam," Lars said. "I thought I had lost my source for bacon when you and Sally left after we killed the neighbors."

"I was mad, and I'm still mad. What you did goes against everything we believe, but we all need each other," Sam said. "Things will never be the same, but we will still trade with you."

Lars and Sam quietly walked to the porch and joined the ladies. Lars told the Lins about the results of their reconnaissance mission sample tests and he was happy to hear this news.

"It seems we have one less worry these days," Lars added.

The guys chatted with the ladies a while; then Lars said it was time to go. Lars grabbed his empty sack and slab of bacon, and he and Eileen strolled back home. Lars and Eileen both loved the smell of the forest. They stopped here and there to take in the beauty and a couple of deer they happened to see. The squirrels and birds liked the warmer weather and chattered in the treetops.

"This is why I moved out here," Lars said. "This and the river. I fell in love with this place the very first time I came here. One look, and I bought it on the spot. All the animals and the wonderful woods! This is great!" Lars took in a deep breath. "This smells like home to me."

When Eileen first came to Lars' place, she saw and experienced danger at every turn. It seemed everything was out to hurt her—mosquitoes, hornets, thorns, snakes, and ants every time she turned around, and she suffered physically and mentally daily as a result. Lars saw everything, the beauty and the dangers, long before they could hurt him. Eileen saw only the sky, trees, and weeds without seeing the insane and infinite intricacies and dangers of the woods. Eileen just needed to open her eyes and see the woods as Lars saw it. Through experience she was learning to avoid most of the dangers which not long ago hurt her badly. She was learning to see past the hazards to see the elaborate design and beauty of Lars' world. Lars would probably see a Van Gogh or Da Vinci as mere paintings if he were to come to what had been her world in the city. This place was fantastic, like a great work of art. This place would never be boring.

"I love it too," Eileen added.

Lars and Eileen made it home just in time to begin dinner and before they knew it, another day was gone. They watched the sunset and went to bed.

James, Melissa, Reggie, and Emily converged upon the Lindgren place the following week to help harvest the corn crop. Lars, Reggie, and James pulled and hauled the ears to the porch where Eileen, Emily, and Melissa pulled the shucks off and filled baskets with the yellow ears. They saved some of the shucks to make tamales when Lars got ready to butcher one or two of the little piglets. Those piglets were growing like weeds and getting quite fat. When all the baskets were full, Reggie and Lars ran the ears through the shelling machine while James held the plastic lined sacks over the spout to fill the bags with clean dry corn kernels. When the bags were full, James tied the end securely with leather cordage and hauled the bags to the root cellar, stacking them where Lars had shown him.

When they had ten bushels of corn stored in the root cellar, Lars said this was enough. They only harvested half the corn. "Looks like you guys are going to get a hefty batch of corn too," Lars told Reggie and James.

The men continued harvesting the corn; then they shelled and bagged it for Reggie, James, and Sam. "The Lins are really going to be surprised," Lars said.

They ended up with nine additional sacks of the organic gold. They each got three sacks, James and Lars running a sack each to the Lins while Reggie stayed with the ladies. Lars and Eileen took the last sack to the Lins the following day. Eileen said she needed the exercise anyway, and another visit with Sally was always pleasant.

Chapter 30

Melissa's tummy continued to grow over the next few months. James had to help her out of bed most mornings and he was always helping her get off the sofa. October had rolled around and Melissa had gone full term. One morning, James hurried over to retrieve Eileen. He didn't like leaving Melissa alone, but he really didn't have a choice. They had gone months without a single intruder after having put in their new security measures, so he was certain Melissa would be fine. Eileen hurried back with James while Lars went to get Reggie and Emily. The trio hurried over to James' place, arriving just in time to hear a baby's cry from inside the house. Reggie waited outside with James and Lars while Emily went inside to assist. After thirty minutes, Lars stepped inside. It had been a long time and Lars was certain someone would have come out to inform them of the good news by now. *Has something gone wrong?* he thought. The baby stopped crying some time ago.

Lars met Eileen at the doorway to the bedroom. She advised him they were not through and to go back outside. Lars stepped back outside and joined the men. He shrugged his shoulders, saying he didn't know what was going on, but the ladies hadn't seemed upset. A few minutes later, they heard the baby crying again. About fifteen minutes later, Eileen stepped to the front door and announced they were through. James went in first and found Melissa in bed with a bundle in each arm. James turned to Eileen and Emily with a quizzical look on his face. "Yes, twins," Eileen said.

"You have two wonderful and healthy boys," Emily added.

James moved closer to Melissa and as he approached she opened her eyes. James had tears in his eyes as he leaned over and kissed Melissa on the forehead. Melissa smiled as she looked into James' face and the tears in his eyes told her how pleased he was.

They left Melissa alone for a while to give her a chance to rest a bit. James fixed coffee, as everyone had missed breakfast as well as their morning java today. Everyone said they were too excited to eat, so James only made coffee. Lars congratulated his son and the others followed suit. After a while, the excitement settled down and James began to fix something to eat. He pulled out a dozen eggs and a slab of bacon. He also cut up some potatoes, which he cooked in the bacon grease, and added the eggs when the potatoes were soft. James also fixed another pot of coffee and they all ate while they waited for Melissa to awake.

James heard one of the newborns crying and went in to check on Melissa.

One of the boys was feeding at her breast while Melissa was positioning the other to have his first meal. Noticing Melissa's voluptuous exposed breast, James felt the pressure of his expanding organ. Melissa was more beautiful than he had ever seen her. James ignored the pressure as he walked over and planted a big kiss on her lips. The boys had brown hair and looked very healthy. Their cheeks were a bit chubby and they worked tenaciously on Melissa's breasts. *I guess I'll have to share now*, James thought. James bent over to whisper, "I love you," into Melissa's ear.

"I love you too, James," she replied.

James joined their guests and informed them the boys were getting their first meal.

"We need to beef up the security around here a bit more," Reggie said. "We need to make damn certain our grandkids are well protected. I'll bring a couple more volleyballs over the next trip and maybe another mine or two."

James agreed.

It wasn't long before Melissa called the ladies back into her room. Eileen took one of the boys to his cradle and Emily made up another makeshift cradle out of a box, into which she placed and tucked the other newborn. Melissa then said she wanted to get cleaned up and change the bedclothes. Eileen told the guys to step outside and they all filled their coffee cups and adjourned to the porch.

Reggie asked if the others needed any fuel or paraffin, but everyone said they were good for a while. Reggie then changed the subject to the state of the nation. He had not heard anything new on the radio but said he thought it would be at least a decade before the country returned to anything close to what one might consider to be normal. The old normal included well over 300 million people; the new normal would maybe include 30 million at most, Reggie estimated. "That's an awful lot of people to die. I will never see a country anything close to what it was," Reggie continued. "In a hundred years, the population will still be much less than what it was," he added.

Lars and James agreed. "But we don't need them," Lars said.

"Exactly," Reggie responded. "Maybe the planet will heal up now."

"If we can keep intruders out," James said, "we can live out our lives in this little valley as happy as pigs in a wallow."

"Yes, we can," Lars said, "but one day your boys will grow up and need women. They need to be trained to take care of themselves in the outside world, whatever that world may become."

Reggie agreed, as did James. "Melissa and I will teach the boys all we can," James said.

"And we will help," Reggie added.

"You got that right, Reggie," Lars continued.

"Never forget about intruders though," Reggie added. "They will never go away completely and if we get caught off guard, the boys may never grow up to become men."

"And the boys need to be constantly warned about unwanted guests and how to deal with them," Lars added.

"They are only hours old," James said with a chuckle.

"Yes, they are," Reggie said, "but we need to be thinking about their security and safety now."

James finally agreed. "I'll do my part," he promised.

A short while later, Emily opened up the front door and said, "Melissa is ready to receive visitors." Everyone filed in one by one and kissed and gave Melissa a little hug. They all congratulated her on her excellent job to produce two fine baby boys.

"A good trick for a lesbian," Reggie sneered and laughed.

"Don't make me laugh, Daddy; it hurts."

As each made their way to Melissa, they all got their first good look at the boys. "They are really beautiful boys," Eileen and Emily said. Everyone agreed and before they left the room, each had tears of happiness streaming down their cheeks.

"This calls for a celebration," Lars said. "How about we give you guys a week to get things in order and we'll be back for a feast which will put our Thanksgiving feast to shame?"

Everyone agreed the following week would be the perfect time.

"I'll make a trip to the Lins and inform them," Lars said.

"Great!" James said.

"You don't have to fix a thing," Reggie said to James, "and you certainly don't need to do anything, Melissa. You take care of yourself and don't worry. We'll take care of everything." Melissa smiled and soon dozed off.

Everyone took this as their cue to head home. The neighbors met on the porch and they hugged and kissed their goodbyes. They congratulated James again and headed home.

Reggie and Emily stopped to visit a bit more with Lars and Eileen on their way home. The weather was warm with a good breeze from the south. The stiff breeze from the south this time of year also signaled to the men that it would not be long before cooler weather would be here again. This year, everyone was ready for winter—more so than they had been in previous years. The smokehouses were full, the root cellars were full, and the firewood was chopped and stacked in the woodsheds, with plenty of reserve outside.

After Reggie and Emily left, Lars brought up the idea of Eileen shooting her first deer. She had become a very good shot and just maybe a little better than

Lars. The only game Eileen had killed was a few rabbits and squirrels and wasn't certain she was ready to take on a deer. Lars assured her it was no different than killing the smaller animals. "You just need a little bigger gun, but the procedure is the same. It's certainly a lot easier than killing intruders."

"The deer are so darn cute," Eileen said. "I'll think about it."

Lars let it go at that.

Over the next couple days, Lars and Eileen spent some time fishing; they caught several nice fish—enough to prepare fresh for the party. Lars kept the fish in a live trap until the morning of the party. He cleaned the fish and then he and Eileen breaded them in cornmeal, ready to fry. For sides, Eileen prepared mashed potatoes and got out a couple jars of pickled beets. Lars didn't know how she did it, but Eileen baked a carrot cake for dessert. Lars began to fry the fish shortly after the Carstons and the Lins arrived. Emily brought creamed corn, jalapeno peppers stuffed with sausage, and some cheese she had gotten from the Lins. Emily also brought some hominy and fudge. Reggie brought a couple of his famous volleyballs. He promised James he would bring a couple mines on the next trip.

"Not a problem," James said.

The Lins brought a smoked ham wrapped in bacon. This was a big hit with Lars. For sides, Sally brought rice with peas and carrots, and onion soup. Sam and Sally told Melissa they were so happy to hear about the newborns and asked if they picked out names for the boys.

"Yes we have," Melissa replied. "The names will be announced right after we finish eating."

Melissa thanked everyone for coming and all the wonderful food they brought. She announced that the boys had just gone down for their nap and they were not to be disturbed. With the boys sound asleep, Melissa explained she would be able to enjoy the meal with the family. The fish were ready in a short time and the group sat down to enjoy the meal.

"The fish are excellent," Reggie said.

"I haven't found a morsel that is anything but superb," James said.

"This is quite a spread," Emily added.

Everyone signaled their agreement.

The table got quiet again as the neighbors enjoyed the delicious food with wonderful family and friends. Lars heard Buster scratching at the door and he got up and stepped outside for a minute to give him some scraps. He was no doubt getting a little hungry after smelling the food.

When everyone finished eating, Eileen brought out her cake. She cut a large slice for each guest.

"This is a superbulous cake," Emily said. "I'll need your recipe."

"Thank you," Eileen said, "I'll be happy to give it to you. I'm really glad you like the cake."

"There's no such word as superbulous," Reggie declared.

"There is now," Emily insisted.

"I think superbulous is a fitting description of the cake," Lars inserted.

"Thank you," Emily said, sneering at Reggie.

Reggie shut up.

When Eileen finished her slice of cake, she got up, found a piece of paper and began writing the recipe. She had improvised a little, but it really didn't matter. Most of the original recipe came from an old cookbook she had years earlier with ingredients modified by necessity. The improvised cake probably didn't resemble the original in the slightest in looks or taste, but it really didn't matter anyway; the only thing that mattered was what the improvised version tasted like. Eileen finished the recipe and handed it to Emily.

"Thank you," Emily said.

"You're welcome."

Everyone had finished eating except Lars, who was on his second slice of cake, and Melissa was waiting for him to announce the boy's names.

"He's finished," Eileen said as she gave Lars a little nudge in the ribs with her elbow.

"I'm finished," Lars proclaimed.

Eileen smiled.

Melissa stood up, grabbing James by the hand and pulling him up with her. "Ladies and gentlemen, James and I have decided upon names for the boys," Melissa announced. "We decided it would be fitting if one of the names was Ronald, in honor of the Westons. Are there any objections?"

"I think Ronald is an excellent name," said Lars.

There were no objections.

"The second name," Melissa said, "is Robert."

Again, there were no objections. "We'll call them Robbie and Ronnie."

"And their last name?" Eileen asked.

It could not have been quieter on the far side of the moon. Melissa paused and looked at James. "Their last name will be Lindgren," Melissa said. "James and I will be married just after Thanksgiving."

"Wonderful," said Sam.

"I just love weddings," Sally added.

"Looks like we'll be having another party," Lars said, turning to Eileen.

Suddenly Buster began barking and there were shots fired. The men grabbed their rifles and told the ladies to get down. Melissa ran to her bedroom and got the boys out of their cribs and onto the floor behind the bed.

"We'll be at the sides of the house," Lars said, and he and Reggie rushed out the back door.

James opened the front door and he and Sam took positions at each side of the opening. Eileen and Emily grabbed their rifles as well and prepared for the worst. They took positions at the windows.

Lars whistled and Buster came running around the side of the house; two more shots fired, kicking up dust at Buster's heels. Buster ran to Lars.

"Good boy," Lars said.

Lars eased up to the corner of the house and looked towards the brush line. He spotted some color near a large tree and then some movement. Lars then backed away from the corner and ran around to where Reggie was squatting.

"You see them?" Lars asked Reggie.

"No."

Lars pointed to where he saw the color; then a shot rang out and Lars and Reggie immediately heard the bullet hit the side of the house.

"I'm going to circle around them," Lars said.

"Okay," Reggie responded.

Lars backed up and Reggie aimed and returned a shower of bullets in the area where Lars pointed out the men. James and Sam zeroed in on the intruders and laid down their own flurry of lead into the area.

Lars ran back to the woods and began a big circle through the brush to where he had spotted the men. As he ran he could hear more shots. It took Lars about ten minutes to get around to where he thought was just to the right of where he had spotted the intruders. Lars paused behind a tree and listened. He could hear flurries of shots from the house followed by shots from the woods just ahead of him. Lars did not know how many men he was going to encounter, but he knew he had made it near their location.

Lars crept forward very slowly so as not to be spotted. As he moved, Lars listened carefully to the shots fired by the men. When he got close enough, he discerned there were two men ahead from the shots they were firing. Lars moved to a position where he was nearly behind the first man he spotted. Concealing himself behind a tree, he watched for a few minutes. Directly, the second man moved a little and Lars spotted him. Knowing where this second man was located, Lars leveled his 30-30 at the first man. As he sighted in on the first man, Lars looked over at where the second man was hidden. Lars could only see a little of the man's arm but had a clear line of sight to his position. He sighted in on the first man's chest area and squeezed the trigger. Immediately Lars sighted in on the second man. Hearing Lars' shot, the second man moved back and looked in Lars' direction. When he did, Lars shot the man in the face. He dropped like a brick. Lars reloaded and waited should there be a third intruder.

After a couple minutes and seeing no movement, Lars moved forward with his gun ready. Reggie, James, and Sam had quit firing. They didn't want to hit Lars. When he got a little closer, Lars could see both men clearly and that they were dead. Lars then spotted a third dead man. Apparently one of the neighbors had taken him out. Lars then let out his signature wolf howl. Reggie signaled back and Lars walked over to the dead men. He poked one and picked up his gun; then he walked over and poked the other two and got their rifles.

A short time later, Reggie and James walked up. James checked the men for more weapons and took their remaining ammunition. One man had a knife. James found a small bag with a bottle of water and a couple boxes of ammunition. They had no food and the men were thin and obviously well on their way to starving to death. This was likely the reason they were so brazen in attacking their house. Satisfied their work here was nearly over, the men walked back to the house. Sam and the ladies met them on the porch.

Eileen had blood running down the side of her face. Lars went to her and looked at the blood.

"What happened?" Lars asked.

Eileen looked at Lars with a strange look on her face. "What do you mean?" she asked.

Lars touched her face and showed her the blood. Eileen looked at it and touched her cheek. "A bullet shattered a window pane," she replied. "I guess a shard of glass hit me."

"Let's get that cleaned up," Lars said and they went inside the house.

"Well," Reggie said, "chalk up three more for the good guys."

"I don't know," James replied. "I'm not so sure we're the good guys anymore, after what we did across the highway. It seemed so necessary at the time, but now I'm not so certain. I know Lars is still struggling with it."

"We had to do what we did," Reggie said. "I still don't have a problem with it. And we are the good guys, dammit."

"I'm glad you think so," James said. "I'm not certain anymore."

"There must be hundreds, if not thousands, of people scavenging the countryside for food, water, fuel, or whatever," Reggie said. "We have killed less than a couple dozen. They may be few and far between, but apparently they are out there and sooner or later they are going to find us and want what we have. The killing is not over."

"I was hoping it would all stop when we got rid of the neighbors," Emily said.

"Me too," Sally said.

"It's never going to stop," Sam stated. "As long as people are desperate for food, they'll keep coming."

"Yeah," Reggie said, "we have been venturing out a little ourselves, but we have roots here in our little valley and don't stray far. These guys probably don't have any roots and will travel until they find us or some other unfortunate souls to try and kill."

"You're probably right," James said.

"I know I'm right," Reggie said, "and we're going to kill every one of the bastards!"

"Yes we will," James asserted, "but we have to spot them first."

"Yes, we do," Reggie agreed.

"And we will," James said. "We will stay alert."

"Yes, we will," Sam said categorically.

Chapter 31

Thanksgiving rolled around quickly. The families were getting ready for yet another big feast. This would be their second Thanksgiving feast this year, but this didn't matter; the inhabitants of the valley used any excuse for another party. They worked hard most days; they deserved a break every now and then. And they enjoyed each other's company. They were all like family. The last Thanksgiving party was at Lars', so James and Melissa decided they would like to host the second.

Lars and Eileen left home early to help Melissa and James with the preparations. They would have loved to have another fine turkey like the one Lars bagged, but this was not to be the case. James had hunted hard the past week, but could not get a good shot at a bird. "Turkeys have very good eyes and are nearly impossible to sneak up on," Lars said. James tried everything he could think of, but the turkeys outsmarted him every time. They would have to settle for venison, but no one objected. Everyone loved venison.

The remainder of the guests showed up a couple hours later, all carrying a variety of food items. Emily brought a carrot cake using Eileen's recipe. Her cake was not nearly as big as Eileen's but more than enough for the party. It didn't take long to set up the table and the guests gathered quickly around the food.

"Let's see if we can get through this feast without killing anyone," Reggie said.

"I certainly hope so," Lars chimed in.

As usual, there was little talking at the beginning of the meal other than an occasional compliment. All the ladies, as well as most of the men, were very good cooks. James was the exception. He could roast a hunk of meat over an open fire and a little bacon and eggs weren't exceedingly challenging for him, but that was the extent of his cooking skills.

When the meal was finished, the men went outside to relax on the porch and took Sean and Debra outside with them. They had all eaten more than they should, which was always the case at holiday feasts. They discussed a wide variety of subjects, starting with James' hunting skills. No one blamed him for not bagging a turkey, but rather shared some hunting tips with the husband-to-be. Sean and Debra played with Buster in the front yard, very noisy as usual when they played. The ladies were making a lot of noise too as they cleaned the kitchen and table. The guys knew they must be making wedding plans. "Ladies are always louder when it comes to weddings," Reggie said. With the guys outside, Melissa fed the twins.

They guys strolled around the house and made their way down to the river, the kids following close behind. Debra was walking fairly well now, but Sean always insisted on holding her hand. She still fell down often and Sean didn't like to hear her cry. The water level was a little low and Lars pointed out the spots where the pier and cleaning table needed some work. James took note, saying he would take care of the problems. Sam looked up into the sky after hearing a flight of geese flying over. There were not many geese so far this year. The guys discussed the unusually warm weather they were having, the probable cause for the lack of geese. They just might have a mild winter, in which case there would be fewer geese.

"It takes several strong northers to drive the geese this far south," Lars said.

As the guys worked their way back to the house, they were met by the ladies. They had finished cleaning up the kitchen and decided it was time to head home. The ladies also informed the men there would be a wedding the following weekend.

The men were delighted—another good excuse for a party and feast. They agreed to meet at James and Melissa's the day before the wedding to make the final preparations, and then have the simple ceremony at noon on the following day. Everyone headed to their respective homes.

The following morning, Lars went outside and was playing with Buster when Eileen came out and approached him about a walk.

"Why not?" he said, and the two strolled off in the direction of the sycamore tree, Buster following close behind. They mostly discussed the wedding, with Eileen smiling a lot and squeezing Lars' hand from time to time. Lars could tell Eileen was in a good mood the way she acted. *Wedding preparations always seem to lift the spirits of women*, Lars thought.

Lars told Eileen he had something very serious to discuss with her. "I have been thinking about this since the twins were born," he said. "When the boys call me grandpa, I just thought it would be nice if they called you grandma. What do you think?"

"I think I would love to be called grandma," Eileen replied.

"You know I love you and I know you love me too," Lars said. "I know you are here to stay and I am not going to send you away, ever. If we were married, the boys could call you grandma."

"What are you saying?" Eileen asked.

"I'm saying we should get married."

Eileen teared up, "Are you asking?"

"Yes I am; will you marry me?"

Without hesitation, Eileen said yes.

"I thought early spring would be nice, when the first flowers come out," Lars said.

"I think that would be a perfect time," Eileen said.

"Then it's settled," Lars added.

By the time Eileen finished kissing him, his face was wet from all her tears.

"When do we tell the rest?" Eileen asked.

"If you can wait, after James and Melissa's ceremony," Lars said.

"I'll wait," Eileen promised.

Lars and Eileen strolled back to the house. Eileen had a little more zest in her step and squeezed Lars' hand at a faster rate now. He could tell Eileen's mind was racing, but neither said a word.

Eileen began lunch and she seemed to have that funny grin on her face, the same one she had accused him of having on numerous occasions. Every time she turned to look at Lars, there was another trickle of tears down her cheek. Lars assumed she was happy; he just didn't know how happy she really was. He could never have guessed how happy she really was. She was off the scale.

It seemed like Lars and Eileen were just at James and Melissa's for Thanksgiving and here they were walking up to their house again to prepare for a wedding. "We must be getting old," Lars said. "The days are going by so fast."

"Yes, they are," Eileen agreed. She didn't comment on the age though, only on the swiftly passing days; she felt younger than ever. She was Lars' fiancée and was almost giddy. She had never felt this young.

It was extremely difficult for Eileen not to say anything about her and Lars, but she managed to contain herself. The men rearranged the furniture for the wedding ceremony. After a few rehearsals everyone agreed it would be a fantastic wedding. Sam would conduct the ceremony, Reggie would give the bride away, Lars would be best man, and Eileen and Sally would be bridesmaids. Sean and Debra would lead the processional. They were set and ready to go.

Emily and Reggie stayed the night, while the rest of the neighbors went home. Emily had to help Melissa with her dress and bouquet, while Reggie helped James with flowers. James and Melissa went over their vows again and again in their heads.

The following day, everyone showed up at the prescribed time. All brought food for the event and Reggie had brought several bottles of his best wine to wash it all down. The men mingled while the ladies attended to the bride. Melissa fed the twins and put them to bed. They fell asleep immediately, after which she got into her wedding dress. It wasn't a real wedding dress, but it was the best she could do with the resources she had. Emily brought some lacy fabric she had intended to use to make curtains, and some ribbons. The veil and train was made out of this fabric. The ribbons were used to make a wonderful bouquet with some of the roses James cut.

Finally, it was time to begin, and Sean and Debra were called into the bedroom. The men took their places and Debra led the troupe out of the bedroom, with Sean following closely. The bridesmaids entered and took their places, then began to sing *Here Comes the Bride…* Immediately, Melissa and her dad appeared in the doorway; they slowly walked out the door and toward Sam waiting for them near the front door. When they reached their positions, Reggie gave the bride away, placing her hand into James' hand. Reggie then took his position.

Melissa looked exquisite in her wedding dress. Emily helped fix her hair on top of her head with curls down each side. She also made a tiara out of some of the flowers James had cut and the ribbon she brought. Her lips were a rosy red from the lipstick Eileen had given her.

James was handsome in his suit. Reggie had several suits from the days when he was a salesman that he never got around to throwing out. One fit James nearly perfectly.

The ceremony began with a few words from Sam. Sam had never performed a wedding ceremony, but Eileen, having been married twice, wrote the words on a piece of paper for him to recite. While she was not overly religious, Emily did have a bible, into which Sam stuck the paper from Eileen. "Dearly beloved, we are gathered here…" Sam recited.

When Sam finished, Melissa said her vows. She had tossed and turned much of the night thinking about what she wanted to say. "James, I take thee as my lawful wedded husband, to love, honor and cherish…until death do we part, hopefully not by my gun or cooking…"

James had also written his vows, but as all men, did not work nearly as hard on his words as Melissa had. "Melissa, you have shown me a new world. I am as happy as a squirrel in a nut tree. I promise to love, honor and cherish you…"

When they had finished, they exchanged rings which were fashioned out of wire. Sam finished the ceremony by pronouncing them as husband and wife. James kissed Melissa and the new couple headed toward the front door. Melissa stopped at the door to toss the bouquet. Of course, Eileen caught the bouquet, she being the only unwed lady in the room. The bride and groom continued out the door and shut it behind them.

The ceremony was not perfect, but Sam did the best he could. Everyone thanked Sam for performing the wedding. No one said a word about the few mistakes he made.

Melissa and James kissed for a little while on the porch. And then they returned to the living room and began to mingle and accept congratulations.

Eileen walked over to Lars with her bouquet and he could tell she was about to burst.

"Let's let things settle down a bit, and I'll make our announcement," Lars said.

Eileen said she could wait a few more minutes but not much longer. Lars gave his son a big hug while Eileen was doing the same with Melissa; then they swapped. Reggie broke out a bottle of wine and made a toast to the bride and groom.

Lars and Eileen finished their wines and Reggie refilled all the glasses.

"I don't want to rain on your parade," Lars said, "but Eileen and I have an announcement to make.

All attention turned to Lars.

"Eileen and I are going to be married in the spring."

The congratulations came from all except James. James leaned over to Melissa and whispered in her ear. She then whispered back into James' ear.

"Why don't you guys get married right now?" James asked.

"Yes!" from everyone.

"Again, I don't want to rain on James and Melissa's parade," Lars said.

"You're not raining on anyone," James replied.

"Yes, you guys must get married too. Everything is ready; let's make this a double wedding," Melissa added.

"Then it's settled, right?" James said.

Lars looked at Eileen, "I'm alright with it, how about you?" Lars inquired.

"I'm good with it," she replied.

Sally, Melissa, Emily and Eileen went into the bedroom to prepare Eileen for her wedding. Emily worked on Eileen's hair while Melissa put the veil and train on her. As the ladies worked on her, Eileen thought about her vows. It wasn't long and she was ready, and Reggie was called into the bedroom as were the kids.

The ceremony was then duplicated with Eileen and Lars as bride and groom. Reggie gave the bride away and Sam repeated what was on his piece of paper.

Then Eileen said her vows. "Lars, thank you for not killing me when I first arrived here. Thank you for being the man you are and taking me in. Thank you for teaching me all you have tried to teach me, and showing me a new life completely different from the one I had in the city. Thank you for loving me and for caring for me and making me feel like I belong here. We may both die tomorrow, but I will die as your wife and am so thankful to you for that. I love you with all my heart and promise I will love, honor and cherish you for the rest of my life. I will cook you bacon and put up with your shit from time to time, if I'm in a good mood. I take you as my lawful husband from here to eternity."

"Damn, how am I going to follow that?" Lars asked, smiling at Eileen. "Oh well, I'll try."

"You'll do just fine," Eileen said.

"Eileen, I was lost when you showed up on my doorstep. I was lonely and my life was dying. What's worse, I didn't care. You have given me purpose, hope and all the love I can handle. You have made my life complete and I love and cherish you more than life itself. I want to spend the rest of my life with you and will protect you the best I can. Yes, we may both die tomorrow, but I will die with a smile on my face. From the bottom of my heart, I take you as my lawful wife, also to eternity."

Sam pronounced Lars and Eileen as husband and wife and they kissed, then exited the front door. Everyone clapped and there was not a dry eye in the room. After a few kisses on the front porch, Lars and Eileen returned and Reggie opened a bottle of wine and the congratulations began—first to Lars and Eileen, and then again to James and Melissa.

Emily reminded everyone they still had food to eat. Sally helped Emily warm up some of the dishes and the venison roast was ready, having finished cooking during the ceremonies. Reggie and Sam helped set the table and they all sat down to enjoy the feast. Reggie opened a third bottle of wine and they finished it off as quickly as the previous two.

Everyone relaxed for a while after most of the food was gone. Reggie apologized for not having another bottle of wine, but everyone said they had enough anyway.

"Maybe we should have some coffee now," Emily suggested.

Sally agreed and the two put on a pot and exchanged the wine glasses for mugs. The party and talk went on for another two hours, before Reggie decided it was time for the newlyweds to be left alone.

"It is time for them to consummate the vows," he said. "That shouldn't be too difficult. You've had plenty of practice," Reggie said jokingly.

Everyone laughed and began cleaning up the mess.

Everybody went home a short time later.

"Christmas is just around the corner," Reggie reminded everyone as they parted.

Chapter 32

The next few weeks, Lars spent a lot of time in the barn at his workbench. He wanted the upcoming Christmas party to be the best ever and he had a lot of gifts to prepare. Eileen asked for numerous items, also to use for making gifts, which Lars supplied if he could. They mostly discussed gifts and food, but at times the discussion turned to their lives. Eileen was the happiest person on the planet, she imagined. Lars wished he had married Eileen long before now.

Lars brought up the idea of Eileen killing a deer again. She was still hesitant. He suggested they go hunting and if she still didn't want to shoot the deer, she didn't have to. They needed a little more venison and someone needed to kill a deer. The following morning, the two got up early, dressing a little warmer as a fresh norther had blown in during the night. The two went into the woods across the river and found a well-traveled deer trail not far from the stream. They found a comfortable and well-hidden little hole between some fallen trees and settled in. After an hour, they had seen nothing. A doe and her yearling wandered by after two hours, but another hour passed and again there was nothing. Lars decided it was a bad day to hunt. Maybe the deer were bedded down and not moving due to the new norther and colder wind. They headed back home empty-handed.

They warmed up by the fireplace and Lars helped Eileen prepare lunch. Lars was bacon hungry and went to the smokehouse to retrieve a slab of bacon. They prepared squirrel, bacon, potatoes, and green beans. Lars felt stuffed as he and Eileen relaxed snuggled up on the sofa while they finished their teas. After their food settled a bit, Lars brought in more firewood and some jerky from the smokehouse to nibble on as he began a new novel on the recliner. Directly, Lars dozed off.

Lars only slept an hour; when he got up, he asked if Eileen would like to take a quick trip to see Reggie.

"I can use a walk," she said.

"Then let's get going," Lars replied and they packed up and headed out the door.

The trip to the Carston's seemed to get shorter every time they made it, since the trail that was getting less weedy and more compacted as they used the path. When they got there, Lars told Reggie he was still concerned about the people to the south on the other side of the barricade.

"I think we should take another road trip," Lars said.

"I'm with you, brother," Reggie said. "When?"

"I'll talk to the Lins and the other Lindgrens tomorrow; then we can go the following day if they are agreeable," Lars said.

"That works for me," Reggie replied.

"Alright then, we'll be on our way and see you day after tomorrow," Lars said.

Then Lars and Eileen went home.

Early the next morning, Lars and Eileen took a short trip to the Lins and Lindgrens. Everyone said they would be there the next day.

The following day, everyone showed up about mid-morning. Lars had his RPG and other necessities loaded into the truck and the truck checked over and ready to roll. James again took the bed while Reggie rode shotgun. Lars carefully negotiated his way around the mines and logs; then the team ventured on toward the barricade.

James got ready in the back with his RPG launcher while Lars got his white shirt and stick out.

"Shoot a few shots into the air, Reggie," Lars asked.

Reggie obliged.

After thirty minutes, no one showed up.

"Shoot a few more rounds, Reggie," Lars instructed.

Again, Reggie complied.

The men waited. After another thirty minutes, no one had shown up.

"What do you think we should do?" Lars asked.

"Maybe we should make some more noise. "James, shoot one of your RPGs into that tree over there," Reggie said.

Lars and Reggie got behind the truck and James aimed at the middle of the large tree and fired. The grenade took about half a second to hit the tree and exploded with a deafening bang. The large puff of smoke rose into the air.

"Well, if anyone is home," Lars said, "they now know we're here."

"Yes, they do," Reggie said.

The men watched the puff of smoke rise high into the air and just hang over them. After another thirty minutes, the smoke cloud dissipated and still no one came out to greet them.

Lars looked at James and Reggie with a queer look on his face. They returned the look.

"Well, what do we do now?" Lars questioned.

"If no one is home, we may as well take a look around," James said.

"I think we have no choice," Reggie said. "Otherwise, we came out here for nothing."

They got back in the truck. "Keep your launcher ready at all times," Lars said and then cranked the truck up.

Lars drove around the barricade and proceeded down the road. Reggie and Lars kept their rifles out of the window this time. Reggie checked his AR-15 first, which was pointed towards the floorboard beside him, and then checked his sniper rifle, which he held out of the window. He was as ready as he would ever be.

Lars drove slowly and all three men kept their eyes peeled for anything—everything. Lars came to the top of one hill and they saw nothing. When they topped the second hill, the scenery was the same—more road and more trees and brush. When they topped the third hill, however, they saw a sprawling city. It was not a large city, but a city nevertheless. Lars stopped his truck and the men sat and watched for any sign of life.

After thirty minutes, they saw no one. This was a fairly large town; there had to be someone there. But after another hour, they still saw no one.

"This is scary," Lars said.

"Yes, it is," Reggie replied.

"What do you suppose we should do now?" Lars inquired.

"Let's just wait a while longer," Reggie suggested.

Reggie pulled out his binoculars and began to look around the road ahead.

"You had those all the time?" Lars asked, a little upset.

"Yes," Reggie said. "I didn't think about them. Sorry."

"Okay, I'll chalk that up to old age," Lars said with a grin. "Well, what do you see?"

"A Wal-Mart sign on one side of the road and an HEB grocery store on the other side," Reggie answered.

"If they haven't been totally looted, these may be a good find," Lars said.

Reggie looked over at Lars and smiled. Reggie then gave Lars the binoculars so he could have a look. James couldn't hear what Lars and Reggie were saying from the back of the truck. He peeked over the side and asked what was going on.

"There's a Wal-Mart store and an HEB grocery up ahead," Lars said.

"Are we going into town?" James asked.

"We are discussing it," Lars said.

Lars could see no smoke, no vehicles roaming around, and no people.

"Let's move in a little closer," Lars finally said.

"Okay," Reggie replied. "We're going in a little closer, James. Be alert and ready."

"Okay," James replied.

Lars started the engine and put the truck into drive. He laid the binoculars on the seat between him and Reggie and eased toward the stores. The adrenalin was pumping in all the men as they pulled within a few hundred yards of the Wal-Mart store. Lars stopped but did not cut the engine off. All three had their fingers on the triggers of their rifles and RPG launcher.

They sat and watched. Lars made a mental note on some of the other retail stores he could see with the binoculars. There was a tractor supply, a lumberyard, a hardware store and a dry goods store. Thirty minutes went by, then an hour. They saw no one and nothing out of the ordinary.

"There could be someone watching us," Lars said.

"It does feel like a trap, doesn't it?" Reggie asked.

"Yes, it does," Lars replied. "I feel like I'm bluffing pocket aces with nine/three off suit and an empty flop."

"Let's get out of here," Reggie said.

"I'm with you," Lars agreed.

Lars turned the steering wheel sharp and turned the truck around. He then hit the gas and they headed back towards home. Lars checked the odometer.

"Stop at the barricade," Reggie told Lars.

"Okay," Lars said.

Lars stopped at the barricade and Reggie got out and pulled out a small can of paint and a brush. He shook the can a few times and then pried the lid off with his Swiss army knife. Reggie then painted a sign on the cars as James and Lars watched. When he finished, Reggie stood back and looked at his art. The paint was overly applied and streaks ran down from each letter, but the message was unmitigated: *Kill Zone - All who enter will die! No exceptions!*

"That should do it," Reggie said as he got back into the truck. Lars agreed and steered his truck around the barricade. Lars didn't stop until he reached the road into his place. There was very little talk on the trip back. Lars then checked his odometer again; he had driven 33 miles. Lars then drove down his road and around the downed trees and minefield. He made his way to the house just as it was getting dark. He honked the horn and pulled up beside the house.

The men were greeted by their spouses and neighbors. Hugs and kisses were shared all around; then they sat on the porch and talked a while.

"I'm sorry it is so late," Lars said.

"Well, what did you guys find?" Sam asked.

"We found a town that appeared to be empty," James said.

"And it had a Wal-Mart store and an HEB," Reggie said.

"But we all got a little uneasy," Lars added. "It looked a lot like a trap, so we turned around and headed home."

"What are you going to do now?" Eileen asked.

"I think we need to go back," Lars said, "but we need night vision goggles."

"A little misstep on my part," Reggie said.

"When?" Emily asked.

"Now. We get the night vision goggles and we go straight back," Reggie said. "James, do you think we can go to my place now?"

"Yes, we can," James replied.

Lars retrieved a lantern from inside the house. "You guys take care," Lars said. "I'll have the truck ready when you get back."

"Sounds good," Reggie said, "we'll be back in a couple hours."

Reggie and James headed off toward Reggie's and Lars got after the truck. He added gas and checked the fluids and tires.

James and Reggie were back in a couple hours. They wore their goggles on the way back and Reggie brought three backpacks as well just in case they found some bounty to haul back. Lars had thrown a couple empty corn sacks into the truck as well.

"These goggles are fantastic," James said. "They made the trip back much easier and quicker."

Lars was just finishing his third cup of coffee by the time James and Reggie got back. Eileen had brewed another pot and filled three thermoses for the men to get them through the night. She then started another pot as it was going to be a long night for them too.

Lars, James, and Reggie kissed the ladies goodbye again. Lars cranked the truck up as James and Reggie got in. Then he backed the truck up and headed towards the sycamore tree and then up the road. Lars made it around the mine-field and trees, and then onward to the highway and checked his odometer. As they were approaching the barricade, the men put on their goggles and Lars cut the lights off.

"Can you see where you're going, Lars?" Reggie asked.

"Better than with the lights," Lars replied. This wasn't quite the truth, but Lars could see well enough.

Lars drove much slower now as he eased his way near the Wal-Mart. He turned his truck around and rolled to a stop, not wanting to touch his brakes as this would light up the taillights. Lars turned the engine off and the men got out of the truck.

Lars, James, and Reggie got their weapons and then just stood at the back of the truck, looking the city over. There were no lights of any kind. They also dis-cussed what they wanted to find in the stores. Salt was the primary item. Though

James and Melissa had found a significant amount of salt in the Weston's store-room, divided four ways, it wouldn't stretch nearly as far. As important as salt was, they still needed more. After that, antibiotics and painkillers, coffee, tea, sugar, and—if they had room for it—toothpaste and deodorant, in that order. They were all but out of coffee, tea, and sugar as well.

"Well, men, we may as well get going," Lars said and led the way.

As they made their way to the Wal-Mart, there was an eerie silence. The sky was overcast, which was to their advantage, and there was just enough moon shining through the clouds that they could see well. When they reached the building, Lars led James and Reggie all the way around the perimeter checking for any signs of life; there was none. Lars found a window which had been broken out and the men entered through the opening.

It was difficult to see inside even with the night goggles, and so Reggie pulled out a light stick, bent it and gave it a shake. The light sticks were not all that bright, but with the night vision goggles on, the store lit up like someone had turned the lights on. Reggie then handed James and Lars each a light stick.

"Again," James said, "these goggles are awesome."

Each took an aisle and when they got to the far side, they reported what they had found. James found salt and took Lars and Reggie back down his aisle. The men filled two backpacks with this precious commodity.

The store had been looted, but mostly what was taken was ready to eat food items and canned goods. The pharmacy was cleaned out. While the shelves were mostly bare, some of the items the men were looking for were mainly untouched.

They then took three more aisles and repeated the procedure. This time they found coffee, but no tea and filled up the third backpack and partially filled a corn sack. "Dammit," Lars said, "I need tea."

They again took three aisles and found nothing and repeated the process. Lars found antibiotics and pain killers and the men put these items in corn sacks. Lars then found toothpaste but no deodorant. Lars only managed to squeeze in a few tubes of toothpaste and they could haul no more. The men made their way back to the broken window through which they had entered the store and, now able to see much better, they tossed their light sticks inside the store and looked around the parking lot before they exited.

The men made their way back to the truck, removed their backpacks, and emptied them out inside the truck along with the corn sacks.

"You guys up for one more raid?" Lars asked.

"Yep," James said.

"Well, guys, we may as well check out the HEB store." The men headed back towards town and the HEB. They did not get all the salt from the Wal-Mart store and there was also more of the other of the items they needed still in the Wal-

Mart, but they needed to at least check out the HEB store before they headed back home.

The men carefully made their way to the store and checked the perimeter before entering. They proceeded exactly as they had at the Wal-Mart store and found more salt, which they collected. This trip, however, the remaining backpack was filled with toothpaste and more antibiotics and painkillers. Lars was also able to find a few bottles of rubbing alcohol, which he also added to their cache. Again, this store had been looted as well, but just like the Wal-Mart store, they were able to find some of the items they needed. Lars was disappointed there was no deodorant, but especially pissed that there was no tea.

Satisfied they could carry no more, the men headed back to the truck. Before they got in, they took another good look at the city. Again, there were no lights. Lars started the engine and they headed back home.

"You know how damn lucky we were?" Lars said.

"I certainly do," Reggie replied.

"It is strange that there was no one around. It was even more peculiar that there were so many items we needed still on the shelves, not just in one, but both stores.

"That is really odd," Reggie said.

The men were quiet the remainder of the trip, each sipping on their thermoses of coffee. *It has to be getting close to daylight*, Lars thought.

By the time Lars made it home, the sun was just peeking above the horizon. Lars honked his horn as he drove up and parked by the side of the house. The men were surprised that everyone was wide awake and on the porch when they arrived. They really should have expected this though. The others couldn't sleep knowing James, Reggie and Lars were out and about. The men could have gotten into trouble the ladies could not even imagine. The ladies greeted the men with hugs and kisses.

Sam and the ladies were surprised and happy with the load of goods the men had brought home. They carried all the items inside and stacked them on the kitchen table.

"What now?" Eileen asked.

"We need to get some sleep; then I think we need to go back again tonight," Lars asserted.

James and Reggie agreed. "We got a lot of stuff, but there is still a lot more we can get," Reggie said.

Sam and Sally said they needed to get home to tend to the hogs, chickens and goats, but they would be back later this evening. They then headed home.

Eileen and Emily fixed a bite to eat for the men; then they got on the recliner and sofa and soon dozed off. Melissa tended to the twins, and then the ladies each took separate short naps while the men were sleeping.

Sam and Sally showed up a couple hours before dark and the men got up and got ready. Lars added more gas to his tank and checked the fluids and kicked the tires. He also went inside and found a couple duffel bags in a closet and two more backpacks. He wished he had thought of these before the first trip.

When it got dark, the men kissed the ladies goodbye and headed back to the highway and headed south. They parked where they had previously parked and donned their goggles. As the men peered across the city, this time they noticed a light they had not previously seen. The men waited at the truck for a while and watched the light. Reggie got his binoculars and looked at it. It appeared to be a vehicle, but it was so far off he couldn't tell for certain. As they watched the light, though, it gradually moved in the opposite direction and did not appear to be a threat.

The men decided to head over to the Wal-Mart store, and they proceeded as they had the night before. Lars and Reggie both took two backpacks and a duffel bag each. James took only his backpack, as he also had to carry the RPG launcher and a couple rounds. They got the last of the salt, more coffee, sugar, rubbing alcohol, and over the counter medications. They also filled a duffel bag with toilet paper. James grabbed a couple boxes of disposable diapers, the last ones on the shelves, for the twins. *Melissa will appreciate these,* James thought. Lars found several pairs of fingernail clippers and took these as well. They then made their way to the truck and unloaded.

They checked for the light they had seen when they arrived, and saw no sign of it, so they headed over to the HEB store. Again, they got the last of the salt, more coffee, and medications. They also got two duffel bags of toilet paper. There was no more sugar, but they found more rubbing alcohol. Then they browsed around for more items to fill the last backpack. Lars got razor blades and razors, hemorrhoid ointment, and toothpaste. James grabbed a few cans of bug spray while Reggie collected writing tablets, pencils, and a few containers of bleach. That was all they could find they could use. They had all the bags filled and headed back to the truck.

They put their booty into the truck and headed home. When the men were well down the road, Reggie began laughing. Lars followed suit. The men had not only secured a good supply of many of the items they felt were necessary for their survival, they had fun doing it. They did not get shot at, the task was relatively easy except the heavy loads they hauled, and they had a sense of achievement. They had ventured out of their little valley and successfully raided a nearby city without getting caught or hurt. They had worked well together and had gained confidence in their abilities to provide for themselves.

The men got back to the house before the sun came up this time as they had left home a little earlier than before. Again, however, Sam and the ladies were on the porch to greet them when they arrived. The ladies prepared an early breakfast and they all ate and discussed their adventure. Sam and the ladies were very pleased with the items the men had secured for the group. Melissa gave James a big kiss for thinking of her with the diapers. "You don't know how tired I get washing and drying cloth diapers," she said.

After they finished eating, the women informed the men that they had had a meeting while they men were off looting the stores.

"We have made some decisions which you will abide by. We had a quorum and voted and passed our measures," Eileen said.

"Oh, you did," Lars replied with a smile.

"Yes, we did," Emily affirmed.

"Doesn't seem quite fair," James stated.

"No, it doesn't," Reggie agreed.

"Well, wait until you hear our new rules," Eileen said. "You may not totally like the measures, but I think you will agree with us."

"Now that we have a good supply of many items we are out of or are getting low on, we are going to make certain they last," Emily stated.

"Yes," Eileen said. "Coffee and tea will be reused three times before it's thrown out, and the amount we use each time will be cut in half."

"You may not always get as much as you like," Melissa said, "but our supply will last much longer."

"You will drink a lot more water," Eileen asserted.

"Every item will be used sparingly," Sally said.

The men did not disagree with the ladies. They had been drinking too much coffee and tea anyway. They were still a little miffed that the ladies had made the decision without them, but they also knew it was for their own good. They agreed with them and promised they would abide by the new rules.

"One additional rule," Eileen posed. "You will need to find a substitute for salt when curing your hides. Salt is too important for canning and food preparation to use in this manner."

Reggie did not tan hides and James had just begun to tan his hides.

"I'm fine with that," James stated, "provided Dad can come up with an alternative."

"I'll figure something out," Lars said.

"Okay, now that this is settled," Eileen said, "come over here and give me a big bear hug."

Lars obliged. James and Melissa, and then Reggie and Emily did the same.

"I am so proud of you," Eileen said. "Thank you for what you guys did for all of us."

"Thank you, darlin'," Lars said. "And thank you, Sam, for taking such good care of the ladies."

"You are most welcome," Sam said.

"We need to make another trip to town," Lars inserted, "but we can do that later. We need to check out some of the other stores, particularly the tractor supply and hardware stores."

"Yes, we do," James said.

"Well, folks, I think it is time we head home," Reggie said.

"Yes, it is," Sam agreed.

Sam, James, and Reggie each took a couple backpacks of their divided bounty. They would get the remainder on the next trip over. They all hugged and kissed, and went to their respective homes.

"Good job," Reggie said as they were leaving.

"Don't forget," Lars said, "Christmas is just around the corner."

"We won't forget," Melissa said.

"We'll see you guys soon," James said as they headed home.

"Did you enjoy your little adventure?" Eileen asked after everyone had gone home.

"Yes I did," Lars replied. "You know, the adrenalin was pumping and the loads we carried out were heavy, but it really felt good. It was great to be able to provide, not only our necessities, but also a few of the niceties in life, particularly coffee. I'm still a little pissed we didn't find deodorant and especially tea, but we'll get by. We may never live like we did before the grid shut down, but we will be okay."

"Yes we will," Eileen said.

"Come here, you," Lars demanded and gave her a big bear hug, then planted a kiss on her lips she would not soon forget.

Christmas Eve rolled around. Lars and Eileen had plenty of daily chores, but both managed to find at least a few hours each day to work on their gifts for the party the next day. Lars and Eileen made a quick trip to take the gift Lars made for the twins to the edge of the clearing at James and Melissa's home, as it was heavy. They hid the gift in the bushes where they would have easy access the following day. The remainder of the gifts could be taken in a single load. By the time evening rolled around, they were ready for the trip the following morning.

Eileen got her shower first, and then Lars. When Lars stepped out of the bathroom, Eileen was lying on the bed wearing nothing but a smile. Lars returned the smile.

"An early Christmas gift," was all she said. She didn't have to say it twice.

When they finished, they rinsed off in the shower together. "Thank you very much, Mrs. Lindgren," he said as he stepped out of the shower.

"My pleasure, big boy," she replied. They went to bed and snuggled up together and fell asleep.

The following morning, Lars and Eileen got up early, eager to get started. They dressed quickly and grabbed their gifts and gear; then they headed to James and Melissa's where the Christmas party would be held. Lars and Eileen were the first there, but the rest of the neighbors were not far behind. Melissa made eggnog, saying she got the recipe from Emily and some goat milk from the Lins. She served a mug to each guest after they finished putting their gifts and gear down. Lars and Eileen thanked Melissa for the eggnog. "Delicious," Lars said.

Eileen asked if she could help in the kitchen, and then followed Melissa to the stove. Lars started up a conversation with James. "It's going to be a very good day," Lars said.

"Yes, it is," James replied.

"How's married life?" Lars asked.

"Fantastic, Dad," was the reply, loud enough Melissa could hear. Melissa looked over and gave James a smile.

Reggie and Emily signaled and Lars opened the front door and waved them in. James did the same with the Lins, hearing them at the rear of the house. The twins started crying and Lars picked up one and took him to the sofa while Eileen grabbed the other and joined Lars.

"How are you boys doing this morning?" he asked.

"They are probably wet," Melissa said.

Eileen laid her twin next to Lars and went to retrieve some diapers. Eileen changed one diaper and then swapped with Lars and began to change the other diaper. The second was more than wet, so Lars got up, taking the dry kid and headed over to the kitchen to retrieve another mug of eggnog. Lars couldn't tell the difference between the twins at this age. He wasn't even sure Melissa could, but she assured him she knew which was which.

When Eileen finished cleaning up the second twin, Lars gave her back the first and took the other to kiss and bounce him on his knee for a bit. At two and a half months, they didn't do much but drool when you played with them, but Lars loved his grandkids anyway.

After a bit, Lars put his twin down and asked Reggie for a little help. Lars and Reggie retrieved the gift for the twins and assembled it at the side of the house. Nearly two hours later, Lars and Reggie went inside, having finished the task.

"I didn't think it would take quite this long," Lars said. "Must have been the assistant," he added with a smile.

"Kiss my ass!" Reggie exclaimed.

It wasn't long before the meal was prepared and laid out on the table. The friends gathered and ate until they thought they would burst.

Everyone thanked Melissa and James for hosting the party. "It's my pleasure," Melissa said. "Thank you guys for allowing me to host the party. This really makes me feel at home here in the valley."

After a little recuperating from the huge meal everyone had eaten, James said it was time to open gifts. They started with numerous gifts for Sean and Debra, mostly clothes Sally and Emily had sewn and a few small handmade toys. While the kids were playing with the toys, the grownups opened their gifts. All the gifts were homemade and from the heart, which made each and every one of them so special.

Sam got a rocking chair from Lars, which he said he would get a lot of use out of the next few years. There were scarves, fancy candles, smoked food, and Lars had gotten a fine hunting knife Reggie made himself. Lars and Eileen presented first a fine carved picture frame to James, and then Eileen presented the painting of James and Melissa to go into the frame.

Melissa was in tears. "This is so beautiful," she said.

Eileen did a wonderful job with the painting, especially since she painted it completely from memory.

Melissa said, "We will hang it there," pointing to the only bare wall in the living room. She then gave Lars and Eileen a big hug and kiss.

Lars opened his gift from Eileen to find a new pair of moccasins. She had sneaked some of his deer hide stash out of the barn. He kissed her and thanked her for the thoughtful and well-crafted gift. "I thought I was going to have to make a pair for myself," Lars said. "The old ones are getting pretty ratty," he said, kissing her again. Lars took his gift for her out of his pocket. Eileen took the little box, held it up to her ear and gave it a little shake. It made no sound. She then tore the paper off and opened the box but saw only paper. She pulled the crumpled paper out and laying in the bottom of the box was a shiny band of gold. Eileen looked up to Lars with tears starting to run down her cheeks.

"I had some old gold coins," Lars said as he took the ring from the box. "I melted a couple down," he said as he slipped the band over her left ring finger. "We are now officially husband and wife." She planted a kiss on Lars' lips he would not soon forget. "I love you" were the only words she could get out; then she hugged him so tight he had difficulty breathing.

"I love you too, sweetheart."

"Well," Reggie said, "that about takes care of the gifts, except one."

"Right," Lars said as he grabbed up one of the twins and Reggie, the other.

They led the group out of the front door and around the side of the house where they set up the swing set. Lars and Reggie sat the boys in the padded box swings and strapped them in. Then they gave them a gentle push back and forth. The boys didn't do much, but at least they were not crying. Everyone stood watching as the boys gently moved back and forth. James and Melissa thanked Lars and Eileen and then her dad for helping put the set together.

"When they get old enough for flat seats, I'll replace the box seats," Lars said, "but for now these seats will keep them from crying for hours at a time. The swings will be especially good when you are working in the garden." They watched the boys for a while. It wasn't long before both boys were sound asleep.

"Guess the swings work," Lars said with a smile.

James and Melissa smiled as well.

Lars mentioned that the tea was a bit on the weak side. "You better get used to it," she said. "This is the third pot from the same tea leaves. Lars frowned but didn't say another word.

The party moved back into the house and Melissa and James put the boys to bed. Lars and Eileen took center seats on the sofa. Lars then called Sean and Debra over, one to his right and the other to the left, as he read *The Night Before Christmas*, which he had brought over from his book collection. By the time he finished with the story, the kids were sound asleep. It had been a long day for them. Melissa and Sally carried them to Melissa's bed.

"The days are certainly short this time of year," Lars said. Everyone decided to head out in order to get home before dark. Everyone thanked Melissa again for hosting the party. This would be a Christmas they would not soon forget, especially Eileen.

Chapter 33

The next few years, there were fewer incidents with intruders in the valley, but it seemed they would never be completely safe from attacks. Sam had said this years ago and his postulation had become fact, at least over the past few years. Fortunately for all, however, Buster always kept an alert eye out for intruders. Their safety also was due in no small part to Lars' numerous skills. He had an eagle eye that was second only to Buster's. Lars always dressed to blend in with his surroundings. His moccasins, which he always wore, allowed him to walk as quietly as any animal in the woods. Lars was also very adept with his rifle and pistol.

Lars never liked killing anyone—he especially hadn't liked killing the Tuckers and Gómezes and this troubled him often—but he never wavered when it was necessary. Well, maybe once. A couple years back, he did hesitate a second when it was necessary to kill a woman when a couple wandered into the valley. This hesitation cost him a finger that the lady shot off. Luckily, the shot hit Lars rifle after hitting his finger, deflecting the slug away from Lars body. Lars killed three more people after that and never wavered again.

It seemed like the twins just had a birthday and now it was time for yet another. Melissa and James arrived at Lars and Eileen's at mid-morning, explaining the boys really slowed them down every time they went somewhere.

"If we get started ten minutes early, it takes twenty minutes. If we get started twenty minutes early, it takes thirty minutes," James explained.

"That's not a problem," Eileen said. "Life always throws something at you from time to time to slow you down. And you can't plan for it. We all know what that's like."

Melissa smiled.

"Reggie and Emily got here only a few minutes ago," Lars added.

Eileen then thanked James and Melissa for making the long trip with the boys, explaining she wasn't certain she could make the trip to their place with such a large birthday cake.

Melissa said it was no problem. "Thank you for making the cake."

Lars knelt down and Ronnie and Robbie ran over to give grandpa a big hug. He picked the boys up and kissed them on the cheek. "Happy Birthday," he said to his favorite grandkids. "My Melissa, what are you feeding these guys? They are growing like weeds!" Lars said with a smile.

He then looked back at the boys and bounced them up and down a little.

"How old are you today, Ronnie?"

"Four," was the reply.

"How about you, Robbie? How old are you?"

"Four," was again the reply.

Eileen came over and gave the twins a big hug and kiss and then wished them a happy birthday.

"What do you say boys?" Melissa said.

"Thank you, Grandma," was the reply from both.

Eileen squeezed the boys again and said, "You're welcome, young men. I can't believe these little guys have grown so much," Eileen added. Eileen stood up and turned to Melissa. "You are doing a wonderful job with the boys," she said.

"Thank you," Melissa replied.

Sam and Sally were along shortly with Sean and Debra in tow. The kids had grown too big to carry everywhere, so with them having to walk, they slowed Sam and Sally down a bit too now.

"Who are these young people?" Eileen asked Sally. "They are growing so fast, I almost didn't recognize them," she added.

"It's probably the bacon," Lars said.

Eileen imagined Lars never saw Sam as a person, but instead only saw a slab of bacon every time Sam approached him. Sean and Debra were only a year or two older than the twins and they played well together. Debra, though she was a girl, thought of herself as just another one of the boys. Sean and the twins treated her as one of the boys too.

"Everyone is here now," Melissa said, "so let's get this party going."

Melissa sat the boys down in the middle of the living room; then everyone else sat on the sofa and recliner while the boys opened their gifts. Lars and Eileen gave each a wooden rifle that Lars made and Eileen put the finishing touches onto. Reggie made each a coonskin hat, while Emily made them moccasins. When they finished opening their gifts, the boys were handed sticks to whack a piñata Sally Lin made.

Sam tossed a string over one of the rafters and tied the piñata to the end. Then he pulled the red, blue, green, and yellow frilly monster up and down for several minutes before the boys finally killed the creature and the candy spewed out. Ronnie, Robbie, Sean, and Debra scrambled to pick up the assortment of hard candies Sally also made.

Eileen served tea, giving the boys time to eat some of the candy until Melissa stepped in saying they have had enough. "You will have cake in a few minutes," she explained.

Eileen announced it was time to cut the cake. The cake was a two-layer oblong chocolate carrot cake with four small candles on each end that Eileen made from one of their larger candles. Robbie and Ronnie's names were scrolled on opposite ends in contrasting chocolate Eileen got from Emily. She and Reggie certainly possessed a marvelous stash of survival foods, which provided a little extra for special occasions, including chocolate.

Melissa sat the boys on opposite sides of the table with the appropriate names facing the boys. James got behind one son while Melissa got behind the other. Eileen lit the candles and they all sang *Happy Birthday*. Then James and Melissa stood the boys up and instructed them to blow the candles out.

Plates were set out for all and Eileen cut the cake, delivering a slice to each, beginning with the two birthday boys. When everyone finished their cake, Eileen refilled all the glasses with a fruity drink she made and the adults retired to the living room for some more conversation while the boys hunted bear with their new wooden guns. The bear was really fierce—with Grandpa playing the part of the bear—but by the time the boys finished with it, it was little more than a bearskin rug, which James had skinned and tanned for them. The boys didn't know the difference between a bearskin and a deerskin at their age, but he would need to come up with another game soon. The boys were quick to learn and couldn't be fooled much longer. After about an hour, the boys were getting tired and it was time for them to take a nap. James and Melissa decided this would be a good opportunity for them to go home, as the boys were much easier to carry if they were not squirming all the time.

Everyone gave each other a big hug and farewell and kissed the boys on the cheek, waking them up slightly.

"Happy Birthday," they all said to the boys.

Chapter 34

Lars and Eileen produced very successful crops most years, thanks in part to their new irrigation system, but maybe a little more importantly to the tender loving care Eileen gave the delicate plants. She worked tirelessly gathering chicken poop, dog poop and composted logs to place around the young plants. The extra nitrogen and minerals gave the young plants a significant boost.

Eileen and Lars seemed to have been made for each other and their love for each other grew daily. They worked very hard and took a lot of pride in everything they did, but everything they did they considered play—hard play, but play nevertheless. They loved their tough lives. Gardening, gathering firewood, and dressing deer, fish and other small animals was their connection to the land and to each other. Taking care of their grandkids was hard work at times, but to Lars and Eileen this was their best playtime. No one told them what to do and when to do it; they simply did what they needed to do to eat, live, and love, and their efforts paid off. They always had plenty to eat, they laughed, enjoyed their hobbies and neighbors, and Robbie and Ronnie were growing up smart, strong, and healthy.

Reggie and Emily loved living off the land but did not completely depend upon what the land could provide. Reggie made certain of this a long time ago. They had a more reliable source of electricity than the others in the valley. While Reggie did provide a substantial portion of their heating in the form of wood for fuel, they had all the food they would ever need with their non-perishable food packets. Reggie and Emily enjoyed the deer and rabbits, but didn't need them. They enjoyed the fruit and vegetables they grew, but were not dependent upon them. The things the land could provide were merely embellishments.

They lived very comfortably in their home and had for many years, long before Lars moved into the valley. Reggie and Emily loved each other very much and this showed in how they looked at each other, talked to the other, and touched each other. It especially showed in how far Reggie went to protect Emily and his property. He loved Emily more than he could describe and he was certainly happy when playing with his guns and explosives. The couple loved the woods and river as much as anyone. They were survivors, but their survival was due more to Reggie's planning than his survival skills.

The Lins came from a different world. They had no relatives anyone knew about. They were originally from Hong Kong. They never talked about their past and no one pressed them for information. They must have had a terrible ordeal because they changed the subject any time someone asked about their past. They were highly skilled in survival methods and their love and caring for each other and the valley spilled over to each and every one of their neighbors in the form of bacon, cheese, honey and black and red pepper. Sam expanded his hog farm for only one reason—to provide Lars with the bacon he loved so much. Sally worked hard to provide the little things which make life worth living like crystalline candy flavored with wild mint and wild berries. She made the best homemade bread and jelly in the valley.

Though Melissa and James' connection was accidental, they were a good match for each other. You could see their love every day in the way they cared for Ronnie and Robbie. Melissa worked hard in and around the house, but she worked even harder teaching the boys how to read, how to do things around the house, and to love and take care of each other. James worked equally hard at teaching the boys about the woods and river. He taught them how to mind their parents but also how to be assertive. He taught them to play hard, which at their age would build their bodies strong and healthy like their hard work would when they grew older. They loved each other, their children, their life, and their valley as much as anyone.

Lars helped James and Melissa as well, by reading stories to the boys often when he and Eileen would visit, which they did frequently. He also helped James teach the boys how to shoot accurately and safely and to take care of their weapons. James showed the boys how to clean the meat they killed and they learned there was plenty food in the forest if they knew where to find it. By the time the boys turned eight years old, they both killed their first deer. They needed help cleaning the deer simply because of the size of the animal, but they knew the basics of the process long before then. Another four years and they would both be master hunters.

One day, Lars and Eileen had just finished breakfast; his favorite meal—bacon and scrambled eggs. He had a second cup of coffee with Eileen before he began his chores. His first task was to fill the wood bins in the house with kindling and split logs. Lars filled the kindling bin beside the fireplace and then went out to get the logs. Lars brought one load in and stacked it neatly in the steel rack, then went out for another. Eileen finished cleaning the kitchen and poured herself another cup of coffee. *Lars should have been back by now*, she thought. She walked over to the front window and looked out toward the garden, and then out toward his truck. She didn't see Lars, so she walked to the door and pulled it open. She still didn't see him.

"Son-of-a-bitch!" She heard, then a shot from around the corner of the house. She hurried to the end of the porch. Near the several cords of wood stacked beside the house. Lars was on his knees with his pistol in one hand, and holding his neck with the other. Eileen jumped off the porch and ran to him. Immediately, she saw the rattlesnake laying on the ground with a missing head. Eileen knelt in front of Lars and looked into his eyes, then she pulled his hand away from his neck. There were fang marks near his carotid artery. Eileen then looked back into Lars eyes. She couldn't hold back the tears.

"Looks like I've really done it this time," Lars said. "That thing got me good."

"I'll get help," Eileen said.

"There's nothing that can be done," Lars said. "He got me in a bad place. I love you darlin'."

"I love you too, baby," Eileen said, hugging him tightly. Then she could feel his body going limp and she could not hold his weight up and Lars fell to the ground taking her with him.

"No!" she screamed. She turned him onto his back and looked into his face; then she put her ear to his chest. She heard his heart beat three times, then it stopped. She hugged him hard as she began to cry out loud. Eileen had spent more hours snuggled against his warm body than she could count, but now his skin was growing cold. Lars was the source of her happiness and her strength, but now Eileen could feel her strength fading and her happiness shattered. "No! Not now," Eileen said out loud. "I need you. Please don't leave me."

Buster came over and lay down beside Lars and Eileen with his muzzle on Lars' arm. Eileen did not know how long she lay there crying on Lars' chest, but though she still felt like crying, her eyes ran out of fluid. She rose up and looked at Lars and closed his eyes with her hand. She didn't feel she had the strength to get up, so she lay back down on Lars' chest, clenching him tightly. *What am I going to do without you?* Eileen asked herself. *You have so much more to teach me. I can't make it here without you. I need you. I need you. Please!*

Finally, Eileen knew she had to get up and get help. Eileen stood up and told Buster to stay and then went inside and got a quilt to cover the body. Having done this, she ran as fast as she could to James and Melissa's. She was tired and crying again by the time she made it to their porch. *This is very unusual*, James thought as Eileen made her way to the house. When she got closer, James could see she was a terrible mess and was crying. Eileen wasn't able to say much, partly from having run most of the way but also due to her crying, but she managed to tell James that Lars was dead. Eileen didn't see them, but tears began to trickle down James' cheek.

James told Eileen to stay with Melissa, who had come to the door; then James took off toward his dad's place. It didn't take long, with James running the entire distance. He checked his dad, with Buster still lying beside Lars, and then James took off toward Reggie's. James told Reggie what happened and Emily and Reggie followed immediately. By the time James made it back to Lars, he spotted Eileen, Melissa, and the boys coming from the other direction. Melissa explained to the boys what happened to Grandpa, though she wasn't quite sure they understood; then she took them inside the house. Eileen went to Lars, kneeling on the ground next to his body, her crying beginning again. "Oh baby, I need you. Please come back to me," Eileen begged.

Reggie told James to go get Sam and Sally and he left immediately. Reggie went to Lars' barn and found a small tarp and some leather cordage. Reggie put them down next to Lars and then knelt down next to Eileen. He put his arm around her. Emily, who was also on the ground on the other side, put her arm around Eileen as well, consoling her. Reggie had no words. After a while, Emily convinced Eileen to go into the house while Reggie wrapped the body. Melissa almost had coffee ready by the time they walked in. Emily took Eileen to the sofa and Melissa brought coffee over a short time later.

By the time James, Sam, and Sally returned, Reggie had Lars wrapped up and secured with leather cord. Sam and Sally gave Reggie a tearful hug, and then Sally went inside with the kids to join the rest of the ladies. Sam knelt down beside Lars, put his hand on his chest and mumbled a few words to himself; then he stood with tears in his eyes. Sam then hugged Reggie and James. James went inside the house to talk to Eileen.

"I know this is tough on you," James said as he hugged Eileen. "I need to know where you want Dad buried."

Eileen looked up, not able to speak at first. "I think below the sycamore tree would be nice," Eileen said, bursting into tears again. "What am I going to do?" she kept saying over and over.

James went back outside and told the men where they should dig the grave. He went to the barn and found two shovels, and then walked back over to Reggie and Sam. Buster continued to guard Lars while the men made their way to the sycamore tree. They picked out a nice spot where the grave would be visible from the house and began to dig. When they finished, they retrieved Lars' body and placed it beside the hole. Buster followed and took his position beside the body. James walked back to the house and informed the ladies of their progress; then he walked back to the barn to retrieve some rope and made his way back to the sycamore.

Eileen stopped crying briefly and decided the inevitable shouldn't be postponed any longer. The ladies worked their way toward the men, Melissa and Emily on Eileen's arms and Sally herding the kids close behind. As they reached the grave, Eileen began crying again and knelt down beside Lars and wrapped her arms around the bundle, saying something which was inaudible to anyone else. The ladies gave her some time and then urged her up and back. The men put ropes around the bundle and lowered it to the bottom of the hole.

Reggie recited a beautiful eulogy hitting on most of Lar's fine accomplishments. There were not enough hours in the day to note all of his amazing qualities, but Reggie touched upon all his main attributes. Everyone was in tears before he got started, including himself, and the tears were still flowing freely when he finished. Reggie and then each of the others gave Eileen a big hug and kiss on the cheek. Eileen picked up a handful of dirt, put it to her mouth—again saying something which was imperceptible to the others—and then tossed the dirt into the hole. "Goodbye, my love," Eileen said.

Eileen and the others stood back and watched as James and Reggie filled the hole. There were not a lot of flowers this time of year, but Melissa managed to find a few and handed most of them to Eileen, reserving a single flower for each of the rest of them. Eileen felt she could not stand any longer and knelt to watch the men finish filling the hole. When they were finished, James helped her back to her feet and she put her flowers on the grave. Then, one by one, the rest added their flowers and said their final farewell.

"I love you dad." James said.

"I love you, grandpa," the twins said.

"Good bye old friend," said Sam and Sally.

Melissa and Emily said, "We'll miss you, Lars."

"Goodbye you old coot," Reggie said.

Everyone looked at Reggie. His farewell sounded a little out of place, but outside of Eileen, they all knew Reggie would miss Lars more than anyone, quite possibly including James.

It was mid-afternoon by the time everyone made it back to the house. Melissa made more coffee and some food as no one had eaten since breakfast, while Emily and Sally continued to console Eileen who took a little coffee but refused food. No one ate much, but there was some nibbling. Sam and Sally offered to stay with Eileen, but Melissa told them she and James would stay.

"It might help if Ronnie and Robbie are close," Melissa said.

They agreed but said they would be back tomorrow.

Reggie and Emily said they would be back tomorrow as well.

Sam and Sally excused themselves saying they would bring some food back and would be prepared to do whatever needed to be done; then they gave Eileen a final hug and kiss and headed home. Reggie and Emily didn't stay much longer, telling Melissa not to worry about food, just take care of Eileen and they would see them tomorrow. Reggie and Emily also gave Eileen another kiss and loving hug.

It had been another long day for the boys, so Melissa put them to bed early and headed back to talk with Eileen and console her. James sat with Eileen until Melissa came back in; then he decided to run home quickly to get them some clean clothes. He said he would ride his cycle back and wouldn't be long, definitely before dark. James did make it back by dark and went in to shower and change. Melissa convinced Eileen to take a shower, and then took one herself. Melissa, James, and Eileen sat and talked for a couple hours before they could urge Eileen into bed.

Chapter 35

It was a long, restless night for Eileen; she woke up several times and then cried herself back to sleep. Having gone to bed early, the twins woke Melissa and James up just before sunrise. Melissa began making coffee and breakfast for the boys. Eileen was still asleep and Melissa tried to keep the boys quiet to let Eileen get as much sleep as she could. James went outside to feed Buster and to bring in a little more wood for the fire.

Buster was in a playful mood after not getting any attention yesterday due to the solemn event. James gave Buster a good scratching and a few words of praise as he gobbled up his food. When he finished, James tossed a stick for Buster to retrieve, which he did quickly. James tossed the stick again and Buster retrieved it again. Buster didn't seem to remember what had happened yesterday, but James certainly did and tired of playing with Buster quickly, thoughts of his dad creeping back into his mind. James went to the woodshed, grabbed a few logs, and went inside. Buster wanted to play more, but James was not in the mood.

Eileen heard Melissa and the boys in the living room despite their best efforts to keep quiet. Eileen got up, got dressed, and joined Melissa and the twins. "Lars," she called out. She looked at Melissa, "Where's Lars?" Melissa walked over and gave her a big hug and held on tight for a minute. Then Eileen began to remember yesterday's events and her tears started up again. She made her way over to the sofa for a little while and sobbed. There was little Melissa could do. It wasn't long before the hunger pangs set in and she decided she needed to eat a little and managed a couple eggs and bacon. As she nibbled on the bacon, she thought of Lars and immediately began to cry again. Melissa gave her another hug.

No one had slept well the night of the funeral. Reggie, Emily, Sam and Sally arrived at the Lindgren homestead early, shortly after Eileen finished her breakfast. The Lins first and the Carstons next asked if Eileen would come stay with them for a while. Eileen told them she would not leave her home. This is where she and Lars made the perfect home for themselves and she wanted to stay near Lars, even if it was only his grave.

Eileen then walked over to the front window and peered toward the sycamore tree. She could see the mound of dirt where Lars was buried. Immediately, she felt the need to go to the grave. Melissa joined her while Emily looked after the boys. Eileen knelt beside the grave and began crying again. Eileen then looked around and saw some flowers nearby; she got up to pick a few and then returned to the grave. She kissed each flower as she laid them on the mound of dirt near those which had been placed there the day before. Eileen knelt at the grave for nearly an hour before Melissa was able to urge her back to the house.

Emily and Sally made tea and gave Eileen a glass. She took the glass and began to take some small sips. Sally led Eileen to the sofa and they sat and talked a while, Sally quoting a few Chinese proverbs. The proverbs didn't help, but nothing would have. The boys gathered around Eileen and she bent over to hug and kiss them. Eileen loved these boys as Lars had, and right then and there she vowed they would know Lars through her. The boys would grow up knowing Lars as if he were here through the stories she would tell them in the years to come. Eileen hugged and kissed the boys again and then continued her crying.

The men moved to the front porch to discuss the situation. There was not a lot needing attention at Lars' place, as Lars kept up with his chores and the homestead was in good shape. They then discussed the need for Eileen to stay here and what they should do about this. The only remedy they could come up with was for James and Melissa to move here. Though they had grown accustomed to the Weston place and had everything they needed there, there was more here at the Lindgren place—more room, a bigger garden, and a place they could call their own, they being no more than squatters at the Weston place. If they could move all their stuff here, they could live here comfortably and take care of Eileen as well for as long as she would have them, possibly indefinitely.

The men continued to discuss the idea. They then pondered the huge task of moving James and Melissa's belongings here.

"It can be done," Reggie said, "if we all pitch in."

Before they could do this, though, they needed to ask Eileen to see if she would accept the idea. They decided this question should simmer for a while and maybe they would ask her tomorrow. Their thoughts then returned to Lars. He was the best friend and neighbor they could have possibly asked for. Even without Buster, he easily could have handled most intruders that came his way. They were all going to suffer in his absence. Most importantly, though, they were going to miss him. Eileen visited the grave again later that afternoon. This time, everyone went with her and they all mourned Lars. Eileen said they needed a headstone. Sam asked Eileen if she would do him the honor of allowing him to make the stone. Eileen agreed. Eileen gave Sam his birth date and Reggie and his phone provided the date of death. Sam also made certain he had the correct spelling of his name. He then promised Eileen he would get started on the project immediately and let her know when the task was complete. Eileen thanked him.

Sam and Sally headed for home a short while later. Reggie and Emily followed Eileen, Melissa, and James with the boys in tow to the house. Eileen made another pitcher of tea telling Melissa she had to do something, that she would go crazy just sitting around. Reggie and Emily told Eileen they would be back tomorrow and headed home when they finished their teas. Eileen went to bed a short time later, having grown tired from her long day and the lack of sleep last night.

The following day, Reggie and Emily arrived as promised. James and Reggie talked a bit on the porch while Emily went inside to be with Eileen and Melissa. When they finally went inside, James asked Melissa how Eileen was doing this morning and said he would ask her about them moving in, which he had discussed extensively with Melissa last night after they went to bed.

James went to Eileen, who had settled in on the sofa. He gave her a hug and kiss and asked if she had breakfast. She said yes, though she was not able to eat much as her stomach didn't feel well.

"I was thinking," James began, "Melissa and I don't think you should stay here alone."

"I'll be fine," Eileen said, not really caring whether she lived or died at this point.

"Let me put it another way," James continued. "Melissa and I would like to move in with you."

There was no reaction from Eileen though James could tell she heard what he said.

"If we move in here, you can help us take care of the boys and we can help you take care of the homestead. You cannot take care of this place alone."

Again, James could tell Eileen was thinking.

"We need you as much as you need us at a time like this," James continued. "Planting time will be here before you know it and the crops must be planted. You cannot do this by yourself. There is so much for Melissa and me to do; you can really help us with the boys and they need you too."

James then sat silent watching Eileen's every little movement and twitch.

"I think it would be wonderful if you, Melissa and the boys move here," Eileen finally said.

James gave her a big kiss and hug. "We need you and you need us," James said. "Dad will look down upon this place and smile. We will take everything he has taught us and make a strong, healthy family he would be proud of."

"Yes, we will," Eileen said, "and Robbie and Ronnie will know Lars as well as they would have if Lars were here. I'll see to it," Eileen said, staring at the painting she had made of Lars on the wall.

James motioned to Reggie to join him on the porch and Reggie followed him outside. James told Reggie he would like to get started tomorrow and when they finished moving in, they would need to build a new bedroom for the boys. The boys could share a room, but it would need to be big enough for both of them, now and when they grow older and need more room. Reggie said he would certainly help with the move and the addition. James said he was going to run over to see Sam and inform him of the move. Reggie and James then went inside and James told Melissa he was going to run over to Sam's.

"I'll be back in a little while," he said.

Melissa gave him a peck on the cheek and James left.

James made a quick trip and when he returned, he informed Reggie that Sam would meet them over at the old Weston place. Bright and early the next morning, as soon as Reggie and Emily made the trip to Eileen's, Reggie and James headed over and began packing stuff back, starting with clothes, guns, and ammunition. They worked hard all day, making trip after trip, and still the chore took an additional two full days. Finally, the task was completed and James locked up the old Weston place, probably for good this time. James and Reggie thanked Sam for all his help and Sam started to head home, saying, "If you need anything else, be sure to let me know."

"As a matter of fact, Sam, we are going to build on a new bedroom for the twins. We could really use your help with that too."

Of course Sam wanted to help.

"Give us a few days," James said, "and we'll be ready to get started."

Reggie helped James move things around a bit to make room for their additional items. Emily helped Melissa set up their new bedroom and made a place for the boys. Everything didn't fit and many things had to be stored in the barn. The only problem was that the barn was already stuffed. In spite of a lack of room, the next day they were completely arranged and ready to begin their new life with Eileen. James told Reggie to give him a few days and he would get started on the new addition. James thanked Reggie for all his help and he and Emily headed home. Reggie and Emily discussed the new addition and were really pleased to see how things were working out. They knew all along the new arrangement would work out just fine.

A few days later, Reggie and Emily returned to help James with the new addition. Sam showed up too as promised. With Eileen's help, they decided on the location of the new addition and James and Reggie marked off the spot with stakes and string. James began digging the holes for the pilings and Reggie or Sam would spell him from time to time. Lars had only one posthole digger. It was an old all steel model and it was heavy. It cut through the hard dirt easily, but the weight of the tool would take its toll on your arms after only a short while. Eileen and Emily kept them in tea and water, alternating between the two. By the end of the day, they had all the holes dug and were ready for posts.

The following day, James found some nice straight trees, large enough for the foundation timbers. Luckily, the sap was down in the trees this time of year and the posts would take much longer to rot. James cut while Reggie and Sam carried them to the holes and dropped them in. This was another all day job and by late afternoon, it was time for Reggie and Emily to head home again. The following day, they tamped the posts in and notched them for the floor joists. James cut a few more trees and then pulled Lars' portable sawmill out of the barn. It was an old mill and James spent an hour trying to figure out how to use the machine. It took another hour to hook it up to the tractor's power take-off (PTO). James greased the machine and checked everything over he could see that might need attention. James then started the tractor and engaged the PTO. The old machine sprang to life.

It took James, Sam, and Reggie a week to cut enough boards for the joists, flooring, and framing. James couldn't find enough nails, but a trip to the Weston place remedied this problem. James found plenty metal roofing in the barn to cover the roof though none of the panels matched. Another week and the new bedroom was nearly finished. They found one good window in Lars' barn, so this is what the room had. They really didn't need more. A coat of paint on the inside and two on the outside and it was finished. Thanks to Reggie and Sam, they finished the chore in less than half the time it would have taken James alone. Melissa thanked Sam and her dad, giving them each a big hug and kiss. They aired the room out a few days until the paint was dry and the fumes from the oil base paint were just barely detectible. They brought over the beds from the Weston house and the boys moved in. Eileen began working on curtains for the window. By late afternoon, she had the curtains finished and Melissa helped her hang them.

"Something's missing," Eileen said.

"It looks great to me," Melissa said.

"Bars, it needs bars," Eileen said, "over the window. James, where's James?"

"He's around here somewhere," Melissa said. "Don't worry, he'll get the bars on the window."

A couple hours before dark, Eileen made her way to Lars' grave, as she did every evening to tell him she loved him, missed him, and goodnight. She cried for a while and informed him of the day's events; then she told him she would see him the next morning.

Eileen insisted on helping Melissa prepare breakfast and dinner each day, keeping busy with small chores. Each day, Eileen seemed to be getting a little better and she especially enjoyed reading to the boys, which she did without fail each and every day. She read stories from one of Lars' books, as she was not able to tell the boys stories about Lars without breaking down into tears, unable to finish the story.

Chapter 36

By the time planting season rolled around, Eileen was doing much better. She worked hard beside Melissa and James to get the corn, potatoes, and numerous other vegetables planted. Eileen even planted a few tobacco plants though no one would use them. Eileen continued to visit Lars' grave each morning and evening, even during planting season, as tired as she was. She also told stories to the boys, mostly about their grandpa, as she was now able to do so without breaking into tears. Everything she did, whether it was planting the corn and potatoes or swinging the kids on their swing, Eileen had a story about Lars.

Eileen also helped the boys hone their hunting and shooting skills. She mostly used the .22 rifle Lars taught her to shoot with, explaining to the boys they needed to be nearly perfect with the smaller caliber rifle to hunt smaller game, which would be their most dependable source of food.

"Your grandpa was an excellent shot," she told them. "He could shoot the eye out of a squirrel a hundred yards away." Then she had to walk off a hundred yards for them so they could determine if this was possible. *These are very smart boys*, she thought after she stepped off the distance. She explained hunting was their way of providing food for themselves; hunting was a necessity. "If you want to eat well, you had better learn to shoot well," she added.

The boys were still young and she would need to repeat the lessons many times the next few years, but she didn't mind. Eileen loved these boys as if they were her own.

Soon after they finished planting, Sam and Sally came over one morning with Lars' headstone. The stone must have weighed a hundred pounds. It was a slab of nearly white sandstone Sam found. Lars' name was perfectly chiseled across the top of the stone in large letters. Below were the dates, followed by the inscription *Beloved Husband of Eileen Lindgren*. On the bottom center was a pair of hearts, one linked into the other. Sam had found some clear varnish to seal the stone to prevent degradation and so it would retain its white color. When Eileen saw the stone, she burst into tears, giving Sam a big hug and kiss.

"It is perfect, Sam," Eileen said.

Sam put the stone on the front porch at Eileen's direction and she asked James if he would mind going to Reggie's to tell them the headstone was ready and that they would be having a ceremony this afternoon. James promptly headed over to see Reggie.

James returned a couple hours later telling Eileen that Reggie and Emily would be there. James then got back to his chores while Melissa, Sam, Sally, and Eileen went back inside the house to chat. James moseyed in after a while and joined the conversation.

It wasn't long before Reggie and Emily showed up.

"Really good job on the headstone," Reggie told Sam.

James carried the headstone to the sycamore tree while Sam grabbed a shovel. Reggie dug a short trench at the head of the grave and James stuck the bottom edge into the trench; then James and Reggie packed dirt around the stone while Sam gathered a few large rocks to place at the bottom to reinforce the headstone. They all gathered at the foot of the grave and again Reggie said some words about Lars and asked his spirit to give Eileen strength.

Sam and Sally said they needed to go and gave Eileen a big hug and kiss. Eileen thanked them for the headstone. "You have gone above and beyond this time," Eileen said. "I am so proud to call you my friends."

Eileen told the rest that she thought she would stay with Lars for a while and gave Reggie, Emily, James, Melissa, and the kids a big hug and kiss before they headed back to the house, Buster following close behind.

Eileen spent nearly an hour at Lars' grave. She would turn around and look toward the house from time to time, hearing the kids and Buster playing. *Buster is so good with the boys*, she thought. He never tired of playing with the boys and he put up with their occasional shenanigans. Eileen was about to get up when she heard a noise in the woods in the direction of the road into the valley. Eileen drew her pistol and moved behind the sycamore tree. A few seconds later, she heard a twig break and peeked around the edge of the tree. As Eileen looked around the tree, she saw a lone man and he saw her as well and reached for his pistol. Eileen quickly cocked her gun and shot the man in the center of his chest. She cocked and shot the man two more times as he fell to the dirt.

Eileen immediately fell to her knees and stared at the dead man. She had not killed anyone since the two men at Reggie's. She had just about gotten over these two men and now she was going to have to deal with shooting someone again. "Lars, please help me get through this," she said looking over to Lars' grave.

Reggie and Emily had gone home but James, hearing the shots, grabbed his rifle and quickly ran out of the front door.

"Eileen!" James screamed.

"Eileen!" James screamed again.

Then James heard her feminine wolf howl and saw her stand up near the sycamore tree. James ran to Eileen and then walked over to the dead man and poked his body.

James walked back over to Eileen. There were no tears in her eyes. She was not crying. Eileen was just standing there holding her pistol in her hands and staring at it.

"You okay?" he asked.

"Yes," Eileen replied. "Just another day in paradise."

"I'm so proud of you," James said, "and Lars would be proud of you too."

Eileen didn't say a word and James walked her back to the house.

"I'll take care of the body," James said.

"Will you take him down the road a ways?" Eileen asked. "I don't want him buried anywhere close to Lars' grave."

"Yes, I will," James replied.

Melissa and Eileen prepared dinner while James buried the body. Eileen acted as if nothing had happened. She was hurting inside but drew her strength from Lars.

Robbie asked what happened and Eileen told him and Ronnie it was time they learned a new fact of life around here. She explained the reality of intruders to the boys. She explained that from time to time someone would come around and it was necessary for them to die. There were plenty of warnings on the way here. If intruders ignored these warnings, then they would die. She was not certain they understood this lesson, but in the years to come Eileen would reinforce this fact. She had to. If she didn't, it might be the boys who died. She didn't think she could handle this.

When James returned, they ate and talked mostly about the quality of the headstone. Eileen made no more mention of the incident and James and Melissa were not about to bring it up.

When they finished with the meal, Eileen went to the sofa with the two boys and told them a story about their grandpa. The boys loved to listen to Grandpa stories. Eileen had such a way with words and the boys felt the love Lars had for them and their mom, dad, and grandma.

James was amazed at how Eileen had taken care of the intruder and now sat with the boys reading as if nothing happened. Lars did a great job of teaching Eileen how to deal with danger and the adversity of life in the woods. She was as sweet as any cake she ever baked when she was with family, but at the same time she was as tough as boot leather in the face of danger and handling the never-ending chores which needed to be done. Simply put, she was remarkable.

Chapter 37

Eight years had passed since Lars' death and the Lindgrens had a wonderful life. There were bumps in the road, however, and the biggest bump was they lost Buster the previous year due to old age. He was buried at the foot of Lars' grave.

The boys grew up smart and strong. Melissa made certain they read from one of the many books in Lars and Eileen's collection most days, while Eileen told them stories about Lars every day without fail. Eileen never tired of telling the boys stories about their grandpa. James worked the boys hard in the garden and gathering firewood as well as most other chores that needed to be done around the place. James also taught them survival skills, like setting snares, building fires, and fishing. The boys were only sixteen, but they had more skills and were smarter than James when he was twice that age.

The boys played as hard as they worked too. They visited Sean and Debra often and the two visited the twins in between. Debra grew up a tomboy and was able to do just as much as the boys could. They spent a lot of time in the river during most of the year, swimming usually but also fishing.

In the past eight years, Eileen never missed a day visiting Lars' grave and talking to him. Often she would take the boys to visit the grave and tell them another story about this great man. Even after such a long time, Eileen still shed many tears for the man she loved and missed so much. His spirit did give her strength; she could feel him in her bones. The boys were a huge comfort to Eileen as well and she could feel their love. She just loved being called grandma.

One day, while Sean and Debra were swimming at the Lindgren place, Ronnie and Sean wandered off into the woods to play while Robbie and Debra stayed by the river. It was a warm sunny day and the two were lying on the riverbank working on their tans. Robbie was lying on his side facing Debra, who was lying on her back. Up until now, Debra was just another one of the boys. Robbie noticed the little scar on Debra's leg where he accidentally shot her with one of his arrows. He then noticed the mole on the side of her stomach near her navel. For the first time, Robbie found himself looking at Debra's breasts. He had seen her breasts many times covered with the skin tight cloth of her swimsuit and never paid any attention. She was just one of them and he had no interest in Debra as a girl, but the hormones had been growing within his body and seemed to have peaked at this particular moment. Robbie looked up at her face and how smooth her skin was. Her silky brown hair, her little button nose and perfectly shaped mouth for some reason became an interest for Robbie. He then felt the strain inside his swim trunks and he reached in to adjust himself.

Debra had nice size breasts and Robbie could see her nipples straining against the fabric of her swimsuit, which again became the center of his focus. Robbie found himself wanting to see more and to touch her breasts. Directly, Debra opened her eyes and caught Robbie staring at her breasts. Robbie didn't notice she opened her eyes as he was focused elsewhere. Debra closed her eyes again and smiled a devious little smile, which Robbie also did not notice. Debra leaned over toward Robbie, still with her eyes closed, and reached around to her back and pulled a string on her bikini top. She then rolled back to her original position. Still with her eyes closed, she pulled at and loosened her top, but let it lay still covering her breasts.

After a bit, Debra opened an eye and took a peek at Robbie. He was still focused mostly on her breasts but noticed when she opened her eyes and his eyes immediately focused on hers.

"Robbie, will you rub some lotion on me?" she asked, handing him a plastic tube.

"Sure," he replied.

Robbie took the cap off the tube, squirted a little on Debra's legs and rubbed the liquid into her skin. He then squirted some on her arms and did the same. Robbie stopped for a moment and Debra urged him to finish the job. Robbie squirted the liquid onto her stomach and continued the task. She asked him, with her eyes still closed, to put a bit more on her stomach. After he had, Debra took his hand and helped him rub the lotion in moving in the direction of her breasts. When his hand reached the fabric, Debra pulled his hand upward, pushing the fabric aside.

Robbie could feel the strain in his trunks as Debra guided his hand over her breasts, nipples pink and erect. When both breasts were completely covered with lotion, Debra continued to hold onto Robbie's hand but stopped on top of her left breast, the other exposed for Robbie to see. And see Robbie did, admiring the size, shape, and color. He had never seen anything more beautiful than the sight he was staring at. But it was much more than this. He had one hand placed squarely on top of the other mound. Robbie squeezed his hand and felt the softness of her breast with the hard nipple poking the center of his palm.

When Robbie squeezed her breast, Debra's eyes popped open. "What are you doing?" She asked. Debra quickly removed his hand, raised up and put her top back on. "You can put that thing away," she said smiling and looking down at the protrusion in his trunks.

Debra stood up, walked over to the water's edge and dove in. Robbie stood up as well, admiring the roundness of the bottom half of her swimsuit as it disappeared into the water. The banana in Robbie's trunks took a while to disappear, but he adjusted so it was not as noticeable.

Sean and Ronnie returned a while later on the far side of the river from Debra and Robbie. They dove in and swam around a bit. Debra climbed out to join Robbie. Sean and Ronnie finished swimming across and then climbed out to join Robbie and Debra.

"What's going on, guys?" Sean asked.

"Nothing much," Robbie replied.

"Anyone getting hungry?" Ronnie asked.

The guys always seemed to be hungry, so they went up to the house. When they finished eating, Melissa sent Debra and Sean home.

"Your parents will get worried," she said.

Sean and Debra were over again the next day. Sean and Robbie walked down the river looking for soft shell turtles as Debra and Ronnie made their way to their favorite swimming hole. Debra and Ronnie sat on some large rocks and talked a while. Debra asked Ronnie several questions about Robbie, which seemed a little strange to him. Ronnie answered the questions anyway, not thinking twice about the questions or the answers. *She should know the answers to these questions*, Ronnie thought. They had been best friends all their lives. Yes, she had to know the answers to these questions, but he didn't pry as to why she was asking them.

Ronnie, getting a little annoyed at Debra for the questions, said they should go swimming now. Debra had not worn her swimsuit and needed to change. Ronnie was already in his trunks. Debra stood up and took her blouse off and then her shorts. Ronnie sat on his rock looking at Debra in her bra and panties, not really thinking she would change in front of him. She never changed in front of him before, but Debra released the clasp on her bra and tossed it onto the rock where she had been sitting, revealing her firm and erect breasts. Ronnie immediately felt the hardness in his trunks. *Her breasts are so beautiful*, he thought; her pink nipples as hard as his manhood. Debra slipped her bikini top on and slid her panties down revealing her wonderfulness. Ronnie had to straighten himself, as his trunks would not allow his hardness to progress without causing pain. Debra slipped her bottom on, gave Ronnie, whom she had ignored up to now, a little smile, and dove into the water. Ronnie stood there dumbfounded by what happened.

Ronnie could not believe what Debra did, but at the same time, he loved every second of it. *Is she trying to tell me something?* he thought. Ronnie's hardness reached its full potential, which he could not conceal, so he did not try. Rather, he sat down on one of the large rocks to watch Debra swim around.

"Are you going to come in, Ronnie?" she asked.

"I'll be in shortly," he replied.

He got into the cool water when his trunks returned to normal. Ronnie and Debra swam around for a while, Debra acting as if nothing had happened, but for Ronnie something major had happened. This would be a day he would not soon forget.

One morning the following week, Robbie told James, Melissa, and Ronnie he was going hunting. Robbie had gone hunting every morning but he never brought anything home. Each time, he headed across the river and directly to the Lin homestead to see Debra. Each time, Debra gave her parents a lame excuse to go into the woods with Robbie. Debra and Robbie mostly talked with a little kissing here and there, but their affections never went any further.

Sam and Sally noticed something was going on with Debra and the twins and decided to confront her. Well, actually Sally noticed something was happening; Sam, like most men, didn't notice anything until Sally brought it to his attention. Debra and her parents had always been good about discussing situations and working through them and this time was no different. "I'm 17 now," Debra explained. "It's time I get married and there are only two available men in the valley." She was trying to determine which of the two were more suitable as her mate. Debra told them she wasn't certain yet which she liked the best. Satisfied with Debra's answers, Sally and Sam let it go at that.

Sam and Sally now knew Debra was seeing the boys on a regular basis on a completely new level. Melissa and James didn't know anything at all about the relationships and Robbie didn't know that Debra was also seeing Ronnie on the same days she was seeing him. After she sent Robbie back home, Ronnie was waiting at a secret location for Debra to arrive. Neither Ronnie or Robbie had a clue about the other meetings, until one day Robbie had forgotten to give her a message from James to give to Sam and went back to catch up with Debra. She wasn't headed home though, and Robbie followed her to her and Ronnie's secret rendezvous location. Robbie was shocked to see Debra and Ronnie together after she had just been with him. Robbie barged in to confront Ronnie and Debra and immediately the boys got into a shoving match until Debra broke it up.

"If you men are going to act like babies," she said, "I'm going home. When you guys man-up, come see me."

Debra stomped off and didn't say another word. The boys looked at each other after Debra disappeared into the woods and then got back to their shoving match.

When the boys got home, James and Melissa immediately knew something serious was going on and confronted them. The boys told their parents what was happening and started to get into another shoving match, but James put a stop to it. James and Melissa sent the boys outside while they discussed the situation. Then James went outside, sending Robbie back inside to talk to Melissa.

James and Melissa basically told the boys the same thing, but thought it would be better if they discussed the situation with them separately.

"Robbie, you and Ronnie are the only two available men in the valley, while Debra is the only single woman. It's as simple as this. You boys fighting will do no good. Debra will decide which of you she wants and that will be that," Melissa said.

Robbie and Ronnie told Sean what was going on with his sister and he was really surprised. Sean also let the boys in on his little secret too. The twins were equally surprised. Sean told Robbie and Ronnie he had been thinking of leaving the valley, that there was nothing here for him. He hated abandoning his parents, but men have needs and his needs could not be satisfied any other way. The boys made a pact to keep their plans quiet until Debra made her decision. When Debra made her decision, the remaining two boys would finalize their escape.

Debra finally made her choice, but took just over a week to do so. Debra chose Ronnie and met all the boys in the woods to inform them of her choice. Ronnie could not have been happier. They confirmed the decision with a big kiss.

Sean and Robbie followed Debra and Ronnie to her house and Sean and Robbie said goodbye to Sam and Sally. They then made a trip to see Reggie and Emily before they informed Robbie's parents of their decision to leave the valley. They knew Reggie was the best person to help outfit them for their new adventure. Reggie filled their backpacks with enough survival food for a week—and this was if they killed nothing along the way, which was highly unlikely. Reggie gave each of them a bulletproof vest, onto which he attached fragmentation grenades, light sticks, a fire starter, and some spare ammunition. Robbie's rifle of choice was his grandmother's carbine. His pistol of choice was his .357 magnum, but he also strapped a .22 pistol he had gotten from Reggie as a gift a few years back on his other hip. He would use it for small game, remembering Eileen's words on the value of a small caliber gun. He might not be able to shoot the eyes out of a squirrel at a hundred yards, but he could at thirty yards with his .22 pistol. Sean also packed a .357 magnum so they could share ammo, but his rifle of choice was his AR-15. The AR-15 gave him more range than Robbie, but Robbie liked the knock-down power of the carbine. Reggie also packed numerous small trinkets into the boys' side pockets on their backpacks and gave them a big hug before sending them on their way. The boys told Reggie they would be back in a year, and then they were gone.

Sean and Robbie showed up at the Lindgren place all geared up for war, it appeared, and Eileen, Melissa and James knew immediately something was up. Sean and Robbie informed them they were leaving the valley. Melissa was immediately in tears.

"You boys know what you're doing?" James asked.

"No, but you know we need to go," Robbie said.

Ronnie was still with Debra at her parents' house, so they could not have known Debra made her decision and the boys shared this news with James and Melissa. Debra chose Ronnie for her mate and now the final decision was up to Ronnie. Ronnie basically had two choices—accept Debra or leave with Robbie and Sean. Ronnie really liked Debra, but he did not love her, even though he thought over time he could. Ronnie chose to stay with Debra to see if they would work out.

Having been rejected by Debra, Robbie saw no reason to stay here in the valley. Sean never had a choice. Neither wanted to leave the valley, but if they wanted to find a woman and happiness, they would need to find it elsewhere. Neither had a desire to remain single the rest of their lives and they certainly were not gay.

"Anywhere you go is a long walk on foot," James said.

"I know, but we don't have a choice," Robbie replied.

"Do you know where you're going?" James asked.

"We thought we would head toward Corpus Christi," Sean said. "I think this is our best option."

"We'll be back in a year," Robbie said.

The boys made a stop by Lars' grave to tell him goodbye and to ask him to keep an eye on them and guide them on their long trek. They also asked him to keep an eye on their parents, grandmother and siblings and keep them safe.

James, Melissa and Eileen knew the boys needed to go, but this didn't make it any less painful. They followed the boys around to the back of the house. Everyone kissed and hugged, and then the boys were on their way. Eileen went back inside and got off her sore ankle. She twisted it a couple days earlier.

Melissa and James made their way to the pier to watch the boys cross the stream and head south into the woods. The couple sat on the pier with tears in their eyes as their baby and his friend left. They continued to watch long after they disappeared into the forest. James gave Melissa a big hug and kiss and finally decided it was time to go inside.

Debra spent most days at the Lindgren homestead with Ronnie, getting to know him better, though she had known him her entire life. She knew he would make a good husband, but could she love him and would he be a good lover? Those were the big questions.

One morning, Reggie and Emily had just arrived at the Lindgren place. Debra came running up to the house screaming. "Come quickly!" she cried, "Mom has burned herself really bad!"

"What happened?" asked James.

"Mom burned herself with a skillet of grease. All over her leg," Debra told them.

Eileen didn't think she could make the long trek on her bad ankle. Reggie volunteered to stay with Eileen while James, Emily and Melissa followed Debra back home.

Sally had burned much of her right leg. Sam had cleaned her leg up the best he could with a cool water and soap solution by the time Debra returned with the neighbors. The leg was burned really badly. Third degree burns covered about half her leg. Melissa and Emily cleaned the leg up a little more while Sam prepared a dressing for her leg. He crushed aloe vera plant he pulled from the side of the house, added water and some of Reggie's wine for its alcohol content, and the liquid from boiled willow bark. They applied the dressing, then wrapped the leg with clean bandages. This was all they could do. The healing process was up to Sally now.

Back at the Lindgren place, Eileen took her pot of coffee off the stove and grabbed a couple mugs out of the cabinet. Reggie was sitting at the table, and when she poured his cup, Reggie noticed the top two buttons were open on her blouse and that she was not wearing a bra. Reggie got a good look at her breasts and he could immediately feel the pressure in his britches.

"How about a little milk?" Reggie asked.

"You don't take milk in your coffee," she said.

"Not normally," Reggie said, "but I think I'd like to have a little of yours."

"I don't think so!" she exclaimed, now noticing Reggie was looking down her top.

Reggie got up and walked around the table. He grabbed Eileen from behind and held her tight. He kissed her on the neck as he grasps one of her breasts and squeezed. She struggled a little until Reggie squeezed her breast, then she relaxed a bit. Reggie turned her around and gave her a big kiss on the lips. Eileen began to cry, then when Reggie had finished kissing her, she retreated into the bathroom and locked the door.

Eileen came back out a short time later. "I'm sorry," She said.

"You're sorry?" Reggie asked. "For what?"

"For not slapping you; for not pushing you away before I did," she replied.

"Then you liked what I did?" he queried.

"Yes," she replied after a short pause and began to cry again.

Reggie walked over to Eileen and started to grab her once more, but she did stop him this time. "We can't," she said. "What about Emily?"

"I love Emily and would never leave her, but our intimacies have all but dried up. She's just not interested anymore," Reggie shared.

"I can't," Eileen said. "Lars…," and she rushed outside and toward Lars' grave.

Reggie followed, and Eileen knelt at the foot of Lars' grave. "Hey buddy," Reggie said looking at Lars' headstone. "I loved Lars' too and I miss him terribly every day. I know I could never miss him as much as you, but the difference is small. Lars would never want you to be a nun the rest of your life."

Eileen never said a word, but listened to every word Reggie said, as she continued to sob.

James, Emily and Melissa returned shortly after Reggie and Eileen returned to the house. "What's going on?" Emily asked, noticing Eileen's red eyes.

"We just got back from Lars' grave," Reggie said.

Two weeks with Ronnie answered all of Debra's questions, and now the final decision was Ronnie's to make. Ronnie spent two days away from Debra talking to his parents and finally came to a decision. He realized that while her body excited him, he really didn't like Debra enough to marry her.

After not seeing Ronnie for two days, Debra was excited to see him again. They went for a walk and Debra held on to Ronnie's hand as they walked. "I like you a lot," he told Debra. "I want to love you, but my feelings for you are no different than my feelings for Sean or Robbie. You are more like a sister to me, so I'm really sorry, but I can't marry you." Debra stopped and just stared at Ronnie for a few seconds, then she slapped him hard across the face. She then ran home in tears.

As Ronnie headed back toward the house, he heard Reggie's familiar wolf howl. Ronnie returned the howl, and met Reggie and Emily at the front porch. Melissa, Eileen and James walked out the front door.

"You guys ready to head over to the Lins?" James asked Reggie.

"Yes," Reggie replied.

Eileen thought she was up for the trip this time as her ankle felt much better. She wanted to see Sally. "I hope she's going to be alright," Eileen said.

Melissa realized Debra wasn't here and asked Ronnie about her.

"She went home," he said. "I told her I couldn't marry her. She started crying and ran home."

"Darn. I was looking forward to another wedding," Emily said.

"Me too," Melissa added.

"You okay?" James asked Ronnie.

"Yes," he said. "She's like a sister to me. I can't marry her." Ronnie paused for a second then said, "I don't know what the hell I'm going to do now, though."

"Things change," Eileen said. "Some changes are good and some are not, but life is always about change. You take and deal with whatever comes at you."

"Life has definitely been altered here in Peaceful Valley," Melissa said.

When the troupe got to the Lins, Eileen, Melissa and Emily removed the bandages from Sally's leg. It didn't look good. "It looks like it's getting infected," Eileen said.

The ladies cleaned and wrapped her leg again. That was all they could do, and they all headed back to the Lindgren homestead.

"We'll check on her again tomorrow," Melissa told Sam as they left.

"Sally may die if we can't get the infection under control," Emily stated on the way home.

"Yes she may," Eileen agreed.

The End

Epilogue

All living things on and within this planet struggle to emerge into existence. All living things struggle to survive. The strong not only survive but thrive; the weak die, as they should. Luck and will play important roles in survival. Ignorance and apathy adversely affect survival. Struggle is a necessary ingredient for strength. Overpopulation of any one species is detrimental to all species. Intelligence has many faces. Animals survive because they have the skills to do so; people are—and always will be—animals. Too many modern conveniences take away the skills needed to survive. It's not the size of the man but the size of the gun. No one can predict when the world will shut down, only that it will. Shit will happen at the most inopportune time. Love conquers all. Man cannot live by bread alone. A good life is built much like a house, from the ground up. Love never dies. Always remember the past; don't continually repeat your mistakes. Proper preparation prevents piss poor performance (6Ps). Nothing ventured, nothing gained.

Characters

Lars Lindgren

James Lindgren

Eileen Branson

Reginald Carston

Emily Carston

Ronald Lindgren (Ronnie)

Georgia Fenwick

Paul Fenwick

Samuel Lin

Sally Lin

Andy Prentiss

Buster

Rachel Lindgren

Ruby Lindgren

Ronald Weston

Sara Weston

Melissa Carston

Robert Lindgren (Robbie)

Dean Fenwick

Ricky Fenwick

Sean Lin

Debra Lin

Richard Tucker

Into Autumn (Larry Landgraf 3-2-2015)

The seed softened by winter rain,
Bursts open and begins to strain;
Spring warmth so encouraging,
Groundwater so nourishing.

Pushing deep and gathering strength,
Growing tall and gaining length;
Spreading wide, leafy arms,
Showing off its intricate charms.

Months go by and the pain begins,
The sun grows warm and intense;
Soothing moisture at night,
Then another day of bright light.

Day in and day out, the heat,
Each and every night, so sweet;
When will the torment end,
How much energy must I spend?

At last, a cool north wind,
It's time to take it in;
One last surge of might,
Everything will be alright.

Thrust upward to give a sign,
Let it out and unwind;
Show all that you can do,
Let them see the color in you.

The beauty of one little flower,
Growing bigger by the hour;
Drawing in friends to help out,
Beneficial to both no doubt.

My fate now to wilt and die,
My seeds shall fall then lie;
Strangers will take some away,

Others will always stay.

We shall snuggle down,
Winter rain, another round;
Waiting for the warmth of Spring,
Then another round of green.

Into Autumn is the first in a series. It was not planned that way. Hell, I didn't plan writing *Into Autumn*. I just woke up one morning with the story in my head and started writing. *Into Spring* is book two and was intentionally written as a stand-alone novel, but best if *Into Autumn* is read first.

Into Autumn, and *Into Spring* (after December 2016), are available on Amazon, along with my second book, *How to be a Smart SOB Like Me*. This book is my autobiography published in 2012. It has been called my rant. You decide for yourself.

My first book, *Dangerous Waters*, published in 1986, is out of print. A few limited copies are available if you really want one. If you cannot find a copy, email me at riverrmann2@yahoo.com, as I have a few copies I'll sell.

My next two books planned are *Into Winter* and *Into Summer*. I plan to write and publish them by the end of 2017 and 2018 respectively.

Thank you for reading *Into Spring*, and I hope you will enjoy my other books as well. They can be found at Amazon as well as numerous other well-known book sites or through one of the links on my sites.

My website: http://www.intoautumn.com

My Pinterest: https://www.pinterest.com/riverrmann2/into-autumn/

Follow me on Facebook: http://www.facebook.com/intoautumn

All my videos including book trailers for all available books:
https://www.youtube.com/playlist?list=PLHAl2COVDW-FIpDB_B8AkoRp3iiaXaKCaC

THE END

About the Author

Larry Landgraf was born and raised in and around the swamp country of the Guadalupe River Delta on the Texas Gulf Coast. After four years of college, not wanting to spend the rest of his life in an office or classroom, he became a commercial fisherman. That played out in the late '80s, and he became a general contractor for another twenty-plus years. Due to a death-defying injury on the job, he turned to writing.

Trying to save his commercial fishing career, Larry wrote his first book in 1986. The career and book were a failure. He didn't write again until he published his second book, *How to be a Smart SOB Like Me*, in 2012. Then he got serious about writing and in 2015 published *Into Autumn* to launch his *Four Seasons* series. The release dates for *Into Spring* and *Into Winter* are 2017, and 2018 for *Into Summer*.

Larry divorced in 2006 when his wife of 38 years decided to walk out. This marriage produced three kids, all grown now. Larry met Ellen in January 2009 after a long search which spanned the globe. They now live together in the swamp where Larry has lived all his life. Much like Eileen Branson in *Into Autumn*, Ellen is a city gal, but loves Larry's swamp. Larry, much like Lars Lindgren in the story, wouldn't have it any other way. He teaches her the ways of the swamp, and she has plenty to teach Larry, as well.

Fresh Ink Group

Publishing
Free Memberships
Share & Read Free Stories, Essays, Articles
Free-Story Newsletter
Writing Contests

Books
E-books
Amazon Bookstore

Authors
Editors
Artists
Professionals
Publishing Services
Publisher Resources

Members' Websites
Members' Blogs
Social Media

www.FreshInkGroup.com

Email: info@FreshInkGroup.com

Twitter: @FreshInkGroup

Google+: Fresh Ink Group

Facebook.com/FreshInkGroup

LinkedIn: Fresh Ink Group

About.me/FreshInkGroup